All the Small Things

© (Sharon Noble, 2025)

All rights reserved.

No part of this publication may be reproduced, distributed, or transmitted in any form or by any means, including photocopying, recording, or other electronic or mechanical methods, without the prior written permission of the publisher, except as permitted by U.K. copyright law. For permission requests, contact [include publisher/author contact info].

The story, all names, characters, and incidents portrayed in this production are fictitious. No identification with actual persons (living or deceased), places, buildings, and products is intended or should be inferred.

1st edition 2025

ISBN 9798345628089

Lana

I'm a sucker for an old Western. And, yes, I'm aware of how non-PC they are. I'm a teacher, so I don't shout about it, but there you have it – my guilty pleasure. When (not if) Hallmark negotiate the film rights to my life, I'll insist on a Western theme despite my suburban existence. My life lends itself to the bleak, high-stakes themes that play out so well in Westerns. I'd want an AI version of John Wayne settling something for me or deciding my fate with that wonderful coin flip that no Western is complete without. I'd want a pivotal scene with slow-motion capture of the coin's rotation, glinting in the sunlight before rolling to a dramatic stop, *everything* riding upon which side it lands.

Heads: All is peachy. Away you go into the sunset.

Tails: Everything's lost. Game over.

Okay. I'm being melodramatic. I have a free pass to do that. Last August I birthed a stillborn infant, a daughter. Forty weeks of waiting, Evie growing to perfection, then at the last minute we flipped tails. We lost. Still. There's plenty in my life that's good. Really good. I wonder somehow if I just wasn't meant to play the grown-up. The home, the family, even a plant that I might keep alive has eluded me.

I was dog-tired but couldn't sleep. The starched sheets were coarse against my skin; red weals had appeared where the drip met my wrist. Thank God visiting was restricted. Wan's face yesterday had been unbearable, his anguished yet furious expression as he tried to make sense of my lying there. Closing my eyes, I tilted my head away from him, unable to offer anything that might begin to explain. He stood awkwardly over the bed for the remainder of the visit until the visiting bell sounded, then leaned in to say goodbye.

'It's so ... unfair,' I managed.

Wan jokes that I'm Barbie to his Ken. Which is amusing, because as an African-Caribbean woman and weighing in around four times the size of lil Barbie (FYI, Wan is no Ken either), we couldn't be less like the glamorous couple. Wan is Joel to everyone else. But he's my Wan because he's quite literally 'white and nerdy', to give him his full title (think anxious-looking accountant, despite his wannabe DJ persona). We've photos of me in 'Military Barbie' mode, as he named me – in full camo from my Yugoslav TA days – and as 'Career Barbie', graduating with (ahem, a respectable 2:2 in Education from Liverpool Hope) hat-throwing pics, my beam visible from space. We never knew 'Suicide Barbie' would make an appearance at Manchester Royal.

I heard snippets of an exchange between Wan and the ward sister. I didn't think they would be allowed to tell him much beyond the facts. I wished they could, because I didn't know how to explain.

Tilda

Onlookers might generously have described me as inebriated. Monumentally so. My mother, bless her freshly deceased soul, would have been furious.

'Not your finest moment, Tilly,' my dad might have offered – had he outlived his unfaithful wife.

'GRIEF-STRICKEN DAUGHTER BRAWLS WITH SIBLING AT MOTHER'S WAKE.' I'm not aware of any headlines, but that would have been the gist. If I were to *try* to capture the jibes and one-liners that resulted in my spectacular launch, it still wouldn't translate. My behaviour, I think, was an effort to silence my pompous supremacist sibling, Archie. I urgently needed him to stop opening his flabby, self-righteous mouth.

Stepping into the hallway of my childhood home brought an unexpected wave of nostalgia. Muscle memory saw me nearly avoid the squeaky hall floorboard – although as an adult, I can come in as late and as drunk as I please. The floorboard would hopefully not be loud enough to summon Mother from her grave. Teenage petulance flooded through me, *almost* bringing tears – the first since I'd learned of Mother's death. As I wheeled our cases into the hall, I heard a familiar and provocative humming – the ancient champagne chiller, hanging on for dear life on Mother's behalf.

The funeral was tedious. I'll spare you details of the freezing church, the monotonous service – I'm sure you're keen to cut straight to the brawl. My mother was a cold fish, and the atmosphere at her send-off was fitting. There was no sobbing, no one throwing themselves at the coffin. We were apathetic at best. 'It's what she would have wanted' was not just a cliché. She would have been furious had there been fuss of any kind.

My grief, in any case, was still reserved for my father, who'd passed a decade ago, worn down by her acid tongue and his profound shame at her blatant philandering. Tears pricked my eyes as I imagined him beside me on the pew, a protective arm around my shoulders. I missed him so much. Even when I was small, I saw his efforts to compensate for her lack of warmth towards me.

Instead, I had Edwin at my side. Edwin's old. *So* much older than me. It had been years since I'd considered our age gap anything but charming. Yes, I was the student who'd shagged the lecturer all those years ago. And somehow we'd largely remained an item – much to my and his then wife's bewilderment. Edwin and I had gravitated back together in recent months – my vulnerable side needing support beyond the reach of Tanqueray.

It was satisfying to hear the gasps from Mother's mourners as I sashayed, after three glasses of recovery-aiding and mind-numbing breakfast champagne, to the front of the crematorium. My carefully chosen 'grieving yet seductive' outfit was receiving an audible response. What's not to like about a British Racing Green velvet bodycon and peach ostrich feathers? My mother would have detested it. And as such, it was the perfect choice. I imagined her, maternal disapproval still going strong in the afterlife.

Two hours into the wake, my tolerance began to reach its threshold. Back at Mother's, black-tie staff diligently waited on us. Pre-death, she'd organised the catering and staff to deploy the strange vol-au-vent-themed buffet – she never did move with the times. Thankfully, the wine was flowing freely. Circling the room, I'd tried without success to attach myself to a group that I didn't want to massacre. Edwin had followed like a lost puppy, his nose more bulbous with each glass of the Rioja he has such a taste for. I'd been pleasant with the God squad, tolerating gibberish about Mother being 'at Jesus' right hand'. I'd been delightful to the charity crew – something to do with saving dogs in Afghanistan. Poor mites. Unfortunately, my 'paw mites' pun was not well received. Either they didn't understand or they thought I was being rude. I wasn't sure either as the Bollinger continued to flow.

Sister-in-law, Babs, persisted in her attempts to 'engage' with me.

'So sad it takes a death to bring a family together.' Placing her hand on the small of my back, she offered her clichés. My non-verbal language was clear, but she wasn't receiving me. Archie waddled over, looking, to my horror, way too much like Edwin. Brothers from another mother. What did that even mean?

'Tilda, Tilda.' Breathing pure alcohol my way, my sibling leaned in for the hug I'd dodged all day. Placing a table between us, I manoeuvred into an unhuggable position.

'It's been such a long time. Too long,' he lied.

'Archie, we avoid each other because it ends badly when we do anything else.'

'I know. Shall we try again? For Mother's sake?' Mother wouldn't give a flying fuck. My trigger point firmly reached, I crab-stepped from the table to find myself in the path of Archie Junior. Fourteen years old and oozing arrogance, a hideous clone of his father. I hadn't seen Archie Junior since he was a fat, tufty-haired bundle, and, other than his height, little looked to have changed.

'Auntie Tilda!' he announced. 'Good to see you.'

I volunteered a mid-travel wave.

'You're here with your partner. An introduction is in order.' He craned his neck around the room.

'Archie Junior …'

'Rupert,' he inserted.

'Rupert, thank you.' Dramatic, alcohol-fuelled pause. 'I'm sure this is well intended, if not remotely doable.' I attempted to wobble off on my Jimmy Choos (peach soles to match the feathers). Rupert's sister, Octavia, stepped forward like a well-rehearsed farce unfolding around me, a sweet-looking girl with wispy hair *exactly* like mine. Hair that could *almost* be lovely.

'Aunt Tilda.' She reached forward in such a genuine way, I found myself meeting her hug. 'Love the frock.' She eyeballed me from head to toe. 'Not sure what Grandma would say.' She raised an eyebrow. Maybe I could tolerate this girl. The feeling was short-lived.

'Aunt Tilda, is it true what they say?' My stomach tightened, sensing her tone.

'That depends on who "they" are and what "they" are saying.' My thirteen-year-old niece had me on the back foot. She smiled as I zoned in on the glass of Bolly she held in her manicured hand.

'Mummy couldn't help but wonder, given what's occurred' – Mother's death? – 'whether you might assume some responsibility.' I was speechless. Let's not forget her age, and she was possibly buzzed from Bollinger. Was this her after-school go-to? In the absence of my *responsibilities*, I wouldn't know.

'Well,' I began, with no clue where my response might be heading. Fortuitously, all eyes were on Edwin, who was causing a timely stir. I should have remained more switched on – more *sober*. Edwin, Man of Science, versus the (Make)-Believers could have been predicted. Pivoting quickly on my heel towards Edwin sent me into a tailspin, only stopping when I steadied myself against Octavia's bony shoulder. We clattered noisily to the floor as Archie came blustering over. Shooting daggers, he dusted off his glassy-eyed daughter, fussing over her and looking accusingly my way.

'Don't look at me, Archie. I've had nothing to do with your daughter's inebriation. She's taken care of that all by herself. You've raised an independent girl. Well done you.' A wave of crimson swept over my throat and face.

'For goodness sake, Matilda. Don't you think that at Mother's funeral you might keep yourself in check? At least you're consistent. Making her as proud today as any other.' He turned to escort his wobbly teenager to a chair as I launched myself at him, slapping pathetically at his chubby jowls, his skin wobbling like a Basset's cheeks.

'And how, Golden Balls, other than being firstborn and male, did you make her proud? That and producing pretentious mini versions of yourself for her?'

Disappointingly, Archie stepped away, leaving my hand and emotions numb from the slap. Shame descended as phones pinged around me. Bursting into tears, I headed for the loo. Would I be sick? It was touch and go. I leaned over the thankfully pristine porcelain. I eyed the door, ready to projectile vomit in the direction of anyone who came to check on me. I needn't have worried. The hubbub of conversation picked up as the wake continued without me. Angry, humiliated tears fell. Not even Edwin showed his ridiculous face. Well, fuck Edwin, fuck Archie, all of them. How dare a tipsy teenager make me feel so insignificant? Why should it bother me what she or anyone thought about me? I shuddered as a bile and wine elixir rode my oesophagus like an elevator. Sweat poured from my brow, and I winced at my ghoulish reflection in the bathroom mirror.

'I have nothing and no one,' I declared aloud. And I never really have.

After heading back to my old bedroom, I hurled Edwin's suitcase violently into the hallway. The case clattered spectacularly against the door casing; my mother would have had a fit.

'Just me,' I muttered, locking the door from the inside and climbing back into bed, the greasy old candlewick bedspread pinning me down with its weight. The radio alarm blinked 17:20.

***

Returning to London did not improve my mood. The solicitor would let me know the outcome of the reading of the will. I was to be contacted only if strictly necessary. I wouldn't be apologising or even referring to Funeralgate, as I was now calling the event. And Edwin, after his failure to respond in my moment of need, could also do one. I'd blocked his number. That had happened before, but there was a finality to this time. I miserably scrolled my phone contacts, pitiful exhalation the only sound in my apartment. How did I have so few connections? The Italian leather sofa supporting my skinny backside provided little comfort, and the view of the Thames was almost unbearable to behold alone. My 'no drinking until I'm back at work' resolve had failed. I use the term 'work' loosely. My mood was only temporarily bolstered by the Chardonnay in my lonely hand. Mother's words echoed from one of our last conversations.

'Tilda, you've been spoiled. We spoiled you and now you're spoiling yourself. You haven't done anything with the loans that your father and I gifted you. You've completely neglected the charitable foundation that we worked so hard to build – how many years ago?' I'd hoped that post-death, I might not think about her quite so much, but here she was berating me from beyond the grave.

I batted away the guilt pangs nudging at my periphery. The Stand Foundation had funded, through the Catholic Society, worthy community projects, helping bridge the ever-growing poverty gap well before my time. Causes included children's counselling, bereavement support, benefits assistance – randomly, an overseas dog shelter. I had to remind myself that I *had* tried hard in the early days, following Mother's retirement, to make the charity work, but she'd effectively refused to let go of the reins. It had become clear as I scratched the surface that all was not as it seemed. The worthy causes were a smokescreen. I learned that staggering sums of money had funded UK pro-life groups, hunting petitions and rallies that I would have no part of. I was also supposed to be a visible ambassador at church, which, quite apart from being too early on a Sunday, was far removed from my value system. My mother believed that being *seen* to attend church would absolve you of your sins, at least in the eyes of others. Sins I had aplenty, but I'd never felt I needed God's opinion of them. As both a child and an adult, the feelings of revulsion I held towards the Church, in part driven by Mother's affairs with various men of the cloth, were still strong. The sanctimonious judgement that pervaded so many of the projects rendered my involvement with any aspect of the charity impossible. Only instead of saying that and folding the charity, I'd pretended. In exchange for the generous salary that I awarded myself, I'd let the Foundation limp along without any direction and certainly no progression. I'm not proud of it, but they're the facts.

Right. Stop this wallowing right now. Who could I find for a cheeky midweek catch-up? There was no one springing to mind. Friends, I was sure, had distanced themselves from me because they were uncomfortable with Edwin. Or I'd been too embarrassed to keep in touch while we continued to be an item. Either way, waves of self-pity crashed over me. Again, I picked up my phone and zipped through the names. Sonya, she was nice – wasn't she? I've known a couple of Sonya's. Oh no, this was University Sonya – done for fraud last year. Chenice – awful name. I can't believe I would address someone with that name, let alone store them in my phone. Shelby. Aw, Shelby was lovely, far too nice for the likes of me. 'Hello, Shelby. Do you remember me? We used to sit together at those awful Business for Breakfast meetings, connected through our shared loathing of them. Or maybe not, seeing as your business now turns over a few million while mine hovers in the U-bend waiting for the flush.' What I needed was a good Facebook stalk. Pouring myself another glass – *really, the bottle's gone already?* – I settled back down with my iPad.

I was bombarded with the usual horrors: friends with perfect Facebook lives, awash with adoring boyfriends, perfect bikini-clad figures silhouetted against sunsets, families tucking into delicious Sunday roasts, cuddling impossibly cute pets, birthing breathtaking newborns. Not a useful exercise given my current mood. *I could look up that guy that was hanging around last time Edwin and I split. What was he called?* Just then a message popped up.

'Hey, Tilda. Long time no speak.'

Alas. It's Ellie from the gym. *Yes, Ellie, we haven't spoken because you're as dull as dishwater.*

'You're online. It's been ages! How are you doing? X'

Things are bad.

'Hey x I'm good. How's you?' I find myself replying.

The 'I'm typing' jiggly thing comes up. My mind maps the fridge, mentally searching for another bottle.

'I'm good, Tilda. So over the breakup. Can't believe I stuck around for so long. If you fancy a catch-up some time that would be awesome.'

I'm so desperate, I respond immediately, despite Ellie's unforgivable use of the word awesome. Before I know it, we've *pencilled in* a date for Friday. A horrific wine bar at the wrong end of town. But a lunch date no less.

Lana

'Have there been any recent triggers?' the tired psychiatrist had asked. A little scripted for my liking, but I was probably his third attempted suicide of the morning. 'Have you had feelings like this before? Any recent trauma?' I had neither the energy nor the inclination to respond. Not that I'd attempted it, but yes, I'd had those thoughts. When we lost Evie. When *I* lost Evie. But I didn't say that. I told him what he needed to hear.

'I thought I was pregnant.' My voice cracked, but I was determined to hold it together. 'It turned out I wasn't. I met a friend; we downed a few drinks. I was feeling sorry for myself.' I'd rehearsed what to say. 'I got home. My partner wasn't back. I needed something to help me sleep. I didn't mean to take too many.' It felt like I was in the headteacher's office.

''So, you *wanted* to be pregnant or … you didn't?' He looked at me expectantly, pen poised, awaiting my response.

I remained silent. *You insensitive prick.*

'Will you try it again?'

Another day, he'd have had a mouthful from me. But all I could do was turn my face to the wall.

My mistake that day? Allowing hope to squeeze through the gaps in my defence, despite my promise to myself that I would *never* do that again. Not after losing Evie. The last few weeks had been strange. Wan's a DJ. Freelance. He rakes money in when there's work and we coast along when there isn't. It almost works. He'd been gigging in Croatia, which had been great. I'd enjoyed the space, just me and my shaky pregnancy belief. I'd missed a period. Mrs Clockwork had missed a period. Despite home pregnancy tests (four) coming back negative, I *knew* this was just down to the shedloads of vitamins and minerals that I'd been shoving down my neck for the last few months. I'd joined the Desperately Seeking Impregnation online army, learning all about false positives and false negatives. My research was inconclusive. But how could I not be pregnant? Tender boobs. Tick. Fatigue. Tick. Nausea. Tick? *This* time I could feel it. The awesome Dr MacKinnon would have my test results back. I was beside myself with anticipation. Veuve Clicquot or Dom Perignon? I would pick up a bottle and surprise Wan, casually perching it in the fridge, an oversized blue or pink ribbon tied around the top.

Metacognition. My every sense making its perfect best guess. Dr MacKinnon looked small behind her enormous desk. No family photos, receipts or abandoned lunch like my workspace. Detecting her cheery vibe, I knew I did not want to hear her news. Mothers of stillborn infants have a highly attuned 'false cheer' radar. My wobbly legs delivered me to the seat opposite.

'So it's a no, then – I'm not pregnant?' I cut in quickly, my voice just holding.

Dr MacKinnon looked at me squarely and wheeled her chair forward.

'Lana,' she began (use of my first name – not good), 'the test *has* come back negative; however—'

I cut her short angrily. 'So why a missed period? Can you do another? I have sore boobs, I have …' I began to list my phantom pregnancy symptoms.

'I'd asked if Joel could join today. Did you not get my message? Is he coming?'

'He can't.' I gestured dismissively, closing her down. 'Listen, it's fine if I'm not pregnant.' I shrugged. We'd just carry on shagging. As we were. Hardly a burden.

Dr MacKinnon's impossibly young forehead wrinkled behind her cropped fringe. She looked again at the screen before her, but this seemed more for distraction than to remind herself of any detail.

'The blood tests have come back with some readings that I wasn't expecting. I'm going to run them again, but it would appear from your FSH and LH levels that there's a likelihood that you're becoming perimenopausal, which means—'

'I'm thirty-two!' I responded, louder than she deserved.

'I'm going to run another set of tests; readings can be wrong, but early indicators are that if this is the case …'

I couldn't hear any more.

'Lana, please sit down. It doesn't mean what you think …'

Wan's name lit up my phone in my open bag. Lovely Wan with his prize-winning healthy sperm – every bit as desperate as I was for a baby.

Prima donna Barbie right there. The details could wait. So could Wan.

'Hey!' a miserable-looking elderly lady shouted as I barged past her. The automatic doors flew apart as I strode furiously through reception. Parking myself across the road, I sat head in hands on a bench in the square, just downwind of the public toilets. If I'd been pregnant, the smell would have been unbearable. But I wasn't. And probably never would be. With shaking hands, I dialled Jodie's number. The only person I might begin to share this with. No answer, of course. She'd be teaching. It was just me who had skipped work today, overwhelmed by morning sickness. The tears began to spill. Shakily, I texted her and headed over to the Railway Arms. The lonely rundown Arms. Perfect.

Jodie came straight from school, although you wouldn't know that. She has one look and it's far removed from any schoolteacher stereotype. The kids love her rainbow dreads and colourful outfits – purple tie-dye harems today. The kids also adore her grounded vibe. It's one of the many things I love about her too.

By the time Jodie joined me, I was well on my way. Given that I'd last drunk alcohol before I was pregnant with Evie, that gives you some idea of my threshold, and even before, I was never a big drinker. Three drinks in and I had a new BFF. I enthusiastically introduced him to Jodie when she appeared, looking alarmed at her usually sober friend. She manoeuvred us into a corner and ushered him to the other end of the bar. When she returned with a soft drink for me and a large glass of wine for herself, she found me sobbing.

'What does that mean, perimenopausal? In English.'

'It means I'm going through the change. But ridiculously early. I'm not going to …' I sobbed.

Jodie hugged me tight and stayed there until eventually my tears reduced to hiccups. If she was quaffing her drink over my back, I wouldn't blame her.

'I thought I was pregnant, Jode,' I whispered. 'I really thought I was … that enough time had passed that it would …'

Jodie listened. And listened some more. Until even I had had enough of my voice. Drinks arrived and we sipped in silence. New BFF had sent them over. Jodie gave a 'thanks, but back off' schoolteacher stare his way.

'What's Joel say? Where is he?'

'He's away. I'm not telling him over the phone. But you know what? The *only* good thing about not being pregnant is that I can get very, very merry with my bestie.' I raised my glass, and she reluctantly chinked back.

My recall was hazy. I remember a nightclub, or at least feeling old in a nightclub, swaying with teenagers in their heels to painfully bad music. There was so much drinking – glass after glass of ropey white wine – with no clue where the rounds came from. Did I pay? My BFF from the Railway reappeared fly. I had an image of him being strongarmed off the dance floor by Jodie. We joined a hen party. Jodie pretended to know the bride from school. Said bride was too far gone to argue, and we scranned the remnants of a dodgy buffet and a rancid cocktail from a plastic bucket. Later there was kebab, but too late to be of any benefit in soaking up the booze. God, I was rough. My shoulder throbbed from my grand entrance into the taxi rank's reception, where I ricocheted from wall to wall until Jodie brought me to the floor in the corner of the filthy office, arranging her coat underneath me. I tried to train my eyes on one spot – the bare bulb suspended from the ceiling – but couldn't halt the violent spin of the room. I'm sorry, Jode, if I vomited on your fake fur coat. Powerful waves of nausea swept over me, reminding the only functioning part of my brain that I wasn't pregnant.

My key refused to cooperate with the lock. Jodie propped my frame between herself and the wall and we eventually burst through the door. Wrestling me free of my jeans, she directed me towards the sofa, dragging my duvet from the bedroom. Pouring water into a pint glass, she gave me strict instructions to drink. The taxi driver honked impatiently outside. Just how I ended up finding the sleeping meds prescribed in those early days of losing Evie, I don't know. I don't think I could have found them sober. But drunken me knew where to look. Wan had stashed them under the bath – out of my reach – in those nightmare early weeks. Dispensed daily under his strict supervision until very gradually, I was weaned off them. Lovely Wan.

***

An aroma of damp hovered just beneath the smell of bleach and laundry. Wan had tried so hard to make the flat less dingy for my return home. The greasy windows were streaked with cotton flecks where he'd wiped them with a lint cloth. He'd even had a go at re-sticking the curling 1970s flock wallpaper.

Perching like a guest on the sofa, I could barely look at the begonia he'd tried to resurrect. The mulched leaves had been cleared from the base; the brass pot gleamed – he'd cleaned each of its dusty leaves. It was too much. My tears fell as the horse racing commentary filled the flat. Like clockwork, every weekday at 2 p.m., the bookies downstairs providing its intrusive yet familiar backdrop. We sat in silence until the race was over, the noise building to its predictable crescendo. Wan had set out two mugs and a teapot, an unused gift from our engagement. I could barely focus through my tears and headed for our room.

He crouched at the side of the bed.

'What did I miss, Lana?' He stroked my hair, which made me feel worse. I felt like I'd betrayed him. It was excruciating. 'After

Evie died it was … horrific. Unbearable for you, for us. But I thought you were getting there. Getting better. I wouldn't have gone away if I'd realised.'

'I thought I was too. And then somehow I convinced myself I was pregnant.' Tears spilled down my face. Wan gently wiped them away.

'Why? How? Why didn't you tell me?'

What to say? Eventually the silence broke.

'Because I knew deep down I *wasn't* pregnant but couldn't bear to hear it. In any case, I'm going through the change. So I thought I'd save myself the heartbreak. And you.' The pain inside was unbearable, but my tone was angry.

'So you thought by topping yourself you would "save my heartache"? Seriously?'

I shrugged. 'I don't mean it like that. But I *cannot* bear another month where you can't quite meet my eye. *"Next time. It's okay, babe."* Well, it's not, is it? It's fucking devastating.'

'I don't know what I can do to make this better. But blaming me doesn't.' Wan was crying now.

Burying my head under the pillow, I sobbed loudly, deliberately drowning him out. He stormed out of the door. Seconds later I heard the ping of the fridge and the snap of a ring pull. *Excellent work, Wan.* I was jealous of his beer strategy when all I had were my spiralling and mean thoughts.

It was about midnight when Wan came to bed. I stirred. I couldn't smell booze, so I guessed he'd only had a couple. I was hurt that he couldn't sit out my pain with me. But I get it. It's way worse seeing someone else's than managing your own. I snuggled into the crook of his left arm, like always. He gently kissed the top of my head.

'We'll make this work. We'll figure it out,' Wan whispered.

'I'm sorry. Truly.'

'I know.'

'I've not *gone* through the change, just going through it, I think. Maybe they can freeze my eggs or something. I don't know. But I *must* have a solution.' I knew that Wan would be dying to use the 'A' word. But he was banned. It's frankly insulting to me that people, usually those who have kids of their own, think it's appropriate to suggest adoption. I don't want *any* baby. I want mine.

'I want a baby with my funky hair and your ...'

'Musical genius?' Wan laughed.

'I want a brother or sister for Evie. If we need input from an IVF doctor who might take all our money, then so be it.' I turned to the wall, my go-to-sleep position.

Wan squeezed me tighter by way of a goodnight.

'Babe.' Moments later, I thought Wan had something important to add. 'Do you think when they defrost the eggs or whatever they do, the docs can screen for the possibility of the baby ending up with my shit hair and your lack of rhythm?'

'Any more thoughts, do hesitate to share,' I whispered back, squeezing him tight, thankful for this man.

***

It's worth the extra ten minute walk to my mum's house. Going via the canal avoids the dodgy precinct. It's not exactly unsafe by the shops, but at best it's hard work saying no to the poor sods pleading for a quid. I'd had a busy few weeks. School was mental, but every spare moment had been dedicated to my own homework – PhD-level research into early menopause and IVF. I'd wanted to be as informed as possible prior to the consultation with Dr MacKinnon. She specialises in fertility outside of her GP role, and I wanted to fully understand all the options open to me.

As we walked, I updated Wan on both my research and the outcome of the appointment with Dr MacKinnon. Obviously, I'd become an overnight expert, having joined several fertility forums and reading a zillion articles on the subject. Dr MacKinnon had referred us to a consultant but couldn't make any promises regarding timeframes. If we needed to harvest my eggs (as per my amateur googling), then that was what we'd do. We'd consider private options if the NHS couldn't help us this side of the decade. It would be costly. Our house deposit was the only money at our disposal, which I would use in a heartbeat. Any other decisions we would deal with as they came up; my priority was to harvest as many eggs as possible before my ovaries decided to call it a day. It felt good to have a plan. Wan didn't interrupt. Neither did he object. I took this as supportive without inviting his thoughts on our sabotaged finances or jeopardised homeowner status.

Standing at the front door of my mum's neglected terraced property, I heard my nieces and nephews long before I could see their willowy figures approaching through the wavy glass.

'Auntie Lana!' announced Syl, bouncing up and down with excitement. He was head and shoulders shorter than his six-year-old twin, but still he beat her to the hug, wrestling through knees to grab my and Wan's legs, pulling us in over the doorstep.

Mum's Sunday brunch is a monthly tradition that when we can, we opt out of. They're lovely but intense. Think survival of the fittest. The quickest get the food, the loudest are heard, the whole experience is overwhelming. It's tough on Wan. As the only child of middle-aged, reserved parents, he often looks shell-shocked. Between my five procreating siblings are *seventeen* grandchildren. Thankfully, they don't all appear every time, but there's usually a fair number, and there's always drama. Girlfriend drama with my younger brother; my eldest brother just out on licence (don't ask); general child noise and mayhem. Mum squished me with a big mama hug, which immediately made me tear up. If anyone was remotely nice to me, I would cry – I'd been at it all week. I hoped there would be drama on offer to draw attention away from me. I followed her through to the cramped kitchen, where she stirred a giant pan of spicy egg and potato.

'You've been holing yourself up there in your flat whilst your man's away – why didn't you come visit? We missed you. It's been crazy without my best girl to keep the peace!' Tears sprang to my eyes – she refers to us all separately as 'her best', but still. Mum eyed me carefully, shifting her focus from the bubbling pan. She would know that something was off. With Wan away, I would normally have popped over. I opened my mouth, about to comment that *she* could have contacted me, but that was old ground – the hierarchy of my siblings' needs versus the 'stable Lana', who doesn't get a look-in.

'Mum,' I began, checking the door was properly closed. I hadn't rehearsed this and had no idea how it would come out. My mum's traditional and uber Catholic, and I had no idea if she would get her head around our news. I went through the motions of prepping a coffee, rummaging for the packet at the back of the sticky cupboard. Anything but eye contact.

'I'm going to say this quickly, Mum, and I don't want you to tell the others, right?'

She shifted her bulk to face me and placed her hand over mine, halting my coffee prep.

'Knew something was up.' Balancing the spoon across the pan, she looked expectant. I had her attention.

'This is a weird question. How old were you when you went through the change? I mean, old, right? Ben is eighteen now, which must have made you about … thirty-six when you had him? Pretty old?'

'He was my surprise boy! Thought I was all done and dusted early thirties, but God had other plans.' She laughed loudly.

'Doctor MacKinnon says I'm going through the change … I'm thirty-two.' My voice broke. The devastation hit me all over again.

Tears filmed her eyes, and she brought me in close. 'Aw, Lana. My love.'

'God, all I ever do is cry these days.' Anger and sadness competed as I wiped away my tears. 'I *don't* want the others to know.'

Mum dabbed my tears gently with a tissue. 'So you're going to need your sister's eggs?' she asked genuinely.

'Mum!' I didn't want anybody else's eggs. Least of all my mental sister's. 'How can you even say that?'

This wasn't the response I'd been expecting. Where were my reassurances? My platitudes?

'I started at around your age and thought I was all done by about thirty-three – so yes, I think I was pretty early.'

'Why didn't you say? You know we've been trying!' I said sharply, immediately regretting my tone. I allowed myself to be pulled in tight to her enormous chest. The door cracked open slightly, but Mum glared fiercely, shooing the figures away.

'I will pray for you, Lana. All will be well. You'll see.' Prayer, I didn't need. Money would have been helpful, but I knew that wasn't on the table. Prayer and love were all my mum could offer.

'We're going to see about harvesting my eggs. Maybe give IVF a go, given that we've been trying for eighteen months since Evie.' I didn't mention the phantom pregnancy or suicide attempt. My siblings had all the drama covered – no need to add my contribution.

'I will pray for your baby and their test tube journey.' Mum gestured crudely with her hands, unbelievably, one as an egg, the other an energetically swimming sperm. 'Yours and Joel's?' she queried.

I nodded. 'Not my sister's, anyway!' I was incredulous that my mum's first thought would be of me carrying one of my bonkers sister's children. Chelsea, my middle brother's toddler, came waddling innocently through the door, reaching her pudgy arms skyward for a squeeze. Scooping her up, we jimmied down the narrow hall towards the main group in search of Wan, who would absolutely need rescuing.

'Top Secret, Mum – I don't want this lot to know. Right?' I popped my head briefly back around the kitchen door. Meaning, of course, my siblings. Mum nodded solemnly, although she indicated that she would need to let God into the loop by her heavenward gesture.

***

I needed to hear my options without Wan's input and attended the first consultation on my own. It felt illicit, like cheating, but this felt more about me than us. Retrospectively, I'm aware of how selfish that sounds. I should have involved Wan more in those early stages, particularly given how things played out.

Wan looked taken aback as I updated him over dinner that evening. He didn't say explicitly *'Do I not get a say in this?'* because he's Wan. He just rolled with it. On some level I was irritated that he didn't, even when I casually threw in that we'd be self-financing, as in not covered by the NHS. He seemed more concerned with his part in the mechanics.

'Let me get this straight. I just need to go in the loo and think about ... you, obviously.' He tried hard to look serious. 'And I need to' – he gestured with a very gentlemanly wanking motion – 'do my thing, then it can all happen? I don't need hormones or too much messing down there?'

'So *good* that you got that GCSE biology back in the day!' I leaned over the table and kissed him gently. He looked around awkwardly, uncomfortable with remotely affectionate behaviour in public.

'Yes, you do your thing.' I mimicked his so-polite wanking gesture. 'It's important to run from the cubicle, get the swimmers while they've got energy. "Live sperm coming through,'" I teased, thoroughly enjoying his discomfort. *I have the tricky job to do. Trying to keep hold of it while it cooks.*

'So, tell me again why we can't go through the doc and get it funded like every bugger else.'

Don't block me on this, Wan. I can't cope if you do. 'Because,' I explained again, 'to qualify for NHS IVF – or ART, as it's called now – we must have been unable to conceive for at least two years. That means we'd have to hang on for another six months before the NHS would even look at us. And I *know* how long the NHS takes for egg harvesting, from the forum. I'll be Gangsta Granny before we get anything sorted. We might get lucky, but I'm worried it'll take too long and we'll be too late. So I think private should be our first option.'

'ART?'

'Assisted Reproductive Technique. Sounds so much nicer than IVF, don't you think?'

'I'm not sure what to think. But I feel a playlist coming on. All things artificial, egg-related? Think sticky situations, fake stuff, but optimistic. What do you think?'

'Oh, now the DJ's interested.' I tried hard not to think about the beautiful playlist Wan had put together to welcome Evie. It was almost too painful to listen to even now. We'd so carefully chosen the tracks to welcome her to the world. Evie's favourite during pregnancy was 'All the Small Things' – Blink 182. A belter from back in the day, and always one to get her moving. If it made him happy to contribute, then it was fine with me.

'"Art for Art's Sake" ... Art Garfunkel ... anything from the Sticky Fingers album. 'I Am the Walrus' -the perfect egg reference - the entire *Harvest* album, Neil Young. A classic.' He seemed genuinely excited.

'Are you sure about our savings, Wan? There's no guarantee that this will work. We might use our deposit and still be childless. Forever doomed to living in the curly-wallpapered dive that is our home.'

'If I never see you again in a hospital bed with tubes every which way, then it's all good with me.' Wan couldn't quite look me in the eye, his distress still raw. The shame of my drunken efforts to not be there, to take away the horrific pain that hadn't shifted since Evie died, was ever present. I'd just found ways to survive. Or so I'd thought. I'd rejected subsequent offers of mental health support, unable to process my behaviour or admit to myself that the pain of surviving was worth it.

The waiter hovered to our left. There was that awkwardness when nobody speaks but you're obliged to make enthusiastic noises about the food, which did not look great. Still, we obliged.

Wan raised a glass as he left. 'To us.' We clinked, his red to my soda. The hollow chink was not lost on me, and Wan's expression fell short of being able to mask his anxiety. Or maybe I'm adding that retrospectively, knowing that everything went pear-shaped.

Tilda

Café Noir was my first real outing since returning to London. The normality of setting the alarm, showering, choosing an outfit and putting on makeup all felt good. Ellie always dressed to impress – making every inch of her curvaceous body count. I'd opted for a vintage checkered catsuit with my funeral heels (who would know?) and ridiculously oversized Mongolian fur bag. At just after 12 the bar was warming up with the lunch crowd. Scanning the room however, I could see no sign of Ellie. There was a loud work group, hipster Uni crowd, Wrinkly Brigade- already quaffing rose- and several mums with pushchairs and whining toddlers. My phone buzzed just as I was about to call Ellie. Her voice boomed in stereo just to my left.

'I'm here!' She shrieked excitedly from a booth. How long had it did been since we'd seen each other? Ellie looked stunning as always – but where had she gone? She'd dropped about three dress sizes and -behold- was breastfeeding a baby! I rushed to hug her, masking my shocked expression.

'So, I won't ask what you've been up to?' I laughed, gesturing at the tiny head perched discreetly underneath her shirt.

'You didn't know about Rosa? I definitely told you. Didn't I?'

'I swear I didn't know that you were even pregnant, Ellie that's amazing,' I gushed. She looked as stunning as ever but was now exuding serene maternal vibes.

'How?' I gestured at her impossibly tiny frame. 'I mean you look great- but then you always did.' I hoped that didn't sound too terrible.

'I had the world's *worst* morning sickness. I was in hospital throughout the whole pregnancy. It was horrific, but I survived-we survived! I got this.... condition,' she waved her hand dismissively. 'Anyway, I thought that Rosa would be really premature or tiny, but she was neither.' Ellie beamed and looked proudly down at the feeding bundle.

I nodded to the barman who brought over a half decent bottle of fizz, despite my initial misgivings about the place. It genuinely felt lovely to see Ellie who seemed far more animated than I ever remembered her when we'd had drinks after spin class.

I was strangely curious to see the face of baby Rosa. I'd always been baby ambivalent; I think. There was one time in my early thirties when Edwin and I had a scare. I was about three weeks late for no apparent reason. I told myself that Edwin was far too old to be a father and that was that.

'So, what have you been up to? Been back to the North at all?' Ellie skilfully unhitched the baby and fastened herself back up.

'I was there a few weeks ago,' I paused to take a gulp of fizz. 'For my mother's funeral.'

'Oh, I'm so sorry.'

'Don't be. I'm not.'

Ellie looked shocked but pursued anyway. 'Weren't you close?' She stood to wind Rosa and swayed on her elegant heels. I'm sure the old Ellie would have hedged politely away.

I found myself attempting a sanitised version of where things were up to, with the potential closing of the Foundation and the shittiness of the funeral but I really wasn't sure that I had the stomach for digging it all back up.

'What about Edwin? How's he doing?'

'We need a proper catch up, preferably over half a dozen bottles of wine- but I've finally ended things with Edwin. Really. Properly. Finito this time.'

'Well, that's interesting. And I couldn't agree more. I can give you the low down on the arsehole antics of Jed. The formerly lovely boyfriend who thought it was okay to sleep with his boss- right through our pregnancy. I even had him back at one point. To my shame!' Ellie teared up and instinctively smoothed Rosa's hair.

'And we haven't missed him at all have we?' Ellie cooed into Rosa's ear; her soft head now perched on Ellie's shoulder.

'God Ellie. That's horrific. I'm so sorry. What a twat!'

I mouthed an apology for my blasphemy to Rosa.

'That's putting it mildly!'

I'd always thought that Jed was a bit of a knob. And Ellie had always been so besotted with him.

'He was always having a pop at my weight, trying to put me on crazy diets. I literally cannot believe that I tolerated it.'

I recalled dreary conversations with Ellie-boring me rigid with details of her latest insane diet and sharing beyond tedious loved-up selfies of her and Jed overlaid with ridiculous heart emojis. Truly.

Ellie deliberated as she saw me eyeing the waiter to bring another bottle. To be fair I'd had the lion's share as Ellie had only politely sipped.

'Not for me, thanks,' Ellie quickly covered her glass. 'I've got to get going; I'm meeting my baby group at two. Would you mind just hanging onto Rosa for a sec whilst I nip to the loo?' Ellie extended the bundled Rosa towards me. I hesitated. The last baby I'd held would have been Octavia. I was completely out of practice. Ellie thrust her my way and made off to the loo. Perching on my chair, not daring to move in case she woke, I peered through the swaddled blanket. I spied her tiny rosebud mouth, eyes flickering beneath impossibly delicate eyelids. Oh, she was a sweetie. What on earth was wrong with me? I have *never* thought of other people's babies as anything but a barrier between myself and their parent having fun. If Edwin could see me, he'd have a fit. An embolism, quite literally. But then Edwin wasn't my compass now. I was.

My mother had bequeathed me an eyewatering amount of money. I knew she was loaded, but even I was taken aback. Of course, I should have been ecstatic, and I *almost* was. I just wasn't sure what to make of it, nor quite what to do with it. Or myself. Since I'd shared with the funders my intention to close the charity, I could no longer pretend to have a day job. My old routine of checking emails and making an art form out of not replying left me strangely without anchor.

I found myself in an unhealthy sleep/wake cycle like an unsupervised teenager. 'Going for coffee' was the only scheduled event in my day. I'd returned to the gym as an added juncture to my routine, but my days were unremarkable. Ellie had joined a gym with a crèche, and without her, my workouts were dull. I'd tried to chat with a girl in my Salsacise class, but it felt clunky and awkward. I think she was Russian, and we struggled to understand one another over the Tijuana beat. I flashed her a smile as she passed through the restaurant on her way out, but I don't think she noticed. I wondered how long I'd been giving off socially awkward vibes. Probably since birth. Wandering home via Harvey Nic's, I found myself dropping decadent items into my basket. Throwing in horribly expensive deli nibbles and an exquisite bottle of red, I somehow found myself – after a quick circuit in Ladies New Season – in a cul-de-sac of first teen, then baby wear, drawn to a delightful silk dress – a christening gown, sheer ivory with antique lace. It sounds hideous but was stunning. I stroked the fabric gently. Would it be weird if it I bought it for Rosa? I mean, not as a christening gown but as a summer dress, a posh picnic dress. No, it was a christening gown. I moved to everyday wear and found a gorgeous Armani dungaree set in violet, the price of an adult outfit and far too cute to leave. Money had no meaning. I left the store giddy with excitement, clutching my purchases and wondering when I might next see Ellie and Rosa.

***

'Hi, this is Ellie and Rosa. Leave us a message.'

I couldn't get hold of Ellie, despite my best stalking efforts. It felt good not to be answerable to Edwin, but there was an Edwin-shaped hole where he'd existed. It had been the right thing to do, though. His apathy towards my distress at Mother's funeral was the final straw. I didn't want to hear his explanation. I'd been there too many times before. But still, I was lonely. The guy I'd been Facebook stalking – the bearded dude from last summer – had messaged a few times. Then I remembered why it hadn't gone anywhere. How to put this? He'd seemed mainstream originally but became increasingly Neanderthal. I was picking up veiled but definite right-wing views. My brother would love him. I, however, would not. There'd been a couple of friends with whom I'd picked back up, but my life desperately needed direction, and soon. *Do I go back to uni? Buy a racehorse? Develop a cocaine habit?* Something needed to happen. I'd got the alcohol abuse comfortably covered, but even that was becoming tedious. My heartburn was off the scale, my skin a daily reminder of the previous night's overindulgence.

I bumped into Ellie before we connected over the phone, striding up Hampstead Heath at around 7 p.m. to stave off wine o'clock. Every step powered me up the Heath while trying to stall the call of the Sauvignon beckoning me home. I didn't notice her initially – a mini version of herself jogging with headphones and a buggy. The epitome of the Yummy Mummy. Doing it all alone without a Tasty Daddy in sight. Such respect.

'Ellie,' I blurted, practically flagging her down.

She hugged me warmly, removing her earbuds and apologising. She'd seen my missed calls but had been really 'caught up'. Did that mean she'd ignored them, as I had when she'd tried to catch me back in the day? I felt a pang of guilt. Baby Rosa pumped her tiny arms and legs and looked ecstatic to see me. I almost filled up. Bending down, I took her tiny fist and jiggled back.

'I've got something for Rosa. It's nothing really, just feel bad that I missed her birth and stuff. Let's get together! What are you doing now? You can come back to mine,' I gushed. Not needy at all. Ellie looked slightly taken aback.

'That would be great.' She nodded. Too enthusiastically? Or was I just being paranoid?

'Literally, I'm free now.'

Ellie paused.

'Sure. If you're not too busy? I'd hate to intrude.'

Baby Rosa would normally have been in bed by her strict 7 p.m. bedtime. Thankfully, Ellie thought it would be fine as a one-off.

As we entered the apartment, I was relieved that I'd cleared last night's empties and takeaway carnage.

'Wow! This is stunning. That view!' Ellie let out a high-pitched whistle as she wheeled the buggy towards the balcony, taking in the dramatic landscape of the Thames, the vastness of Tower Bridge. Normally I would have been falling over myself to show off the vista; however, baby Rosa was stirring. Ellie's attention was immediately redirected. I remembered my mother's famous quote at baby Rupert's christening – 'The feeling you have for your firstborn' – thanks for the clarification, Mother – 'is like a drug. If you could bottle it, you'd be a millionaire.' Your second-born would always remember those words and the second-class sentiment that came with it.

I busied myself making tea for Ellie, stopping myself from reaching for the chilled option. I could have tea too. How was it possible to lose hours simply meeting the needs of a tiny human? By the time Ellie had fed and changed her, then generally faffed about delighting over her, we decided takeaway might be a shout. Tiny Rosa was centre stage on her blanket in my living room, living her best life, staying up late and beaming like she approved wholeheartedly of the rule-breaking. I was smitten.

'They're beautiful! Look, Rosa – your favourite colour!' Ellie held the dungarees towards Rosa kicking on the blanket and squeezed me tightly. 'You're too kind!' She beamed. Her hug felt more genuine than any I'd tolerated at the funeral.

'It's nothing, really. I can't explain just how cute this little girl is.' I could feel my face flush. *Did that sound weird?* 'I don't think I've ever noticed other people's babies before!'

'That's because she's the most amazing bubba in the world!' Ellie laughed, blowing a quick raspberry on her belly, generating an infectious giggle from Rosa.

Ellie asked the inevitable. That was okay. There was a time in my early thirties when I'd had badges made so that when people asked me, in their various direct or indirect ways, if I wanted children, I had a punchy response. I kept a handful in my bag and looked forward to handing them out when the situation demanded. The bright pink badge read in green font: *'I'm fond of sleeping in, drinking shitloads of wine and watching daytime porn.'* They were spectacular. As I'd gotten older, people seemed to have stopped asking, which was disappointing. My response was different this time.

'You know, I did think about it one time. But I was with Edwin, and his children were adults before we'd even gotten together. I guess the time was just never right,' I said as steadily as I could, the memory of my badges seeming so flaky as Rosa cooed and kicked before us.

'You still could?' Ellie ventured gently.

'I could, I guess, technically.' I laughed.

'If I can do it on my own, anyone can,' Ellie said emphatically. 'It's been the making of me. It's changed everything about me as a person. At one time the idea of being a single mum would have been unthinkable – for me, anyway.'

'With respect, it must be incredibly challenging on your own. I don't have a partner and I'm not looking, so it's probably a non-starter. I was thinking I'd maybe do something radical with my mother's money – I don't know, create a kibbutz, open a women's refuge, something useful, seeing as I've been Chief Procrastinator for so long. Maybe something closer to home but less virtuous – I could buy a vineyard!' I was telling Ellie more than my current counsellor had managed to extract in the last four expensive years.

'Tilda. You need to do whatever makes you happy.' She placed her arm gently on mine. 'We only get one go around, so if it's remotely on your bucket list, you need to do it before you leave it too late. And there's nothing more radical than having a baby. Besides, you could have a baby and do the other stuff too. Go on, indulge me. What would you want, a boy or girl? I was desperate for a boy, but when Rosy Rosa came out, I couldn't imagine having anything but her.'

It wasn't something I'd ever given conscious thought to, but immediately an image appeared. A mini-me. A little girl with wispy blond hair, blue-grey eyes and dimples.

'I don't know, but if Mr Right appears any time soon and I find myself impregnated, you'll be the first to know! And I promise you can organise the baby shower.'

I laughed a tinny laugh, suddenly feeling like I needed my own company. Not even so that I could open that bottle of white I'd been craving the last few hours. Ellie and Rosa took an eternity to get their gear together and vacate the apartment, yet the moment they left, I felt strangely alone. What on earth was wrong with me?

The following morning, I made an appointment with Jenna, my on/off counsellor. I'd seen her for years following a voluntary stint in a detox. My drinking at the time had been completely off the scale – blackouts, bruises, waking in strange beds, you name it – my increasingly erratic behaviour forcing drastic action. Against Edwin's wishes (because it challenged his own alcoholism), I'd stayed in a high-end clinic for two months.

hobnobbing with B-list celebrities and the like. It had cost a fortune, but I'd left feeling much improved. I'd seen many therapists over the years, but for the first time I began to build a relationship with the counsellor there.

After several sessions I found myself stepping towards the root of my problems, which I'd been unable to verbalise to anyone previously. Which prompted my self-discharge. A close call in revisiting aspects of my childhood that I'd sworn I never would. The counsellor had referred me to Jenna for follow-up. She turned out to be an extremely poor second, and I was unable to build the trusting relationship that had developed within detox. I was supposed to see Jenna to explore further the issues that I'd only scratched the surface of in the clinic. However, the safety bubble popped as soon as I got out. Drinking with Edwin again became the norm, and I hedged neatly away from Jenna's efforts to further open the lid on memories too painful to acknowledge while trying to function in the real world. However, seeing Jenna intermittently had been helpful in keeping my drinking levels from tipping from high to dangerous. In theory, at least. A timely cancellation that afternoon saw me squeezed in and resuming my old position on her couch just a short hop from my apartment. I felt sheepish updating her that Edwin and I had resumed and again abandoned our relationship when my game plan last session had been to never see him again. But I was sure she was used to 'dogs returning to their vomit', as I used to (openly) describe my continued return to him. Jenna listened as I glanced over my shameful behaviour at mother's funeral.

'I feel like I need to do something really radical with my life. I'm just not sure what. I feel very empty is the best way I can describe it. Embarrassingly empty. Take this morning. I know that forcing myself to do stuff should make me feel better but I don't think I can keep doing it. I found myself crying mid-workout at the gym. Everywhere I looked there just seemed to be …' Words failed me. 'Humans with connections – the kind of connection that has *always* eluded me. Even with Edwin, I never really felt connected – fully understood. It's devastating.' Wiping away my tears, I was aware of how utterly miserable I sounded.

'Again, last week. There was an older guy together with a younger woman, in her twenties, I think, probably his daughter. She was matching him on the treadmill. He raised an eyebrow every time she picked up the pace but stepped up to match her every time. You could see the love that sat between them. I was close to my dad, but never in a way that meant we spent time together. We just had each other's backs as we shouldered my mother's unpleasantness between us. Mother and Golden Balls versus my poor father and me.'

Jenna nodded and jotted something on her pad, which irritated me.

'After my workout, I was changing and a little girl wandered over, about three or so, ginger spiral curls – she liked my neon leggings. I could see her grandmother watching in the mirror, looking so proud of her granddaughter's confidence. I will never have this. Never had. It's not fucking fair.'

Jenna offered tissues.

'No, it's not, Tilda,' she soothed. 'We've acknowledged many times the impact of your mother's behaviour upon both your childhood and your adult life. It has been significant, her criticism, her infidelity and disapproval of you, immobilising you. You've struggled to build trusting relationships of your own as you've convinced yourself that partners would be unfaithful to you. Now, however, your mother has passed, and you will be reflecting on several levels. Whilst this will be painful, it will also provide a space for growth. If you allow it.'

I pondered for a moment. 'You're right. I have a friend, Ellie; she has a baby. You know the little people that I've always held in some kind of derision? Suddenly, that's all I can see anywhere. Babies, people in relationships, families. I think it's what I'm missing.'

Jenna attempted to maintain a neutral expression. And failed, her eyes wide like a constipated pug. On cue, she gestured towards the clock.

'Let's discuss this next session. For now, proceed slowly, Tilda. Decisions following a bereavement – even one you insist to be unaffected by – should be carefully considered. I had a Methodist client once in the aftermath of a complex bereavement. He'd donated his house to charity, joined a cult and developed substance-related psychosis within four months of his loss.'

'Sounds like a plan!' I grinned. 'I'll give it some thought.'

Jenna looked taken aback. 'Talk to your nearest and dearest. People you trust. I would, however, recommend against Edwin.' She was quick to clarify.

That wouldn't take long, then.

My homework was to consider a range of futures and map these to preferred outcomes. 'Talk with someone who knows you well. I don't think you're clinically depressed or anxious but at a reflective point in your life. This is normal, if uncomfortable.'

Her disapproval at the very mention of my having a child and strict clock watching at what could have been a pivotal moment for me felt off. Not to mention her bizarre comparison to her former Methodist client. Fighting strong feelings of irritation, I still found myself making an appointment for the following week. I was that desperate.

***

'Auntie Ellie!' Pippa hollered from the highest point of the climbing frame. Ellie waved manically and stuck out her tongue. Pippa squealed with delight.

'Remind me who she is again?'

'It's complicated. She's my brother's daughter's friend who's like family but not. Her family are batshit crazy. We help where we can.'

I was struck by a ridiculous pang of envy. *My* family were batshit crazy. Where had been my Auntie Ellie to scoop me up and love me? Ashamed of my pettiness and seeming inability to move forward, I busied myself making faces at Rosa babbling in her car seat.

'So, she told you to what? Imagine your preferred futures? God, you're lucky, Tilda.'

I felt stung. How was I lucky? My misery and loneliness were consuming me alive.

She continued, 'my 'preferred future' options are that the council might grant me a parking space outside my flat or, if I was really pushing it, that Rosa would be considered within the catchment area for the only decent school within five miles. The sky's the limit for you. So, what do you think?'

'I think I'd trade for what you have in a second.'

Ellie proffered her hand. 'Deal!' She laughed but dodged as I thrust my hand her way. 'You're wadded, Tilda. You can do anything. Why are you even here in this mangy playground on this dismal London day? Why aren't you on an exotic beach with a hot waiter plying you with cocktails? I know I would be.'

'Edwin and I used to go on dock-off holidays all the time. I've done it. They bored me rigid I don't know what I want, but that's not it.'

Pippa had slithered from the climbing frame and was bouncing energetically at Ellie's side. 'Auntie Ellie! Look how long I can hop on one leg for! Watch!' she shrieked with so much joy on her small face, her plaits bouncing in rhythm. 'Auntie Tilda, look!' she continued. I was annoyed for a moment at her interruption before I remembered that adults are supposed to be kind to giddy children. I felt a strange flutter at the 'Auntie' reference, despite having no relationship with this child.

'That is impressive one-leg hopping, Pippa. The best I've seen!' Ellie laughed. Pippa's nose wrinkled in delight as she sped up the hopping.

'I don't know what to do, Ellie. My Google history is beyond random. Over the last three days my searches have included, and I quote ...' I held my phone aloft.

'Buying a vineyard in Chile – FAQs. Can you open a kibbutz if you are not Jewish?' Ellie roared with laughter; Rosa joined in.

'And my personal favourite, "Do nuns have to take a vow of silence?" I mean, how do I choose?'

Pippa, still mid-hop, offered a solution. 'Auntie Tilda, when I can't decide if I want to play with Meesha or Lucy, I hop and say their names until I mess up. Whoever's name it lands on, I play with them. Sometimes I do it on purpose if I really don't want to play with Lucy because sometimes she's mean …'

Ellie grabbed Rosa from the car seat to join in the chat. 'Pippa, you're such a smart girl. Why didn't we think of that? Tilda, let the hopping decide!' Ellie shrieked as loudly as Pippa.

'If you think I'm hopping in public, you're wrong. In fact, I don't think I'd hop in private either. I prefer the considered approach!' I could feel my cheeks burning as amused parents looked on.

'Shall I do it for you, Auntie Tilda?' Pippa so wanted to help, bless her.

Ellie interjected. 'Well,' she volunteered, 'it's between vineyard, kibbutz, baby or nun, it seems. Let's practise!' Seeing my horrified expression, she brought her voice down. 'Vineyard, kibbutz, baby or nun!' she whispered to Pippa.

'Yard, butz, baby or nun. Yard, butz, baby or nun!' Pippa understood completely that this needed to be discreet. She chanted quietly under her breath as her hops became quicker, her left foot moving at an impossibly high speed.

'… butz, baby!' she whispered, turning to both of us before collapsing dramatically to the floor. She lay panting, full length across the foam flooring, her legs trembling with the challenge. 'Are you having a baby, Auntie Tilda? Will she be friends with Rosa?' she exclaimed.

'I think you did that on purpose, Pippa, because somebody is rather fond of babies, maybe?' Ellie teased. Pippa got to her feet and sped back off to the climbing frame. Thankfully, the attention of the nearby parents seemed to have migrated elsewhere.

'Well, that's that sorted, Tilda!' Ellie laughed and pushed my shoulder playfully. 'Out of the mouths of babes and all that.'

'Who knew it would be so simple! Thanks, I'll let you know what Jenna makes of the methodology.' I laughed. It felt surreal. To be even talking about having a baby made me feel both anxious and elated at the same time. Was it a ridiculous idea that I might have a child? Probably. Or would it be the best decision I would ever make? Edwin and my mother would scoff. Which made the idea most appealing.

Wan

'The world breaks everyone and afterward some are stronger at the broken places.' Hemingway. Not sure where I pulled that one from, as you know I'm no reader. I'd love to believe it was true, though. But the bit of me that broke when Evie died has not made me stronger. It's created a wound that I don't think will ever heal. Then, seeing Lana attached to tubes, physically and emotionally shattered after her overdose, did not make me stronger. It introduced a new vulnerability, a set of fractures that I can't figure out how to mend. I think I'll end up like one of those broken cartoon characters, walking around until the fractures merge and I crumble into a million pieces.

When Evie died there was an avalanche of support.

'How's Lana? How's she coping? It must be terrible for her.'

Friends checked in, sent food, cards. But they had no clue what to say to me, nor I to them. 'Keep strong for Lana' was the message. Reference to my feelings seemed beyond people's reach. Maybe it's because I'm reserved, particularly compared to Lana, or maybe it's what people think blokes should hear. Lana nailed it; she said I'm made of 'different stuff' to her and her family. Lana's mum literally wailed out loud when she heard that Evie had died. My parents told me that they were devastated. Well, they didn't; they wrote it in a card. How can I show Lana how much I'm hurting when I literally don't have the words?

It's irritating watching your partner grieve. That sounds harsh, but it's true. After we lost Evie, Lana took to her bed. I took to my studio. To cry where Lana couldn't see. It was beyond her that I could seemingly 'carry on as usual', the implication being that I wasn't as devastated as she was. But if we both sank, who would keep us afloat? Instead, I threw myself into work. When

I wasn't gigging, I was mixing, making new playlists. Trying hard to offer a smile to lift Lana's frown.

So, here I am, pretending to feel strong so that I can be strong for Lana. Because I don't know what I will do if she tries to kill herself again. I've joined a grieving dads blog. Lana doesn't know and I need her to think I'm doing just fine. I can handle her thinking I'm not as upset as her if that makes it easier for her.

'It's different for the mother,' I've been told many times. But I would tell you that's not true. If I had the words.

Lana

I was so ashamed of my behaviour. Aware of how selfish, indulgent, narrow in its thinking it was. I didn't *have* to have my own child. We *could* adopt. We could foster. I could do something completely different with my life, an alternative to being a mother. Literally, Wan would support me in any direction I chose. So why was I hauled continually back to the belief that a life without my own child was not a life worth living? I felt guilty that I didn't love Wan enough to stay alive. But that was the truth. And I didn't love myself enough either.

Early menopause. The words made me feel masculine, but something about the news didn't surprise me. Stigma does that. It forever taints you, and no matter how hard you try, you can't quite decontaminate yourself. I *think* I had happy memories from before my dad died, but I'm not sure if I've made them up. I do remember days out as a family, trips to the seaside, a night when we went to the park with a family from over the road. We didn't know them very well and it felt awkward, so I've no idea how that came about. I remember Mum and Dad hanging back, laughing with the parents, whose names I can't remember. Joe and Sam were the kids, older than us and moody. My sister and I couldn't believe they called their parents by their first names and were allowed to swear. Even the F word. I can remember trying to create distance between my siblings and the boys, trying to walk ahead while keeping them in sight. One, two, three, four, a constant headcount. My parents had had a drink, and although Mum would deny it, her guard would be down. That was okay because I was there, pushing my youngest sibling in the pram while watching that the others didn't stray too near the stream or wander too far ahead. I'm guessing that life was okay – non-traumatic at least – because nothing really stood out. But after Dad died, that changed.

Mum was adamant that she never asked me to look after my siblings. It was just something I did because for a time after he died, she couldn't. My twelve-year-old understanding was that Dad had lost control of the bus he was driving through the midweek rush-hour traffic. The bus had somehow careered across the road and collided with a truck going in the opposite direction. Mum reassured us he'd been killed instantly. I have no clue if that was true or if the same could be said for the elderly passengers that passed with him. Had they felt fear and pain in their last moments as they swayed at the front of the bus waiting for their stop? Passengers had raised concerns just moments before the fatal crash as the driver sped and weaved erratically through the traffic. Toxicology tests would confirm elevated alcohol levels, of which my mother never spoke. But neighbours – and the community – did. Kids at school found out and never let me forget it.

'To kill yourself drunk driving is your own funeral,' Auntie Stella slurred. I'd have been about fourteen and eavesdropping on the stairs, avoiding creaky stair number seven to avoid detection. It was late, but always worth an earwig when Auntie Stella visited. Mum never drank again after Dad died. Auntie Stella did, though. My God. I heard the clumsy top-up of her glass.

'Sylvia said they'd just celebrated their *fiftieth* wedding anniversary. They were Methodists, you know. Never touched a drop their whole life,' she whispered, referring to the pensioners that had passed that day, hoping to get off a stop early before heading to the market. Mum sniffed and I heard the familiar rustle of a tissue.

'God will resurrect them in the fullness of time.' Mum clung to her faith and by extension our only source of support – the Church. Given that we'd been ostracised by most of the community, it made sense. For her, anyway.

In the months following Dad's death, Mum would wordlessly scrub the graffiti from the front door every morning before we left for school. I would hear the furious to and fro of the wire brush as she vented her anger in those early mornings, long before my siblings woke. She'd march us all, heads held high, down the path to school, her efforts to shield us from the hecklers almost successful. But for me, as the eldest, the damage was done. I would always be 'the daughter of the drunk bus driver'.

It wasn't lost on me that Wan believed he could 'shield me' from the horror of our situation, that he could make me happy, with or without children. It was me that couldn't move forward. Having my own family would allow me to start again. To rewrite history. I would raise untainted, non-stigmatised, happy, whole children. If IVF was my shot at doing that, then bring it on. We would be skint, happy and whole.

***

I became obsessed. It was all I could think about. Jodie wasn't impressed.

'The world continues to turn while you find a clinic. Girlfriends need a pub quiz partner; school children need a teacher who can remember their name …'

'I know, Jode, but it's such an important decision.' I'd bored her so many times telling her the same thing. I knew she was just worried, like I'd be about her. 'So, what was it we used to talk about before my stillbirth and hot-off-the-press menopausal news?' I asked sweetly.

Jodie hugged me tightly, pretending to strangle me in the process.

'You're right, I'm wrong. As usual. Tell you what, if you help me choose the clinic, I'll stop harping on about it. Deal? Give me twenty minutes of your time. Seriously, I need this.' Brew bribery gets you everywhere in the world of education. I headed to the staff room and put the kettle on. I loaded my impressive spreadsheet of clinic contenders. Jodie heaved her rucksack onto the table and gave me her undivided, if reluctant, attention.

'I've pretty much narrowed it down. There are two clinics in central Manchester and one in Bradford, which is forty minutes away.' Making room by my side, she peered at the website reviews.

'This one looks promising. I quote,' she read aloud, '"There's no clinic I'd rather have ferreting around in my wife's fanny." From the partner of a successful IVF birth.' Her deadpan expression gave way to laughter.

'It's bad enough with Wan taking the mick every two minutes!'

'I'll be sensible. I can do this.' She continued to scroll through my phone while I pretended to make my way through the exercise books at her side, trying to match her dodgy handwriting.

'It's a no brainer,' she said at length. 'Clinic number one has a man with a dodgy 'tache. Looks like something from *The Joy of Sex*.' I looked at her, bewildered. 'Before your time,' she muttered.

'Clinic number two doesn't have any mixed or even *borderline* reviews. They're clearly all fake.'

'Whilst clinic number three has it all. *Seemingly* genuine reviews ... a few "they're hopeless, never answered my calls" ... plus there's a team photo of them looking like regular people. The others are clearly stock photos of impossibly attractive staff with gleaming teeth, and I think some cultural over-representation. And they're slightly cheaper. What's not to like?

'Quick and dirty, my friend. I like it. Thank you. I'll discuss with Wan. And I'm as good as my word. Do you fancy a coffee/drink/other on this fine Friday? My guarantee that all fertility-related conversation will be banned!'

Jodie hugged me again. 'Usual terms and conditions apply!' It's a given between us that if a better offer presents, as a single person, Jodie can legitimately bail at the last minute. Her quest for Ms Right remains ongoing.

'And yes, the F word is forbidden. Fertility talk strictly off the table.'

***

Harvesting was no worse than I'd imagined. Hormone injections to 'pump up the eggs' (Black Box's 'Pump up the Jam', replacing 'jam' with 'eggs' – thanks, Wan) made me feel strange but not exactly unwell. Focusing on where the procedure could lead – a sibling for Evie – kept me grounded. The five-day wait while egg and sperm did their thing was painful. Wan and I kept busy and had an agreement that whatever the outcome, we would discuss next steps together (strict 'Lana, don't top yourself' instructions). Returning to the clinic, we were ecstatic to learn that there had been eleven 'viable' eggs – nine of which had been frozen for potential future use. Two would be transferred to my uterus for my safekeeping. No pressure at all.

The days after insemination were difficult. Despite being told to continue 'as normal', I did no such thing. Feigning a migraine, I took to my bed, worried that I might dislodge my cargo with even the slightest activity. I was rumbled as Wan rounded the doorway bearing a cup of tea, seeing my ridiculous pose, last used when we were trying to conceive, to absolutely no effect, my legs high in the air, cycling style. What Wan couldn't see was my other strategy: manic completion of pelvic floor exercises, on the hour, every hour, to 'hold' the zygote in place. Then panic set in. Could pelvic floor exercises trigger miscarriage? I lost a further half day hyperventilating and scrolling through 'evidence' for and against both possibilities. There's loads of evidence around the role anxiety plays in predicting IVF outcomes. And none relating to possible excessive pelvic floor lifts. Anxiety – or cortisol – is the enemy, which is the ultimate oxymoron; it's impossible for anyone whose financial and emotional future depends upon a successful outcome to be anything but anxious. Otherwise, we stuck strictly to consultant guidelines – avoiding sex, caffeine, alcohol and extreme exercise or sports. Midweek schoolteacher life right there.

Because you're reading this post-event, I can do this. I'm sparing you details of the rollercoaster we endured, our lives punctuated by injections, blood tests, hormone-hiked mood swings veering from ecstatic to utterly miserable. It was exhausting. In short, the first cycle was not successful. Emotional weeks passed by, and we tried again. A false dawn of a positive test saw us again travelling hopefully, only to miscarry early at three hopeful weeks. I cried and I cried some more. Together and separately, we grieved. I imagine even the bookies turned up their commentary to drown out my sorrow. Like an exotic mourner, I shredded my T-shirt one morning. Wan wordlessly placed it in the bin with his fake-beer empties.

I wasn't sure how much more emotional energy Wan had, his vigilance over my mood well intended but painful. My efforts at feigning positivity left me exhausted. And yet. The last round of harvested eggs took us miraculously to a single female fertilised egg. I hung on to her for dear life. We were equally terrified and delighted. At the three months mark, we began tentatively sharing our news, feeling more confident as the weeks passed. Only close family and Jodie were aware of the IVF route we'd used to get there.

I wasn't sure if having a girl would be difficult, like we were trying to replace Evie, although I tried to hold in my mind just how excited Evie would have been to have a sister. I'd often sense Evie looking on, and I tried hard to picture her excitedly waiting for her long-awaited sister. Looking back, it was hard to know when I first started seeing Evie or if it was initially my imagination. As my pregnancy progressed, she appeared more frequently, which I understood as her approval.

While we'd plenty of time to land on a name, I felt like she needed one now. Evie had been 'Windy' – predictable, I know – as her first movements I'd mistaken for gas and the name had stuck. Tinkering with variations on our own names, Wan came up with Wala. I worried it sounded like she was wailing and wasn't going to tempt fate and risk a screechy baby! The name somehow morphed into Koala, which was much cuter.

***

Our first real parenting argument took us both by surprise. I was used to Wan rolling with whatever I decided. This was new.

'The gender reveal business is absurd. We will look back on the activity with shame one day.' I could not believe that Wan would want such a thing.

'You are completely overthinking this, Lana! Koala can become whatever she likes. You're losing sight of what the event is about,' Wan argued.

'They will be exactly what they choose. It's not for parents to do that before they're even born! Only crazy people have a gender reveal. Look at the people we know who've had one!' Wan knew exactly who I was talking about. 'The drummer in your last band, Wan—'

The doorbell rang loudly, stopping me mid-rant. We'd been going in circles for a good half an hour; Wan was showing signs of tiring and sounded more deflated than angry. After the third ring, Wan stomped downstairs. Hearing an exchange of voices, I peered from the window. My view of our door was eclipsed as usual by the enormous Ladbrokes sign. Wan returned, looking amused, and I saw a pair of middle-aged women saunter away from our door.

'I don't think I've ever been pleased to see a Jehovah's Witness before!' He grinned sheepishly, waving something that looked like a *Beano* at me.

'Hope you didn't pretend to be too interested; they'll be back. Did you ask them where they stood on gender reveals?' I laughed, relieved that Wan seemed to be backing down, and proffered a steaming brew his way. 'Olive branch,' I said, grinning. Wan rolled his eyes but accepted the drink.

'Anyway, I don't want my nutjob family members having too many scoops and the whole thing degenerating into a debacle.' There would be a diverse mix (euphemistic language) of my not-right family members, Wan's irritatingly puritan parents, my fab colleagues and friends, and Wan's cool but not substance-averse music crew. It had all the hallmarks of an event that I would not want to marshal. 'Think about my sister's gender reveal. The dreadful firing of cannons and ambiguous-coloured smoke – mass confusion about whether it was pink or blue. Just vile.'

'There's no need for early stereotyping, Lana; you of all people ...' Wan assumed a shocked expression as I threw a cushion his way.

'Let's compromise,' I ventured, sounding like the reasonable person that I'm not. 'We'll just have it my way. You get to choose *every* track on the "Welcome Koala" playlist, how's that? I'll even let you have your cheesy Stevie Wonder track, because I know how much you love it – even though everyone knows how clichéd it is!'

'Okay, you win,' said Wan, defeated. 'But I trump you whatever our next argument is over. How's that?'

I thought carefully. What if the next one was a biggie? Even bigger than this?

'No, I think I get to decide *every* time. Mum's prerogative.' We didn't know the decisions we'd face in the months ahead. But I'd set out my stall, mama tiger claws flexed, ready to defend at a moment's notice. My way or no way.

Tilda

I'll be brief here – very like my session! Jenna tried to help me flesh out the potential future selves that I'd brought. However, I had already decided by the time we met again that the baby possibility was my only source of happiness. Evidently Jenna felt it her professional duty to stall me on this. I'd overheard my mother telling my aunt once that she thought I was too selfish to have a child. I'd been earwigging on the stairs, aged twenty-three at the time. Putting myself first at that age seemed – and seems – sensible to me, but on some level I'd come to believe it. Was this why I'd never chosen to have a child? Had it been easier staying with Edwin and sparing myself the decision with another partner?

Jenna pushed me: what did I hope to achieve by having a child? She was hedging me towards naming my loneliness. I could easily own that, and in some ways, having a baby may well open doors of friendship, but it felt deeper than that. This seemingly unexpected desire to *nurture* felt like something I'd been sidelining for some time. Had my efforts to distance myself from Edwin on all those occasions been an unconscious attempt to create a future with children? I'd never really been without a partner, even in my brief separations from Edwin. It's so easy for women. I can turn a head in a bar; I can flirt. But this time it didn't feel like a partner I was looking for. I needed something to fill this void inside me. Or did that mean my mother's hypothesis was correct? If I was considering a child to meet my own emotional needs, did that make me selfish? Fuck knows.

I was keen to tell Jenna that since this strange possibility had been quivering away, I had considerably reduced my alcohol intake. I wasn't sure what I was trying to prove or to whom, but surely that wasn't a bad thing. And if I did go ahead and buy a

Chilean vineyard, I'd be dead from liver failure in six months. Jenna nodded her agreement a little too readily for my liking.

'Conversely, procreation is good for you. It diverts your best efforts at self-destruction if you've to stay alive long enough to protect your offspring.' I'm not sure if that was my theory or one I'd repackaged from my sociology undergrad years.

'Tilda. I'm going to be blunt here. Do you remember the rescue chihuahua?'

'That was completely different. How can you compare that?'

She was referring to the handbag dog I'd thought I could care for a few years ago. I'd overlooked the fact that I would need to be home 24/7 to meet its every pampered chihuahua need. After three weeks of the creature shitting all over the cork tiles and destroying two-thirds of my designer kitchen, I decided I wasn't the rescuing type. That's fair. However, this was a child we were talking about. And that was *years* ago!

'Food for thought,' Jenna mused aloud.

There would not be a further appointment. Despite the hour not being up, I got to my feet, tucking my Prada handbag under my arm.

'You've overstepped your doctor/patient boundary,' I said simply.

'Tilda, I'm therapeutically challenging you. I'm sorry if that offended you. It's my job as a therapist to help you name what *might* be happening here.'

I paused. 'Maybe you're right, maybe you're wrong. But with my mother dead, I am free of her judgment of my every decision. I don't have to listen to opinions that offend me anymore. And I certainly don't need to pay for the privilege.'

***

Shifting from curious googling to booking an initial IVF consultation took just twenty days. Moving quickly meant less chance of a U-turn. I'd convinced myself that the appointment was merely an information-gathering exercise. However, once the appointment was booked, my emotions and hormones switched from 'dormant' to 'live'.

I could reach the Manchester clinic in less time than I could cross London in rush hour. Opting for an out-of-area clinic would, I hoped, afford some privacy. I didn't want my IVF status to be common knowledge, preferring to leave others to their best paternity guesses. Although I would be keen to clarify that Edwin wasn't the father. The clinic came highly recommended by my GP and was, bizarrely, not at all far from my mother's home. The clinic's website was generic; however, I was assured the establishment had an impeccable record for pre- and post-clinical support. The GP —despite her best guess that my drinking far exceeded my reported units – had been happy to share documentation with the clinic stating that I was indeed mentally well and accessing mental health support in a preventative manner.

Receiving a one-to-one consultation initially, I was then introduced to a group of 'IVF curious' (yes, really) others. Nodding awkwardly, conscious of my solo status, surrounded by couples of all types, I grinned nervously around the group. In *Brave New World* style, I tagged on alongside a gay couple towards the end of the tour and tried my best to be charming. We convoyed through a Disney-style tour of the 'baby hall of fame' narrated by a David Attenborough soundalike. There was a near evangelical atmosphere as we were led slowly through the clinic's 'timeline tunnel' – an incredible construction where we were immersed in hi-tech learning about the early beginnings of IVF and the commissioning and research that had led to the first IVF birth (Louise Brown) in a Manchester-based hospital in 1978. In short, it felt like we were in safe, pioneering hands. I thought of the badges still languishing at the bottom of my bag. Would I be escorted from the building if I started handing badges out like a religious apostate? I wasn't about to try. The idea of Mini-Tilda was beginning to germinate.

The information from the consultation and tour was overwhelming. My head was spinning with the volume and pace of it all. So much of the language was alien to me. The clinic provided us with a glossary of IVF terms and procedures in simple language, but there was a lot to take in: options, costs, psychological and genetic assessments, sperm donor options, rafts of glossy literature. There was much to ponder. But on an emotional level I was hooked. I was in. This was it.

The decision to proceed with IVF changed everything and nothing initially. Mentally, I felt a powerful disconnect from my previous non-child-oriented existence. Ellie coined it OT and NT – old and new Tilda. I've had Fluoxetine, Citalopram, Sertraline, so many chemical helpers over the years that never gave me this high. I woke each morning with a feeling of hope and excitement. My outlook and behaviour were changing.

I noticed a removal van outside the apartment block, a steady flow of boxes being loaded into the apartment to my right. Not an infrequent occurrence – it's a busy building. New Tilda scribbled a moving-in card and took a lovely bottle from the rack, placing it on the doorstep to welcome the new tenants. I may need to be in their good books if Mini-Tilda turned out to be a screecher. It could pay dividends, so potentially the act was not from altruism. But I felt positively awkward

.

For regular non-IVF couples I guess the fun bit is conception. Without a partner, the closest I got was perusing the catalogue looking for a worthy donor for my formidable egg. Ellie – my new partner in crime – was keen to contribute. Armed with a delightful wine that I'd nabbed from Mother's redundant chiller, we spent an evening at hers – Rosa in bed – generating a 'Top 3' from the donor choices that the Manchester Clinic had sent through.

'This feels like a cross between Tinder and speed dating. Not that I've done either!' Ellie squealed, swiping through the images of impossibly hunky guys beseeching you to use their sperm. You could tell by the glint in their eye. Literally. 'Have you ever done speed dating? I'll bet you have!' Ellie poured us a generous second glass.

'I have indeed. Never again!' I laughed. 'There were about forty of us seated in a circle at the back of a revolting bar. A buzzer goes and you get five minutes to "sell yourself", but the pressure means that you come across like a crazy person. Then the buzzer goes again and you all swap places and off you go again. Everyone was either mad, sad or criminally insane, and there was certainly no one that I wanted to speak to! Half the people left in the first hour, which just made those of us who stayed feel even worse.'

'This is perfect; you don't even have to speak to them. Just swipe if you fancy my sperm!' She giggled raucously.

'Surely there are a few regular blokes here. I'm not opposed to superheroes, but where is the nerd section?'

We pored incredulously over donor details. Height, weight, religious views, education, occupation, personality, even voice type. Obviously there were photos, but also pictures of the guys as babies.

'Whoa, look at him.' Ellie jabbed her finger at the screen. 'Hot or what?'

'It's not about whether he's hot. What's his aura like?'

'He looks like he's got a really big aura.' She raised her eyebrows suggestively.

'That's Mini-Tilda's potential father you're talking about!'

'Just think – no interfering mother-in-law, no weird best friend. Have you noticed guys always get jealous when their bestie has a baby? Jed's friend did. I swear he went into overdrive with man-stuff-only invitations when I was pregnant with Rosa.'

'Now that's what I want to find in a father!' I almost spat my wine out. 'Simon has *well-proportioned limbs*! He'll do. God, they must be scraping the compliment barrel if that's all they've got! Poor Simon!' We howled with laughter, grabbing the screen from each other to zoom in. We scrolled for a further hour before I'd narrowed it down.

'Right!' I yelled, heading for another bottle. 'I've got my top three. Here.' I thrust the iPad in Ellie's direction. 'What do you reckon?' Leaving her to peruse my choices, I peeked very quietly round Rosa's partially open door, unable to resist a quick look. To think that I might have a baby too seemed incredible. Rosa stirred briefly and I backed away.

'Could it be contestant number one?' announced Ellie theatrically as I entered the room. 'Roger. A stunner. Australian. Blond, six-four, non-religious. A poet in his spare time. He looks like a model to me, but he's a plumber. Whoo!' she shrieked, inviting me to join her.

'Ooh, could you bob over and check my pipework, Big Rodge?' I dutifully whooped, popping the cork on the bottle.

'Or contestant number two? Meet the hunky super-spunky Jay. Jay's Norwegian, but we'll let him off. His hobbies include snowboarding and flying. He's a vet specialising in marine animals.'

'Whoo, brains and money. An attractive combination. Easy on the eye but in a slightly ginger way?' I queried.

'Or the very lovely contestant number three? Phillip. Tall, dark and very handsome. Check out those biceps. Runs marathons, but his real passion is his day job. He's a doctor. Specialising in children's oncology. He is a babe!' she shrieked.

'I think you're getting confused. I'm not dating him, just receiving his sperm.'

'I know, I know. Shame, though, isn't it? So, who's it to be?' Ellie produced an unconvincing drum roll sound. I swiped each picture and back again. 'And the winner is ...'

'Roger,' I yelled. 'Cheers!' We raised our glasses, chanting his name like schoolgirls. I zoomed in on his lovely profile. A sprinkling of freckles covered his nose and cheekbones. Platinum blond hair glowed bright in the Aussie sunshine. The possibility that he hadn't come from money (plumber by trade) appealed to me. One in the eye for my family. He looked like a masculine version of me, which I hoped wasn't weird.

Ellie's shrieking had roused Rosa, and we quieted immediately as stirring noises came through the monitor.

I floated home with an image forming in my mind of Miri-Tilda/Roger. Freckles, alabaster skin, long blond hair, tiny rosebud lips. I could not have been more excited.

Lana

I'd forgotten just how fun-deprived it was being pregnant. Wan was gigging at a festival where normally I'd have joined him. I did debate it, but it was baking even here in the north, and I didn't fancy frying all weekend in the south. Jodie and I found ourselves instead trawling Manchester's charity shops, which felt a poor second on such a lovely weekend. I'd winged it for as long as I could in leggings and baggy tops. I was sporting a Peter Rabbit post-radish-binge look, belly bursting through the seams of my clothing. I needed something new and roomy. With two hands for dramatic effect, Jodie held aloft an enormous psychedelic kaftan. I gave her my 'maybe' face. It looked huge. At five months with Evie, I'd been barely showing in comparison to my current size.

It wasn't purely a money thing, charity shop purchasing. We have landfill sites the size of Wales full of unwanted clothing that there's nothing wrong with. This was my nod to the green agenda. I beamed as the cashier ran our items through the till. Jodie had thrown in a gorgeous sleepsuit with an embroidered 'Manchester Bee' at the shoulder. A rollercoaster sensation washed over me whenever I bought or received something for Koala, a vertigo-like blend of fear and hope. I was terrified that those tiny clothes might go unworn if history repeated itself. Jodie picked up on my mood and delivered a huge unsolicited hug as we stepped onto the pavement.

'Lunchtime,' she declared, and we headed to our usual Jamaican café with its tired interior and incredible smells wafting from the kitchen. Jodie ordered while I pinged a photo of the sleepsuit to Wan. He'd sent a pic of last night's gig, complete with messy dance floor and shiny young things in wellies and braids loving his tunes. To the right of the pic, I saw what he was really showing me – a guy dancing with a tiny baby strapped to his chest wearing oversized ear protectors (the baby, not him). The flip-flop of emotion was always there. I don't think the fear was the same for Wan.

'Oh my God, that's cute,' squealed Jodie, and in a moment I was hopeful again, trying to banish my unhelpful thoughts. 'So, remind me – due date and last day of work, you lucky human.'

'Well, it's half-term next week.' I gestured at an imaginary calendar. 'When I'll be five months and will be stopping as soon as I'm able – which will be July the 1st, with a tantalisingly close due date of the 28th of August. Which will obviously mean a no-show until mid-September, so that Koala can cheat the school year and get an extra year at home with me.'

'You know, I fancy some mat' leave myself. Why should it be only for the pregnant? Surely that's discrimination. I could be really constipated, have a *massive* poo and call it "shat leave".' Jodie spluttered into her Coke at her own wit. 'Who doesn't need recovery time after a really big poo?'

The lady at the next table glared, peering over comedy half-moon glasses. Jodie tipped back in her chair, rubbing her imaginary belly.

'I'm driving myself crazy, you know. I really want to sit back and just enjoy being pregnant – here and now – but at the same time I need to fast forward and have Koala right here. Sat there.' Pointing to my left, I imagined her in a baby chair beside us. Healthy, whole and breathing. All the things you want from your new baby.

'I get that.' She paused gently. 'How are you doing?' A catch-all question when what she really meant was, *Any suicidal thoughts you need to talk about?*

'I'm good.' My stock response. Which is what people need to hear. Although if anything happens to this baby, I have no intention of hanging around for more pain.

'Course you are.' Jodie's response was predictable. She felt a level of guilt that I'd tried to kill myself after spending the evening with her. What had she missed? She didn't miss anything. And if I feel that desperate again, there still won't be any sign. It will be because things haven't worked out. That I'm childless despite my pregnancies. And I will have to do something more drastic, because I cannot endure that pain all over again. I can't and I won't. Seeing children come into my class day after day, watching them grow, their siblings following the next year, is unbearable. I see amazing parents, okay and good-enough parents. I see really crap ones and evidence of their neglect on the forlorn children I teach. I try hard with those kids. *Their* burning shame reminds me that I'm only ever a step away from mine, its cruel visibility still there for all to see. Lined up alongside the 'regular' kids with parents who love them, those kids stand out a mile. Of course, I don't mention any of that to Jodie – even she gets the people-pleasing version: I'm good.

'So, can I do another mural?' Jodie looked uncomfortable, unsure if she should even ask.

'Evie would have loved her butterfly. And it's going nowhere. If you could do a koala companion, that would be ace.' Producing my phone, I showed Jodie the cutest koala images for ideas.

'Aw, I was going to *surprise* you with a koala,' she groaned but nodded enthusiastically at the pictures.

'I'm well ahead of you. But get ready, because by Easter, I'll be ready to roll – paintwork done and raring to go.' The next few months were nicely mapped out, largely around the primary school curriculum – Easter, May Day, midsummer; landmarks and celebrations punctuating my life as I waited for my new one to begin. The fear that I didn't voice – even to Wan – sat heavily on my shoulder. Fate could still rob me of my hope if she felt inclined.

Tilda

Treatment began. Ellie did a sterling job of getting me through the first incredibly tough weeks. She had supported a friend who'd gone through IVF (ultimately unsuccessful, I prised from her), so she had some idea of what to expect. I felt like I'd ridden out the worst (so naïve), braving the onslaught of daily injections by my own trembling hands, artificially stimulating my ovaries to produce as many eggs as possible for harvesting. The effect of these injections and the oestrogen pills I was taking resulted in a speedy weight gain of around seven pounds. Each pound made its way exclusively to my backside, resulting in a porridge-like texture. No glamorous J-Lo derrière for me. Aside from the weight gain, I was by turns ecstatic and tearful, fuelled by a hormonal tsunami that could sweep over me without warning. My self-imposed no-alcohol resolve was sorely tested. I persevered, but the days were long and the evenings longer.

Who knew that I would be a natural at egg production? A first attempt yielded an impressive twenty-eight eggs. I couldn't help but feel proud of my bumper crop. The daily injections thankfully ended, but my mood did not reset. I was Snow White and the Wicked Queen in consecutive breaths. Of the twenty-eight eggs, thirteen were declared 'good', eleven of which were frozen and two of which were sent to get jiggy with Aussie Roger's sperm. The days in between were spent keeping everything crossed. Retrospectively unhelpfully, I'd opted to receive daily updates on their progress.

'I picture them in petri dishes or whatever they use. I *so* want there to be chocolates and red roses strewn around the laboratory. Maybe some Barry White to set the tone.' Ellie had popped over with Rosa and found me in overdrive. Ellie laughed. My manic behaviour was not dissimilar from her friend's at this stage. I hoped that was where our common experience would end.

'I really want to ask,' I continued, 'but it's clear that the technicians have all had their sense of humour surgically removed. They already think I'm a bit weird, so I don't ask about the lab environment or offer helpful suggestions.'

'Why do you have this idea that others have a "weird" view of you? It's not healthy, you know.' She laughed, passing Rosa to me while she checked her phone.

'Accurate, though. I see the side looks every time I go in. Perhaps it's because I'm doing this solo. But I get a *vibe*.'

Somehow, I was completely unprepared for an unsuccessful first attempt. On day three, two of the eggs had not progressed to fertilisation; by day four, one more was looking iffy. By day five, all four eggs were declared non-viable. I'd taken the train from London to hear this news. After the high of travelling hopefully, I left the clinic feeling utterly deflated. Why I'd thought that my first effort would be successful - when it's statistically so unlikely – I don't know. I sobbed quietly on the rush-hour tram. Rather than staying at Mother's house as planned, I took the tram straight to the station and the next train back home, grabbing two mini bottles of Sauvignon Blanc and a large tube of Pringles from the train trolley.

My weeping became louder and unashamed. Without a plastic cup, I swigged straight from the bottle. Placing my headphones on to deter strangers' concern, I turned my head to the window, the bump of the train leaving red weals on my forehead with every jerk of the track. God, I'd missed Sauvignon, even this hideous economy version. I texted Ellie an update and placed my phone on mute. After three months without alcohol, the wine did not touch the sides. I soon drifted off to sleep but woke at Euston, where 'this train terminates'. *Like my eggs*, I thought, morosely gathering my belongings and the wine and snack debris. Fitful sleeping had done nothing to improve my mood.

Ellie – God bless her – was waiting outside the station, brazenly jockeying for position with the taxis. I exited through the doors, hearing the frantic pipping of a horn and seeing her waving furiously through the car window.

'I clocked which train you were on. And yes, I'm an amazing human and banking significant brownie points for future use. Babysitting favours, designated driver delegation, I have a list!' she joked.

Fresh tears coursed down my face as she joined an extensive line of traffic. Rosa was fast asleep in her seat; God knows how long they had already been in the car.

'It's stupid to be devastated.' I rummaged for a tissue. 'I just felt so optimistic. Rooting for each one of those eggs, my babies, then hearing one by one that they'd not made it.' I sniffed loudly, wiping my nose on my sleeve.

'Do you want to come back to mine?' Ellie asked, her hand hovering over the indicator where she'd normally turn into her road.

'No, I'm good. I'm okay. I need to be tough. Tougher.' We drove in silence through the jammed streets.

'Thank you for coming out to get me.' My words were genuine and generated fresh tears. After queuing painfully through the endless temporary traffic lights, we finally pulled into the drop-off zone outside my building. I half hugged Ellie goodbye through the open car window and made my way slowly to the lift. It was impossible to avoid my reflection in the mirrored walls; orange Pringle crumbs clung to my oatmeal woollen coat, and my puffy face was a mixture of crying and hormone-fuelled pounds.

It had been just a few days since I'd been home, but a belch of stale air greeted me at the door, riding on a wave of heat. Had I forgotten to take out the rubbish as well as leaving the heating on? Adding brain fog to the list of side-effects over the last oestrogen-drenched fortnight was depressing. Could I really do this? On my own? I wasn't sure. Maybe the eggs not surviving was God's way of telling me that I wasn't mother material. I headed straight for the fridge and wrapped my hand around the lovely chilled Bollinger that I'd resisted all these months, an almost sensual thrill as I lifted the bottle from the shelf. The cork made an exquisite pop in its bid for freedom. The champagne was as delicious as I'd imagined it would be throughout my alcohol-deprived months. And then some. Every drop.

***

Well, I haven't missed you, Han Gover. Not one bit. Bile travelled up and down my oesophagus as I staggered from my bed. My hands trembled as I attempted to spoon coffee from the packet, scattering it across the counter. I tried again. With little success. Trailing black coffee across the carpet, I headed back to bed. The mid-afternoon sun woke me several hours later. The coffee was untouched, as was the stain that would now be impossible to shift. A familiar feeling of shame washed over me as I attempted for the second time that day to get up.

Despite feeling wretched, it was good to be home. Although the neglected state of the apartment further threatened my precarious mood. Post and flyers littered the hallway. I stooped to open the only item of interest, a pastel-coloured envelope containing a pretty William Morris card.

> Dear Tilda
>
> I've moved countless times and never has someone put a note through, not least left a sumptuous bottle of wine. I drank it all – on my own in one sitting – but can testify to its loveliness. I've knocked a few times to say thanks but haven't found anyone home. Give me a knock at some point or text me (number below) and we can get together for a neighbourly coffee/other. When I move again (and I'm a serial house mover), I'm going to pay the gesture forward, so consider yourself having done a fine deed!
>
> Yours, Vic
>
> xxxx

My yo-yoing mood soared. It's the small things. How lovely of me. And how lovely of Vic. Male or female? Based on the neat and rounded handwriting, my feeling was female. Not that it mattered. I would give Vic a knock when Mr Gover eased. Retreating to the sofa armed with co-codamol and coffee, I checked out 'next steps' in my IVF chat group, my iPad cruelly reflecting the extra layer around my neck. Bring on Phase Two.

I'd never contoured before. My cheekbones had always held their own, but I looked like an over-fed hamster. I was only popping to the shop and knocking at the neighbour's, yet life suddenly depended upon the emergence of my cheekbones. *How do people find the time and patience for this daily?*

Emergency cleaning products jutted from carrier bags as I paused at Vic's door. I hadn't texted the number on the card. If

Vic turned out to be an axe murderer, I didn't want him/her to have my mobile number. That would not help me now if I went in and axe-murdering was the objective. *Stop overthinking, you maniac*, I told myself sternly and rapped on the door. The knock echoed loudly. I felt my fragile mood hover. Fucking hormones. I was on the point of leaving when I heard the key turn in the lock.

A stony-faced guy, mid-forties at a guess, whipped open the door. My internal lift quivered.

'Hi. Is Vic home? Are you Vic? I'm Tilda,' I gushed, pointing in the direction of my apartment. I should have rehearsed to avoid presenting as a crazy person.

'I'm so sorry …' he started.

'Don't be. I'm used to being me. A cross I bear.' So much for my usual poise.

The guy belly laughed to the point I thought he was being sarcastic.

'No. *I'm* sorry. You're here because of the noise! I've had a builder in today knocking lumps out of the walls – I would have let you know, but I couldn't catch anyone home.'

'No, I'm not here because of noise. I was just saying hi.'

'Oh, you're too kind!' He stepped back, offering me into the apartment. 'I'm Vic!' he bellowed. Did he think I had additional needs? Was that why he was shouting? Or maybe he did. Either way was fine.

'Thanks for your card. Thanking me for mine.' I laughed nervously.

'Come in, come in,' he urged, opening the door wide and diving forward for a hug. A lovely gay vibe radiated from him.

Stepping into the apartment, I began to relax slightly. As a gay man, would he be *less* likely to be an axe murderer? Or more? The apartment felt welcoming despite open boxes spewing their contents and a thick film of brick dust on every surface. So far removed from my clinical abode. Vic rummaged for the remote and switched off the enormous TV that filled the wall.

'My guilty pleasure, I'm afraid.' He laughed. 'Weekend soap catch-up for my shame.' He ushered an ancient-looking Basset hound from the sofa – 'Eric, meet Tilda!' – and gestured for me to sit, attempting to brush away the greasy fur that clung to the sofa.

'It's fine. I don't want to intrude.' I wasn't sure I wanted to perch my Gucci outfit on Eric's sofa spot. Clutching my carrier bags, I raised them as my excuse. 'I'm just saying hi and welcome. Checking if you need anything. I hope the other neighbours have been nice!'

'Well, I was disappointed not to receive Chateauneuf-du-Pape from the other residents! That was so kind.' He beamed.

'A neighbour once did something similar for me, so I thought I'd do the same.' This was a lie. For no apparent reason. I'm going to blame the hormones.

'Can I tempt you? I've nothing as luscious as the Pape, but I could rustle up a cheeky cocktail?' Vic placed his right hand on his hip, cocking one eyebrow in a staggeringly camp fashion. Upstairs would be sober and lonely.

'Well, just a quick one. That would be lovely.' I beamed. My precious pantsuit could always be dry cleaned. It had been such a challenging few weeks. Non-pregnant and hungover me would love a drink. The carriers were gently lowered to the floor.

The 'quick one' led to a steady stream of Tom Collins, mojitos and espresso martinis. Vic was a delight, part cocktail waiter, part raconteur and part comedian. Wobbling back to mine later, my mood had stabilised from the elevator-dropping sensation I'd experienced earlier. I hadn't gotten so tipsy that I'd mentioned anything about IVF, in part because I wasn't sure if Vic would judge me for drinking while trying to conceive. Paranoia only ever a step away. I thought there'd been a connection with Vic, which was great. I'd even told him about my mother's charity.

'So how come you didn't do anything with it?' God, he was direct.

'To be fair, I tried hard. Initially. It's a long story, but in essence the main funding came through the Catholic Church, who had a vested interest in charities that I could not endorse. Although they supported worthy projects, there was a palpable right-wing undercurrent and funding of groups that I could not be associated with. Think Tory fox hunting, pro-life groups, blatantly homophobic, horrific Catholic misogyny.'

'No!' cried Vic dramatically, clasping his hands to his face in an exaggerated fashion.

'My mother made it impossible for me to sever ties with the seedier aspects of the charity. She just wouldn't let go of the reins, critical of my every decision. My efforts to influence the kind of organisations involved and causes of the charity were completely vetoed. And you would not believe the misogyny that exists within the Church. I was surrounded by conservative patriarchs refusing to embrace my ideas, instead suggesting that

I "get into bed" with theirs. I'm sure their turn of phrase was deliberately provocative, given Mother's philandering reputation.' I elaborated upon her penchant for infidelity, surely requiring confession. The problem was that her confessor would be the same man of the cloth who had shared in her sins.

'What?' Vic looked genuinely aghast.

'My mother had taken lovers from amongst the commissioners for decades. It wouldn't surprise me if she thought I might do the same. This went on until she was well into her sixties, long before my father passed away. She wasn't even discreet, sparing my father nothing.'

'She sounds like a peach!' Vic looked suitably appalled.

'In the end, apathy became my only weapon. A kind of "fuck you" gesture, calling out her behaviour in a way that my dad hadn't felt able.'

'We should have a "bad-mother-off". I may be able to trump you, but that is a tale for another day!' Vic crammed the last of the delicious cocktail into my glass, surface tension at the maximum.

As a journalist, Vic shared that he had lived and worked all over the world since his twenties. He alluded to heartbreak, tearing up at one point but not sharing further. Our conversation shifted to neighbour gossip – of which I was a poor source of information. Vic had learned more this week than I had as a resident of seven years. We became sufficiently inebriated to start planning a housewarming for Vic. We would invite all the neighbours – something Old Tilda would *never* have done.

I was beginning to like this reinvention of self, I decided, as I made my way home, passing the mirrored panels in the hallway.

It was lovely to have passed hours without thinking about fertility or eggs that never became zygotes. Or Edwin. I was more drunk than I thought, because as I (third attempt) engaged the lock, I saw eight missed calls from the new number that I thought was Edwin. The ugly old fecker. How had I devoted my fertile years to him? Could he not have foreseen that I would resent him for it? He'd *had* a marriage, a life, children, for God's sake. I opened a bottle of tepid Sauvignon and simultaneously made a mug of tea; I promptly fell asleep before consuming either. Another sun would rise with my nemesis, Han Gover, perched on my sorry shoulder.

***

I was better prepared second time around. My hormones were settling, and I'd banished booze from the house to avoid impulsive consumption. Although I wasn't physically present, I lived vicariously day to day through my freshly defrosted eggs' journey, again being introduced to Roger's sperm; the process of five more Mini-Tildas attempting to fertilise.

Distraction was my main strategy. The gym, the coffee shop, Ellie. My options were limited, but I clung to them with my every fibre. Offloading to Vic about the Foundation had resurrected old feelings of guilt and frustration. Of course, Mother had made things difficult, but surely I could have found a way. It didn't make sense. Had I been depressed? Or was that a cop-out for my apathy? Either way, with her now out of the equation, maybe there could be a way forward.

'I'd like to speak to someone in Charitable Foundation, please. It's in connection with the former Stand Foundation.' I'd dressed as if attending an interview despite sitting at my breakfast bar on the phone – sharp kitten heels, Karen Millen woollen suit and high-necked silk blouse in teal.

'Tilda, is that you?' The female voice was friendly but wasn't one I recognised.

'It is. How are you?' I gushed, with no clue who this could be.

'I was *so* sorry to hear about the passing of your mother.'

Ordinarily I'd have been unable to pass up an opportunity for a derisive comment or quip, but instead I graciously accepted her condolences.

'So, the Foundation has folded after all these years. Such a shame.'

'That's actually what I'm calling about. I'm wondering if Richard is around to have a chat?'

'Absolutely. He'll be thrilled to hear from you, I'm sure.'

I wasn't sure if that was genuine given my seeming apathy for the Foundation all those years, but I nervously waited to be transferred. Richard's voice boomed down the line.

'Good to hear from you, Tilda. I tried to call after your mother passed to offer my condolences. She was truly a unique woman.'

I concurred with all that euphemistically meant.

'Richard. I feel a bit of an idiot. As you know, there were professional differences that prevented me from being able to get on board with the Stand Foundation.' I paused, struggling to find the right words. 'Given the nature of some of the beneficiaries it supported.'

'I understood that you held different values to your mother,' Richard offered diplomatically, aware of the tension between our polarised views.

'I know that technically I'd requested that the charity be dissolved, but I've had some ideas with my mother's passing. Instead, I've been wondering about a rebrand. I don't know – something far removed from the religious aspect. I don't know if that's remotely doable, these are just my early thoughts ...' I was floundering, hoping he would jump in and save me, but even from usually excitable Richard there was an agonising pause.

Just as I could bear the tumbleweed no longer, he saved me.

'It would not be without its challenges, but I'd be willing to have a look. It doesn't actually have to be linked at all with Stand. You could set something up from scratch, just as your mother did before you.' he enthused.

'I was hoping to cherry pick the charities – maybe something in a completely different area.'

'What area are you thinking?'

'I have had some thoughts but have no clue if it's an area you could help me with. Either way, I want to move as far away as possible from everything that Stand stood for. You're aware – how do I say this? – that my mother had some rather *right-wing* opinions, opposed to anything that vaguely stepped outside of the nuclear family and traditional norms.' I paused, aware of how vague I was sounding. 'Actually – and please keep this strictly between us, Richard – I'm having IVF treatment at the moment. And truly, without my wealth – or my mother's wealth – I wouldn't be. I'd be on an eternal waiting list until I'm officially too old to access NHS treatment. The postcode lottery for IVF treatment is spectacularly unfair. And the rights of single gay individuals, well ...'

Richard made a noise in his throat. I couldn't determine its direction of travel.

'I think, given that, that trying to resurrect the Stand Foundation would be difficult. Essentially, it's a Catholic charity, and I would be surprised if they would support the cause. However, very recently, there has been a wave of European funding linked with the area, and others, that you've touched on. I've actually just returned from the European Health Commissioning Conference in Lisbon where that was one of the big agenda items. I can get Pauline to send over some details if you like. I can't promise it will be exactly what you're after, but it would be a start. It's pretty heavy going, just a heads up – systemic reviews, shortfall, geographical areas of need, that kind of thing.'

'Perfect. That would be fabulous, Richard. Do me a favour, though – please don't shout about this for now, particularly about my own IVF treatment. There are few people who know.'

'The very soul of discretion!' He laughed. 'And I'm thrilled for you, Tilda. You will make an amazing mother.'

'I've many hurdles to clear before I'm a mother, but I'd like to have a shot. Thank you. I'm going to let you go.'

'Let's meet up when you've had a look through the commissioning information. If you still have the appetite!'

My mind was already rolling. I could combine a meeting with Richard with my next clinic trip for the all-important fertilisation update.

'Thanks Richard. Let's do that.' Butterflies of giddiness somersaulted through me as I cut the call.

***

Turning my key in Mother's front door for the last time should have felt significant. Yet there was no sense of loss or sadness, just ambivalence. Travelling up the night before the clinic, I'd decided to stay at my mother's despite the place being practically empty. The only item left remaining a made up bed in the single room for this purpose. I hoped I might excise my mother by doing something that she would find ridiculous. I pictured myself snake-like, shedding a tired and uncomfortable skin, a new physicality waiting for me after this life that I'd long outgrown. I was a blank slate, with my mother no longer alive to remind me of all that I wasn't.

The clearance company had been thorough. The house had been emptied of everything, including Mother's personal effects. I'd wanted nothing. Archie and I had accepted an offer, and the agent was hopeful for completion in the next few weeks.

'Maybe I'm just a really late starter?' Mobile tucked between shoulder and ear, I chatted with Ellie as I multitasked, pretending I wasn't uncomfortable in the echoey single room and narrow bed, highlighting sections from the consultation papers that Richard had sent over. I was trying to keep myself occupied until I could fall asleep and focus all my energy on the clinic results tomorrow.

'Better late than never. Look at me, putting up with Jed the Eejit all those years. Mental. So, massive day tomorrow. Let me know as soon as you do. Am I allowed to say I have a good feeling this time?' Ellie ventured.

'You said that last time.' I laughed.

'No, I didn't. But I can *feel* it this time. I've worked out your dates. Mini-Tilda will be due at the start of September, making her one of the oldest in her class, which always makes them super smart comparatively. Unlike Rosa here, who'll be bringing up the rear with her August birthday.'

'It is what it is,' I muttered, steeling myself for disappointment tomorrow while desperately hoping Ellie would be right. I'd opted out of live egg updates this time. Instead, I would be told the outcome face to face at the end of the five days.

'Anyway, I've loads to keep me busy. I met with Richard today. He's put me on a business start-up course. If it's not good news egg-wise, then I'll just try again and keep busy in the meantime.' I was preparing for a potential mood crash and planning accordingly.

Rosa's background wailing was cranking up and we agreed to cut the call. Vic had texted to see how the business meeting had gone, and as I was replying, I saw the missed call log. Again, calls from the same unidentified mobile number. I shivered. Why was I only now waking up and choosing a life for myself after all these years? It was puzzling. But exciting.

***

Just one of the five fertilised eggs was still in good shape. One minute I was hearing the mixed news and the next, I found myself fabulously legs akimbo having said embryo inserted into my uterus. It wasn't actually as terrible as it sounds. I've had worse smears – memorably one by a student nurse years back.

This journey home was far removed from the last. Seating myself in first class, I caught sight of my reflection in the window. I was taken aback to see the beginning of furrows across my forehead. How long had they been there? At one time I'd have been straight on to my dermatologist, obsessing over this new ageing symptom. I leaned further towards my image, smiling broadly. *Bring on the laughter lines.* Conscious that the zygote still had a long way to go before it would be considered viable, I was still beyond excited. Arranging myself across the double seat, I relaxed into the movement of the train, conscious of my early and precious cargo. The next few days again were pivotal. Would the egg attach itself to the uterus lining? The waiting would be agony. I exchanged text messages with Ellie and dared to dream. The places I would go, the things I would do, an entire world of possibilities there for me and my child.

Lana

Jodie had pulled out all the stops for my surprise marsupial-themed leaving party. Loosely following the curriculum of classification, she'd commissioned the kids to create all things marsupial. Koalas joined wallabies, kangaroos and snapper jacks as they manically bounced and hopped. Spectacular garlands and vines festooned the sports hall (props from last year's end-of-term play) and looked incredible. Apart from minor casualties involving kids in oversized kangaroo hoods, all was fabulous.

'We are, of course, very sorry to see our lovely Miss Edwards leave.' Lynda, my headteacher, was proposing an orange cordial toast. I heard lovely, if romanticised, claims about my teaching abilities and how I'd be missed. Reception were impossibly cute, and Miss Grant, their wonderful teacher, led a 'koala conga' that snaked its way around the perimeter of the hall, joined by each successive year group. Staff and children mingled, bobbed and jigged to the funky tunes that the caretaker and Wan – yes, Wan – had rigged to the sound system. Even Wan sported a kangaroo pouch and, to the delight of my class, joined in the dancing. As if on cue, the music faded.

'Speech,' shouted Jodie as I graciously accepted the vouchers from her collection. The children joined in the chanting. Stern teacher voices brought the children into line and a hush fell over the room.

'I cannot tell you how excited I am. And I've still got *ages* to go!' I laughed, gesturing at my sizeable belly protruding from the multicoloured kaftan that had become the mainstay of my maternity wardrobe. 'Each and every one of you has been amazing. You've all been so kind.' I smiled at the Year 6 kids trying to look cool while sipping juice through their koala masks. 'Even Mr Peterson has been nice!' The kids roared with laughter. The whole school was aware of Mr Peterson's retirement countdown and his struggle to raise a smile in these last few weeks. His lips turned upwards at the edges, causing him to look like a terrier with wind. 'I will miss you all, and we will be back to see you in September for baby cuddles. Be good, be kind. Thank you so much for all your koala-based efforts. You are fabulous. I do need to clarify – for Reception's sake, mainly – I *am* having a baby, not a koala!'

There was only one feeling finer than finishing school for summer: finishing two weeks early. Bliss. Koala was in fine form, booting and elbowing like the self-respecting foetus she was. Every afternoon she would come alive as the racing commentary started. Encouraged by the crescendo of excitement, she really went for it, her cartoon fist visible through my stomach. The open windows afforded a breeze that filtered deliciously through the flat. The trade-off was traffic noise and dust.

I would look back nostalgically upon those long afternoons, so much excitement and hope incubating there. Finishing work marked another step closer to all being well. The gnarl of anxiety had reduced but remained a constant. I'd been here before, waiting so patiently, with no baby at the end. I tried to keep my mind from focusing on the worst outcomes, but the possibility of losing her was only ever a step away from my thoughts. I'd read a bit and drift off again, sometimes novels or school stuff, half-heartedly glancing at the scheme of work for Year 5, whom I'd not taught before but would probably pick up when I returned to work. Wan would appear periodically from the cupboard under the stairs we generously called the 'studio'. Quite what he did in there for so long I'm not sure – nor how he could bear the intense heat. He'd emerge, blinking mole-like, headphones draped around his neck, looking every bit post-snooze rather than successful in his quest for the perfect set. I'd wander around barefoot, wafting voluminously in my kaftan, enjoying the nothingness of it all. My days were busy – trips to the loo, peering round the nursery door to check in on koala, right shoulder leaning protectively towards Evie's butterfly, who glowed with life at 4 p.m. as the sunshine burst through. There was Rightmove scrolling. The interior of every three-bed property within a 5-kilometre radius was imprinted on my brain. I coveted everything, jealous of kitchen islands, utility rooms bigger than my front room, wistful for lush gardens – yards, even – planning in my mind's eye which we'd have should a deposit materialised. Wan had hinted heavily to his parents, but without a lottery win I had no clue how we would become homeowners. Would they surprise us at the birth with a generous donation, falling impossibly in love with their grandchild, just as they would have with Evie? A child needs a garden, surely?

It was a routine visit to the midwife in early August that saw the first domino shift.

'Protein's a tad high.' The midwife held the amber specimen up to the window. 'Nothing too worrying. Just something to watch. Are you resting enough? Are you still working?' The locum midwife, whom I did not recognise – Zara, according to her badge – tapped away into my notes. She reached for the blood pressure cuff and gestured towards my sleeve.

'I couldn't do less if I tried.' I laughed nervously. 'What does that mean? Protein? I've not changed my diet.'

'No, nothing to do with diet. Your bloods are fine, blood pressure seems okay-ish.' She nodded towards the monitor. 'Elevated protein levels usually link to your kidneys. It's hot;

make sure you rest in the afternoons, drink plenty of water.' She was businesslike compared to my usual midwife. Not unfriendly, just professional. 'Any thoughts about a birth plan? I can't see one in your notes.' She scanned the screen.

Had she seen my history?

'It's on there, but I'm open-minded. Just get her out in one piece,' I said, my face serious. 'You know I can't go over, right? If I get to thirty-eight weeks, they will induce. Mr Coleman is overseeing my care at the hospital.' My pitch was high, anxiety creeping in.

Zara's expression altered as she read the screen. Forty-week stillbirth primigravida, uncomplicated labour. Non-hereditary, no birth defects, no familial difficulties known. No signs of meconium or distress. My version: she'd gotten so caught up in the excitement of birth, she'd forgotten to breathe. One minute sailing down Birth Canal and the next propelled by powerful contractions, a delicate shade of lavender as she landed.

'Lana, I'm sorry … This isn't my usual clinic.' Her mask momentarily fell, and she looked for all the world like Jodie when she's worried about me. It wasn't a look I wanted to see on my midwife's face.

'It's fine. So, what's with the protein levels?' My heart hammered.

Zara looked again at the screen as well as at the sample bottle where she'd left it on the windowsill.

'It's borderline and I'm pretty sure nothing to worry about. That said, let's do another test. If the protein level rises, it could indicate pre-eclampsia – highly treatable, but we'd need to be straight on it. Which we will be.' She waved the sample bottle my way. 'Come back and see me tomorrow. In the meantime, any swelling, dizziness, headaches, get yourself to A&E. Here's a leaflet. I'll drop a note to Mr Coleman so that he's aware.'

Did Zara look less confident in the delivery of her words than earlier? She helped me from my reclining position, jamming flip-flops onto my swollen feet.

If rest is good for pre-eclampsia, how is exercise too? Get your act together, NICE guidelines. An afternoon googling all things pre-eclampsia left me confused rather than expert. Declaring my most swollen foot (the left) pregnancy puffy as opposed to clinically puffy (in my non-clinical opinion), I took my sofa-weary body the long way round the park, feeling smug as I overtook an elderly jogger, taking my pregnancy small win where I could. I tried hard not to catastrophise about a common and manageable *possible* pregnancy complication.

'Cortisol is the enemy,' I reminded myself as I headed back, breathing away my stress. Four weeks to go. Ignoring the slight pain under my ribs, I resolved to get fitter using the jogging buggy I'd bought with work's vouchers. If Koala popped out right now, all would be fine. *Four weeks early is doable. She's a good weight.* But still the niggle in the lowest pit of my stomach suggested otherwise.

Tilda

Perched on the edge of the bath, I peered anxiously, searching for the faintest line.

'Ellie, it's blue. The line's bright blue. I'm pregnant!' I shrieked down the phone, not daring to believe, sending Ellie a shaky photo of the result. As we squealed loudly in our separate locations, I jigged wildly around the bathroom. Baby Rosa came to the phone to join in. There'd be four of us doing that soon.

'We should toast for luck.' Ellie disappeared and I heard the delightful sound of a mid-launch cork. Opening my fridge, I reached for the sparkling water, breathless with excitement.

'To Mini-Tilda!' I shouted and jumped around the kitchen island. Giddiness like I'd never known.

'Really? Does that mean that's it? Good to go from here on?'

'I've a slightly increased risk of miscarriage, but studies vary. I prefer to believe the studies where there's little difference between IVF and standard conception.'

'You *have* to let me come to the scan. Ooh, I can feel myself getting broody!' Ellie squealed. 'You will make the most amazing momma!'

My heart lurched as I recalled my mother's thoughts to the contrary, but I chinked the thought away with my faux champagne toast. The moment felt surreal.

'To us – to all of it! Yay!'

'Oh my God,' I yelled immediately after cutting the call to Ellie and Rosa, wondering what Vic would make of all the shouting. Although he'd have to get used to a bit of noise if all went according to plan.

***

Conceiving in January, my year unfolded into trimesters matching the months. The first travelling-hopefully trimester was a pure white-knuckle rollercoaster. Between early vomiting bouts and quashing miscarriage-related anxiety, I tried hard to channel my mind and energy into the start-up.

I'd identified a very relevant gap in the charity sector based both on my research and my own experience. It was not lost on me how fortunate I was to be financially comfortable and able to access IVF. For so many in society, IVF is not an option. Same-sex couples, older couples (who aren't old at all, just outside NHS criteria), singletons and couples without financial means to pursue IVF, individuals in geographical areas where they've used their meagre NHS allotment of IVF cycles but have been unable to conceive. Could I offer funding support to people unable to access IVF privately but excluded by the rigid NHS criteria? I hadn't figured out quite how I'd offer this. I clearly didn't have a bottomless pit; however, if I could establish a framework that might shape a set of fair criteria, it would be a start. And then perhaps I could pursue additional funding. Stress is one of the biggest threats to successful IVF. In an area where the odds are already stacked against favourable outcomes, this seems particularly unfair. Removing the element of financial stress for vulnerable individuals and couples seemed like a worthy direction and a step towards a levelling of the playing field – ambitious, I know. Richard was incredibly helpful in setting up contacts between IVF legislators and NHS commissioners, even meetings with individuals impacted by the postcode lottery of treatment. Again, all possible for me simply because I had the money to make this happen.

If I'd been remiss in the past and not used Mother's money as a force for good, I was trying to make up for it now. I enjoyed the fact that that my mother would not have remotely approved of the cause. I could imagine her caustic words and criticism, reminding me that the Tilda of old was only ever a step away. From beyond the grave she could still make my veneer of positive thinking feel dangerously thin.

I resisted alcohol right through my first trimester. Likewise, I only fleetingly thought of calling Edwin – or the number I assumed was him, since I'd blocked his original one. I almost called one metaphorically dark night when the enormity of my decision covered me like a cloak. In a moment of self-doubt, I deluded myself that Edwin could take on a grandfather role. More likely he'd persuade me to have an abortion. I shuddered and moved through the moment, texting Ellie and remembering the image on my phone that I used to stall myself in these moments. A border collie tucking into a pool of its own vomit. Very apt in the first nausea-filled trimester.

The second trimester felt a little easier. The risk of miscarriage was beginning to reduce, and I tried hard to worry less. My strange weight distribution was beginning to play fair. I had a bump. Not an 'I've had too much Indian buffet' bump but a genuine early pregnancy bump, making me ride the waistband low on my jeans or unbutton slightly with a longer top. I was delighted. Slowly I began to let people know, my grin announcing the news to anyone who cared to look before I officially told them. Like an adolescent in the early throes of a crush, I was consumed. I went to sleep every evening with a grin across my face and woke each morning delirious to find myself still pregnant. The marionette smile lines were fine by me.

'Vic!' I hadn't seen him for a few weeks. We'd exchanged messages and talked about getting together without arranging a date. We passed fleetingly in the hallway.

'Drinks?' He gestured enthusiastically. 'We never did sort my housewarming! Let's get together and plan.'

'Sounds good.' I offered a thumbs-up, but rushingly, as I had a midwife appointment. We agreed to meet the following night at mine. Old Tilda would have been half cut before her guest landed. New Tilda was cleaning the loo (again. Better watch that OCD) and drinking fizzy apple juice.

Vic blustered through the door, clinking bottles. Frustratingly, he had Eric with him.

'Didn't want to him to get lonely hearing us have all the fun!' I hoped Vic hadn't caught my horrified expression as the greasy hound padded slowly across my expensive flooring.

'Of course not.' I could clean later. *Please God, don't let him sit on my sofa.* I tried hard to look convincing and managed to extend my hand to his matted fur.

'This apartment is to *die* for. How did you *do* this? You've seen my place. Why does mine look so shit? Seriously, can we swap? I'll throw Eric in!'

'I'll get the paperwork sent over first thing.' I laughed. 'It was nothing to do with me. I bought it with the walls knocked through and glass everywhere. I do like it, though.'

'No, it's more than that.' He looked around again. 'I know what it is. It's clean. It's my Achilles heel. I just can't be arsed!'

'At least yours is homely. Even I can see that my place is a little ... austere. That said ...' *Here goes ...*

'That will alter over the course of the year. I'm thinking of doing some work to the spare room.' Leading Vic and Eric into the small bedroom, I opened the blind using the remote. Sun poured into the magnolia room, creating spectacular light refraction from the mirrored furniture, the low Japanese bed frame contrasting elegantly with the high ceiling.

'I think it's a little clinical for a nursery at the moment, don't you?'

Vic did not disappoint.

'My darling!' he shrieked loudly, squeezing me tight. 'You dark horse. Shagging away all these months and not a word!'

'I haven't been, actually!' I laughed, conscious of how that sounded.

Vic looked puzzled. 'An immaculate conception? I *knew* there was something about you!'

'Kind of! I've gone for IVF. There's just me. No partner.'

Vic stopped mid-sip, almost spitting out his drink. 'And you never said a word? So that's where you've been beetling off to!' he exclaimed. 'So there's no dad on the scene?'

'Anonymous donor,' I ventured bravely. Vic was clearly shocked, his body language communicating his discomfort.

'I won't have any of the headaches that men can bring – just us,' I said simply. Vic opened his mouth to say more but seemed to check himself. We somehow quickly segued to Vic sharing gory details of Eric's conjunctivitis and a long-winded conspiracy theory that greedy vets are complicit in unnecessary treatment. Before we'd even stepped back into the lounge, Vic had steered the conversation clear of any further discussion around my pregnancy. I was about to talk about my due date when he set off on another rant about being banned from Waitrose after sneaking Eric in when the weather was bad. Maybe it was because my social exchanges with Vic to date had been alcohol fuelled, but something felt off.

Vic topped up his drink and we retreated to the sofa. Vic played text ping-pong with a friend, which interested him more than my company. He again entered into various monologues – all Eric related – and I couldn't help but feel slighted that he hadn't asked about my pregnancy. My small but visible bump was clearly the elephant in the room.

Feigning tiredness at 10 p.m., I asked to call it a night.

'I know we haven't even discussed your housewarming, but we will. Next time!' Vic was out of his chair before I'd finished my sentence. Closing the door behind him, I wondered why he'd behaved as he had – why he'd shifted so radically after my pregnancy news. Maybe being gay had led to difficult conversations or experiences around conception and children. Although it hadn't been my actual pregnancy that seemed to throw him – it had been the IVF detail. Was he Christian? Did he consider IVF immoral? I hoped that next time we got together, he might feel able to share. He hadn't explicitly said he was gay, but that was my assumption. I'd somehow banked disproportionally upon Vic being a supporter. Ridiculous, I know, and a reflection of my loneliness. Even though he was a newcomer, I'd hoped we might become friends.

I texted a thank you around 11 p.m. but didn't hear back. I had a stern word with myself about not overthinking and opted not to be offended but understanding. I hoped there would be a logical explanation for his distance. Pulling out the conference notes I'd annotated earlier, I began to read. Misery loves misery.

Mother's words chimed in my head as I read the gloomy statistics relating to IVF pregnancy outcomes and linked clinical levels of low mood in the sample from the north of England. If Edwin were here, he'd pour me a glass of something delicious and we'd watch an old movie to take my mind off things. I resisted the urge to text back on the mystery number that I still presumed was him, despite my lonely state.

***

The last trimester was unfeasibly hot. In between wilting, I consciously tried to fill every moment to pass the time. I'd worked hard to make the apartment less sterile – nothing radical, but adding colour to my laboratory-style space. Vibrant throws, cushions – items I'd previously considered to be clutter, I hoped were creating a homely feel. Funky prints were ordered online, moved to various rooms, then eventually shipped to Ellie's when I couldn't quite find the right spot. Mini-Tilda's room was sublime. Ellie had helped me create a beautiful space: whisper-grey walls with a bold fuchsia chimney breast and contrasting fairy-themed prints. A stunning crystal fairy mobile hung from the ceiling. Not fragile, ethereal fairies, but fairies with attitude, just as I knew Mini-Tilda would have.

I ought to have put in a little research before choosing an antenatal group. I'd opted for the National Childbirth Trust, mainly because they were on the doorstep, which I thought would be good for the children keeping in touch longer term. However, without being unkind, they really were the most banal bunch of people I'd ever encountered. Probably products of trysts between schoolteachers and Methodists. It sounds mean, but it's accurate. Blander than budget vanilla ice cream. Or at least my group were.

I walked into the second meeting and was met by a wave of excitement. I was disappointed to learn that this was because the guest speaker – Taryn, discussing home birth – had brought her toddler along. Of course she had – she was still breastfeeding despite said toddler having a full set of teeth and being so long that he lay across two chairs as he fed. The child looked about three years old, and no one in the room reciprocated my discreet eye roll as he fed noisily from alternate breasts throughout his mother's presentation. The room was full of prissy Tarquins and Maisies – all couples – bearing the most sincere expressions. Even when Taryn comedically paused the home birth footage – father-to-be behind labouring mother in the birth pool – no one would meet my eye. It was clear to anyone with eyes that the image looked like a still from a porno, but nobody would take me on. It was priceless. Edwin would have been beside himself. Clearly, they weren't my tribe – nor I theirs. Which was a shame and a missed opportunity to meet what I'd hoped would be like-minded mothers.

I experienced my first IVF haters. Who knew they even existed? After Vic's distance following my IVF disclosure, I'd thought he must be an exception for personal reasons. What was wrong with people?

The start-up was really taking shape, and together Richard and I had created an early draft of the charity's aims, aptly named the Nurture Foundation. Richard was presenting at a conference we were attending and referenced Nurture within this, which was met with interest. Forming a steering group and recruiting members was taking time, but I was excited by the possibilities. I passed on the opportunity of presenting myself but glowed with pride as Richard passionately described what we hoped to achieve. At lunchtime I stepped out for fresh air and found myself mobbed by a sea of middle-aged women shouting and waving placards.

'Leave playing God to God,' they chanted angrily. 'Not your choice!'

A woman who looked disconcertingly like my mother blocked my path as I tried to reach the bridge to make my escape.

'Will you tell your child the truth about their conception?' Her mean, bird-like eyes bore into me accusingly. In the absence of a timely one-liner, I welled up with tears and pushed her out of my way. I fled, completely taken aback by what I'd just experienced, their vile chanting still ringing in my ears. I made my way back to the building using a side door.

'Have you seen them outside? It's mental. How is that legal?' I fumed to Richard.

'Their protest is apparently legal, but I don't think approaching pregnant women and being rude is remotely ethical or kind.' Placing an arm around me, he steered me towards a chair. 'We will never win over groups like that, but we can put it on the Steering Group agenda – how we meet the challenge,' he soothed, placing a coffee in my still-trembling hands. 'And breathe,' he joked, knowing that would irritate me further.

'Name the agenda item "dealing with fucking mental self-righteous right-wing bitches". I'll lead on it.' I laughed, my pulse rate beginning to slow. 'If they're still there on the way out, I'll have something to say to them!'

They were nowhere to be seen when the convention ended, which in hindsight was no bad thing.

Walking home from the conference, I tried to put the incident behind me, keen to feel the high I'd felt that morning watching

Richard speak and the energy behind his words. Nurture was bringing me vitality and motivation, making me feel both relevant and determined. It would be incredible if I could attract funding and shine awareness on the injustice within the system, helping those who fell between the cracks of self-funding and the NHS lottery. Even highlighting their plight would be something. Conscious that I was getting ahead of myself, with Nurture in its earliest stages, I still felt excited. The altruism jury was still out as I wondered, not for the first time, if this was about me feeling good about myself or about helping others.

Clutching a bulging file of literature and business cards, I headed to the café on the corner of the Heath before heading home. As I carried my cappuccino carefully between the crowded tables, I spied a free chair. Two guys were hugging goodbye, which opened a space.

'Tilda!' Vic waved his friend off and sat back down at his open laptop.

'What a lovely surprise!' It was certainly an *awkward* surprise given that Vic had U-turned in his early friendship overtures. I'd resigned myself to him not being friend material, but maybe I'd just caught him on a bad day. New Tilda would give him the benefit of the doubt.

'Look at you!' He gestured. 'Increasingly pregnant!'

'As pregnant as it gets!' I laughed nervously.

We made small talk about the cost/benefit of Vic's freelance journalism job versus a salaried position. Still pumped from the conference, I dared to update him on the progress of the charity. I explained about the financial barriers for so many facing IVF, seizing the opportunity for a little publicity.

'You could do a piece for us, Vic – give us a platform!'

Vic's left eye began to twitch. He turned his attention to his coffee.

'I'm sorry, am I making you uncomfortable by talking about this?'

Vic hesitated, searching for words.

'Do you know what the statistical outcomes are of planned parenthood without a partner?' A red flush crept up his neck.

Boy, I was getting both barrels today. 'No, but I think you're about to enlighten me.'

'I was raised by an alcoholic mother who was as far removed emotionally from me as she could be –an only child that she'd deliberately chosen to raise solo. She never even told the father about me. A quick shag in the loos because *she* wanted a baby – that she could care for neither emotionally nor financially. And when I tried to come out as a teenager, well ... she was having none of it. I just don't think it's fair to bring a child into the world without both parents. I'm sorry, Tilda. This isn't personal.'

It was incredibly personal. He was judging me, implying that I was selfish. That I would fail my child in a repeat of his own experience. How dare he?

'I'm sorry things were so difficult for you,' I offered. A generous response.

'People never think about the child, particularly when the baby's "engineered" through IVF. It's complicated for me. I wasn't what my mother "ordered". I don't know what she wanted, but it wasn't me.'

I placed a hand on Vic's forearm. 'I'm sorry,' I said as gently as I could. 'I'm not asking anything from my baby. And I'm prepared to be both mum and dad.'

'Everybody says that, and it *never* pans out that way. It might be different for you, with your ... financial situation.'

Feeling the physical rise of indignation for the second time in as many hours, I took a breath. I wasn't there to persuade, inform or defend myself, my finances or my situation. Getting to my feet, I placed the money for my drink on the tray, too angry to speak.

'You asked me. I'm sorry. I just feel strongly.'

'So do I,' I muttered, grabbing my bags and bundling myself quickly through the door. I was shaking with rage but wasn't going to give him the pleasure of seeing that.

***

'What a twat!' shouted Ellie down the phone as I walked, updating her on the exchange with Vic, as incredulous as I was.

'So much hate in one day.' I explained about my encounter with the self-righteous right-wing bitches from lunchtime. She commiserated.

'What gives them the right?' I demanded; I was shocked that those women felt they could behave like that. In the short walk to my apartment, I tried to expel my fury. Ever cortisol conscious. Mini-Tilda didn't need to hear or feel this. 'It's awful what happened to Vic, but what's that got to do with me?'

I strode onwards past the lovely wine shop. Exquisite bottles of Bombay Sapphire glistened provocatively in the window.

'I could murder a gin and tonic,' I fumed.

'Not much longer and you can do just that,' Ellie said with a laugh.

'I think I'll pinch your empties and display them in the recycling tub outside the apartment. Then we'll see what Vic the Prick has to say!' I could feel the anger beginning to subside as I vented.

'Don't give him or his views a moment's thought, Tilda. Crack on doing what you're doing with Nurture and becoming a mum. It's an amazing concept. And don't doubt yourself for a second,' Ellie lectured.

'I know. I'm not going to let his angst become mine. I'm declaring him a massive tosser and drawing a line under it. I'm leaving it at the door.' Turning the key in the lock, I stepped into the apartment. Sun streamed through the balcony window, catching the dazzling fuchsia colours on the embroidered cushions. The new linen drapes beautifully outlined the majesty of the windows without blocking any of the view. The smell of paint from the nursery felt fresh and clean.

'This apartment is officially *homely*,' I decreed. Mini-Tilda nudged her approval, on the move, as was her wont at this time in the afternoon.

'We will be just fine, won't we, little one?' Patting my shifting stomach gently, the question – or statement – hung in the air. I'd bloody make sure we would.

Lana

Was it really over a year since I was here (post-*incident*)? Still those ridiculous hand-washing posters everywhere. *Who are these people that need reminding to wash their hands? I have Reception kids who've mastered it.* That middle-aged guy, looking so much older than his years, propped at the entrance to A&E – the same greasy pyjamas, chain-smoking. He'd looked on the verge of death a year ago, so maybe not the same guy, but the same papery skin emitting that near-death glow.

Wan checked me in as I weaved my way through the crammed seating area, mouth-breathing through the unhygienic bodies. Perching on a moulded plastic chair, I focused on the pan balanced on my knees and its peeling non-stick coating. The vomit/bile combination I'd been producing for the last hour probably hadn't done it any favours. Was this pan an engagement gift from Wan's mum or auntie? Not that it mattered. Dizzy, I leaned forward, head between my legs, breathing in an exaggerated manner, braced for a new stream of vomit. Koala wasn't happy, all arms and legs. I drummed my fingers reassuringly on my belly. If this wasn't a bug and was pre-eclampsia, she'd be making an appearance sooner rather than later. Would they induce me or do a section? A pain shot through my ribs followed by the most powerful vomit stream, hitting the half-full pan and spraying everything within a three-metre distance. Those seated within spraying distance recoiled immediately. Wan joined me, clutching my pregnancy notes like a scroll.

'Probably that Chinese from last night. I've felt off all day …'

The fear that it was something more worrying was terrifying.

'Wan, I need a section. Tell them. Something's not right.' I grabbed his hand.

'You're in the right place. If you need a section, they'll do it.' Wan looked unconvinced but kept up the chatter until the porter whisked my wheelchair away to triage. Bloods, monitors and scans occurred in quick succession. The lovely (if elderly) porter ferried me smoothly but at high speed. His English wasn't great, but his watery eyes looked at me so kindly, and he respectfully looked away each time I needed to empty the pan.

Around 2 a.m. I was admitted to a hushed maternity ward. The vomiting had finally subsided. I was mute with exhaustion. And fear. The nurse wordlessly attached me to a monitor.

'Shouldn't you be doing a section?' I pleaded.

'You don't need a section, Ms Edwards.' The nurse's tone was patronising. 'Your protein levels and blood pressure are down; you've responded to medication, which is why you're no longer vomiting.' Her tone was brusque. As she attached the last of the cables to the foetal monitor, I felt relief course through me, the hypnotic whirring matching my heartbeat like a tag team.

'Love you, Lana; love you, Koala.' Wan leaned in, carefully dodging the medical paraphernalia around me. I'd forgotten about Wan. My lips were so dry, my skin clammy; I was exhausted, unable to respond. If I felt this bad, how was Koala? The thought was terrifying. I tried to relax, my vice-like stomach muscles still so tight from the vomiting. Wan quietly unpacked my spare clothes. I imagined his lovely brown eyes full of concern. I felt his gentle squeeze and a whispered promise to text as soon as he was home. Only he didn't, because he was so very tired. Wan headed straight to bed, leaving his phone charging in the kitchen on silent. No matter how frequently or desperately it rang, he wouldn't hear it.

***

If I'd had a detailed birth plan, I'd have been really disappointed. I remembered my words to the locum midwife days before: *Get her out. Do whatever it takes.* And they did. At 5.02 a.m. Just a few hours after I'm wheeled in, I'm back out again. A flurry of activity and apparent consent to a caesarean section. Stitch-like pain racked my body and now a searing headache. Why hadn't they listened to me? Clearly the meds had only stalled the pre-eclampsia march. The solution: delivery. I was so glad they didn't induce me. I had zero energy to push even if our lives depended on it.

'Let my husband know,' I urged the staff nurse. Desperation swept over me. Was this the moment I'd been dreading? The bit where I would lose my second-born child? 'Get her out, please.' I heard my voice, high and wavering. The nurse nodded reassuringly. 'Her sister didn't ... make it,' I cried as a terrible pain shot across my forehead.

'Hush,' soothed the nurse. 'Listen to me.' She moved in closer. 'This baby will be with us before you know it. She won't be impressed. She's pretty comfy where she is, but we'll get her out. Okay?'

I nodded, unable to voice my spiralling fear, so grateful for her reassurance but filled with a certainty that things would not end well. Wan needed to be here. I attempted to use my phone, but my stupid trembling hands refused to cooperate. The kind anaesthetist tried to call, but the phone rang out. A nurse detached me from the reassurance of the foetal monitor and wheeled me quickly from the ward. How would I know if Koala was okay without the monitor? I tried desperately to implore the nurse to plug it back in. The anaesthetic covered my thoughts like a cloak.

***

Who knew Koala would actually look like a koala? That *had* to be self-fulfilling. Jamming my pillow against the nightstand, I tried to gain a better view. Koala was whimpering, more puppy than infant. Was that normal? My breasts throbbed, ready for her again. It was so frustrating to be at the mercy of the busy nurse to allow me to feed. I'd tried to get her myself earlier only to find myself in big trouble from the ward nurse. Wan appeared as I was about to ring the bell.

'Babe …'

Had he practised those spectacular words all the way to the hospital? After his extended lie-in, refreshed by the midday sun and oblivious to the frenzied log of missed calls and messages?

I beamed from my semi sitting position at his mortified expression. He looked from the plastic crib at the side of the bed to me. And back again, his mouth wide open. Tears fell down his cheeks and he darted over, not to Koala but to me, burying his face against mine.

'Are you … okay?' Wan was tearful.

'We're good,' I whispered, tears streaming down our faces.

Wan stepped over to the snuffling Koala, taking in her shock of fair hair, furrowed pink face, eyes tightly shut. He put his hand to his mouth in disbelief, shaking his head. Like he couldn't quite believe his eyes.

'Isn't she lovely?' he sang softly to her, as he'd sung to her so often in the womb.

'Pass her over, then,' I whispered.

Wan looked panicky. 'Should I ask a nurse? She's …'

'Seriously?'

'She's so tiny.' Wan sat back on the edge of the bed.

'She'll stay that way unless I feed her.' My breasts stung, anticipating her hungry mouth.

I guided Wan through picking her up, supporting her neck – just like we had with Evie. Carefully, he passed her over. Without opening an eye, she latched quickly on. Our tears continued to fall as we gazed at her perfect jaw and impossibly tiny hands pulled tight into her still-curled body, drinking in the moment with her.

A nurse bustled through, oblivious to our moment, performing her checks.

'Would you look at this wee one?' She nodded, recording her readings. 'Could you ask your breast-feeder there to have a word with the baby opposite? Don't think she got the memo like this one.' She laughed, looking softly at the nuzzling Koala. Wan and I laughed politely but were reluctant to let anyone into our bubble.

'She actually *looks* like a koala.' Wan giggled, stroking her soft spiky hair and peering into her perfectly shaped almond eyes. 'She needs a eucalyptus leaf! Where can I get one?' he whispered, not taking his eyes from hers. 'I am *so* sorry I didn't pick up all the calls. I completely crashed out. I totally forgot to unmute the phone after I left the hospital last night.'

If he hadn't looked so devastated, I might have been annoyed, but all that mattered was that we were all here. Alive and well. Nothing else.

'Who've you told?' I glanced down at my messages and missed calls.

'My parents and your mum. Was that right? I knew your mum was desperate for an update ...' Wan looked panicky again.

'You can tell anyone you like. Now she's here.' I truly didn't care how people found out. I had no inclination to see or speak to anyone. My world consisted of just the three of us. 'They're not visiting, are they?' I groaned.

'I said I'd see how you were. I didn't know if you'd be conscious, let alone breastfeeding.'

'I might look the picture of health,' I said, 'but I'm actually knackered. I'll be out for the count as soon as she is.'

A familiar voice boomed from reception. Someone hadn't needed inviting. The no-nonsense clack of Mum's boots came down the corridor.

'I will not stay more than two minutes; you won't know I'm here,' she boomed ironically, alerting the ward to her presence. 'I prayed for this koala bear and both of you too.' She beamed. 'And here you are, all safe.'

'Could you not have asked God to unmute Wan's phone? He might have been here earlier,' I teased, watching him squirm. There was going to be so much mileage in this.

'What is this?' she cried, placing her bags on the end of the bed and nudging Wan out of the way. 'A blond baby, well, my stars! Look at that fair skin!' she marvelled, peering closer. Mum's other grandchildren had Jamaican fathers and were much darker. Even Evie had been darker, so obviously Koala had taken her father's share of DNA this time.

'She's her own person already.' I prickled. A perfect foil to her older sister. Also slightly premature and blessed with the exotic gene pool of the white and nerdy one and yours truly.

'She's perfect,' mum breathed and planted a gentle kiss on the top of her head. There were hugs for Wan and me as she gathered her bags to leave, hearing the frosty nurse coming down the ward. She leaned in for a last look and spoke quietly.

'Lana, of my five children you were the fairest, the lightest colour at birth. You were also – it turned out – the smartest, the most resilient. And – do not tell the others – my closet favourite. God has blessed us!' She gestured theatrically heavenward.

Wan and I grinned, relieved that her visit was brief, enjoying the sound of her and the nurse's footsteps as she left the ward.

***

Jodie was phantom-like in the early days. We didn't see her, but evidence of kind and practical deeds was left in her wake. Aside from texts and calls, she struck the perfect balance of being supportive without being full-on. She came over twice and cleaned the entire flat. She baked, she shopped, she screened visitors, acting like a bouncer when she saw me tiring, encouraging guests to leave before I knew I was flagging. Everybody should have a Jodie.

Wan had a busy gigging schedule – not having anticipated an early Koala arrival – and we weren't in a position to turn down the money. I adored those early weeks, Koala gradually unfurling, her old-lady frown relaxing day by day, her downy skin losing its impossible fragility. I immersed myself completely in her newness. There might not have been room for Wan had he been around more. I get that new mums are supposed to sleep when their baby sleeps, but I couldn't. I was captivated by her. I even thought about setting up cameras to capture every moment, knowing how fast the early weeks would pass. Yet, amidst this Disney version of motherhood there was a nagging angst which I just could not shake off? A foreboding that I would wake and there would be no baby. That I'd either imagined the whole thing or she'd been there but had gone – taken in some way.

I had been surprised at Koala's complexion compared to Evie's, although it wasn't something I verbalised, even to Wan. Wan joked that I seemed happiest when there was no one around – even him. Which was true. I would have done anything to create distance in those early weeks between myself, Koala and others. I heard Wan and Jodie talking in whispers. Could I be postnatally depressed? It was quite the opposite. I could not get enough of her. She was *all* I wanted. I didn't want to dilute or share her, even with Wan. Retrospectively, I think I was always waiting for the comment: *Isn't she fair? She takes after Joel, doesn't she?* Feelings of rage simmered whenever anyone mentioned it.

'You can't call her Koala forever.' Wan's mum, Jean, hovered over the Moses basket, willing her to wake. I hadn't trained her to sleep when they visited, but it didn't displease me that she seemed to save her waking moments for us.

'We could. I mean, she does look like one,' I said, defensive of what we could or couldn't do with our daughter.

She began to stir, opening her eyes to check out her visitors. I generously passed her to Jean, who swayed with her by the window.

'I'm trying to think whose eyes she has.' Jean stared intently, angling Koala towards the light from the window. 'Who was that cousin on your dad's side, the one with the really blue eyes, reddish hair?' Wan's dad had no idea. He couldn't bring the name to mind. Jean continued to worry at it. Of course she did.

'They're all born with blue eyes, Jean. We've a picture the same of Joel at a few weeks old.' They bickered between themselves, but Jean was adamant it was neither Joel nor his brother but a more distant relative. I couldn't give a rat's ass whose baby it was, and it was all I could do not to share that.

'She's a suspicious-looking baby with the air of a grumpy old man. I keep seeing Winston Churchill but with Boris Johnson's hair! They are much of a muchness at this age, Mum.' Wan was quick to divert the conversation, as every guest who visited had commented similarly. Wan could see the conversation was wearing thin for me.

'She's a good feeder, isn't she, Lana? You must be exhausted!' A typical glass-half-empty Wan's mum comment.

'Wouldn't have it any other way.' Scooping Koala back, I quite deliberately prepared to feed.

'Feeding on demand, is it? Not like back in my day. She'll be using you like a dummy before you know it.' Where was Jodie the Bouncer when I needed her to remove guests *before* they outstayed their welcome? Wan saw my mood dipping and made wrapping-up noises to close the visit, thanking them again for the baby gifts.

As the door closed behind them, we sighed in unison.

'I owe you one.'

'No sign of that house deposit, then.' Wan rolled his eyes. Our hopes were dashed.

'Maybe we need to be nicer to them,' Wan suggested gently. Meaning that *I* needed to be a little nicer.

'Wan, I'm sorry. I'm tired, and the next person who mentions how she isn't "dark" like me, I'll fucking punch them. Family or not.' How could people be so insensitive? They never saw Evie in the flesh, but I knew how much darker she was then her sister. It felt like a knife turning whenever someone commented. In that moment I realised why it rankled so much – where the source of the hurt came from.

'Let's call her Koala just to prove a point.' I kissed Wan fleetingly, aware that I'd just been short with his mother. Again.

'Whatever you say, dear,' Wan mock-patronised.

'I'm torn between a name that sounds like Evie and something completely different.'

'Well, that narrows it down, doesn't it?' He laughed.

'I'm used to calling her Koala now. Everything else feels wrong.'

Wan opened the parcel he'd collected from the post office that morning. His brother, Jake, had been on the phone from Oz, checking it had landed.

'Seriously cute,' Wan declared the oversized plush koala bear, freeing it from its box and scattering the floor with tiny foam pellets.

The name tag introduced 'Stevie the Koala.' Wan and I looked incredulously at one another. 'Did you tell Jake we were thinking of an Evie-related name?'

'I don't think so. The last time we spoke – and probably when this was posted – we were hovering between Niamh and Evangeline. Probably thought he'd spare her either! I think it's my new favourite. Let's see how it goes. What do you think, Stevie-lady?' I whispered in her perfect ear, gently nudging her back to wakefulness after her mid-feed snooze. She opened an eye, a clear indication that she'd give it some thought.

Tilda

The September sun dipping over the Thames was incredible. Busy with tourists but without the intensity of the summer months, the vibe was chilled. The evenings were still warm enough to sit outside as the sun slowly set on the Embankment. I felt privileged. My antenatal class and I were having dinner not too far from my apartment. I'd been vague with my baby friends regarding my address, aware of my privilege and not wanting to shout about it. The group was mixed. Sadly, nobody was standing out as a friend-keeper, which was one of the main reasons I'd joined a group. They were nice enough in their own way and I'd hoped that we could allow the babies to keep in touch, but I was getting a distinct feeling that, for me, that might not be the case. I felt like a different species to them. All of them had partners. And they were all so *wholesome*. There was also the added complication of my IVF. What would they say if they knew? Would the NCT even approve of IVF? I was hardly the poster girl for natural childbirth, was I? At least, the conception was anything but. I grew irritated listening to tedious tales of supportive partners and helpful mothers-in-law. I began to fidget. Maybe I would join a single mums group. Or set one up. An *old* single mums IVF group; covering all the bases. Looking around the table, I was astonished to see a couple of the group drinking red wine.

'A glass a day keeps the doctor away.' Steph laughed, draining her small glass, revealing wine-stained teeth as she beamed around the table. 'When you get to our stage, it's fine. I didn't drink for the first four months. Not a drop. But truly I don't think there's any harm in the odd glass.' A non-verbal response divided opinion around the table.

'Years ago, Guinness was recommended by midwives.' Jess chipped in, trying to remain liberal despite her abstinence.

I resisted the urge to list the harmful substances and foods that the health profession discourages while pregnant. I imagined Vic opportunistically strolling past, attempting to wrestle glasses from their swollen hands and alerting the authorities.

'How long, Tilda?' asked the lady who always wore the same outfit and whose name I could never remember. Steering the conversation away from controversy seemed a grand idea.

'Two weeks left and counting,' I breathed. My swollen ankles reminded me of the daily countdown.

'Any advance on Mini-Tilda yet? Not that I'm judging. We've still not got past Bunion, and unless we agree on another, he'll be stuck with it!'

'Well, I love the name Rosa, but unfairly it's been taken by my friend. I like the idea of a variation on my own name but can only think of Hilda, which is unlovely!'

'I'm obsessed with old-fashioned names. And yes, Rosa is so pretty. Can't help but think of Rosa Parks. What were your grandmothers' names?'

'Well, Kay.' Same outfit lady's name came to me from nowhere. 'Not that I met either of my grandmothers, but I believe they were Phoebe and Leah. Phoebe Rose would be pretty.' I'd turned that over in my mind more than a few times. Mini-Tilda fidgeted wildly, to the amusement of the table, my enormous stomach holding court. There was only so much baby small talk that I could maintain enthusiasm for, and I was reaching my threshold. The group was showing signs of breaking up anyway, and we bid our goodbyes, agreeing to meet again, post-baby for some of us.

Taking the long way home, I avoided passing the wine shop. Had this been a subconscious decision over the last few months when the pull was strong? I was so sensible in my old age.

As I entered the apartment, the sun was just dipping over my small balcony. Pulling up a chair, I enjoyed the last of the rays. I pictured my group, all going home to partners offering back rubs, foot massages and lovingly drawn baths. Loneliness overwhelmed me. Would anything ever fill my strange discontent? I thought of the girls boldly enjoying their wine. You are never too old for peer pressure. I was thirty-six, a very respectable thirty-eight weeks pregnant, and bloody craving a gin and tonic. The mixer I poured came a poor second, yet I savoured every drop, proud of my resolve even at this late stage.

'To us, Phoebe Rose.' I raised my glass, liking the way the name sounded aloud.

Lana

Baking weeks turned to months. Keeping cool became a national obsession. Teething babies aren't fans of hot weather, and neither are their parents. At just nine weeks, Stevie's first tooth appeared, coming as a spectacular relief. The sleepless nights had tested even my maternal limits. Wan and I were a well-oiled shift-taking team. The only advantage, however, to not being 'on duty' was that I could *listen* to Stevie's wailing instead of being involved in the effort to make it stop. I'd end up taking over, unable to listen to her misery.

Joining the Sing and Learn baby group caused me more anxiety than any teaching observation. It made no sense, but I just didn't know what to expect. Would they like us? Or would it be cliquey and awkward? I hadn't lost *any* weight since Stevie's birth. How was that even possible? The textbooks had clearly lied. As a breast feeder, my weight was not 'dropping off'. Could I really wear my pregnancy kaftan? An image of skinny teen mums huddled over their phones or Yummy Mummies in expensive sandals, oversized jewellery and posh accents worried away at me. Which would be worse? I'd never know unless I went.

As it happened, we were minor celebrities.

'She is gorgeous!' gushed the tutor, whom I immediately warmed to, an earth mother with a gravelly voice and a strong aroma of amber oil. She also had the most incredible dreads. If Jodie's mum were alive, it's how I would imagine her.

'Welcome, Stevie and Lana.' She introduced us to the group as they gathered around to check out the newest member. Most of the babies were around one, so there was lots of fuss and cooing. Stevie lapped it up, her eyes dancing as she waved her small fists around excitedly.

'Her dad's a DJ; she's obviously got his rhythmic genes.' I explained.

Bert the toddler was fascinated by Stevie. It was almost sweet, but the mucus thread that connected whatever toy he was holding to his upper lip made me gag. Despite this, snotty Bert and his mum Ali turned out to be lovely. Bert sent a steady stream of (mucus-drenched) toys in Stevie's direction, which I was largely successful in intercepting. The group was a mix of regular mums, childminders, a token dad, and a grandma with her twin grandsons. We belted out Old MacDonald as if we were tipsy on a hen do; it was ridiculously good fun. I exchanged numbers with Ali – like a desperate dater – delighted to have found a new baby friend. I pictured a parallel existence. One where I had both my girls. Evie, central to the toddler mob, stealing toys and the clear ringleader. Her pudgy hand holding tight to the buggy as she marched, singing loudly as we walked home. I tried to embrace the image rather than fight it, taking comfort from the thought that in a parallel universe we were doing just that.

***

Going to the last festival of the season wasn't a decision I arrived at lightly.

'Babe, loads of people go with kids. We've seen more than a few newborns at festivals!' Wan so wanted to convince me.

My withering look let him know exactly what I thought of the idea.

'She's sleeping about six hours a night, yes? You've your boob at the ready if she needs a night feed. What's the problem?'

'I'm not opposed to the idea; I just want to make sure that …' I didn't know exactly what I needed to make sure of. 'She's such a good girl. I don't want to mess up her routine.'

'Really? Lana, we used to *love* seeing families at festivals. It's how you get them used to it. We can put little lights on her pram, baby headphones …'

Wan whisked her from underneath her jungle gym. Wandering over to the studio, he unplugged the headphones, loud tuneage blasting. Stevie's eyes lit up, alert. Wan 'stood' her on the window ledge so that she could see out.

'You've got your answer. Stevie has spoken!' He laughed as we performed a window dance right there.

It's clear to me how women might become addicted to having babies. It's intoxicating. Like you're a celebrity – people talking to you, smiling, crossing the road to peer into your pram. How *clever* you are to have birthed this creature. As they grow – and become less cute – I understand why you would crave that newborn elixir all over again.

***

We whiled away the afternoon wandering through the festival site. Giant bubble-blowing – which mesmerised Stevie – family hula hoop and bongo drum sessions, all were lovely. The weather was finally breaking, and the drizzle was refreshing. Everything felt dreamlike. Stevie and I headed to where Wan had his teatime set in a tiny woodland venue. Grabbing drinks, I followed the sound of unmistakable Wan tunes, a mix of old school, new stuff, funky house. I held our pints aloft and made my way across the dance floor. Wan must have been watching for us; his face lit up behind the decks.

'The next tracks are for Lana, Stevie and the lovely Evie.' Wan's hammy DJ voice was thick with emotion. He blew a kiss our way. The first beats of Evie's track filled the air. Stevie and I began to sway as a group of teenagers charged onto the dance floor, recognising the track. I tugged Stevie's legs in time to the beat, misty eyed.

'All the small things …' The happy base notes vibrated through the ground and the dance floor came alive, all ages loving the tune. I pictured Evie holding her space, busting her best moves. Wan was right to insist we came here as a family. My cheeks ached from all the smiling. I shifted Stevie to face outwards just in time for her own track, which I swear she sensed before the beat even hit, slowing the pace right down. The song she'd heard from conception.

The unmistakable guitar intro. *'Isn't she lovely.'* Wan was really going 'mushy-all-out', seamlessly weaving the two tracks, just for us.

I felt like the luckiest, happiest woman on the planet. Stevie and I sashayed over to the DJ booth, planting a kiss on the nerdy DJ's lips. A cheesy ripple of applause went round the dance floor. An older guy wobbled over with a request. Wan leaned towards him, kindly steadying his shoulder, somehow deciphering the drunken guy's words. In that perfect movie-still moment, I pressed pause. Life couldn't get any better. It was pause-worthy. We had no idea what was in store and just how much we'd need to hold on to every precious memory.

Tilda

I was most disappointed to find myself attending the late-September IVF conference with Richard. Instead of queuing for coffee and squeezing into uncomfortable plastic chairs, I'd hoped to be feeding on demand and lamenting a sleep-deprived existence. I found myself instead ten days over my due date, forcing open-toed sandals onto hideously swollen feet. How could it still be so warm? It was interesting timing to find myself in early but definite labour just as the keynote address was reaching its conclusion. I'd felt off all morning, hoping it wasn't the buffet from the day before with its retrospectively metallic-tasting anchovy dip.

I'm a firm believer in science rather than old wives' tales, that babies' births are driven hormonally rather than by a drop in air pressure. However, Phoebe Rose chose the moment of the first cloudburst to let me know she was on her way.

Though I say it myself, I was impressive. The proverbial swan right through to the first push. I cruised elegantly while my legs paddled furiously beneath the surface. Ellie was beside herself on my behalf. While I didn't feel I wanted her present at my labour, I kept her updated by text throughout. Labouring in a very sophisticated private room, I tried hard – bizarre as it sounds – to enjoy the process. With a little help from the on-tap gas and air, I breezed it. Five hours start to finish. A phenomenally giddy bubble grew in my chest by the second. I knew Ellie was waiting downstairs excitedly. I imagined her ecstatic face appearing round the door, clutching a fine bottle of Bollinger and two glasses. I'd be the picture of serenity, Phoebe Rose nursing quietly from my breast.

The scene couldn't have been further from reality.

'One more push,' Bella, the wonderful Irish midwife who'd stayed throughout my labour, ordered firmly. 'When I say, Tilda! This is the last one. You've got this,' she cheered enthusiastically.

On the count of three – like something from a film – Phoebe Rose slithered into the world. I was on the right side of the pethidine – not so much that I was out of it- and could still feel the weight of Phoebe Rose on my stomach, cord attached. My legs were shaking like I'd run ten marathons, but the exhilaration was incredible. I looked from Phoebe Rose to Bella and back again, my face a mask. Holding her body close, skin on skin, I peered into her wide-open eyes.

'What? How? Is this ... my baby?' My voice sounded disconnected, like it was someone else's entirely.

Bella was momentarily taken aback. 'She's all yours, every inch,' she soothed. 'We've just got the placenta to deliver. You hang tight to baby while I cut the cord. Would you like a photograph?'

'Open the blind. As fully as you can.' Body and voice had reconnected. My words came out more harshly than I'd intended.

'Everything's okay, Tilda' she said gently. My heart was beating so fast, I thought I would faint, panic flooding my chest. I couldn't form my words. Bella walked agonisingly slowly to the window. Bright sunlight filled the room as she tilted the slats.

'She's beautiful,' Bella breathed, gazing at the still-wriggling baby in my arms, her coffee-coloured skin, dark eyes and lashes contrasting with my lily-white complexion. Unfeasibly thick dark curls coiled tightly to her head.

'How?' I breathed. 'I ...'

The baby began to cry softly, and Bella smoothed my hair. 'Would you like to try a feed? I can help if you like.'

'How?' I stammered, beginning to cry. 'Why is she so dark? Is it because she's overdue? Is she okay?'

I'd so longed for this moment yet here I was, *desperate* for reassurance. Something felt very wrong.

'You're exhausted is all.' Bella plumped my pillow as I resisted the urge to punch her patronising efforts. Clearly, I was bucking the trend for mother/daughter first moments. 'I need you to lean back while I deal with the cord and baby. Hush now.' I tried to speak again, but Bella gestured for quiet as she performed her post-natal duties.

It felt like forever as I lay motionless, the baby whimpering slightly still across my stomach. Eventually, Bella washed her hands. 'May I?' She gestured towards Phoebe Rose. I nodded mutely. Gently swaddling her in the blanket I'd brought, she placed her in my arms and perched on the end of the bed.

'You don't understand ... why is she this *colour*?' I gazed down at her in bewilderment.

'Babies are all shapes and colours when they first pop out. She may have been running out of room in there or maybe she's a little jaundiced, but nothing to be alarmed about. You can check with the doctor, but she looks fine to me. Beautiful, like her momma.'

'It's not that I don't think she's beautiful.' I sounded petulant. 'It's her ... colouring. I gasped, looking at her impossibly dark skin and the covering of downy dark hair across her shoulders. I was aware of how insane I sounded given that I'd clearly just given birth.

Bella was unfazed.

'Does she favour her father?' she asked gently. Roger's pale freckled skin, platinum hair and bright blue eyes sprang to mind.

'No,' I breathed. 'I'm just … I had this image …' I felt numb.

I took in her tiny fingers and toes, her mouth now searching like a landed fish.

'It can take a while to adjust. There are no textbook first moments. Relax. You'll be grand,' she soothed. 'Now shall we think about latching this wee girl on?'

I stared as Bella wedged Phoebe Rose with a pillow and encouraged me to prise her tiny mouth open, latching far back on my nipple. She immediately began to feed.

'Ah, she knows what she's doing.' Bella laughed and tentatively rose from the bed. 'A cup of tea for you and you'll be away.'

God, what was wrong with me? I couldn't even bond properly with my newborn, our first moments ruined. Was this a dream, a nightmare? I felt so overwhelmed. How could this child be mine? This was simply not my family's alabaster colouring. Closing my eyes, I flopped my head back in frustration. My phone was alive with text messages, vibrating on the bedside cabinet. Bella returned with tea for both of us. Completing her paperwork, she kept a vigilant eye on us, looking out for delayed bonding between mother and daughter.

'Is there someone I can call? Anyone you'd like me to contact?'

'My friend's downstairs in reception, just waiting for word. I can text her to let her know.'

'Grand,' she breathed. 'We can sneak her in while I get this paperwork done. Not strictly allowed in the birthing suite, but I'm no stickler for rules!' She laughed.

'That would be great.' I felt like a robot, mechanical and numb. 'Thank you.' Reaching for my phone, with the help of autocorrect, my shaking fingers invited Ellie up to the room. I practised an ecstatic newborn mum face, tears spilling down my cheeks. Poor Phoebe Rose. God, what was wrong with me? I could almost hear my mother's sneer.

'Do you think I'm terrible?' I asked, interrupting Bella for about the fourth time as she tried to complete her notes.

'I think you're a mum who's laboured like a pro for five hours. And now you're feeding like a pro. And you need a good sleep, a bath and – as if on cue – a hug from your friend.' A knock at the door announced the arrival of Ellie. She hovered in the doorway, her face alive with joy, clutching a bouquet of lilies and a bottle. Tears from both of us. Even Bella wiped her cheeks.

'Clever you!' Ellie squealed, trying to get a peek. Phoebe Rose had finished her feed and was dozing while still latched firmly on. The soft pink baby blanket I'd waited so long to wrap her in was tucked tightly around her tiny body. I kept my eyes trained on Ellie's face.

'She's gorgeous, Tilda!' Clearly picking up on the mood in the room. Despite her words, she eyeballed Bella.

'How is she so dark, Ellie?'

I saw her eyes look from mine to the baby, taking in the contrast in colour before her. She shrugged and laughed. 'I don't know! But she's gorgeous. She's so long! Willowy like you.' Clutching at straws given the obvious lack of resemblance. 'And so chilled!

Rosa did not stop wailing for a whole two hours after she was born. Oh, Tilda, she's incredible!'

Even Ellie looked like she could do with a drink. 'Speaking of chilled ...' She giggled nervously. Without asking permission from Bella, she quickly uncorked the champagne, thoughtfully chilled in a makeshift ice bucket she'd fashioned in her bag. Bella 'didn't notice'. Thank God for Bella.

'To Phoebe Rose and her very clever momma!' cheered Ellie. The plastic glasses gave a suitably hollow 'thunk'. As we gulped the champagne I tried to look the part – for the sake of Bella, the world's most lovely midwife; Ellie, my fabulous friend; and Phoebe Rose, who deserved so much more in her first few moments.

I took the option of an overnight stay despite a quick turnaround by the team. While Phoebe Rose was sleeping, I nipped to the bathroom. I could barely look at my reflection in the mirror. I felt in shock, unable to generate words that might describe my emotions.

Jenna would have asked me to try.

'Label it,' I imagined her demanding. 'What are you feeling?'

'Confused.'

'A start. What else?'

'Guilty.' That I wasn't this minute gazing at the undeniably beautiful infant beside my bed, willing her to wake and feed. Instead, I was talking to my reflection like a crazy person. A terrifying thought came over me. Was this the start of psychosis? A loud rushing sound filled my ears; an incredible feeling of pressure began to build in my head. I'd be predisposed given my previous mental health struggles, surely. I'd read about postpartum psychosis and the car crash that your life can become. *Is she even the colour I think she is? I'm losing it. I should never have thought I could be a mother.* I remembered the awful conversation I'd had with Vic. Even as an adult, his feelings of maternal rejection were still so painful. How had he described himself? 'Not what she'd ordered.' He'd referred to IVF as 'engineering'.

Ashamed. That was how I felt. Utterly ashamed. Turning, I vomited into the toilet, tea- and champagne-tinged bile. The stench was hideous. I lingered over the basin. Grabbing my mobile from my dressing gown pocket, I dialled Jenna. We hadn't parted on good terms, but I had no clue who else to run this by. The call rang out. What would I say?

'Hi, Jenna. So that you know, I've had the baby. She's black. I have a black baby. If I pay you enough as a therapist, would you ask the world not to mention it? It's going to be very awkward otherwise. With what you charge, I'm hoping you can somehow make this happen. Thanks.' I didn't leave a message. Flushing the loo, I engaged in magical thinking. *The flush has changed everything. Phoebe Rose will be sleeping softly in her basket. She will be the same colour as I am, undoubtedly mine.*

I sobbed quietly underneath the duvet as the handover midwife, Jamie, came into the room. I wondered what her brief had been. *Watch out for Tilda. We've called Psych. She's hanging in there, but she's a crisis waiting to happen.* Jamie closed the blind that Bella had tweaked earlier.

'It's not her colour....' I began, bypassing the niceties of introduction. Bella had clearly alerted her, as she capably took this in her stride. She sat patiently on the end of the bed in the same spot as her colleague had earlier.

'She's an IVF baby,' I blurted out. 'I think there's been a mix-up. I'm not racist!' Aware of how unstable I sounded, I continued, 'I didn't opt for a black donor. I don't think she's mine!' My voice cracked as I began to cry again. Phoebe Rose stirred, her tiny starfish hands spread wide as she cried out. Like she needed her mother. Any mother, really. My breasts tingled, but still I sat, waiting for the midwife to understand. Jamie held my gaze for the longest time, refusing to look away. Eventually I nodded, defeated. Jamie reached into the bassinet and handed over the hungry infant.

Unbuttoning my nightdress, I attempted to feed as I had earlier.

'There you go! Get you!' Jamie looked relieved. She hadn't responded to the doubts I'd just aired or even the fact that Phoebe Rose had been conceived by IVF. It hung there between us, like it might go away if Phoebe Rose could just latch on. She fed noisily. I was shocked to find milk jetting from the non-feeding breast. Wordlessly, Jamie grabbed a breast pad and placed it against my chest. Looking down, I hoped to feel a glimpse of what I was supposed to. Nothing.

'IVF,' said Jamie. 'That must have been tough.' Bless her. I was pathetically grateful. At 1,600 quid a night, I should have expected some TLC, but still.

'No,' I breathed. 'Actually, it was fine. A bit bumpy at the beginning, but really quite okay.' Reaching for the remnants of the Bollinger, I attempted to explain myself to poor Jamie. 'She's gorgeous. She's perfect. She's just … It's just … she's not what I expected.' I tried to find a positive. 'Better than my burn-in-the-sun skin, I guess. But what if something's gone wrong? What if she isn't mine?' My voice cracked. There. Jenna would be proud. I'd captured exactly what I was feeling. I was processing.

'God. That would be a nightmare!' Jamie exclaimed. In that moment I was so thankful for her honesty. Her validation. I began to laugh, and Bella joined in, reaching her hand out to mine.

***

Mr Andrews was odd. Why are mental health professionals so strange? A psychologist with letters after his name but few social skills. Arriving just after breakfast, he asked if he might eat the croissant that remained untouched on my tray. He'd not had a chance to eat this morning, he informed me mid-bite. Between mouthfuls he pulled no punches with some very direct questions. After about ten or fifteen minutes, he turned from me and bizarrely began to speak into a voice recorder; a summary of the conversation we'd just had. I was incredulous. Noticing pastry crumbs on his shirt, he dusted himself down while sharing the outcome of his assessment. In his opinion, I didn't appear suicidal or intent on harming myself or others – in particular Phoebe Rose. If I changed my mind and started hatching plans to do those things, he provided numbers I could call. I explained the source of my anxiety, and how even I could see how unstable I seemed, doubting if the child I had clearly given birth to was mine. He headed to the bassinet where she lay sleeping. Peering closely, he nodded, taking in her undoubtedly lovely and undoubtedly dark skin. He stated that my concerns *could* be considered reasonable; the baby was not of my colouring, nor the father's, based upon my report. Rather, he mused aloud my anxiety could be understood within the context of my dilemma. Unless, of course, I was not being truthful, in which case I *could* be delusional or holding a false belief.

'However,' he stated, 'I wouldn't read too much into the child's colouring. Genetics love to keep us on our toes. She could just be a strange genetic throwback.' Again, his bedside manner left me open-mouthed in disbelief. 'I'm sure the IVF clinic can respond to your concern if you feel that they need to.' He stated this in a matter-of-fact manner, looking curiously from me to Phoebe Rose, seemingly fascinated by the difference in skin tone. A new possibility joined the others tumbling in my washing machine brain. A small surge of hope. I would contact the clinic and go from there.

Mr Andrews left, satisfied that I would meet Phoebe Rose's needs and would ensure that my concerns were shared with my GP and community midwifery team. Despite his odd way with words, it was a relief to be taken seriously. Refusing to acknowledge the elephant in the room would have been unbearable. I clung to his volunteered possibility; that Phoebe Rose was mine and that way back in my gene pool – or Roger's – was an ancestral line that was raising its head. Wiping away my tears, I held on to this possibility. *Of course she's mine. But what if she isn't? How would I know? Should that even matter?* I sat on the side of the elevated bed, trying to steady my outstretched legs. I tried hard to see any resemblance to me, but there was nothing. The set of her eyes, the breadth of her nose. She could not be further removed from how I'd expected my daughter to look. Did this mean that the sperm I'd received was not the one I'd opted for? Was it even my egg that she had come from?

'Take your – or someone's – beautiful baby home, Tilda, and reset,' I told myself sternly. 'She deserves better than this.' How different it would be to have a partner to shoulder my worries. Not that I wanted Edwin there for a second, but if he were, he'd listen to my worries – as random as they were – then explore them in a logical, non-hysterical manner. He'd then offer me a glass of something to calm me while he headed off to cook dinner. Wobbled off actually, given that wine o'clock had arrived earlier and earlier the longer our relationship had gone on.

'Lord, things are bad. I'm romanticising Edwin's listening abilities!' I told Phoebe Rose. She sighed, and fleetingly I wondered if I had finally made a connection with my strange genetic throwback.

Frustratingly, I had missed Jenna's call. The voicemail she left informed me that she wouldn't be available until after clinic hours, as she was seeing clients all day. Placing my anxiety very deliberately on the back burner, I resolved to behave like any normal new mum. *Fake it till you make it, Tilda.* Phoebe Rose began to make whimpering sounds that would build to a crescendo sharpish, based on last night's feeding, if I didn't attend to her. Lifting her out of her crib, I forced myself to do what I should have done the first time I laid eyes on her. Placing her on my breast, I gently stroked her soft cheek, her beautiful eyelashes blinking away her hungry tears.

'And breathe, Tilda.' I remembered Richard's words at the conference and how patronising they'd sounded. I'd take anybody's words of comfort right now, patronising or otherwise.

***

We strode confidently through the lobby of our apartment building. The image in the mirrored doors gave me strength; a woman like any other, holding a brand-new baby in a car seat.

The apartment was gleaming. I was glad I'd booked the cleaner to give it a spruce for our homecoming. I arranged Ellie's flowers in a vase as Phoebe Rose slept peacefully. The late-September sunshine was weak but filled the room with a lovely glow. Leaving Phoebe Rose in her car seat, I crept to bed to squeeze twenty minutes of shuteye before she woke. Id almost forced my anxiety of the last twenty-four hours into a compartment. I wasn't ignoring the situation and would do whatever it took to address it in time. But right now, I needed to look after myself and this baby. For survival's sake, I would park it for the moment. In the meantime: *Of course, Phoebe Rose is my baby. I gave birth to her*, I chanted like a mantra. However, the vice-like anxiety in my stomach was less straightforward to compartmentalise. It continued to grip, leaving me as nauseous as I had been in the early weeks of pregnancy.

The first few days merged, night and day blurring into an endless loop of feeding and changing. Ellie came over and looked after Phoebe Rose for an afternoon of blissful uninterrupted sleep. Flowers and cards filled the apartment from the Nurture team and baby group members, although I didn't remember receiving them. I placed glorious blooms into vases with no recollection of who'd sent them. The visiting midwife responded to Mr Andrews' notes with the recommendation that the mental health team offer a further check-in.

'I'm fine. Truly.' I dismissed her concerns. 'I had a bit of a meltdown is all.' I was embarrassed and trying hard to shelve all thinking around the subject. I needed to survive, not think, and could not do both. However, I knew what she needed to hear. I'd been in detox and rehab enough to know how to reduce concern.

She persevered. 'I had my first baby on my own.' I did not need her pity. I busied myself with restocking the nappy pile. 'It's incredibly hard work,' she continued. 'Get all the help you can.

There's no shame in it.' It was frustrating that I couldn't quite get the nappies to stack neatly. 'Who've you got around you? Family? Friends?'

'I've got support, thanks. I'm snatching everyone's hand off. My mother is coming to stay in a few days. But thanks. I'm good. We're okay.'

The midwife looked only marginally convinced. Although she couldn't exactly challenge me, could she? Smiling stiffly, I reluctantly handed a sleeping Phoebe Rose over for her check-over. The fact that she'd nodded off not five minutes before the midwife got here was beyond unfortunate.

'I'll try and check her over without waking her,' she said apologetically. Thankfully, no doubt picking up on my teetering mood, she then said the checkup could wait until the next day. My eyes filled with tears at her act of understanding, as well as from relief that my peace could continue, if only for a little while longer. I turned to hide my tears and began to fold the load of laundry that was heaped beside us on the sofa. Breezily ushering her out of the door took all my energy. I slumped against it as it closed, head in hands, listening to the everyday sounds outside. The lift pinging, people chatting, busy with their lives and going about their business. *This is normal day three blues, Tilda. It will pass*, I told myself. *The griping of your stomach is not anxiety but your womb contracting. All will be well.* Phoebe Rose began to stir, and I wondered how long I would have from gurgling to full pelt screaming. Not enough was the answer.

***

'It's a gorgeous day for a walk, Tilda. What do you reckon? Buggy stroll down the Thames? Or is that too ambitious?' Ellie had suggested a walk the last few days on the bounce.

'I've got my two-week checkup tomorrow. We could go after that?' I was hedging her again. What was with her insistence that we leave the apartment? I'd just given birth, for God's sake. Had she forgotten how that feels?

'Just thought it might do you good. Lift your mood.' Placing coffee before me, she halved the giant cream cake that she'd brought between us.

'What does that mean?' My tone was sharper than I'd intended. I'd felt so bombarded the last few days.

Ellie looked taken aback. 'I just remember it becoming quite a big deal for me to go out after I'd had Rosa. My mum kept taking her out in the pram to give me a rest, but when I finally did get out there, I felt loads better. I think I'd developed a bit of cabin fever,' she ventured gently.

'I'm sorry,' I snapped. 'I'm just tired and don't think I have the energy to push the pram. Not and smile at the same time.' I grinned weakly by way of apology.

'Nobody said you had to smile. Anyway, scowling is underrated, don't you think?' She laughed.

We hadn't discussed my post-birth hysteria since I'd come home. I think Ellie had optimistically put it down to hormones, and after the initial minimising response from her – no doubt her attempt at reassurance – I'd no appetite to raise it again. I didn't know what to think other than the certainty that something wasn't right. But I wasn't ready to open the compartment and explore exactly what that might be. I knew Ellie felt it too. And it remained unspoken.

'I do need to go out, though, if you could have Phoebe Rose for a couple of hours next week. I've an appointment. With Jenna.'

'Jenna?' Ellie looked surprised.

I exhaled loudly. 'Probably a terrible idea given the abrupt end to our last session, but I don't know who else to call. At least she knows me. Maybe she can help straighten out my thinking. Because I'm going in circles here on my own.'

Ellie nodded, the unspoken issue of Phoebe Rose's colouring and my ambivalence towards her the oversized elephant in the room.

'Of course,' Ellie stated, looking relieved. Leaving the house and acknowledging a problem was progress, surely?

Lana

The Stevie Loves game was a hoot – for at least the first twenty minutes. It wasn't complicated. We'd wander, randomly naming items prefixed by 'Stevie loves …' It's easy, as Stevie loves everything in life, giggling like it's the funniest game she's ever played. Every time.

Stevie still loving the Christmas tree (despite its presence since mid-November) was our current focus; 'Stevie loving' the baubles and all things tree related. Exhausting that, we made our way to the hearth, where the Halloween invitation from Mum's firework party still perched. With a slight deviation from the game, I proffered, 'Stevie *loved* …' (never too early for tenses). Stevie looked expectant, holding her breath. 'Fireworks!' I whispered. 'Boom!' Again, she dissolved into hysterics.

It was after 4 p.m. and already dark outside. After lighting our new cinnamon candles, I drew the curtains. Wan would be home about 10.30 p.m., not a late one. I thought of my looming return-to-work date and constant plan-hatching to avoid having to go back. Handing Stevie to either of our mothers did not fill me with joy. But then I was no more comfortable with the idea of nursery. Childminders were out – far too many horror stories. I thought again of the figures I'd come up with when I'd looked into tagging onto the festival thing, doing workshops with kids. Pin money, not enough to pay a mortgage. It was depressing. I glanced at my phone. Maybe there'd been a Rightmove miracle and the house of our dreams had just halved in price. I checked my emails: nothing but the latest properties and their ever-climbing prices. I'd missed a run of calls. Telesales callers had been relentless since I'd not been working. I had no clue how they'd got my number or how they realised I might be available. The call log showed the same number. Someone had been persistent. Three calls yesterday and two today. Telesales people don't usually leave messages, yet the icon flashed.

'Mrs Edwards, Mr Edwards. Just a call checking in and following up. Please give me a call when you get the message. Would be good to touch base.' It wasn't a voice I recognised. Stevie had nodded off – not ideal at this time of day, but it allowed me breathing space before sorting dinner. I googled the number. It was the Manchester Clinic. But not on the number they'd previously used, which was still stored in my phone. Were they after another sale? I laughed out loud; unless this one was a freebie, they'd be out of luck. We could afford neither the conception nor the upkeep of another baby. And I was emotionally full. I had no desire to dilute the love and energy that went Stevie's way. Wan and I hadn't discussed it, but we didn't need to. It was a non-starter financially. I pressed delete but then heard the same voice leave a further message, slightly more formal.

'Mr Edwards, Mrs Edwards. Please call the office when you receive this message. We've tried several times and haven't been able to reach you.' The message ended. I'd no intention of calling back to hear their hard sell. If I was being honest, a tiny part of me knew instantly what the clinic wanted. It was unthinkable and a fear that I couldn't give words to. *The clinic wants their baby back.* It was irrational, I knew, but the 'too good to be true' bubble had always felt so precarious. *She's not yours. You need to give her back.* The fear that stalked me had found a voice. I would not be returning any calls. If Wan asked, I would stick to the marketing theory. The harvesting of more eggs would not be something I would be pursuing. Putting Stevie's playlist on low, I grabbed a candle and ran a bath. How dare someone try to rob me of my domestic bliss?

Wan arrived home to a wife pretending to be chilled, trying to quell the anxiety triggered by the clinic's messages. Stevie and I attempted to binge watch a box set, but my preoccupation was real. Stevie enjoyed the cheesy soundtrack and was content to gnaw on the edge of the remote between tracks. She went down for the night easily about 8 p.m., and I attempted to doze on the sofa. Wan looked uncomfortable from the moment he appeared at the top of the stairs, a tension around his eyes that's rare for him.

'You okay?' I propped myself against the cushions, taking in his agitated expression. My stomach contracted. Had the clinic already spoken to him? 'Is that guy messing you about over your gig payment?' Please let it be something solvable like money. Wan could be a pushover when it came to chasing payments. He'd leave it for weeks, then feel too awkward to ask. He looked momentarily confused.

'Yes. No. That got sorted. Got the cash last week.' His voice was tight. 'Bit of a weird one today,' he began. 'I had a load of missed calls from the Manchester Clinic.'

My world teetered. 'Me too. I think they're trying to sign us up for baby number two. Were they pushy? They're sharks. Probably want another 15k for another baby. Hope you gave them short shrift.'

Wan took a breath and perched on the end of the sofa.

'I called them back because they said it was important.' My mouth fell open, a dizzy feeling engulfing me. 'They've asked if we will meet with them next week. The woman said she was from the legal team.' A terrible sense of foreboding crept over me. I knew as Wan spoke that I didn't want to hear another word.

'Is there something we should have done with Stevie's IVF? Registration or feedback or something? It's probably ...' I blinked back tears, unable to voice the insane notion that the clinic might want Stevie back. Wan would say I was being ridiculous, deranged.

Wan shrugged. 'They sent a card and those flowers but never mentioned anything. Have they sent us paperwork that we haven't returned?'

'Of course not. If this is their idea of a jugular sales campaign, I'll have something to say.' I knew this was nothing to do with sales.

'They said they needed to see us both. Together. Wouldn't say what it was about, but that it was important that we see them early next week.'

'I guess they're not open over the weekend ...?'

Wan interrupted. 'They gave me a number. Said we could use it anytime.'

'Do you think there's a health problem? Do you remember that medical screen? Maybe they've missed something. It must be urgent if they've given you a number for weekend use.' A further wave of anxiety gripped my stomach.

'Lana, that is catastrophising at its finest! It could be anything at all. I don't know what it is, but we will call first thing and find out.' Wan's tone was stern, trying to head me off.

'Maybe they've heard how amazing Stevie is and want to clone her free of charge?' I said weakly, allowing myself to be pulled into Wan's hug, trying his best as always to make things okay.

'Will she wake if I go and peek? I've missed her today. How long's she been down?'

'She *should* be well away.'

Wan gently nudged the door and we gazed at her snuggled in her favourite koala suit, listening together to her delicate breathing, as besotted at four months as the first time we'd met her. Wan hummed her signature song quietly. The words were so apt; she really was *so* lovely. Still queasy with anxiety, I decided I'd sleep on her floor until we knew everything was okay. What if there was a problem, she needed me, but the monitor didn't pick it up? I could see Wan peering in the darkness, checking her colour, gently assessing her temperature through the poppers on her suit. Our whole fragile world right there in the crib.

***

'Mrs Edwards, thank you for calling. We've been trying to reach you. It's Holly Barnett from the Manchester Clinic. How are you doing? How's little Stevie?'

I cut her short. 'You spoke to my husband yesterday. Is there a problem? Is there a health issue? Joel wondered if it was something paperwork related?' My words tumbled out, desperate for reassurance. I could hear my anxiety amplified through the phone speaker. Wan paced by the window.

A pause.

'We've contacted a small group of parents who received treatment around the same time as yourselves at the clinic. We've been made aware of some irregularities in care and are trying to identify any patients who may have been impacted.'

Stevie bounced gently in her bouncer, the chair jangling noisily. I took the call into the kitchen.

'It's not health related, then?'

'It's completely unrelated to any physical health concerns. However, it is important that we speak personally and explore possible deviations from protocol which could have repercussions for other families.' Her tone was sugary. And hollow.

'So this isn't a hard sell for another baby? Because we can't afford it. There's no possibility of that changing any time soon.'

'Mrs Edwards, this is absolutely nothing to do with sales nor consultation for future possible pregnancies.'

'Sorry, can you be clearer? Has one of your practitioners been inappropriate? Are you asking me if I was happy with our care? We only ever had very respectful—'

Holly cut me short. 'I can explain fully the situation on Monday if you're able to pop into the office. The appointment will be with myself, a representative from the legal department and Mr Brown, the consultant who has overseen your care. How does 4 p.m. sound?'

Wan was nodding in agreement. Nothing in our diaries that we wouldn't be moving.

'We'll see you then. Thank you.' I ended the call curtly.

'Irregularities in patient care?' Wan ran an anxious hand through his cropped hair. 'Has there been an allegation? Something sexual? Do you remember that male health worker who'd been fitting contraceptive coils without using gloves?' I did. 'Was anyone ever weird with you? Made you feel uncomfortable?'

'Nothing whatsoever. Always a chaperone in the room when an examination was occurring. They were all lovely. And completely professional.'

'Well, it must be an admin process or paperwork issue, I don't know, but on that note, I declare this weekend officially "open". With a packed agenda of Peppa Pig and the Stevie Loves game. What do you reckon, Koala Wala?' Wan sprung Stevie's bouncer, her giggles filling the room.

Wan caught my reflection in the hearth mirror. I looked terrified.

'We're refusing to let you catastrophise, Lana. You're setting a very bad example for our daughter.' Wan unhooked Stevie from her bouncer and chased me around the room pretend scolding me with Stevie's index finger, the mirror now reflecting our little family cavorting around the front room.

Had this all been my fault somehow? Wan could insist all he liked that I shouldn't catastrophise, but that was easy for him. Had I just been too happy? Since Stevie had been born, I'd felt the opposite of post-natal depression – love bordering on mania. The uncertainty of pregnancy, the terrible feelings of pain and loss that we'd endured had melted away. The waiting, the money, all of it worth it. Had I known on some level that it was too good to be true? That *happily ever after* did not work out for people like me?

The racing commentary started early, filling the room with its bizarre backdrop. I'd remember that moment in the days and weeks to come as our last moment of normality, when our lives had become anything but normal.

***

'Smile!' Wan beamed, snapping away on his phone, his grin as wide as Stevie's. Stevie was dressed in her sequinned elf outfit, sparkling in the winter sunshine. The Manchester vista from the top of the Eye wasn't wasted on us. Stevie batted her arms excitedly. Wan tried not to look queasy.

'She's got your head for heights, not mine,' he muttered, gripping the overhead rail, eyes cast downward.

The Eye was packed. Sandwiched in tightly, we were unfortunate to have in the carriage an inconsolable baby, his fraught parents trying everything to placate him, willing the ride to be over.

'OPB,' uttered Wan quietly as the screeching reached new heights. Our code name for when 'other people's babies' were behaving badly, smug baby parents that we were. Squeezing nearer to the couple, I wondered if the baby would be interested in Stevie, for the sake of everyone's eardrums. The baby quit almost immediately, and a curious exchange occurred between the two of them.

'Is she always this easy?' the mum asked, transfixed by the interchange between the babies.

'We're lucky, actually; she is pretty easy.'

The father of the boy was too harassed to make eye contact but at the same time radiated gratitude for the hiatus.

'Our first was a doddle. Don't know what went wrong here.' The woman looked exhausted. 'Is she your first? You're lucky.' She reached out and ruffled Stevie's fair, becoming-blonder-by-the-day hair. Anxiety throbbed from my stomach as I smoothed her poker-straight locks back down.

'No, she's our second,' I added quickly, much more skilful than Wan at responding to the well-worn baby question. 'They've both been great.'

'Well, you're doing something right,' piped a voice from the back of the carriage. A fellow smug baby parent no doubt taking credit for the sunny disposition of her child. I leapt to the poor couple's defence.

'Don't think it's anything we've done or not done. Luck of the draw, I think.' I pulled a face in the direction of the smug mum's voice, and we laughed, as did both babies. Wan squeezed his arms around me and I felt overwhelmed with love.

We enjoyed a whistle-stop tour of Selfridges to see Santa, standard pic of traumatised-looking child, Santa's beard askew as Stevie's efforts to grab it were realised. Glühwein and a hot dog on the Christmas markets and a short trip to Piccadilly Records, the highlight of the trip for Stevie and Wan. Wan doing the cool dad thing with Stevie in her sling, all gummy grins to the music.

Entering the clinic felt strange. None of the travelling-hopefully optimism that we'd experienced all that time ago. Stevie was dozing fitfully in her pram. The glamorous Holly introduced herself, extending a perfectly manicured hand and escorting us to a consultation room. Holly peered into the pram but didn't look disappointed that Stevie was asleep. She tapped away at her keyboard until we were joined by Mr Brown. Shaking our hands a little too firmly, he looked uncomfortable, his hair greyer at the temples than I'd remembered.

'Thank you for coming in at short notice. Apologies – we've been trying to reach you and do need to move this matter forward.' Holly sat back while Mr Brown talked. He'd seemed so composed and sure of himself at previous contacts, exuding capability. Today this wasn't the case.

'Things have moved on apace since we tried to contact you initially, and the remaining patients have already been interviewed following our concerns. We set out to talk to a small group of parents who received treatment within the same time frame as yourselves. As Holly discussed with you on the phone ...' He faltered briefly. 'There is no easy way to say this. A patient of ours, Ms X for the purposes of the conversation, has received confirmation that the child she birthed two and a half months ago is not in fact her biological child.'

There it was. My unthinkable shared aloud. I reached for Wan's hand.

'Further investigations have confirmed that this child is not biologically related to either Ms X or her sperm donor.'

'We thought that this was about an allegation of misconduct. Holly referred to a deviation from protocol.' I listened in freefall, knowing *exactly* where this was heading.

'The other identified cohort couples have consented to blood tests and DNA-matching exploration. All of whom were found to be the biological parents of the child that they birthed.'

A bewildered expression ran across Wan's face. Stevie sighed heavily in her sleep and for a moment we all looked her way. A throbbing noise filled my ears, a blood rush like I'd never experienced.

'So, are you saying that we need to do blood tests to prove that Stevie's ours?' Wan clarified.

'I don't think so, Wan.' I was on my feet. 'Stevie is our baby. Not somebody else's – ours.' My tears brimmed. All Wan ever wanted to do was toe the party line, follow procedure. Was he agreeing to a blood test?

'Mrs Edwards.' Holly reached her taloned hand my way. 'We don't have any evidence to suggest that Stevie is anyone's but yours, but it is our duty to fully explore this and conclude our investigation. Not least to establish the whereabouts of Ms X's baby, but also to consider which aspect of the procedure may have led to this unfortunate situation.'

'So we're the last parents you've contacted? The others have come back with the results you expected?'

'That is the case; however, this is merely procedure, with every possibility that yours and Joel's results will confirm that Stevie is your biological child, just like the other families.'

Rage ran through me. 'How dare you call me and my husband into these offices and state that you are "merely" conducting a procedure of such ... magnitude? How dare you minimise the pain that you have caused these families? And with respect, my only concern is my family. I'm sorry that this has "happened" to Ms X—'

Holly interrupted and tried to backtrack on her colleague's choice of words.

I was on my feet.

'Wan, we've heard enough. We don't need any more details.'

'I need to ask,' Wan said. 'Why did this mother think the baby wasn't biologically hers?'

Mr Brown coughed. 'Ms X is Caucasian, as is her sperm donor.'
A wave of nausea spread through me.

He continued. 'The baby that Ms X birthed has at least *one* parent of non-Caucasian origin.' Stevie chose that moment to open an eye, looking suspiciously around her.

'We can run tests quickly; this won't be a drawn-out process. But please can I ask. Is there *any* possibility that you might feel similarly – anything that might make you query Stevie's biological status?' Mr Brown asked, looking awkwardly in our direction. The million-dollar question right there. Holly couldn't meet my eyes. I felt exposed. Like they both knew already.

'None.' I was straight in. 'Stevie takes after her dad and his side. They're all pale. Scottish ancestry, haven't you, Wan?' My tone was shrill. 'I too was fairly pale at birth – less dark than my siblings but with the same white father and African Caribbean mother ...'

Holly and Mr Brown nodded in unison at the lady protesting too much.

'So there won't be any need for a blood test. That's not something that we'd like to be involved in.' I nudged past Wan, eyeballing him to do the same. Briskly turning Stevie's pushchair, I exited the room and strode down the corridor. I jabbed at the shiny lift button impatiently, my sweaty fingertip leaving a smudge. The lift arrived and still Wan didn't appear. I wasn't waiting. Storming from the building, I brushed past a couple in the revolving doors, spinning them comedy style around the turnstile. I practically ran across the main road, a lorry driver angrily blasting his horn. Stevie was wide awake now and fussing. In need of a feed. Spying a bench, I plucked her from the pushchair with trembling hands and latched her on underneath my poncho, the jingling bells on her outfit making her chuckle, her grin too wide to feed. Wan eventually joined me, looking like a ghost, his pale skin leached of colour. He clutched a business card 'from Holly'.

'You can say what you like, Wan. I'm *not* giving consent for any blood tests. She's going nowhere. Don't tell me you're prepared to go along with this? You know what DNA tests are like. Unreliable at best. Ms X will have just somehow been given the wrong donor. That's where the mix-up will have happened. It's nothing to do with us,' I cried, wiping away the tears now falling onto Stevie's hat.

'Nobody's going to make us do anything, Lana.' Wan attempted to hug us, but I sat stiffly at arm's length. Mr Brown, with Holly as passenger, purred past in his immaculate Jaguar.

The bright Christmas lights we'd passed earlier now seemed dull. Energy drained from us with each passing moment. Stevie was excited by the Tannoy announcing the tram stops. I went through the motions of joining in. Ordinarily, we'd have had a game of Stevie Loves – all things tram related. We made our way silently through the litter whirlwind circling the precinct towards home. Wordlessly unlocking the temperamental flat door, we began the tedious negotiation of getting Stevie's pram up the narrow stairs. Wan clicked the kettle on, which immediately tripped the electric.

'I don't want a drink, Wan. I don't need anything,' I said angrily. 'Do you think they can make us have the test?' I tried unzipping Stevie from her snow suit, but my trembling fingers couldn't work the zip.

'I don't know,' Wan said softly, leaning in and freeing Stevie from her snow suit. She babbled back at him, keen to join in the conversation. Wan crouched alongside her, grinning manically.

'I love it when she talks back!' His voice filled with emotion. I went to reset the fuse box to hide my tears.

Tilda

'I can't fucking believe her,' I raged to Ellie. 'She's supposed to be non-judgemental! Seriously, I pay her a fortune. I could have her struck off. The look on her face was unbelievable. She actually had an *I told you so* expression; the lifted eyebrow, slight lip curl, the whole lot.' I attempted a version of Jenna's unprofessional expression.

Pacing furiously up and down Ellie's kitchen, I gave her the session highlights. Phoebe Rose watched suspiciously from her car seat. She'd slept the whole time, apparently, waking as I knocked the door. Here she was, looking every bit the world's most serene baby, when at home she wakes and bawls within seconds.

'I'm confused. Why would she judge you?' Ellie asked tentatively.

'Oh, she never thought I was mother material. She as much as said that before I even conceived,' I snapped angrily. 'She thought my decision to have a baby was a bereavement response.'

'That's not fair,' Ellie cooed and hugged me tightly, halting my angry pacing. 'Did you tell her what you thought of that?' She stroked my hair, which immediately triggered the tears that had been brimming since I arrived.

'In that moment, in her high-rise office – resisting the urge to leap out of the open window – I think I agreed with her.'

'It's her job to listen and understand. She's no right making you feel that way.' Ellie paused awkwardly. 'Did you tell Jenna what happened after Phoebe Rose was born? That you struggled with her …'

'What am I struggling with, Ellie? I'm all ears.'

'Colouring. Complexion. Your doubts in those first hours,' she managed. I didn't think for a second that Ellie thought my doubts had done anything but increase, but we'd both found it too difficult to broach the subject. Maybe we were protecting one another, or Phoebe Rose, or some combination. I don't know. But I was certain that every time someone looked at my baby, the first thing they queried was whose she was. Let's be honest, she didn't look like she had mixed heritage. She looked black. Like she wasn't mine.

'Of course. That was all I wanted to talk about. I showed her photos of Phoebe Rose, but you couldn't really tell from the picture how dark her skin is compared to mine. She kept talking about attachment. And *my* "complex attachment" with my mother!' My voice was rising steadily in volume, incredulous. 'She suggested increasing my antidepressants. How will that help?'

I could see Ellie deliberate. She so didn't want to say the wrong thing. Phoebe Rose began to fuss, clearly triggered by my presence. Ellie unclipped her from the seat and she hushed immediately.

'How's she sleeping?' Ellie stepped away, sensing that anything she said could trigger me. 'Still okay?'

'Terrible,' I replied flatly, staring out of the window at the school run chaos. There were pink-cheeked children being scolded for running ahead. Another mum scrolling through her phone with a glazed expression, oblivious to the chattering child beside her. *Why did I think it would all be rosy? How could I have been so short-sighted?*

***

The first six weeks were tough. I didn't think things could get much tougher. But they did. My GP, alerted by Jenna, had asked to see me. Referral details, I learned, consisted of concern around 'postnatal mood and *irrational beliefs* regarding the biology of her child'. How dare she? I went to her to explore my concerns, not be held hostage to them. Knowing the system, I graciously accepted the Fluoxetine increase offered. It would no doubt lift my mood, which was clearly impacted by sleep deprivation, postpartum hormones and my sketchy support network. It wouldn't, however, alter my belief that Phoebe Rose wasn't mine. The GP session wasn't completely unhelpful, giving me space to further voice what I already knew. I'd not dared give it headspace after leaving hospital other than confiding in Jenna. I'd hoped to reach a point where I didn't feel quite so vulnerable before I went there. I'd hoped to fall so in love with Phoebe Rose that I wouldn't care whose baby she was – even if she wasn't my biological child – what would it matter as long as I loved her? I'd held her inside me for 9 months, surely that made her mine in some way? Only I didn't fall in love with her. It was like caring for a child through glass. I could see a woman tending to and feeding a baby. She would dress her, ensure she wasn't too cold or too warm. She would sometimes kiss her belly, because babies need affection. But it was perfunctory. And it was exhausting.

Breastfeeding Phoebe Rose was for selfish reasons. I was determined to return to my pre-baby weight, and the thought of prepping bottles was overwhelming. It was purely mechanical. I felt no emotion other than a flinch of disgust as I offered my breast to her hungry mouth. However, at around six weeks, Phoebe Rose went from an infant who would sleep at night for five hours at a stretch to waking hourly. It was hell. Ellie suggested keeping her awake more during the day. We could go to Rosa's toddler group together; I could meet other mums. But I hadn't the energy. We'd arrange it and I wouldn't show. I'd cancel, pretending one of us was ill or making up some other flimsy excuse.

I didn't begin to drink because of any craving, I must be clear on this. Truly. I was too exhausted to enjoy a drink. And the thought of a hangover, well. I felt like I'd explored every possible solution to Phoebe Rose's unrelenting night-time waking. Many mothers will say it's cruel to let your baby cry, but I had no problem doing that. Occasionally she'd cry herself back to sleep, but more often than not the crying did not stop. The only thing that stopped it was picking her up. She didn't even want food; she wasn't hungry. She was testing me, seeing how far she could push me. And she was winning. At around seven weeks in the zombie-like small hours, I found a mum's blog. Sensible advice from normal mothers, not the obsessed NCT 'never leave them to cry' advice either.

> *My first two babies were in a sleep routine within three weeks of birth. Seven hours a night. The only way I could get my third (and last!) baby to sleep was via a nightcap. Sometimes two. Time it so that your drink is still in her system from your breast milk by night-time and you're away. Just don't quote me on it! (Anonymous)*

I quivered with excitement as I read and reread the anonymous and spectacularly wise words. Most women don't have the balls to say it like it is. Thank God for those who do. As there was no alcohol in the house, after our afternoon stroll, we returned via the lovely wine shop. The bell rang invitingly as we entered, and I felt a wistful pang of nostalgia as I stepped through the doorway. Edwin and I had been daily customers at various points. Jeremy was on the till.

'Well, we've missed you, darling!' He beamed and came over for a peek at Phoebe Rose. 'Beautiful!' he declared. Was that a hint of puzzlement in his voice? He quickly busied himself unboxing the Christmas stock while I steered the buggy around the cramped aisles. Christmas music played and my mood begin to lift, surrounded by the familiar bottles and displays. So, a nightcap. Did that mean it needed to be a short, like a whisky or a Baileys? Or would a glass of Chablis be as effective? Or maybe a festive snowball? My attention was drawn to the fake snow sprinkled around the bright red-and-yellow giant bottle of advocaat. I trembled with anticipation as Jeremy wrapped the bottle in tissue paper, adding a flourish of red ribbon around the top. Hurrying home, I caught myself humming the carol that had been playing in the shop. I wondered if that was down to

A. the antidepressants beginning to work (three weeks in, so possible),

B. the large and inviting bottle of advocaat underneath the buggy, or

C. the possibility of a night where I might sleep longer than an hour at a stretch.

A feeling of calm descended as I entered the apartment. The evening would consist of the usual bath at 7 p.m. and down for 8 p.m. A couple of early evening drinks should be sufficient for a chilled evening but without overdoing it and still being able to look after Phoebe Rose. It should leave time to get into her system for a healthy sleep stretch, hopefully past the small hours. I'd taken care to blend the thick eggnog with lemonade, adding a dash of lime and a neglected glacé cherry prised from a long-forgotten jar from the fridge. I was giddy with excitement. Even Phoebe Rose enjoyed her bath time, her long legs swaying in the water. Her expression was still serious, but she wasn't protesting or crying. I could feel the alcohol course through my system. I imagined it spurting from me, my breasts gushing with snowball-flavoured milk. I'd missed this lovely tipsy feeling. I polished off my allotted glasses in the twenty minutes that it took from running the bath to closing the poppers on Phoebe Rose's babygro. Taking care to feed her from both sides, I made sure she took the richer hind milk from each breast. It wouldn't be until the later feed – hopefully around eleven – that any sleep-inducing alcohol would reach her. If she could then sleep until four or five, we would both wake in better humour in the morning.

Stretching out on the sofa, I basked in the advocaat glow. The last drink I'd had had been the champagne at Phoebe Rose's birth. The anxiety associated with it felt far removed from my current relaxed state. How sad that that would be my champagne association. I'd have to address that sometime soon.

It was 8.30 before I put Phoebe Rose down for the night. We'd quite enjoyed a slightly later bedtime. She'd lain contentedly on her playmat as I scrolled through my phone, rather than the now-routine clock watching and bedtime countdown. I made it halfway through the first series of a drama that Ellie had recommended before I flaked out myself, but not before I'd treated myself to a further medicinal measure. I missed everything about drinking. From holding the glass to swirling the liquid, from the first sip and feeling of relaxation to being a bit buzzed and sleepy.

Waking around 11 p.m., Phoebe Rose fed as well as ever. Using textbook strategies, including 'night-time is not playtime', it was easy to settle her back off. With prompting, she fed fully from my hopefully sleep-inducing milk. She looked pretty, her long eyelashes blinking away, beseeching me to talk to her as she fed.

Awkwardly, I patted her coiled hair. I could do this. It would all be okay. Settling her gently into her crib, I climbed back into bed but found myself frustratingly alert after Phoebe Rose had settled so quickly. Half an hour passed and I still I lay there. Maybe *I* was hungry. Did I have dinner? Heading for the fridge, I found leftover pizza. Hungry work, this breastfeeding business. I found myself pouring a sizeable measure straight from the bottle into my stale glass. The bottle was unfathomably almost empty. Might as well finish it off. A pang of nausea suddenly washed over me. *What is the alcohol content of advocaat? Is it whisky? How strong is it?* A sharp pain darted from one side of my forehead to the other. Probably exhaustion. I returned unsteadily to bed. God help me if the five o'clock feed didn't get pushed back. 'Anonymous but wise mum' had better be right on the money.

***

Thump. Thump. Thump. A dull thudding travelled from the adjoining wall. There it was again. *Bloody Vic. What's he playing at? The man's unhinged.* Making my way to the crib, I plucked up a distressed Phoebe Rose and quickly tried to latch her on. Her cries were ear-splitting, like she was being tortured. With trembling hands, I placed her on the bed and checked her over – was she in pain? She was beside herself, her body heaving with distress, incapable, despite my efforts, of even attempting to feed. The thuds came again, three of them in quick succession. *Fuck off, Vic. She's a baby; they cry.* Pacing the floor, I tapped Phoebe Rose's back rhythmically, shushing with each step. Gradually her sobs began to subside, giving way to hiccups, racking her tiny body at random intervals. Finally, she settled and fed hungrily, her face wet with tears. Her small hands flexed; panicked fingers spread wide. I glanced at my phone. How could that be? 9.02 a.m. No wonder she was hungry. She'd last fed at 11 p.m. My head throbbed. My threshold for alcohol was clearly at an all-time adult low, my oesophagus burning. How much advocaat had I drunk? I wandered, Phoebe Rose clutching me tightly, into the kitchen. My stomach lurched at the empty bottle on the counter. I was going to need a strategy rethink. My mouth was dry and stale, pressure pulsing behind my eyes. And I deserved every dehydrated throb.

By lunchtime I was *beginning* to feel more human. Having had more sleep in one stretch last night than the previous week combined, I was determined to have a more positive outlook despite feeling rough.

'Shall we go for a wander, Babba?' After an age of faffing, I managed to get Phoebe Rose into her new baby sling. My fuzzy head was not a good combination with the appalling instructions. Phoebe Rose seemed to like it – at least she didn't protest, and I put a bag together for our outing. I was still musing about how I would tackle the bizarre behaviour of my neighbour, but I wouldn't need to wait long to find out. Heading out of the apartment, I gave Phoebe Rose's harness a final check. Vic opened his door at that moment. He'd obviously heard my door close behind me.

Vic stood squarely in his doorway, arms folded across his chest.

'This is not okay,' he spat angrily as I rounded the corner.

'You are spot on there, Vic. What the fuck was that about at nine this morning? If you think sounding a wakeup call for a newborn and her mother – clearly already struggling with sleep – is your department, then I'm not sure it's going to work out your living next door. I'll be speaking to Stan today, making a formal complaint.'

'How dare you,' he growled. 'For the last three weeks, all that I – and your wider neighbours – hear at night is your daughter. Crying for hours on end …'

'She's a newborn – they do that, you know. As you're aware, I have no partner to share the care.'

'*This* isn't about a crying baby, Tilda. I get that you can't pick her up every time she cries. Nobody would expect that. But last night was child abuse!' he shouted. 'She cried nonstop from 6.30 until 9 this morning when I finally managed to rouse you. I know because as you step out of bed, the floorboard creaks. That's how.'

'God, I have a stalker for a neighbour. Listening and spying on my every move!' I screamed.

Phoebe Rose joined in the chorus of screeching, no build-up. I gestured towards her.

'So, who's the one abusing children? Sort yourself out, Vic. If you wake me or my child again, I will involve the police. This is harassment.' Shaking with rage, I turned on my heel and strode towards the staircase. Taking two stairs at a time, both Phoebe Rose and I were still tearful as we left reception and turned onto the main road. A new emotion joined the anxiety and fear marinade: guilt. Great waves of it. I'd crossed a line last night. If it happened again, I had no doubt that Vic would involve social care. If he hadn't already called. Gripped by a terrible stomach pain, I found myself doubled over, retching bile (or was it advocaat?) into the gutter, my hands attempting to shield Phoebe Rose from the violent stream .

Phone in hand, we headed for the Heath. The urge to call Edwin was strong, simply out of desperation. I didn't want him back, but would he support me, platonically? Because I was drowning.

With shaking hands, I dialled the mystery number. No response. An automated voicemail, no name given. Was it even him? Thankfully, Phoebe Rose had nodded off, content with the rhythm of my angry stride. I was a disgrace. A monster. I'd been desperate to shower my baby with love and yet look at me. Physical symptoms of panic began to wash over me, my breathing fast and shallow. Heading for the café, I spied a free table. Dialling Ellie's number, I felt the strongest sense of shame. What on earth could I say that she might begin to understand?

Ellie's kind voice rendered me practically unable to speak. Through my tears I explained my whereabouts. She would be there as soon as she could. Ignoring the stares of those around me, I pretended to scroll through my phone.

'She deserves better, Tilda. Stop being a fuck-up,' I told myself over and over. Not the most reassuring mantra, but somehow the panic began to subside.

'I can't do this, Ellie,' I cried unashamedly, tears moving steadily down both cheeks. Wordlessly, she guided us from the café and towards her car. I buckled Phoebe Rose in next to Rosa and we drove in silence. Had Ellie seen the crash coming?

Back at Ellie's, she propelled me to her spare bedroom.

'Get some sleep and we'll talk later.' She drew the curtains and headed back downstairs to the girls. Ellie brought Phoebe Rose in for a feed at some point, but I had no clue how long I slept for. I woke with rock-like breasts, the sheets sodden with breast milk. Pushing powerful feelings of shame aside, I joined Ellie and the girls in the front room like a regular person. Rosa was busy bringing blocks over to an oblivious Phoebe Rose, and Ellie was cooking dinner. Chopin played gently, and the smell of roast chicken and thyme was incredible. I was unworthy of such care.

My words came tumbling out over Ellie's lovely roast dinner. I'd been so anxious about letting Ellie know what had been happening, but once I started talking, I couldn't stop. I could hear how freakish my behaviour sounded, how abnormal. Labelling my inability to feel the *slightest* affection towards Phoebe Rose felt like the most honest thing I'd done since her birth. Phoebe Rose stirred in Ellie's lap but quickly settled back off, snuggling into her chest for comfort. I confessed about the advocaat and Vic's accusations – actually labelling my neglect of Phoebe Rose. My shame was overwhelming, but Ellie needed to hear, and I needed to share just how low I had sunk. I craved understanding.

'She's not mine, Ellie. I don't know whose she is, but I can't pretend, and I haven't grown to love her – so where does that leave me? If Phoebe Rose is someone else's child, where's mine?' Ellie's face was a mask. As the proverbial earth mother, she must think me a monster.

The food before me remained untouched. I was hungry but nauseous at the same time. 'I mean, she could be mine, but I don't see anything in her features that resemble mine. I've scrutinised old baby pictures that I rescued from my mum's. I need to know. And if she is mine, I need to get my head around that.'

Ellie's face softened a touch. She pushed her chair back from the table and held Phoebe Rose to her chest.

'I'm glad you've told me. I was worried sick anyway. I didn't know it was this bad, though.' Despite her expression, I searched her face for signs of disbelief or horror.

'It sounds like you have two scenarios. Well, kind of three. Phoebe Rose might be yours and Aussie Roger's child, with a throwback gene which explains her colour.'

'Which is fine. My best-case scenario. But I don't think so. She's got to be someone else's. And I know it might sound weak but there's also a part of me that's trying to protect us both. If we bond and it turns out she isn't mine, how dreadful would that be? I'm raising someone else's baby, then I have to give her back?'

Ellie continued. 'Or she is your biological child – your egg, but it isn't Aussie Roger's sperm, some randomer's, which is also fine, because she's still your baby. Right?'

'Absolutely. I'll take either of those. It's the third possibility that's causing me the biggest problem. If Phoebe Rose isn't mine, where is my child? What became of my fertilised egg?' That isn't strictly true, but it makes me sound marginally less monstrous.

'Which leaves you with only one option. Contact the clinic and do all you can to get to the bottom of this. For Phoebe Rose's sake,' Ellie couldn't help but add. If the boot was on the other foot, I knew she would not be behaving like this. Ellie would have loved the baby she delivered either way.

I nodded solemnly, relieved to have captured the dilemma. It sounded simple stated aloud. Yet I'd been drowning underneath it all these weeks, falling apart.

'Can I listen in when you make the call?' She half grinned.

'Let me stay tonight. I can't face going back to the apartment. And I'll let you listen in when I drop the bomb over the phone to the esteemed Manchester Clinic tomorrow!'

'Deal!' She laughed, for real this time, squeezing me and Phoebe Rose tight in her bear hug. For the first time in weeks, I felt a glimmer akin to hope.

Lana

Jodie appeared on Tuesday teatime. She never 'pops in' after work, and I suspected Wan had given her a heads-up. She hugged me awkwardly; all very non-Jodie-like behaviour.

'So, what's occurring? I sense all is not well in the Edwards household!' Jodie scooped up a babbling Stevie. 'This is new, Mrs Chatterbox. I'm impressed!' She blew raspberries on Stevie's cheeks, causing chuckles of delight; that wonderful sound of the people you love laughing together.

Wan somehow found the words and brought Jodie up to speed with our predicament. She listened, looking more and more horrified as he spoke.

'She's the double of Wan,' I stated, still refusing to entertain a blood test. 'I think they've singled us out because I'm black, which is clearly unethical. Why aren't they first querying the donor side? Wouldn't that be a more logical place to start?'

Mr Brown had explained to Wan after I'd left the room that parallel investigations were occurring, hoping not to find any irregularities within their clinic.

'By "irregularities" you mean embryos that have gone astray or to the wrong woman. Let's not dress this up,' I clarified.

Stevie looked towards her normally zen-like mother. Bringing myself back in check, I joined Jodie on the sofa.

'It's a bloody nightmare. I'm damned if I do and damned if I don't.' I tried to keep my tone and language even for Stevie's sake.

Jodie nodded, looking devastated.

'But we can't unknow what we know, can we? If we didn't agree, what will we tell her when she's older? If she learned that there was a query, but we never took things further? Then there's the issue of my egg – our fertilised egg. If Stevie isn't ours, whose is she? Is Ms X her mum? Or is there a wider chain? If we have a child somewhere, how will we find her?' My anger again gave way to tears.

I'd been in overdrive since the appointment, googling IVF mix-ups – of which there are more than you would imagine, particularly in the US. The only thing certain was that until we did a blood test, there would remain doubt.

'In any case, what are our legal rights? If Stevie isn't our biological child, she shared *my* womb; *I* birthed her, breastfed her. We love her. Parenting is more than biology.' My pitch again crept higher, making Stevie fretful, my previously calm baby now anxious. How would I carry on being a smug baby parent if this continued? I strode to the window, using breathing exercises I'd not used since labour.

'What do you think, Wan?' Jodie asked gently, my opinions dominating as usual.

'I think we need some legal advice,' he said. 'And the clinic had better be covering the costs.' For the first time since these conversations had begun, I considered the cost implications as well as worst-case scenarios. Wan halted my pacing, trying to hold me.

'We'll work this out, Lana. We are Stevie's parents. We always will be. She's going nowhere.' His reassurance brought little comfort. I'd lost Evie. I *could not* lose Stevie. It was that simple.

'I'll speak to Dr MacKinnon. She'll know what to do.'

'Can I take Stevie for a mooch in her pram?' Jodie loved a brisk walk through the park, giving us a break and enjoying time with just Stevie.

'Thanks, and I know it seems bonkers, but until all this is sorted, I need Stevie right here. With me.'

'It will be sorted.' She squeezed my shoulder. 'You'll see.'

***

Holly had responded to Wan's text and come over to talk further. Apparently, legal costs would be covered by the clinic, irrespective of outcomes. I chose not to clarify what that meant.

It was humiliating to see Holly's poorly disguised attempt to control her expression as she took in the threadbare carpets and cramped front room. It was impossible for anyone to find the racing commentary anything but ridiculous, but she tried hard to look nonchalant. I'd tried for a morning appointment to avoid the racing at 2 p.m., but it wasn't to be the case. I explained the temporary nature of the flat while we found our own home, imagining her undoubtedly swish apartment in hipster Manchester somewhere, or maybe on the Quays.

'From a legal perspective, you cannot be *forced* to take the blood test. This conversation could end right now and there would be nothing that either the clinic or Ms X could do. However, I'm sure you and Joel have been over every possibility, including that Stevie *is* your biological child, just like the other couples we've tested, which will allow you to move forward without doubt. If, however, you decide *not* to go for the test, then doubt remains. Which brings its own emotional cost. If Stevie *isn't* your biological child, then whose is she? Which raises the question of where *your* fertilised zygote may be – where's your baby? If you decide *not* to proceed with tests now and in the future a situation arises, Stevie needs blood or an organ or some other health issue – and I know that that's unlikely – but it emerges that Stevie isn't yours, how will you talk to her about this? It's a personal decision if you choose to share the science behind Stevie's conception with her – there are no rules around disclosure – but the conversation might be more difficult if it emerged you both knew there was a query but never pursued it.'

The magnitude of the decision hung over us.

'I'm talking too much. I'm sorry. This must be such a difficult decision.' Holly shifted awkwardly.

'And there's Stevie's rights in this,' Wan said, clearing his voice. '*She* should have the right to know who her parents are. She can't assert those rights at the moment – she's just a baby. But she would have some tough questions for us if we hadn't advocated for her.' He spoke gently, for the first time expressing a view that wasn't in favour of not testing.

'I'm alert to all the possibilities of this fucking impossible situation, Wan.' My voice cracked and Holly shifted awkwardly in her seat.

'What would a judge decide? If this is a direct embryo swap, Ms X's fertilised egg for ours, are we expected to just exchange? Of course I want my biological child, but I can't lose Stevie. I love her. I can't just let her go. You know we lost Stevie's sister at birth, don't you?'

'I do. And I am terribly sorry for your loss,' Holly offered gently. She paused, not long enough for my liking, before carrying on with her spiel.

'It's a relatively untested and ambiguous area of law. A judge will take factors into consideration with nothing certain, either from precedents or previous decisions bound by the law as it stands. It would be unprofessional of me to comment or offer an opinion that could influence you.'

'Can you tell us more about Ms X? Does she not want the child in her care? Has she not bonded with her? Does she, like we would, want both children? Or does she just want her baby back?'

'I am unable to provide details regarding Ms X or her child. I am governed by client confidentiality, just like you are assured.'

There was so much at stake. It felt overwhelming and unsolvable. We agreed a further date to convene and consider 'next steps', as if we were debating finance small print. Read the Terms and Conditions. Holly encouraged us to speak to our networks – GP, friends, family. Being sure in our decision would make it easier for us. I needed to get this woman out of my home. Her platitudes and empathic efforts were not landing well with me.

The days following the bombshell were impossible to navigate. I could neither think nor talk about anything else, driving both myself and Wan mental. Wan diplomatically suggested that we somehow limit our endless and circular conversations – which always wound up back where we started – through a pact, without which we'd probably have come to blows. We agreed 'protected' times when we would discuss the infinite possibilities and solutions. Outside of these times, we could make voice or paper notes so that we didn't end up completely consumed or locked in conflict, which had begun to be our norm. It didn't stop me thinking about it 24/7, but I suppose it stopped our endless to and fro.

Despite Holly's suggestion, I didn't want family members involved in our decision, on either side. I spoke with Dr MacKinnon and vented endlessly to Jodie. Wan talked with his brother on the phone for hours, swearing him to secrecy but welcoming, in fact *needing* to talk things through, to go over and over the same ground again and again as if the more he told the story the more he could process what was happening to us.

We arrived at our decision through the eyes of Stevie. How would we ever answer her questions if it emerged that we hadn't found the courage to know the truth? We would take the tests. Becoming parents had made us braver than we knew we could be.

***

It angered me that Mr Brown and Holly learned the result ahead of us. Had it had been obvious all along? Our fair – becoming fairer by the day – infant, her clear blue eyes showing no signs of changing any time soon. The contrast was more apparent every day in the arms of her African Caribbean mother and dark-eyed, dark-haired father. The innocuous envelope plopped through the door, sandwiched between the gas bill and a Farm Foods flyer. We'd had the option of confirmation by phone call, but I'd overruled Wan. I didn't want to hear the news with a third party present. I was grateful for the smallest element of control in this nightmare.

'There's no Christmas miracle, then,' I said flatly as we read and reread the facts. Neither Wan nor I was the biological parent of Stevie Edwards. The clinic's letterheaded paperwork, dated December 23rd, had decreed. Stevie tried to grab the letter in her tiny fists, intent on stuffing it into her mouth.

'Eating the evidence won't help, Bubba,' I said, gently removing it from her grasp.

Wan and I stared at the paperwork for an age. We had no words. I'd cried so much in recent weeks, it didn't seem possible to cry any more, but there they were, pouring down my cheeks and chin. I was too exhausted to remain furious at Wan for responding to those calls. But I absolutely knew that I wouldn't have. Deep down, maybe I'd *already* had the thought. Could Wan have protected us from this? Hid the letters, deleted the calls? Yet there we were, after doing the 'right thing', now left with the possibility of losing our baby all over again. First Evie. Now Stevie. I was wretched with hopelessness. I thought of the tablets I'd taken all that time ago. Would I find myself back there? If Stevie was taken from me, I would. No question. I couldn't see any way I could cope, having lost two children, despite my love for Wan.

'Do we need to have this conversation during "protected time", Wan?' I asked sarcastically. 'Or are we good to talk now?' Being mean to Wan was easier than blaming myself.

'Fuck, Lana, it's not my fault or yours. It's the cock-up of that shitty clinic.'

I focused on a Stevie sick stain on the threadbare carpet, my breathing audible, body trembling. Stevie was whining, her bumblebee toy just out of reach. On autopilot, I nudged it towards her. Did she whine before all this? When she was still the centre of her parents' universe, our every moment dedicated to making her happy? We'd become those attention-hijacked parents. Non-smug baby parents, doing their distracted best.

Wan's phone rang. Holly's number, a death knell. Today at 2 p.m.? He didn't need to check.

Wan hovered above me as I continued to stare at the stain. It was a vaguely foetus-like shape, but then I thought about foetuses more than most people. I could hear the torrent from the bath tap. I guessed that was for me. Why was Wan so kind to me when I just wanted to be horrible to everyone?

'Holly will be here at 2 p.m. I'm running you a bath.' Crouching beside me, he lifted my chin gently. 'We've got this, Lana,' he said through his tears. 'It's a shitter. But we can do this. We'll fight and we'll make it work.' Bollocks euphemistic talk. What I needed to hear.

'We could ask my mother to put a word in with God. Surely *he* can help?'

'How would he fix it for us?' Wan asked. 'What would he do?'

I thought carefully. 'We'd keep Stevie. And discover that our baby has been cared for but her "womb mummy" is ill. Gravely. We will have both girls within our care for longer and longer periods of time until she's too unwell to care for her at all.'

Wan laughed. 'You're all heart, Lana. You're hoping for the death of Stevie's mother!'

'You asked!'

'Do you think she'll look like Evie?' Wan asked, wiping his and my tears.

'Hang fire, Wan; we don't even know if Ms X's baby is ours. Maybe the clinic has royally fucked up and this child isn't ours either. Maybe it's the start of us trying to find them. But Stevie will never stop being our baby.' The bath water sounded close to full, not unlike my current ability to cope. I headed for the bathroom, depleted of energy.

***

And so we entered phase two: consenting to a DNA test to establish if Baby X was biologically ours. Mrs Jennings, our newly appointed solicitor, updated us over the phone. Mrs Jennings came recommended, having successfully (whatever that meant) dealt with previous complicated IVF cases. The more we researched, the clearer it became that IVF queries arising post-birth were hardly rare. Never at any point in our treatment journey had this been discussed – not a mention within the glossy Manchester Clinic literature.

Stevie was fond of her trips into Manchester. The same wasn't true for Wan and me. What should have been such an exciting time, the build-up to Stevie's first Christmas, was decidedly strained. My mood fluctuated wildly. I was short with Wan. I ate. A lot. Those post-pregnancy pounds showed no signs of shifting. It was all incredibly shit.

Mrs Jennings talked about a 'significant' amount of compensation to which we would be entitled, but it meant nothing. If becoming financially comfortable meant being without Stevie, I couldn't see a future. We needed the DNA results back from all parties to allow a plan to form. The feeling I carried during this time was not dissimilar to the awful charity tandem skydive that I'd done at uni. A feeling of never-ending freefall and a belief that the chute would fail.

Mrs Jennings invited us to her office. The results were back. The neglected offices were stale and dated, far removed from the Manchester Clinic's polished veneer, which was no bad thing. Mrs Jennings looked way past retirement age, but we warmed to her no-nonsense manner.

'Are you sitting comfortably?' She smiled. 'I shall cut to the chase.' Stevie fussed in her baby sling, having resisted sleep all the way into town. Mrs Jennings leaned over, offering a heavy paperweight from her desk. She was clearly from an era when safety kite marks hadn't been invented. Stevie was delighted with it.

'The DNA tests show that the IVF error has *not* involved a third party. Your Joel-and-Lana-fertilised egg was transferred to Ms X's uterus. Incorrectly by the Manchester Clinic. Baby X is both of your biological child. He's a little girl' She paused as we attempted to process the news.

I reached for Wan's hand, would she look like Evie? I *knew* it was a girl. Wan's eyes brimmed.

'Stevie is the biological child of Ms X. Wan is not the biological father of Baby X. Her father is logged as an anonymous Caucasian sperm donor accessed through an anonymous clinic.'

'What does that mean? That Ms X will want to take Stevie, I'm guessing? Well, she can't,' I breathed, kissing the soft spot on Stevie's head. The enormity of the DNA test decision felt so heavy.

'Can she legally?' Wan asked the question I could not bring myself to ask.

'It's an emerging area of law, which means that each case is anything but cut and dried. That said, using old legislation, legally, neither child is the property of their current carers. Legally, they should be exchanged; Stevie is not yours. However, the judge takes each case upon its own merit. He or she will decide what is in each of the children's best interests. There will probably in this case be a psychological evaluation of all parties to guide the judge's decision.'

'What do you mean?' Wan sounded panicky. 'Why would you say that? Is there something wrong with Baby X or her mother?' Fear gripped me. What would a psychiatrist make of my suicide attempt? Would I be deemed fit to care for my own child? Let alone Stevie?

Mrs Jennings chose her words carefully. 'There is evidence to suggest that Ms X has experienced some emotional difficulties – all this will inform the judge's decision. But effectively, yes, Ms X wants to "swap" babies. It does not violate client confidentiality to inform you of that. I'm not saying she's not a fit mother – please don't misinterpret that – but her wishes are that a swap occurs. I'm aware that although you want to gain custody of your biological child, you also wish to retain care of Stevie. Psychological assessment will be a potential tool – *if* you wish to challenge this. I must warn you, however, that Ms X's solicitor will be suggesting the same thing.'

'So we've avoided the worst-case scenario of this baby not being our child but still with an obligation to relinquish Stevie.' I attempted to process everything.

'Some couples find that they can come to an agreement in the best interests of the children and their care. I had one case where effectively two families blended, with children responding to all parents given their existing attachment prior to the error coming to light.' It all seemed surreal. 'If you want to go down this route, we recommend contacts begin in a neutral venue where you can get to know one another as couples and children. We can then regroup and see how everyone is feeling.'

'Do you have any photos?' The question felt huge. Would she look like Evie? I dared for the first time to think about that possibility.

'Until initial contact has been made, the physical identity of the children will remain confidential. Whatever you do – and I've had clients badly burned by this before – *do not* give your address to Ms X nor attempt to elicit hers. Contacts must occur at neutral venues. Flight risk cannot be overlooked. I'm sure you wouldn't consider anything other than a legal route, but emotions can run high. I knew of one family that effectively kidnapped their biological child and left without trace, leaving one couple without either child, which did not end well for them. Am I clear?'

Wan and I nodded solemnly. The paperweight fell to the floor. Stevie was asleep at last. The tears I'd been holding began to fall.

'Don't give yourself too much of a hard time overthinking this.' Easy for her to say. 'As much as you feel you shouldn't have to relinquish Stevie, conversely there are her rights to consider. We need to remember that there is another mother here with her own emotional needs and rights. It's complex, but I'm sure you will want to act in the best possible interests of both children.'

No, it isn't complex. And it's my needs that I will be prioritising. I want both children. I am the flight risk. It's beyond unfair that I am battling to keep Stevie after I've already lost her sister.

***

Doctor MacKinnon agreed to see me after clinic. The warrior-like receptionist wasn't happy when I checked in.

'GPs have lives too, you know, Ms Edwards. It'll be gone 7 p.m. when she leaves here.' Bitch. I'll bet she's had loads of kids and grandchildren and hardly bothers with them.

My anxiety had been off the scale from the moment we'd left the solicitor's office. I needed to clarify what Dr MacKinnon would share when approached by the courts. When Mrs Jennings had mentioned that Ms X had experienced 'emotional difficulties', all I could think of was my own suicide attempt. Did that make me an unfit mother? I'd barely slept since the original thought had grown like a weed.

'Lana. I'm so sorry that all this has turned into such a nightmare. How are you doing?'

'Well, I'm not sleeping, and I'd like to say that I'm not eating, but …' I gestured at my bulk.

'That's completely normal given what's happening.' Dr MacKinnon reached for my hand across the table. 'Let's deal with one thing at a time.'

'Okay. I'm terrified that my mental health will be exposed and it will go against me. Apparently, Ms X has her own stuff going on – but I'm worried I'll come off worse. How will it look? I tried to take my own life before Stevie was conceived. I'm guessing you'll have to disclose that if asked?'

'Well, I would have a duty to disclose relevant health history if requested. Which would include the isolated incident you described. Context is everything, though, which I would be keen to make clear. You were struggling in the aftermath of losing your daughter. You don't have a history of mental illness. You were distressed in the context of an extraordinary situation. You sought help, managed your mood. You are an amazing mum to Stevie and have taken everything in your stride. What's there to say?'

'It sounds awful, but I'm hoping to query Ms X's mental health in order to retain custody of Stevie.' I was almost embarrassed to say this out loud. We'd found the courage to give the children the correct information around their identities and the right to be raised by their parents, but I still hoped to avoid losing Stevie, whatever it took.

'Given the circumstances I don't think there are any rights or wrongs about how you should be feeling. All of it's valid.'

'So, you think I'll come out okay if there's an assessment?'

'You're probably saner than I am, and I'd be happy to testify to that!' She grinned.

'Should that worry me as your patient?' I joined her laughter, feeling the weight I'd carried into the room shift.

'I'd be happy to prescribe something if you think that would be useful. Again, it's an extraordinary time you're going through. I can confidently say that you won't be judged for accessing help.'

'I'll try some meds. It might help. If it only reduces my trips to the fridge, that's got to be helpful!'

'When this settles, you can address your weight if you wish, but for now, be kind to yourself. And from what I can see, you're managing amazingly well. If you could make an appointment during clinic hours next time, that would be even better. It would reduce how cantankerous my front-of-house is with both of us!'

Dutifully promising to make an appointment through official channels in the future, I left, feeling slightly more hopeful.

Tilda

Things moved quickly. From the first impossible phone call to waiting for the results of the DNA test it was ten days. If I hadn't just experienced the worst few weeks of my life, this week would have been a contender. Waiting felt like an eternity, although the relief of simply being listened to was overwhelming. The clinic's theory that Phoebe Rose was mine but a recessive gene was driving her colour was so far off my radar. In my bones I could not reconcile the child in front of me as mine. If DNA came back suggesting otherwise, I would demand a further test. For the first time since her birth, I attempted to enjoy Phoebe Rose. Instead of the flinch that had become my norm whenever I looked at this baby, I tried to begin to genuinely care for her. And she was so desperate to be loved. Her eyes widened as I whirled her through the air, early gummy half smiles hijacking her face. It was painful. It was bittersweet. Knowing that my own daughter was doing this with someone else was heartbreaking – an impossible conundrum I'd been attempting to manage by keeping an emotional distance. Ellie didn't care whose baby she was. She adored her.

'Phoebe Rose's nose,' Ellie would sing and zoom in to gently pinch her nose. She'd take her from me and prop her on her hip, looking as comfortable as she did with her own child. A baby on each side, she'd wander around humming contentedly. She was *everything* I aspired to be, and the struggle was real. Every day I tried to be a better mother to this child, a better person generally, but it was so hard. If I forced myself, would it become second nature?

It was the weekend again. Vic would be home. Putting my big girl pants firmly on, I knocked on his door. I would do the right thing. I would thank him for his concern and attempt to explain myself.

Vic's expression shifted from relaxed to stony as he opened the door.

'Vic, I'm so sorry. I don't know what to say other than that....'

'It isn't me you need to apologise to, Tilda,' he said coolly. 'It's the infant strapped to your chest who needs you, not me.'

'It's been so much tougher than I thought it would be. I thought being on my own …'

Dang, if there was a wrong thing to say to Vic, it was that. I deserved his eye roll.

'I've seen the GP. I'm … it's going to change.'

Vic's disgusted expression did not alter. He wasn't giving me an inch. I sensed him itching to close the door.

'Thank you for your concern. It's appreciated. Truly,' I offered weakly. I tried to make my apology sound genuine despite Vic receiving it with little grace.

'Are you done? I've something on the stove.' Vic closed the door without a goodbye. Stepping away, I felt proud – strange in the context of my shame, but facing Vic had been no mean feat. I shuddered at where things might have led had I gone unchallenged.

***

'You *have* to have a tree. It's Phoebe Rose's first Christmas!' Ellie scolded. It was inconceivable to her that I might not.

'It's November, Ellie. Nobody normal puts their tree up before mid-December *at least*. It's a hallmark of the not-right.' I laughed, knowing that Ellie was firmly in the November camp. 'And besides, I'm not really a Christmas kind of person.'

'Well, maybe Old Tilda wasn't, but New Tilda needs to get her act together, because Phoebe Rose definitely looks like a festive kind of girl.' Ellie dangled a bauble in Phoebe Rose's direction, which she tried to track with her wobbly gaze. 'You're too cute!' Ellie giggled and tickled her tummy, eliciting a twitchy half smile from Phoebe Rose. 'So, blood test results come back when? Thursday?' Ellie knew as well as I did when they were due back. She'd lived and breathed the last ten days with me.

'You don't have to kid glove me, you know. I'm ready for whatever the results are. You can open the letter with me if you like. In fact, it would be great to do that together. Lord knows how I'd have managed this without you. I'd have ended up one of those mothers who leaps from her balcony if you hadn't been here for us.' It was a well-worn conversation by now, but still I couldn't say it enough.

'You'd do the same for me.' She waved away my words as usual. 'Besides, you've done me a favour. I was considering IVF for a possible sibling for Rosa. I'm sufficiently traumatised to stick at one now, saving me a fortune, financially and emotionally.'

'I'd like to say "don't let it put you off". But how could it not? I'm hardly the poster girl for the Manchester Clinic, am I?'

The relief of humour after the consuming darkness was palpable. And it was entirely down to Ellie.

***

Thursday came slowly. The grainy images of Mr Brown and Holly appeared on the screen from the office. Team Tilda consisted of Ellie, Rosa, Phoebe Rose and me; we huddled around the laptop in Ellie's front room, the tension unbearable.

I'd like to start off—' Mr Brown leaned forward into the screen, and I cut him off abruptly.

'Stop!' I almost shouted, and both Holly and Mr Brown looked taken aback. 'Enough!' I held my hand aloft. 'Holly, what is the result, *please*?'

'Phoebe Rose is not biologically yours, Tilda. There is zero possibility that the egg transferred to yourself was biologically related to you.'

There. The relief. The vindication. What I'd known from the moment Phoebe Rose was born. *I'm not mad or a monster. I'm a mother whose baby was taken.* Shaking with rage and frustration, I was determined not to let these polished, sleazy characters see me cry. I took a moment to gather myself.

'I'm sure you *can't* imagine, Mr Brown, but the result evidencing that I am *not* the biological parent of Phoebe Rose is exactly what I expected. If any other result had been returned, I'd have asked for a retest. It's a fact I've known since her birth. The impact is beyond measure.' I struggled to manage my ragged breathing and hold my voice steady. Ellie gripped my hand off camera. 'I want to know exactly what this means for myself and Phoebe Rose and how you plan to 'resolve' this, because I'm unclear as to how this might proceed. The … damage you have caused …' My precarious emotions threatened to overwhelm me.

'We cannot express how sorry we are that you and your family are having to go through this experience. I know we've spoken previously about this, but I must reiterate that we are working hard to identify where the error or indeed errors have occurred.

We will find a resolution to this situation, although we fully acknowledge the challenges you've faced over the last few weeks and months.' All I could hear from Mr Brown was self-protection.

Phoebe Rose began to fuss almost immediately, sensing the tension in the room. Handing her to Ellie, I moved to the centre of the screen.

'What's pivotal is how *quickly* you can identify exactly *where* my egg is, fertilised or otherwise. Minor details like: if my egg was transferred to another woman's uterus, where is she now? Who is the sperm donor? And most importantly, if my beautiful Mini-Tilda has become a flesh-and-blood whole, when can I have her back?' I hadn't rehearsed the words that tumbled from me, my voice trembling with rage.

Holly spoke before Mr Brown could spout further corporate speak.

'Tilda, we're so sorry. From a legal perspective, financial compensation in its various forms can and will be offered. As you so eloquently outlined, the pertinent matters are finding out how the error has occurred and tracking down Phoebe Rose's biological parents and the whereabouts and status of your egg.'

The possibility that my egg had not progressed to fertilisation or been carried to term was terrifying. Obviously, I'd been aware of this as a possible outcome, but hearing it in such stark terms was brutal.

'We have sent letters to all the patients receiving care at the same time as yourself at the clinic. We have initiated an internal audit of our processes and requested an external investigation into every aspect of care. Clearly this extends beyond our clinic given the wider elements of the chain, including the clinic where the sperm donor originated. We have used this clinic many times and only ever had exceptional service.'

It felt beyond me how we might establish what had happened. Ellie had taken the girls through to the bedroom, as Phoebe Rose had continued to contribute, making concentration difficult.

'The external enquiry, overseen by the IVF Association, will scrutinise the process followed using IT logs and dates, lab camera footage, liaison with all services within the donor's chain of care, and any third parties involved in the shipping and transfer of the sperm. No stone will be left unturned.' I was not reassured by Mr Brown's political spin. 'Let's have faith that the enquiry will shed light onto exactly what's occurred.'

'I had faith last year when you took 15k from me in exchange for a child. For *my* child, not someone else's. I no longer have faith. I suggest you do not insult me further by suggesting that I should. I do not wish to meet with you again – not professionally and certainly not personally. I have appointed a solicitor with whom all communication will occur moving forward.'

Mr Brown nodded solemnly. I could see Holly trying to discreetly alert her colleague to the fact that the meeting had run its course.

'I expect this situation to be resolved by Christmas. It's mid-November. You can't reverse the harm that's occurred, but damage limitation is possible if you act swiftly. We all deserve this. No other parent or child deserves to go through what we are currently.' Emotion finally broke through my voice as I declared the meeting over. 'You've a lot to do and I won't keep you.' I closed the call before they could respond.

Ending the meeting felt like another milestone had been met. Sadly, a bureaucratic milestone, not the kind of milestone that matters: the first smile, the first giggle, your baby's personality subtly emerging. It was, however, the first step towards getting the right child to her biological parent. Because currently I was missing out on those all-important experiences. My own daughter would be becoming attached to another family. And Phoebe Rose was desperately missing out on a mother who should be delighting in her, instead of my failing attempts to bond with her.

Lana

I met my biological daughter on a grey January afternoon. It was surreal to feel so connected to Stevie while knowing there was another child – my own child – needing my love. Feeling previously unable to find emotional room for anyone but Stevie, it felt strangely effortless to discover a whole new channel, ready and waiting there for Phoebe Rose. Wan and I were by turns excited and overwhelmed, our lives unfolding in this bizarre way. I craved Phoebe Rose's presence from the moment I knew she existed. On the flip side, I was a dog with a bone. I couldn't let it go, internally wrestling, unable to forgive Wan for his role in this – returning the clinic's calls had been the catalyst for everything since. From the first message from the clinic, I'd known instinctively where this would end. I'd known that my 'happy ending' – the life that others take for granted – was ending. The stigma that had always perched on my shoulder had never left. I was doomed. Maybe it was my dad's fault, maybe my mum's – but I couldn't outrun it. I couldn't say that directly to Wan, so instead I was unkind, passive-aggressive with him on any given subject. Why hadn't he just deleted the calls? How could he risk losing Stevie? Well, I couldn't. What the alternative was I hadn't quite figured out, but I could not see a future without her.

The morning of the first contact, I made short work of the chocolate log that Stevie and I had made the night before to share with our daughter's carers. I found myself 'trying' a corner, which swiftly led to whole log consumption in about twenty minutes.

As Wan checked in at reception, I scanned the Children's Centre waiting room. Where was she? I'd know for sure. Wan grabbed an instant coffee and Jammie Dodgers from the kitchen. I concentrated on my breathing and on studying the children around us. I could see babies that I instinctively *knew* weren't mine. A family worker came over and led us to a side room. As the door opened, I saw the profile of a slim woman, expensively dressed, a bundle on her lap. To her right was a younger woman with a toddler reading a peek-a-boo book. The older woman turned and smiled nervously our way. Her mouth dropped as she took in Stevie propped against my hip.

'I'll leave you to it, then.' The worker asked us to let her know when the room was available.

Stepping nervously towards the women, I struggled to take in what I was seeing.

'Oh my,' I cried. 'Oh, Wan!' The infant on the older woman's knee was the image of Evie.

'She's beautiful!' I cried, wiping away tears that I'd resolved not to shed. Ms X – I presumed – was equally blown away.

'Ellie, it's my baby! It's really her!' she gasped to the woman at her side.

Awkwardly introducing ourselves – for the first time learning names – we introduced Stevie and Phoebe Rose. It was surreal.

I didn't offer Stevie and neither did Ms X, or Tilda, but the desire to scoop up the Evie double was so strong. Awkwardly, we placed the children beside one another and stood back. Stevie's pale arms flapped alongside the undoubtedly darker Phoebe Rose.

'Can I hold her, please?' I asked through my tears.

'Shouldn't we wait until we're not quite so emotional?' Tilda put her hand out as if I were going to make a dash with her baby – my baby.

I backed up. 'Of course,' I said, feeling slightly stung.

We knelt instead, leaning over the children, taking in every detail.

'You have your daddy's eyes and the Edwards nose,' I sang to Phoebe Rose, who sized us up through suspicious dark eyes framed by impossibly long lashes.

'She's exactly as I thought she'd be,' whispered Wan. Without asking permission, he reached for her tiny hand and waved as he sang.

'All the small things ...' Both babies' faces lit up and their arms bashed as they turned to Wan's voice, Stevie's babble filling the room.

'Isn't she lovely, ...' I crooned to Phoebe Rose, helping her join in the fist-waving. So much for holding the tears at bay. All four of us streamed.

'I think they're ready even if we're not.' Tilda gently picked up Stevie from Phoebe Rose's side. My heart lurched, my every fibre wanting to snatch her from this stranger and run. Both babies, actually. It wasn't fair, but I *had* to have Phoebe Rose too. In that moment I knew there would be a fight. This wasn't going to end amicably like the solicitor had mooted.

Wan and I held Phoebe Rose sandwiched between us. She clung to us tightly, mainlining the love that she should have had from us, making up for the lost months.

'So much hair!' Wan patted her soft coils.

'She got the combo. My hair and your sense of rhythm. Close call, Phoebe Rose.' I giggled into her tiny ear.

Being torn between focusing on Phoebe Rose while monitoring Stevie was dizzying. Stevie was fussing slightly, and the other lady – Ellie – leaned in to play peek-a-boo, making Stevie chuckle loudly. The sight of these women holding *my* child was unbearable. After a few moments, Stevie began to fuss again, even with the distraction of the toddler. Stevie was usually smitten by other children, but she was having none of it. Wan and I made our way over, relieved to be closing the gap between us.

'Are you being fickle, Miss Stevie?' I brought Phoebe Rose within grabbing distance of them. Stevie obliged by trying to place Phoebe Rose's hand into her own mouth.

'Is that tasty?' Tilda tried. Stevie released it and began to cry – a real bottom lip wobble followed by a loud burst. Ellie initiated a baby swap and exchanged her toddler for Stevie, allowing the four of them to look through the toddler's book. We backed off again into two parties, giving Phoebe Rose the stuffed koala we'd brought. Phoebe Rose didn't seem nearly as advanced as Stevie, and she resisted our efforts to show her Stevie's ragged board book. She seemed only to want to be held, clinging tightly to my shirt.

A knock at the door gave us a heads-up; the room was needed for the next session. How had an hour passed already? We eked out a further five minutes, to the disproval of the family worker, who tutted as we gathered our belongings. Stealing a final squeeze of Phoebe Rose, bittersweet emotion coursed through me. I had Stevie back in my arms, but leaving Phoebe Rose was overwhelming.

***

As we buckled our seatbelts, I waited impatiently for Wan to offer a first opinion.

'Doesn't exactly seem the maternal type, does she?' he offered, his eyes focusing on Stevie in the rearview mirror. The possibility of losing her was unthinkable.

'Wan, she *cannot* have Stevie, she can't! She's an ice maiden. And don't tell me I'm imagining it. How beautiful is Phoebe Rose? She is the *image* of Evie! Did you feel how hungry she was for our love? Could you sense it? She didn't want toys. She wanted us.' My stomach churned violently.

'She was cuddly,' agreed Wan. 'Maybe that's what she's used to?' Bloody Wan and his bloody positive slant.

'No!' I hissed. 'Did you see who comforted Stevie when she was upset? Not Tilda but her friend, Ellie, was it? Do you think they're a couple? She seemed close to Phoebe Rose. Wan, she's not having Stevie, she's not!' I shouted.

'It's the first time we've met the woman. You can't judge her ability to love Stevie based on that last surreal hour. Don't do a Lana catastrophisation!'

'I thought Ellie was okay. If we had to give Stevie to Ellie, I might be able to bear it. But I can tell you how Tilda made me feel – deliberately, I think. Inferior. Her posh accent and expensive clothes. She even smelled expensive. God, I hate her!'

Stevie began to whine.

'I'm sorry, Bubba.' Bringing my tone back in check, I reached my arm around the chair to wiggle her feet. 'Phoebe Rose, though! Those eyes!' I scrolled slowly through the photos we'd snapped.

Wan wiped away tears as he drove but volunteered little. How was he not raging? What was wrong with him?

Instead of heading home, Wan turned off for the reservoir. The weather was grim, the exposed area windswept and gloomy. It perfectly suited our mood.

'Don't bother with the sling,' Wan said, opening his parka for us to join him. Squeezing Stevie's little body between ours, we walked slowly together over the wet grass towards the water's edge. The thought that we wouldn't always be together was terrifying – just unthinkable. I would do anything and everything to keep us together.

***

The ten-day wait for next contact felt never-ending. Stevie filled my every waking second but received a watered-down version of myself. I couldn't focus, my thoughts pulled back to our daughter – the double of her sister – in Tilda's cold care. My dreams were dominated by thoughts of Phoebe Rose – where she might be, what she might be doing. Was she sad? Did she need us right now and we couldn't comfort her? I tried to listen to Wan and keep an open mind about Tilda. The artificial nature and emotional build up to the 'contact' had been tough to navigate. Maybe the next session would be easier.

The Children's Centre had felt sterile, and I hoped being in a park would make things feel easier.

'No friend this time?' I enquired. Tilda was seated in front of the swings on a bench, Phoebe Rose in her lap. She was wearing a bizarre outfit of wedge heels and combat pants, looking like a *Love Island* reject as opposed to ready for a play date.

'Ellie? No, not today. She's taking her mum to a hospital appointment.' She paused. 'We're not an item, by the way.' An amused expression spread across her face. 'Did you think we were?'

Both Wan and I shrugged. We weren't sure. 'She seemed great with Phoebe Rose,' I needled.

'She's an amazing friend and, yes, like a second mother to Phoebe Rose.' As if there weren't already enough mothers.

I nodded my agreement. 'I've got a bestie. Makes a difference, doesn't it?'

'Absolutely. I don't know what we would have done without her.'

I wanted to dig further, find out exactly what she meant, but left it. *Play nice, Lana.*

'I'm not sure what protocol is here, I'll be honest,' Tilda ventured. 'I couldn't find a chapter covering it in the IVF handbook.' She laughed.

'Me neither,' I agreed, warming to her honesty.

'Are we supposed to get to know one another, or is this just about getting to know the babies?'

Tilda didn't strike me as someone used to not being in control. Compared to Wan and me, she seemed so self-assured. From the outset last session, it had felt like she was in charge, even deciding when we could hold the babies. Tilda was the one who had initiated this, the entire process her call. She oozed money. Her accent, a hybrid of north and south, was so composed. I tried hard not to feel inferior. She was older than me but had clearly looked after herself; she looked in good shape. *Probably sticks Phoebe Rose in the crèche every day while she works out. And yes, I know I'm being a complete bitch.*

'I suppose it's a combination of the two.' I proffered Stevie and we awkwardly exchanged babies. Trying to assert myself, I suggested we play on the park and then have a stroll with the buggies – a statement rather than a question. Stevie complained less this time, and Phoebe Rose snuggled in like she'd never left our side. Playing with babies on a park requires creativity. I enjoyed watching Tilda flounder and lamely copy whatever we were doing, pretending to be propelled down the slide, playing tig between the monkey bars. She looked awkward at best. Wan and I nudged each other, watching her awkwardly negotiate the bark on the playground floor in those ridiculous wedges. It was satisfying to receive Phoebe Rose's gummy grins while Stevie seemed only to tolerate being manipulated around the park. I hoped Tilda was aware of the contrast between the children's responses. Was she deliberately screening Stevie from our view with her body?

Tilda looked cold after about twenty minutes. Not enough meat on her bones, obviously. Also she wasn't running around like a loon like we were, so she would be. Wan suggested a walk to the café at the top of the hill, like two regular families catching up.

I reached for Stevie's pushchair. The concept of having even an element of control felt powerful.

'So,' I asked bravely, 'how soon did you know or query that Phoebe Rose wasn't your biological child?'

'Well, she was born at 3.30 in the afternoon. At 3.32 she was placed in my arms. And I queried!' She managed a smile, but it must have been horrendous. To Tilda's credit, she didn't ask us if we'd had doubts. Both Wan and I had never voiced them even to one other, although for me the niggle had always been there, constant in my periphery. People's endless colour-related comments chipping away at my fragile foundation.

'I'm sorry this has all landed on you. To be honest, I didn't know if I was being mad or bad in questioning Phoebe Rose's identity. Eventually I realised, for my sanity and hers, I had to find out. It must have been awful getting the call from the clinic, the process unfolding in this way.'

'It's been horrific.' We nodded emphatically, the adjective not coming close to describing our ordeal. *Ongoing* ordeal. Tilda's word choice suggested that her trauma was easing. She'd found her baby and was getting her back. She really had not bonded with Phoebe Rose – that was clear – deliberately or otherwise. She didn't seem to conceive how we might be feeling, her lack of insight staggering. How could she be so … clinical with our daughter? What harm was her apathy doing to our child? Clearly, we'd bonded with Stevie – she was *ours* as far as we were concerned – yet Tilda was behaving as if she'd taken the wrong suitcase from a carousel and had now tracked down the owners. The hatred I felt towards her was overwhelming. Wan didn't seem to feel the same level of venom as me, which I found baffling.

Tilda strode ahead, Phoebe Rose's buggy facing out. No interaction, no warmth. She didn't even seem that interested in Stevie. Finding indoor seats at the café, we settled the girls, and Tilda headed for the loo without a backward glance. Wan queued for coffee.

I swear it wasn't premeditated. It was purely an impulse thing. With trembling hands, I found myself un-poppering Tilda's baby bag. The usual wipes and paraphernalia were there in immaculate order, far removed from the bomb site that is my bag. At the bottom was mail, some opened, others not. It looked like business paperwork. I recognised the HMRC logo from Wan's self-employment. My heart racing, I glanced briefly at the bathroom door. Catching only the top line of the address on the letter, I struggled to read it in my quaking hands. Miss Matilda Asquith-Hyde, Nurture Foundation, and what looked like a London postcode. The inner door to the bathroom swung open. Quickly pushing the paperwork to the bottom of the bag, I only partially managed to close the poppers. I grinned nervously as Wan approached with the coffee, giving me his most discreet *what the hell, Lana* look. He took his seat just before Tilda joined us.

The rest of the contact again flew by, but the awkwardness was still there. Tilda propped Stevie on her lap like she was a doll. It was like she wanted Stevie to 'make the first move', to initiate play or communication ... God, she was weird. I removed Phoebe Rose's socks and tenderly kissed her tiny toes, triggering painful memories of doing the same thing with Evie in the precious few hours we'd shared.

'You had a big sister, Phoebe Rose,' I crooned quietly into her ear. 'Oh, she was beautiful, just like you.' I ran my lips over the nape of her neck. 'She said to say hello!' Phoebe Rose squeezed me close. Tears fell. I quickly wiped them away.

Phoebe Rose loved the hissing toy snake we'd brought her. We were careful not to let her use Stevie's toys, not wanting to create anxiety for Stevie. Phoebe Rose's eyes grew excited as we 'hissed' the brightly coloured snake into her ear. Tilda had brought no such gifts or toys for Stevie. I ached to create a version of life where Tilda would leave and we'd head back home with two children. I thought about the solicitor's reference to the IVF family who'd seamlessly blended, swapping the children around between both sets of parents. Well, that wasn't going to work here. Ice Queen Tilda was not going to be raising my daughter – correction, daughters. Ideally her only contact would be photos of both girls sent to her at Christmas and birthdays. There was something off about her.

Tilda

I dared to hope that things were beginning to travel in the right direction. I wasn't an unfit mother, unable to bond with my own child. I was the opposite; I'd known from the word go. Lana and Joel were okay. Stevie could have done worse, but thank God I'd found her before weaning had finished. *The woman's huge; my daughter needs rescuing before she too becomes a sumo. Lord only knows what they eat.* And yes, I was being judgemental, but like so many of their *kind*, they revelled in their 'Northeness' far too much for my liking. One thing I don't miss about the north – apart from the dreadful weather – is their 'down to earth'/'take us as you find us' behaviour. I find it vulgar. The trip to the park had been excruciating. The pair of them shrieking and running around with Phoebe Rose, not caring that people were watching. Thank God contacts occur there rather than London, where I might be seen.

Walking into the Foundation office block had felt amazing. Head held high, Phoebe Rose strapped to my chest in her carrier, we looked every inch formidable IVF advocates. If only people knew the reality. Everyone would in time, I reminded myself. When my own flesh and blood was where she belonged, the exposé would begin, blowing the veneer clean off the ugly IVF truth. I intended to feign progression of the original business plan, temporarily keeping things afloat, then use the platform I'd created to shed light on what the brochures don't tell you. I'm not suggesting IVF is not helpful – clearly, for most, it's a viable solution to having a child. But how could I not raise awareness after what had happened?

Of course, the team made a fuss of Phoebe Rose, passing her around like a parcel. No clingy behaviours for this sociable child, happy to go to anyone offering a cuddle. Goodness knows what

Lana had done to Stevie to make her so clingy. With the legal process in place, the unspoken shame that I experienced introducing Phoebe Rose to new people was beginning to reduce. The 'Is she adopted? Who's the father?' query, the processing that inevitably occurs when we meet someone new, would not be my life. My own daughter shared my peaches-and-cream complexion and her father's platinum hair – the Tilda Mini-Me I'd imagined. I must go via Harvey Nic's next time we were home for some outfits. Stevie was always so practically and casually dressed – cotton leggings and those cheap jersey tops. I thought of the stunning christening robe I'd fallen in love with all those months ago. Lana would never choose clothes for Stevie like that, even if she could afford to.

My mobile rang. I proffered Phoebe Rose to the receptionist and stepped into a side room to take the call.

'So how is it all feeling?' my horribly expensive and slimy solicitor, Mr 'just call me Dean' Dreyfuss, purred down the phone. His fleeting resemblance to Daniel Craig seemed to have affected his ego, feeding a delusion that women found him irresistible. I believe he's the best of the best professionally, so I tolerate it. Opting out of the Manchester Clinic's legal recommendation, I'd hired him based on reputation. He was ruthless and won his cases.

'Excellent,' I breathed. 'We've had several contacts, which I think are going well. How quickly can you make this happen?'

'Based upon my last few clients in a similar situation, and providing the other couple—'

'Lana and Joel,' I volunteered.

'Thank you – don't oppose or have an imbecile for a solicitor, then I hope to wrap this up in the next six to eight weeks. In the meantime, we should start extended contacts, contacts beginning to occur between just yourself and Stevie without Lana and Joel present. Even an overnight if we think that would be helpful. Everyone's different, but I favour the Band Aid approach. If it's inevitable, then crack on – the sooner the better. I'm pushing for a court hearing and hope to hear back by the end of the week with a date.'

'I couldn't agree more timewise, but I'm not sure about sleepovers. Is that not complicating things?'

'The vibe I'm getting from their solicitor is that they would like the transition to be lengthy to reduce impact on the children. We're going to need to manage that. Lana is particularly attached to Stevie. Leave it with me; nothing I can't handle.' He laughed suggestively. I imagined his ridiculous Daniel Craig pout effort, even on the phone, feet propped on his leather desk. I asked that the next contact be arranged as soon as possible to fit in around my work commitments. How responsible did I sound?

***

The next few weeks were busy. My calendar and inbox filled quickly with interest in the European Union funding bid that Richard was optimistic we would win. The angle of IVF and same-sex couples was a seemingly hot topic. It felt conflicting promoting an intervention that had practically derailed my mental health, but in time I intended to use my position at Nurture as a force for good. After my exposé, I would use our case to identify failures within the process and demand that these be addressed. Still radio silence from the Manchester Clinic regarding their investigation. I would take great delight in taking the clinic to the Court of Human Rights if it emerged that they'd failed to follow procedure or even continued to use partners where there were known issues. Of course, Richard knew nothing of my complex situation – as far as he was concerned, I was still its grateful ambassador. *Watch this space.* I was excited by the possibility that European funding could lead to overseas links and opportunities to travel. Richard had already pencilled into speak at a conference in Madrid in a few weeks time and I was trying to manoeuvre things so that I could shadow him there. It would be a great learning experience and an escape.

The deceit, of course, made me feel uneasy. I was hoping that when Richard learned the extent of our situation, he would still feel able to support the trajectory. It was a necessary means to an end to prevent this happening to others. Was I becoming altruistic? If the Madrid trip came off, I would have three whole days without having to care for Phoebe Rose, so maybe not completely. Ellie had had Phoebe Rose often over the last few weeks while it had been full on with Nurture. I paid her well, and she was clearly in need of the money. I could offer her a position within the charity, if she was interested, when the funding came through. Jobs for the girls, obviously, but she'd be amazing. Although that could lead to childcare issues. It would need thinking through.

***

I was unfortunate enough to meet Stan's eye as I made my way through the lobby. Stan's a delight in exceedingly small doses. But I had no desire to hear another long-winded story about one of his grandchildren's bowel movements during my precious childfree time.

'Where's the little one today?' Stan always made such a *fuss* whenever he saw Phoebe Rose.

'She's on a play date and sleepover, Stan. I've been working,' I stated proudly, looking every inch the businesswoman in my sharp heels and suit.

'Again?' Clearly old school. Probably thinks children should be permanently attached to their mother's hip. 'Well, it's suiting you. You're looking well.' He smiled. 'Better than I've seen you look in a while, if you don't mind my saying so. '

'I am good, thank you,' I responded sincerely. 'She's back tomorrow. We'll come and say hi if you're around?'

'That would be lovely.' He beamed. 'Don't enjoy yourself too much, though – while the cat's away and all that!' He laughed.

'I won't do anything you wouldn't,' I replied breezily, grateful to hear the hiss of the lift, my smile fading before the doors had met. Why people think you aren't entitled to a life after a baby I'll never know.

It was delightful to be home alone in the apartment. No guard in place, no pretence. Just me being me.

I had coped so much better over the last few weeks; I could feel the 'old me' returning. With the end in sight, like things might just work out. It had been a close call, and I just had to keep going. Opening the fridge left me dissatisfied. I'd stuck to my no booze rule – quite rightly – after the night of the advocaat. But still, it felt an incomplete evening without a drop of something. The evening was to be devoted to the completion of Nurture's marketing strategy. I'd promised the document to Richard a week ago but had lost all stomach for it. Going through the motions was a skill I'd become an expert in of late. Completing the strategy was the next step towards the IVF platform that would provide the perfect stage when the time was right for my exposé; I had to remind myself of that regularly. I felt so uncomfortable being dishonest with Richard; however, I hoped he would understand in time. Research on/exposé of all things IVF was far more interesting work than the strategy; it was hard to stay focused. I could lose hours at a stretch pulling together sad stories, tales of cover-ups and deceit within the lucrative world of IVF.

Fixing myself a chilled glass of tonic in a pre-frozen glass – a hark back to my champagne days – I wistfully added a slice of lemon, pulling up the document on my laptop. I'd spent so much time on it but had barely made a dent. The course I'd attended had covered the basics of marketing, but I felt woefully inadequate as I looked *again* at the template. Surely I could pay someone to do this? Richard, however, had insisted that I personally develop the plan, because it was 'my opportunity to shape the business from the ground up'. Whatever that meant.

Foster Strategic Communication

Step One …

'I have no clue what this means!' I flung the laptop across the bed. This was not doable.

My phone glowed: three unread messages. Two from Ellie with pics of the girls 'baking'. How do babies bake? Would this ever come naturally to me? There was a message from the WhatsApp Start-Up chat. My fellow newbies sharing resources, ideas, whinging, ranting – there was nothing you couldn't post.

'Struggling with this bloody marketing strategy … help??!!' I typed.

The fidgety 'I'd like a drink because I'm home alone' feeling continued to course through my body. Again, I googled 'Idiot's Guide to Developing a Marketing Strategy'. Reams of articles appeared that this idiot had zero chance of understanding.

Heading for the shower in the absence of anything better to do, I hoped for a reply and divine inspiration from the group.

Stepping out of the shower, I found myself humming – small glimpses of the old me returning. It felt so good, having felt so very desperate.

A quick call to Ellie and I was ready to have another chop, albeit with a heavy heart. The WhatsApp group was pinging. Links to all sorts of baffling and lengthy documents were being sent, looking every bit as bewildering as those I'd already seen and failed to understand.

Dani: I had a mare with mine, but got it sussed eventually. I'm happy to discuss it if that helps. But I warn you, it was painful!

Tilda: That would be fab. Really helpful.

Dani: I can send you mine over but I'm in architecture so transferability might be limited.

Tilda: I'm snatching your hand off, thank you, anything will help.

Dani: Happy to chat about it first. I've some time later this evening, Friday morning or an hour just before the meetup on Tuesday if any of those work.

Tilda: I've only really got tonight with childcare so I can nail this beast!

Dani: Then tonight it is. You're Tower Bridge end of town, aren't you?

Tilda: I am, but I'm happy to come to you. I'm just grateful for your help.

Dani: No worries, that's what the group's for. It's my night off too if you fancy combining it with a drink that would be very civilised!

Tilda: Civilised is my middle name! The Boat House at 7pm?

Dani: Perfect. See you there. I'll bring my laptop and ping any other documents we might need first.

Giddy with excitement, I headed to my wardrobe, jammed with unworn work clothes, still wrapped in plastic and eager to start their new life. Swathes of them. Grabbing a pair of silky culottes and a body suit, I laid them out on the bed. *A chilled glass as a girl gets ready is one of life's pleasures. One I've been deprived of for too long.* Almost without conscious thought, I found myself throwing on joggers and practically sprinting down the apartment steps. A cheeky glass of fizz – worthy of the occasion – from the lovely wine shop was needed. A toast to my business success and pending exposé of the IVF world. Maybe they'd make me a dame or something. And all this pain would be worthwhile.

Freshly coiffed and stepping out into the crisp early evening, I wobbled precariously on kitten heels. The prosecco had gone straight to my feet. Still, if I had front loaded, that was fine; I'd be working, not drinking, for the next few hours. The fizz would add creative flair to my writing.

I'd met Dani only twice before. She'd joined the group late but seemed to know what she was doing with her business, oozing confidence and vision, ahead of most of the group, many of whom were still floundering like me. Dani had also got into town early and had a couple, so we were level pegging by the time I joined her. The Boat House is a funky establishment. I'd been there once with Edwin a long time ago. It wasn't cheap, but I recalled Edwin observing, 'unlike some of the clientele'. He could be droll sometimes. When he wasn't being a twat.

Dani was equal parts party girl and capable entrepreneur. Between us we quaffed the prosecco that inexplicably landed on our table but still managed a good hour working on my template, with Dani taking control of the keyboard. Through a combination (lots) of copying and pasting from other documents, we were able to lay down the bones of Nurture's strategy. Oh, the relief.

'Dani. You're a star! I owe you a drink. Several!' I stated, searching for my purse. 'I, however, must be careful. My threshold is low, and the spirit is keen. A dangerous combination!' I laughed.

'It's a school night for me too, so it won't be a late one. But we *should* celebrate a little!'

Taking care to save and back up the document, I zipped my laptop back into its case and we headed to the next bar. Dani knew the new owner and figured we'd get some freebies. My oesophagus prickled at the thought. I'd make sure to drink plenty of water when I got home. The bar buzzed with energy. Dani knew everyone, introducing me as her 'friend and fellow entrepreneur', which made me sound far more interesting than I felt. Her people were lovely, really welcoming. I wondered fleetingly if I'd dipped a toe into this kind of world sooner, would I have even considered IVF? Not a comfortable thought. After Mother's death and finally leaving Edwin, I had been so lonely. Had a baby just been a solution to my loneliness? Had Jenna been right? Sipping my second free glass of fizz, I swatted the thought away.

I definitely had my laptop as we left the bar. I remember clutching it tightly, proud I'd remembered it through my wine haze. And I remember tucking it under my arm as I took in concrete steps to a neon-lit basement bar.

'The best juke box in London!' Dani shouted above the music and dragged me over to select some tracks. I had flashbacks of dancing around handbags and laptop cases, old school style. There were more drinks, but I'm not sure what they were or who ordered them. Shots, I do remember. A group getting rowdy. Or was that us? Dani dancing with some weird guy, off his head. The toilet bowls. My lovely culottes spattered with saffron-coloured vomit. I crashed hard against the toilet door, hitting my head. My phone rang.

'Hello.' I was able to accept the call but couldn't make out the caller in the semi darkness, my eyes refusing to focus.

'Tilda?' It was Ellie.

'Ellie!' I tried to sound sober.

'Where are you? I've been trying to reach you for hours.' She was tearful.

'I can't hear you. Ellie?' What time was it? I had no clue. The basement reception was poor; she sounded like a robot. The robot continued briefly, then broke up altogether. I willed the phone to reconnect.

'This is important,' I told myself sternly, aware of the immediate need to function. The cubicle began to spin, and again I retched violently into the bowl. Wedging my backside against the side of the cubicle, I closed my eyes, resting my head against the cool cistern. I would find my feet. I would go upstairs and call her back.

'Anyone in there?' A rap at the door vibrated through the cubicle, sending shooting pains through my skull. And again. Trying to speak but unable to, I attempted to rattle the door in response. *Don't leave me locked in here.* An angry voice demanded I open the door. Slowly I slid back the latch. A Rottweiler in female form scowled down at me.

'We closed. An hour ago,' she barked. How long had I been here? She opened the door quickly and I tumbled from the cubicle, landing heavily on the flag floor. Rottweiler steered me past the sinks and up the stairs like a rag doll. Breathing deeply, I tried hard not to vomit, but a violent pain shot from my stomach, strongly suggesting I might.

Ellie. I didn't call her back. Waves of shame swept over me. I could bear being led from a toilet an hour after closing. I could live with being abandoned by my new friend. What was unbearable was knowing that I hadn't sobered up and called a clearly distressed Ellie back. Next level shame: was Ellie okay? Did she need me? Was Rosa okay? Phoebe Rose?

Rottweiler was calling a cab. 'Where to?'

The address that sprang to mind was an old Manchester address. I began to recite it like a lost child. She rolled her eyes and asked again, shaking my shoulder hard. 'I need an address.'

I don't recall the journey home, but it was lengthy. The first two cabs refused to take me when they saw the state I was in. Lord only knows how they got an address from me. I had a recollection of Doorman Stan receiving me as I was ejected from the taxi. Like the gentleman he is, he accompanied me in the lift, propping me in the doorway while he fetched a spare key. Did I imagine Vic's fat face looming in his doorway, poking his oversized nose in as always? I remember being sensible, drinking a pint of water when I finally got into the apartment. And the subsequent trips to the toilet as it came back in instalments.

'Please leave a message. Rosa and Ellie will call you back.' Her voice sounded far removed from her distress last night. 10 a.m., 11 a.m., noon. Between vomiting bouts, I tried. I must have been spiked. All those free drinks, shots and other non-legal freebies. Oh, it was bad. Why wasn't Ellie picking up? Worst-case scenarios tore through my hungover head. All of which I completely deserved.

Staccato rapping burst through the apartment. Moving carefully, I reached the door, sick bowl at the ready.

My stomach muscles contracted as I heard Rosa babbling away outside the door. I braced myself. Rosa sat in her buggy and Ellie had Phoebe Rose in a sling. She looked terrible.

'Ellie. I am *so* sorry.' I opened the door wide and attempted to explain. 'I was spiked. I've been so ill. I passed out.' I knew I looked rough but not as bad as Ellie. Her hair was dishevelled, eyes red rimmed, yesterday's crumpled outfit.

'I'm so sorry you were ill,' she said sarcastically. 'Rosa was *really* poorly yesterday. We've been at A&E all night – in fact, that's where we've come from now.' Her voice shook with rage.

'Is she okay? What's the matter?' Rosa sat in the buggy, babbling, looking flushed but not obviously unwell.

'She had a seizure, Tilda.' She started crying but backed off when I tried to hug her. 'Not now. It was terrifying. They're ... doing further tests.' Tears fell angrily down her face.

'And the last thing you needed was Phoebe Rose in tow. I'm so very sorry. How did you manage?'

'Well, I took care of *your* daughter while the doctors took care of mine. I couldn't be with her because I had Phoebe Rose with me.' Her sobs became louder. For theatrical effect, Phoebe Rose joined in. Ellie unclipped her and unceremoniously handed her and the overnight bag over.

'Can I do anything? Can I have Rosa while you get some rest?'

'I don't think there's *anything* you can do now. It was last night that we needed you.' She chewed her lip awkwardly, refusing to meet my eye and swivelling the buggy round.

'If you change your mind, please shout. I'm truly sorry. I really was spiked, you know.' How pathetic I sounded.

Ellie strode angrily towards the lift. The buggy wheels caught the contents of someone's randomly discarded breakfast, sending coffee and pastry flakes flying. I could not have felt more wretched.

Lana

'Can you explain what you were doing in Tilda's bag?' We'd only just closed the car door. Wan looked incredulous.

'Truthfully, I don't know. It was completely random. Maybe I thought I'd find something incriminating?' I shrugged. 'She's odd, Wan. Isn't she? Something more than weird about her.'

'What did you expect to find? Drugs? A flask of gin? A knife? This is madness. She's a bit odd, Lana, a bit uptight, but we have no reason to believe she's crazy or dangerous. Seriously, what were you looking for?'

'I don't know. I just thought I'd nosey. She's so skinny. Do you think she uses amphetamines?' Wan rolled his eyes skyward. 'What I did find, though, through cunning and enterprise, is the name of her business. I found a tax letter. Ironically, the business is called Nurture. Not that she'd know anything on the subject. What on earth do you think she does?'

'I've no clue. Christ on a bike, Lana, so what?'

'Well … I know our solicitor said we weren't to disclose our addresses, and obviously I'm not going to give her ours, but we can find hers. Through Companies House. If it's the same one that I've just seen.' Wan didn't look remotely enthusiastic about the idea.

'She's hardly likely to have her home address listed, is she? I don't. I have the accountant's, not mine.'

'Well, I'll find out right now.' I began loading the Companies House website, but the internet kept dropping.

'I don't understand, Lana. How will finding her address help matters? Are you planning a kidnap? Shall I sort fake passports and flights to Brazil?'

'Now who's being ridiculous? I just thought if we could see her in her own environment, we might feel more comfortable about who she is. What she does. This is Stevie's life here; her future depends on this. And please know I'm not being manipulative, but you need to hear this. I don't know how I will cope if we lose Stevie. I love Phoebe Rose and want to be her mum, but I can't promise what I'll do if … I don't know if I can …'

The words hung in the air. Wan looked wounded. Wordlessly placing his head on the steering wheel, he sat for the longest time. The circling traffic warden eventually knocked and pointed at his watch. The prick. We drove home in silence.

***

'I knew it was a London postcode.' I showed a disinterested Wan the Companies House search result. 'Just because she attended the Manchester Clinic doesn't mean she lives there. She has a London solicitor too, so that would make sense. How can I check if it's her address or someone else's? It could be an umbrella agency or, like you said, her accountant's.'

'What would Scooby Doo and the gang do in this situation, Lana?' Wan mocked.

'Velma would get right on Google Maps and Freddie would be so supportive!' I said pointedly.

According to Google Maps, the address looked to be in a residential area.

'This looks promising; it's an apartment block. Posh part of London. Bloody hell, I knew she'd have money, but ...' I whistled through my teeth.

'It could still be her accountant's address, or a friend or business partner's.'

'It could, but it's a start. Nothing us pesky kids can't figure out,' I replied in an impressively realistic Velma voice. Stevie chuckled and I was forced to continue my terrible cartoon accent until she'd exhausted her laughter.

'Listen. We need to think about this. We can't afford to end up looking like the bad guys. Stalking's an offence, you know. This is exactly why they don't allow an address exchange.' Wan knew he had zero chance of changing my mind.

'I'm not going to stalk her. I'll just make some discreet enquiries. I'd hire a private investigator if we had the money.'

Wan shook his head and escaped to his cupboard/studio with a beer. Stevie and I busied ourselves scrutinising stills from Google Maps, cross-referencing them with Google Earth. Somone had serious money.

'Jodie, how long is it since we went away together? We used to do weekend breaks all the time. How did we get so boring?' I whined. Jodie had just returned with Stevie from a trip around the park. I was consumed with my 'Tilda info finding obsession' and was currently looking at accommodation close to her address. Even if it didn't end up being Tilda's home, it wouldn't be a wasted trip if we got a break from it; at least this was how I was rationalising it to myself. I was economical with the truth with Jodie. I knew she wouldn't approve of my amateur sleuthing, so I failed to include it in the weekend itinerary I was mooting. Of course, I'd sworn Wan to secrecy or probably between them they'd have banned me completely.

'*I* didn't get boring. I go away with my other friends all the time. It's just you, all loved up in your domestic bliss, who became boring!' she teased.

'Guilty!' I agreed. 'What do you think? I've found a Groupon deal – an undoubtedly mediocre hotel in a crappy area that's almost affordable.' I swiped through the options on my phone. *Everywhere's so expensive in London.* Like us, Jodie was always skint.

'What, just me and you? No Stevie?'

'Course I'll be taking Stevie. But we can still have fun. She'll love it. And she'll behave, won't you, Kookie Koala?' She didn't respond, as she'd nodded off mid-feed. 'I can't express enough milk for a whole weekend and won't leave her otherwise. And besides …' Every moment was precious given our situation.

'Why London? You hate cities.'

'Trying to embrace new things, darling. Thought a bit of culture would be good for Stevie,' I lied, cringing. 'I'll keep on looking, but I don't think I'm going to get much cheaper.'

'Just book it, Lana – let's do it. Wherever's good.' The unspoken timeframe was looming.

***

We had just finished delicious Thai food from Spitalfields. Jodie had had a few glasses of Chablis, as well as a couple on the train journey. I seized the moment to enlighten her regarding the additional itinerary items now that we were safely in London.

'Jode.' I tried to keep a neutral tone. 'How do you fancy tomorrow afternoon a bit of sightseeing, just you and Stevie?

This sounds random, but I've a few things to do. Just for an hour or so.'

Jodie stopped mid-chew.

'What do you mean? What things?'

'Promise you won't get mad?'

'That depends.'

I quite deliberately topped up her glass before I spoke.

'So, I have an address. I think it's Tilda's. I want to have a look, see for myself what the neighbourhood's like ... maybe I'll glimpse Phoebe Rose and Tilda living their best lives. Maybe Tilda's completely different when we're not around. Maybe she's a wonderful mother and I can stop being paralysed with anxiety when I think about Stevie being in her care.'

'Lana, that's mental and you know it. The solicitor specifically told you: no exchange of addresses. For this reason. As an aside, it's also a bit rich to pretend you want a weekend away with me when that isn't the case at all. Actually, Lana, no, I'm not going to help. Because I don't think it will – quite the opposite.' She looked furious. 'You've lied to me all this time! You must have been itching to disclose the real reason for our "cultural excursion", but you thought you'd lob the bomb after I'd had a few. Or maybe tomorrow morning there'll be another update. The whole weekend will become a stakeout and the touristy bit's a complete front.' Jodie wasn't happy.

'You're making this sound a way bigger deal that it is,' I argued. 'In my defence, I *did* want to come away for a girly weekend.' *One half-truth or two, what's the difference at this stage?* 'The timing just meant that if it was London, we could kill two birds with one stone.'

'Killing birds with stones isn't what I came for. I'm here to do cheesy tourist things with my friend and her baby.' She and Wan share the same exasperated expression when they disapprove of my behaviour; it's almost comical. I'm careful not to smirk.

'That's fine. I'm sorry. If you don't feel comfortable, I can come back midweek. No biggie. I don't even have to stay over.' I eyeballed the waiter for another bottle and tried to look genuine.

'*What* are you hoping to achieve?' Jodie shrugged at me, looking incredulous.

'I don't know. Maybe if I saw Tilda in her own environment, I'd be *reassured* she's not this vile cold fish, which is all I see when she is with the girls. The thought of handing Stevie over to her is making me physically and mentally unwell. If I thought she'd love her, it would make this easier, but it's like she has no maternal feelings whatsoever. Certainly not towards Phoebe Rose – it's heartbreaking. It's like she sees Phoebe Rose as inanimate, like a doll. On one hand I want to speed up the process so I can be a mum to Phoebe Rose, but in the same breath it's my worst outcome, because it means I have to give up Stevie in the process. It's like some horrific biblical conundrum. The whole "wise King Solomon chopping the baby in half" nonsense.'

'And what if you see something worse? What if you see her shouting, or ignoring her, or being physical with her? You'll lose the plot!'

'Well, if there was anything that bad, I'd film it or something. I could hand it over to the solicitor. But I'm probably not going to, am I? I'm hoping for peace of mind – that I'll see her being amazing with Phoebe Rose, loving her, taking her to the park, just like I do every day with Stevie.' *Half-truth number three. I'm such a bullshitter. That isn't what I hope to find at all. I want to find any excuse to find her unfit.* Jodie looks suitably sceptical.

'It doesn't make sense. But nothing about this situation does, does it?'

'Do we get to wear full camo gear? Tell me you've brought your old TA uniform!' Jodie giggled.

'If it's a deal breaker!' I laughed, relieved. *I bloody love this girl.*

'But seriously, Lana. Don't lie to me again.' Jodie drained her glass, and I could see from her expression how much I'd hurt her.

Finally I could be honest with her. 'I won't. And truly, I'm sorry.'

***

The day started early, not least because Stevie, without blackout curtains, woke at dawn. Tower Bridge, Big Ben and other dull must-sees filled the morning. I was desperate to begin the afternoon sleuthing. If the address turned out to be the accountant's, I would be more than deflated. Not done but deflated. How would I find out whose address it was? I needed a strategy. Why I was so confident that things would fall into place I'm not sure, but I had little option than to travel hopefully.

'So, the Brownstone Development has a concierge system. Which means it's off-the-scale swanky. No offence, but we're going to stick out like a sore thumb.'

'Listen to yourself with your northern chip on your shoulder. You could be an eccentric millionaire for all anyone knows,' Jodie offered, acknowledging the wafty kaftan and sandals I was sporting.

'I look eccentric, do I? Well, that's good to know!'

'You know what I mean. It'll be full of all kinds of people. Even northerners. Just pretend you're swimming in cash. At least someone looks the part, anyway!' Jodie jiggled Stevie's stripy leg jutting from her carrier. Her best outfit for the occasion, bought by Jodie.

The building was impressive – polished floors and a spectacular entrance; the door guy even had a posh dress coat to greet you. Which was unfortunate if you wanted to discreetly sidle in there and dart up the stairs to flat 725. I had a half-formed plan that, if challenged, I was concerned about a friend I'd been trying to get hold of. Which wasn't far from the truth. I really didn't have the people skills for this – Jodie would have been much better but not nearly as determined or open to deviance. It wasn't her children at stake. Catching sight of myself as I strode into reception, I reassured myself; I looked wealthy and eccentric rather than badly dressed.

'Stan', according to his name badge, was the epitome of the twinkly eyed grandad. If there was a single female resident and baby in and out of reception, he'd have noticed.

Adopting the look of concern I'd practised in the greasy hotel mirror a few hours ago, I began.

'Hello.' I grinned, nervously stepping forward, having waited patiently behind a painfully slow delivery guy. 'I wonder if you might be able to help, please?' My expression was deliberately anxious.

Stan gave me his full attention. 'I will certainly try, Madam.' He beamed.

'I'm trying to get hold of my friend. I don't live here. I live the other side of town,' I gushed. 'It's a bit delicate, actually.' Lowering my voice, I moved in slightly. 'She's had a bit of a tough time recently, and I'm beginning to worry, because she's normally really good at returning calls.' I took a moment to mist up, allowing his paternal concern to kick in.

'I'm sorry to hear that,' he offered, looking genuinely concerned. 'I've worked here almost forty years and fretted about residents of this building like they are my own family. But they care about me too. We're just a big blended family!' He was like an extra in a B-movie, manna from heaven.

'I shouldn't have come over. She would hate a fuss. In fact, you know, she'll be so embarrassed.' I hoped my nervous rambling would add to my authenticity. 'I was just passing and thought I'd knock. It's fine; I'll try her again on her mobile. She's not that long had a baby. Probably up to her eyes in it. Sorry to have bothered you.' I moved from the counter and misted up again. 'Please forget I was here.' I grinned weakly.

'Miss, if you're worried, I can be very discreet. When you've worked here as long as I have …'

'If I could just give her a knock, that would be amazing.'

He deliberated. 'Can I leave your details for her to contact you? I'm not supposed to let anyone through without a fob.'

I hadn't thought this far ahead.

'No. She'd be uncomfortable with that. I'll just keep messaging. Can I ask? You probably know her; she's lived here for some time.' I was blagging, obviously. 'Please don't feed it back, but she's a single mum caring for a small baby on her own. She's managed amazingly well. But the last few weeks have been difficult. It's Matilda Asquith-Hyde – Tilda to her friends. Do you know her?'

'Tilda? Of course I know Tilda! And her daughter – what a beauty!'

'Isn't she? You mustn't say anything, but how does she seem to you? In the interests of the baby, of course.'

Stan looked compromised. Bless him.

'I just really need to know that the baby's okay … and Tilda, of course, but without looking like I'm interfering …'

'What's your name, Miss?' he asked gently.

'Wendy,' I blurted. No idea where that came from.

'Wendy, if I tell you this, I'm trusting you'll receive it in the right way. As a friend of Tilda's?'

'Hand on heart. I have only Tilda's and Phoebe Rose's interests here.'

Stan lowered his voice and moved in despite us being the only ones in the vast reception; his moustache was clogged with dandruff that couldn't be seen from a distance. A queue was forming behind me, but his attention was all mine.

'It's been tough. How could it not be, a baby on your own? When my daughters had their babies …' I willed him not to enter grandad ramble mode. The possibility of exposure should Tilda pass through reception was terrifying. I steadied myself on the mahogany desk.

'I've seen her come through some difficult times. You remember Edwin? She's made of strong stuff. But to be fair, I was worried. After the baby was born.' *Keep going, Stan.*

I nodded knowingly and empathically.

'I have had concerns and so has her next door neighbour , Vic. They did seem friendly, but he doesn't have a good word to say about her now, but I think he's a little harsh on her. That said, the last few weeks, she's seemed more like her old self. No, better. I don't see as much of the baby now she's back working, although – and please don't quote me on this, but last night …' His eyes rolled. 'She was in a hell of a state. The baby wasn't there, thankfully, but I don't think I've seen a girl as drunk in many a year. And I've seen some things in my time—'

I cut in. 'Poor Tilda. It's so hard on your own. Probably just letting her hair down. But the baby wasn't there, was she? Are you sure?' My stomach clenched violently.

He nodded. 'Probably why you couldn't get an answer this morning. I doubt she'll be up to visitors right now. No, the baby was at her friend's overnight.' His expression remained concerned.

'If anyone knows how to take care of a hangover, it's me!' I laughed. 'I'm time served! I'm going to nip over the road, grab some coffee and pastries and give her a knock, if that's okay. If I don't get an answer, I'll leave the bundle at the door with a note. At least she'll know I was thinking of her. Give me ten minutes.' Giving Stan no opportunity to decline, I made for the exit. For someone with few people skills, I'd done a sterling job.

Jodie and Stevie were feeding geese on the edge of the lake at the side of the apartment block. As I approached, the enormous geese honked angrily. Stevie seemed strangely at ease with the terrifying creatures, hungry for the loaf they were doling out.

'It's *her* place,' I whispered, delighted that the address had not been that of a third party. I updated Jodie with Stan's information, a queasy feeling growing in my stomach. Jodie rolled her eyes as I outlined stage two of the plan – casing Tilda's flat.

'Her neighbour is concerned. God, Jodie, she sounds unhinged. Everything I feared. She's never there with Phoebe Rose. She's a drinker. I knew it.'

'So. She likes a drink when she doesn't have care of her child. And your problem is …?'

'No, you didn't hear him describe her, Jodie. There's more – there must be. I *need* to speak to the neighbour.'

'How the hell can you do that, Lana? It's mental to even try. What if you're rumbled? She'll call the police! I would!' I was already walking away. Nothing Jodie could say would stop me. The geese escalated their efforts to regain the bread, pecking aggressively at Jodie's heels. Stevie squawked as loudly as the birds, desperate for Jodie to cast more bread.

'I'll be sensible. In any case, I think you're in more danger from this lot than I am! Be careful with my daughter!' I shouted, adrenaline racing through me.

Loaded with hangover refreshments, I strode once again through reception. Brazenly tailgating into the lift, I beamed in Stan's direction. My heart hammered as we rose through the floors. If Tilda were to appear – hopefully the hangover would prevent that – I had no clue what my defence would be.

Tilda's flat was the second one across from the lifts, but which side was 'concerned' Vic, left or right? Even the hallway was ridiculously plush. I'd only seen places like it in films, let alone stepped inside one. I halted momentarily. The flip-flop of emotions, wondering what my biological daughter's life might have been like surrounded by wealth; the contrast with our car-crash finances without even a hope of becoming homeowners.

Trying hard not to spill the coffee in my trembling hands I walked past Tilda's door and tried to casually see if there was a name on either of the neighbours buzzers. No such luck. Making my way to the end of the corridor I tucked the food parcel and coffees around the corner. I'd just need to take a punt. With hammering heart I knocked gently on the door to Tilda's right before I chickened out completely. Why hadn't I thought what to say? I need to speak to a guy called Vic? But why? Could I pretend to be a Mormon spreading the gospel? How would that help? I could have a delivery for Tilda. Holy fuck, *think*. A dog barked inside.

'Hello.' I smiled pleasantly at the Basset hound and his owner who appeared in the doorway. Guy and pooch looked expectant, which was reasonable given that I'd just knocked their door. *Don't panic*, I told myself.

'Hi. I'm Jeannie from the Brownstone Building Committee. I don't think we've had the pleasure.' I reached out my hand. (Jesus, my lying tongue seemed ever looser.)

'I'm still pretty new, I guess. I'm Vic.' He pummelled my hand vigorously. 'And this is Eric.' Thank God he seemed the friendly type.

'Well, Eric, aren't you a beauty?' I leant down, reluctantly fussing his mangy ears. 'I had Bassets as a kid,' I lied smoothly. 'The most loyal pets!'

'Aren't they just? He was a rescue. Can you imagine, the most loyal breed in the world abandoned by his owner?' Vic reached down and placed his hands over the old animal's ears. 'We don't talk about it now. It's all behind him!' he said in hushed tones.

'A very warm welcome from the Brownstone Building Committee. We're a large accommodation provider but pride ourselves on being personally invested in each of our residents.'

'Not sure I've heard of you before, but I've been made to feel very welcome so far.'

I grinned inanely, looking expectant, desperate to leave the doorstep, where I might be recognised at any moment.

'Would you like to come in?' I quickly stepped inside.

I was the queen of small talk. I was interested in his job, his previous house moves, his revolting on-the-verge-of-death dog; I was all things to everyone. 'So, have you joined our community activities or been to the residents' section of the restaurant? We have so much going on,' I enthused.

'I keep to myself, really. It's lovely that there's a community vibe, but I'm not looking to make new friends.' He smiled awkwardly.

'I understand.' Bringing my voice down, I leaned in slightly. 'I am aware that you had a small concern regarding a neighbour, which will remain *completely* confidential. I spoke with the concierge, who mentioned that you had raised an issue. I'm just checking that you were happy with the outcome – that it had been resolved. The last thing you need in your own home is neighbour angst.'

'Uurgh. I suppose that's okay.' Vic flushed slightly. 'It's fine. I think it's been dealt with. I wouldn't have mentioned anything – God knows I've had my share of parties and been a pain-in-the-arse neighbour to many, I'm sure. I'm usually very "live and let live", but when the safety of a child is at stake, well, I couldn't not get involved. God forbid anything happened.'

'I'm sorry?' I stuttered; had I heard him correctly?

'You said that you knew about the complaint? Stan and I were concerned?' Vic looked puzzled.

'I deal with a large number of queries and disputes. I'm sorry, I didn't get chance to review the case notes on my computer before I left. Stan just mentioned it again now downstairs. That you'd had a problem.' Trying hard to steady my voice, I leaned heavily against the sofa arm.

'Well, there hasn't been anything since things came to a head about a month ago, but I don't think she's at the apartment as often now. I certainly don't hear the baby as much as I did. It *was* awful. I'm not paternal by any stretch, but her cries went on for hours!' I tried to still my visibly shaking legs.

'How awful. So not a regular noise nuisance, then? The neighbour has a baby?'

'She does – I don't know, a few months old now, I think – she's small, anyhow. I really wrestled with it. I know babies cry, and, with respect, the apartments don't have the best sound insulation, but I swear Tilda wasn't even getting up to her in the night. The whole block would hear, but not her own mother! One night it went on for hours and hours. I was clear, if I heard it again, I'd be contacting the authorities.'

'And these details were logged in your original complaint?' I felt lightheaded to the point of fainting. 'Could I trouble you for a glass of water, Mr …?'

'Vic, of course. Mr Vic!' He laughed and headed to the kitchen. 'I'm sorry. If you're a mother yourself – and I don't know if you are – it's probably difficult to hear.' He passed me the water and I sipped slowly, hoping he'd add further detail.

'Was she harming her? That must have been horrific to hear.'

'No, I just think she was out of it. She wasn't waking when the baby was. Lord only knows how – or she was deliberately leaving her, I don't know. I think on the night I became involved she'd been drinking.' Vic gestured a tipple with his hands.

I fucking knew it.

'But you didn't report this to the authorities? What about your duty of care?' Vic looked taken aback at the switch in my demeanour.

'I did my citizen bit, thank you. I hope you're not accusing me here, because—'

'I'm sorry.' Swift revert to friendly mode. 'No. It's just shocking to hear. Did you say there haven't been any further problems?'

'I let her know I was on her tail. Anything else and I would alert the authorities. And there hasn't been, so hopefully she's got her act together. I'm watching, though – the slightest hint and I'll act, don't worry. If you do want feedback, though, I can truthfully say that I've never lived an apartment block with such poor noise insulation. It's the worst! I can even hear when she steps out of bed, it's that bad. That's how I knew she wasn't getting up in the night.'

'Vic, would it be okay if I checked in again with you in a week or so? Obviously, we more generally look out for residents' concerns relating to the building; however, we wouldn't expect you to shoulder a safeguarding concern on your own. If you could jot your contact number down for me to save me having to look up your records, I can give you a call to check in case anything else comes up.' I couldn't ask for his number, because my hands were shaking so much, I wouldn't have been able to write. It was all I could do to steady my trembling legs.

'You know what, I don't feel comfortable with that, Jeannie. No offence. It's sorted; I'll speak to Stan if anything else comes up. I don't think I've ever been part of a building who are so interested in their residents.'

Vic held my gaze, and I thought for a terrible moment he'd seen through me. Was he being sarcastic?

'Of course. Confidentiality is important to us, and I would ask that you do not feed back to your neighbour about our discussion. If you do have further concerns, please don't hesitate to let Stan know. We will support any next steps.'

He looked directly at me again. 'He'll be the first to know.' My paranoia was now raging that I'd been rumbled. Vic waved from the door. I barely managed to hold off vomiting until I'd rounded the corner of the stairwell.

***

I couldn't stay another night. I needed to get home to Wan. Poor Jodie. She decided against staying the last night on her own, probably doubting my emotional ability to get safely home.

'But Stevie's only glimpsed the culture!' Jodie mocked, frustrated but thankfully understanding, considering what we'd learned in the space of a few short hours.

Jodie held Stevie until she fell asleep, rocking her to the rhythm of the train. I was too upset to hold her, desperate to protect her from my distress. I hadn't updated Wan that we'd aborted the trip but landed back home unannounced. Wan's distress was every bit as acute as mine as I detailed what I'd learned from both Stan and Vic. We held each other and sobbed.

'The thought of our daughter being in her care right now is unbearable, she needs *me*, her mother,' I sobbed into his shoulder. 'No wonder she clings at contacts! I can't bear it. Fuck!' I shouted. 'I should call social care right now.' It was all I'd thought about since leaving Vic's.

'And say what, Lana? That you have third-hand information that around four weeks ago a baby cried at night and a neighbour commented? But it's been okay since. And incidentally, you're heavily invested in this because the child is actually your daughter. And you've initiated an illegal investigation into a woman you're also engaged in a legal battle with.'

'The event is on record somewhere. Surely that's evidence?'

'Of what? That a baby cried. A neighbour complained. No further issues.'

'You're not listening! What about Stan's story? She was practically unconscious last night!'

'And she'd made provision for her daughter to be elsewhere. Had she not?'

'Fuck, Wan, why are you always so "reasonable" about everything? This is Phoebe Rose we're talking about!' I yelled, beginning to cry all over again.

'Lana, I'm as concerned as you are. I'm just being realistic. Or maybe you're right and we call it in now? I don't know.' Wan and I held one another, sobbing quietly. 'I don't have the answers, any of them.'

Stevie was thankfully still asleep in her buggy. She'd slept through supper, and I prayed she'd stay that way as I carefully lifted her into her cot. I never wanted her to glimpse our distress. The desire to protect her always was juxtaposed against the awful question: *How much longer can we do that?*

Tilda

I deserved every shred of the shame that sat heavily on my shoulders. Ellie was the only good friend I had. Ever really had. She had been *amazing* to both Phoebe Rose and me throughout our ordeal. I could barely look at myself – even my reflection in the microwave door made me wince. I was a despicable human. I felt bad about the girls; they'd no doubt have been upset, and poor Rosa really distressed and needing her mum when she was so poorly. But the worst of my shame was how I'd treated Ellie. Losing her was more than I could bear. She would *never* have done that to me. What could I do to make amends? A horrific thought occurred to me. Had I ever been anything other than a financial support to Ellie? I'd taken so much from her, but what did she get back from me? Had my only offering been material? I had showered Ellie with gallons of exquisite wine, delicious Harvey Nic's food. I had treated Rosa to streams of clothes and toys. I'd paid her well to look after Phoebe Rose. Maybe she would accept an apology, if only so she didn't lose that? *Who am I fooling? Ellie is the most genuine person I know. Money would not cut it for her.*

Phoebe Rose continued her low-level whining from the floor, where she'd remained in her chair for most of the afternoon. Maybe Ellie would take pity on Phoebe Rose – could that be my 'in'? Phoebe Rose adored Ellie; in fact, I think Ellie would have had custody of her too if she could. It was just me that lacked the maternal gene. The possibility that I was every bit as selfish as my mother had suggested sat there. The thought washed over me – not for the first time in recent weeks – that both Stevie and Phoebe Rose deserved so much more than me. Maybe the solution was simpler than I was making it.

I texted Ellie again; I was going to go to the doctor. I couldn't stop vomiting. Untrue, but I certainly felt wretched, probably guilt-related rather than a hangover. Could the doctor give you something for that? Just the antidepressants I was already on. Dani hadn't messaged. Some friend she was, new or otherwise. The girl code always stands; don't leave each other on a night out. I messaged her anyway, fleetingly anxious that she'd gotten in a worse state than I had. I was *trying* to be nice.

Why, if things were heading in the right direction, was I so royally fucking things up? The 'one foot in front of the other' approach should be working, yet here I was taking five back. God, I needed Edwin. He would know what to do.

'Enough!' I said aloud. This was dangerous territory. I needed to remind myself on a loop: I only missed the *thought* of Edwin. The reality was spectacularly annoying, and in the grand scheme, he'd cheated me out of my shot at normal motherhood.

I found myself miserably reading the last text exchange we'd shared. It had been the morning of the funeral. Edwin had headed into town to get a paper and a bakery loaf. I was having major outfit hysteria. Garments were strewn all over the bathroom like we'd been ransacked. I'd snapped a pic of my current outfit and sent it his way.

Me: Too much?

Were the feathers overkill? I feared that Mother would feel compelled to make an announcement at her own funeral. That she'd gain access to a heavenly Tannoy – one last pop at my outfit before she was off to the great orgy in the sky.

Collie Vomit: You look divine. You are divine. Glad you're mine x.

Why had I removed the only consistently supportive person from my life? I wiped away angry tears and tried to focus on the job at hand. As impossible as it was, I reminded myself that Edwin was an arsehole.

The weather was depressingly drizzly and windy, my mood worse. Strapping Phoebe Rose into her buggy, my head throbbed as I bent to buckle her in. I hurried from my apartment with no destination in mind. Anywhere but my blame-filled walls. My phone vibrated, offering short-lived hope. It was neither Ellie nor Dani. It was the Edwin-likely number. My thumb hovered over the missed call symbol. Was I so low that I would play the proverbial dog and return to its vomit? I cast my mind back to the last time I'd felt this lonely, gravitating back to Edwin because nobody else wanted me. I couldn't imagine that Stevie would want me. My own child. Tears streamed down my flushed cheeks as I strode up the Heath. An image came to mind. A lovely roaring fire – Edwin always had the knack of knowing when I needed warmth, and not just physical. He'd light a fire – irrespective of the weather or temperature – and open a lovely bottle of red. We'd bring down the duvet and watch an old film. When everything seemed shitty, Edwin could make it less so. The halcyon haze I looked through had blurred his edges, made him bearable. If I called him, would that be so terrible? It would feel awkward at first, but maybe I was just meant to be with him. Sixteen years on and off is a long time. I didn't feel that I could trust myself to call in case it wasn't him. The idea that *maybe* Edwin cared was just about keeping me afloat at that moment.

'Fuck!' I yelled, abruptly halting the buggy. Phoebe Rose was hearing far too much of that word. I punched my head hard with my closed fist. My laptop! Where was it? I hadn't seen it in the apartment before I left. Had I parted company with it during the carnage of the evening? It could be in any number of bars, toilets or taxis. Quickly U-turning the buggy, I headed back down the hill. Sod it. The call of the wine shop was too strong. Hair of the dog was needed not a serving of Edwin flavoured vomit. Literally, alcohol was my only constant and solution.

***

The sense of relief was fleeting. Ellie's text was lengthy but it's tone from the outset clear. Phoebe Rose lay in her cot, still wearing her day clothes but dozing lightly. I wasn't drunk but weak; the Viognier had robbed me of volition completely. If Phoebe Rose woke, I would not be able to tend to her. I was done. I would have to wait for Vic to appear. Maybe he would break in when he could bear her cries no more. Or I could instead end the process right now. No more court, no more solicitors, no more pretending I wasn't an alcoholic who thought it was a good idea to have a baby.

Tilda. I see your missed calls. By now you will be realising that I won't be picking up to you. I can't see you anymore and by extension poor Phoebe Rose. Without being cheesy, this isn't about you. It's about me. I can't let you – or anyone else – hurt me or Rosa again. I've never found it easy to make friends, I think I told you that. Growing up, I was always on the edge of someone's group without there really being room for me. I think that's why I took all that shit from Jed for as long as I did. Like you with Edwin, I was lonely. I've known in the past that friends have used me. I used to think I was the token 'fat friend', and I'd take that if it meant not being on my own. Other than size, though, I don't know that much has changed. Or maybe I'm just happier in my own company. I'm not sure. I'd never been anyone's 'bestie' until we became friends. I genuinely thought that's what we were – or were becoming. But no, you've used me only to let me down when I needed something in return. You will never know how much that hurt me.

The problem is, even if I forgive you, I can't trust that you won't do it all over again. Only there might not be enough of me left to carry on if that happens. The only person I will be trusting is Rosa, and I realise how sad and isolated that sounds. Please don't update me regarding Phoebe Rose. I love your daughter – irrespective of whatever words you use to describe her – and the pain of that decision is almost unbearable. However, I need to prioritise my mental health so I can carry on being the best mum that I can for Rosa. I worry for Phoebe Rose. She needs so much more than you are giving her, even in this temporary time frame. I hope in time Phoebe Rose gets all the love she deserves from her birth parents. I hope your own daughter completes you and that you will find happiness. I'm sorry if this feels sterile in a text, but I don't know that face to face I could communicate this. The hurt is almost unbearable. Take care. But please don't contact me again.

***

It's not new for me to struggle to piece together an evening or sequence of events, but quite how Edwin ended up in my apartment, pacing the floor with a swaddled Phoebe Rose, I genuinely could not account for. Ellie's text hit me hard. Shame and guilt jostled for centre stage as I battled to quite literally not nosedive from the balcony. I'm not sure what happened in between. It was probably just as well. But I was correct, the mystery number had been Edwin. If it had turned out to be a persistent 'had an accident, not your fault' sales person, with no interest in rescuing an alcoholic that could no longer care for her baby, then things might have ended differently.

Was that the Cub Scout song? Ging Gang Goolie? There was only one person I knew who ever hummed that song. From my supine position in bed, I saw a slimmer, more sober version of Edwin than I remembered. Was this a dream? My life had become so surreal recently, it was hard to know. Edwin moved slowly across the floor, humming and tracking a strange circuit that I worried would annoy Vic.

Bits from last night were missing. Had *I* called Edwin? Or did he call me? Either way, here he was.

'Edwin,' I whispered, half expecting him to disappear before my eyes. He turned, humming softly while patting Phoebe Rose's back. I buried my face in the pillow, unable to take in the scene. Why did everyone have the caring gene but me?

'How are you feeling?' His tone was hard to place, unfamiliar. Almost paternal?

'I'm okay. Thank you. For coming ... Edwin, did I call you?'

'Thought you might be hazy on recall.' Edwin half smiled, but the stress line that appeared when he was anxious darted across his forehead. He looked leaner. And older. 'Yes. I have thirteen voice messages that you can listen to when you're sober if you like.'

I cringed, able to listen to only the first two. Not even a memory jolt. I must have been hammered. A pang of guilt shot through me as I wondered how on earth I'd been able to care for Phoebe Rose during that time – clearly I hadn't. Had she woken? I pulled the duvet over my head, ashamed again of my appalling behaviour. And my neediness. That I would reach out to Edwin; that he was the only human in the world that I could call.

For the first time since Phoebe Rose was born, I allowed myself to cry. Properly cry, wailing pitifully into my pillow. Because for the first time, there was somebody there to cover, someone who knew me of old, who knew my addictive weakness and how easily I caved. I sobbed – for me, for Phoebe Rose, for Mini-

Tilda, for Lana and Joel, for Ellie and Rosa. And for the car crash that my life had become.

Lana

'Thank you for seeing us at such short notice.' Wan and I took our seats. Mrs Jennings cooed briefly in Stevie's direction and, much to Stevie's delight, again placed the dodgy paperweight in her eager hands. 'I was about to call you, actually. We have an initial hearing date from the courts. It arrived this morning.'

'Well, that's timely, because we have information to bring to the table too, and we will be led by you as to the best way to progress this.'

Mrs Jennings did not try to disguise her incredulity when I shared the details of my unethical behaviour in gaining Tilda's address.

'I specifically told you—' She looked furious.

Before she could get into full venting mode, I jumped in. 'I hoped not to "catch her out" but be reassured that she was a good mum. I didn't set out to frame her or influence this. I'm just letting you know what I've learned, and it's concerning.'

Despite what Mrs Jennings was hearing, her expression did not alter. An angry red flush travelled up her neck.

'Should I have recorded it in some way? I only thought about that on the train home. Why does she even want a baby? Why is she pursuing us for Stevie? She clearly has zero maternal instinct or desire to nurture.'

'Lana, you could have seriously jeopardised your case here. I thought I'd made it clear.'

'I couldn't just wait though, Mrs Jennings. I don't think you understand. The waiting is killing me.'

'I can't imagine how much this must hurt Lana, but this isn't a helpful move you've made. Even if we were to use this – and I'm not suggesting that we do – Tilda's solicitor will counter that it's the pressure of the situation that's driving this. He will argue that when she gains custody of her own child, her care will be completely different – that she will be more than able to meet her needs. And the "evidence" that you have, Lana, is third party. Purely hearsay. It's certainly nothing that would reach a safeguarding threshold based on the report of a one-off crying bout and Tilda being intoxicated while she's arranged appropriate care for her daughter.' Mrs Jennings looked weary, even older in that moment than her advanced years.

I was completely deflated. What did this geriatric know anyway, giving unsafe items to my daughter to play with? 'If you don't feel that you can help us, Mrs Jennings, then we probably need a second opinion. A fresh view …' My voice cracked, and within a moment I had dissolved into a pool of tears, head in hands.

Wan and Mrs Jennings allowed me to cry. The more reasonable Wan picked up.

'I'm sorry. Lana is completely shell-shocked,' Wan tried. Mrs Jennings nodded imperceptibly and turned her gaze to the papers in front of her. 'It just feels off. Like we should be able to do more,' Wan said calmly, rubbing my back as I continued to sob. 'How do we challenge this? You'd feel the same if it was one of your children in similar circumstances.' A bold statement for party line Wan.

'If I had the same attachment you clearly have to Stevie I'd be doing everything, legally, that I could to avoid relinquishing her and getting access to the child I should have. Tilda does not have that same attachment to Phoebe Rose but will fight just as hard to get Stevie in her care. She's invested a lot of money in her legal representation. It's just as well I'm better than her representation despite charging a fraction of his costs.' She smiled but looked weary. Sighing heavily, she finally gave me eye contact. I hoped she wasn't defeated.

'We need to think tactically. I've not had a client before who has so recklessly flouted rules. If I use the information you've given, it could look worse for you. We may have to think creatively about a version of the truth that doesn't involve your rifling through Ms Asquith-Hyde's bag and casing her address.' Mrs Jennings seemed to be rallying with a burst of positivity that I could not be more grateful for, despite my dressing-down.

'This might sound really random.' Wan was attending to a fussing Stevie – no doubt responding to the tension around her. 'Does Tilda *want* to gain care of Stevie? Is there not room for further exploration of that? Would she do a deal or a plea bargain – I don't know how you'd describe it? Does she need to save face but doesn't actually want Stevie?'

'She hasn't bonded with Phoebe Rose, that's not up for debate, although this doesn't imply a lack of care. She will assume that attachment will develop naturally when Stevie is in her care rather than a lack of maternal drive. I haven't had any indication of such from her solicitor. I could raise this if you like; I'm just unsure how it will be received, no matter how sensitively we approach this. But at this stage, we can challenge any aspect of the case and look at all options. And should.' Mrs Jennings began to scribble on her notepad, suddenly energised again.

Through the office window, I saw what looked like a mother and baby group chatting in the park, babies staggering comedically like drunks. I imagined taking Phoebe Rose and Stevie to our baby group. It felt dangerous to even think of such a thing.

Mrs Jennings stopped writing and looked pointedly at me. 'I need to tell you that Tilda's solicitor has enquired about overnight stays for both girls to reduce the impact of separation over the next few weeks.'

'Stevie's not going there overnight.' I aid emphatically. My anxiety rocketed at the very suggestion. 'How can we agree to that, knowing what we know? Obviously we don't want this to look like a bribe or a threat, but if we voice safeguarding concerns which are then corroborated by Stan and Vic, she could end up losing both girls and contact with either of them.' I literally couldn't help myself; I was on a loop.

'As I've just stated, there's no firm evidence of an insufficient level of care. However, given *your own* actions, you could end up losing both girls for stalking and potentially sabotaging contact – in your *perceived best interests of the children*. It's all very messy, without any precedent other than the babies being returned to their biological parents. But that will not necessarily stop us from trying.'

'Obviously, our ideal is that we gain custody of both girls. We don't even want money from her, although God knows she has enough. I guess if we must agree to some contact for Stevie, then maybe that's something we can live with providing we don't lose custody of her.'

Mrs Jennings nodded, making noncommittal noises and continuing with her indecipherable scrawl.

I returned to the possibility of Tilda not wanting either child. Looking desperately from Wan to Mrs Jennings, I said, 'Can *we* speak to Tilda about this? Would it seem less threatening coming from us?'

Mrs Jennings looked uneasy. 'My anxiety – if you raise this at all – is that she could accuse you of intimidation – that you've behaved unethically and in breach of the arrangement that has been put into place to protect you all. It could get tricky. But if there is any possibility that you could come to an amicable arrangement, then now's the time to explore it. Delicate does not even cover this.' Mrs Jennings's gaze reminded me that I had already overstepped the line.

'We're damned if we do and damned if we don't,' I stated flatly.

'Don't do anything immediately. Let me have a think. I have a colleague I'd like to run this by. I'll try to get back to you before the end of the day tomorrow. Irrespective, the court date is for two weeks' time. Can I advise you, Lana? For what it's worth, again – do *not* engage in any further breach of the legal agreement. It is in place to protect all of you. I don't want my client exposed as a stalker, hiding in the bushes of the esteemed Brownstone Building. You might not get away with it next time around,' she scolded, keen to rule out further rogue behaviour.

***

Somehow a version of life continued. I tried hard to remain on the planet for the children's sake. Wan and I were struggling, although neither voiced it to the other. Caring for Stevie was overwhelming. I had no surplus energy, emotional or physical, to give to Wan. Jodie tactfully tried to take Stevie to give us time together, which made it worse. She'd call in on her way home from school around 4.30 just as I was coming round from an afternoon nap. I'd pretend not to hear the door, but she'd persist. Such an annoyingly caring friend. She'd make us both a brew and watch Stevie while I sorted laundry.

'Sit,' she instructed, placing the brew in my hands, and joined me on the sofa. 'What can I do, Lana? Seriously, I feel useless. Do you want me to have Stevie for an evening? I could even do a sleepover here. You two could get away for a night or something.'

'Jode, don't take this the wrong way, but when you mentioned that to Wan last week, my heart sank. All we ever do when we're not around Stevie is mull everything over and then fall out. I *loathe* his optimism, and my pessimism is driving him under. You know he's started running? Reckons it's helping. Spending shedloads of money we don't have on overpriced footwear.'

'Wan running?' Jodie laughed.

'You tell me. Where's that come from? I'll tell you where. It's his way of having a go at my weight. It's nothing to do with coping. It's so he can be holier than thou; a silent but significant dig at my … whatever this is.' I gestured to the bulk under the fabric of my joggers, sitting low beneath my belly. 'He had a right go at my cooking last week. Breaking news: shepherd's pie is now off the menu. The carb/fat ratio is a big no-no. He's even drinking "Lite Beer"! I ask you!'

'Now that's messed up,' Jodie agreed.

'It won't work, because the more he pushes the health thing, the more I eat. On principle. I can't even go for a walk with him and Stevie in the pram without him trying to turn it into some aerobic workout. He's driving me nuts, Jode.' I was only just managing to keep my tears at bay.

'So, what have you been up to, or is it really just wall-to-wall misery?'

'Well. Seeing as you've asked. Every day is shit. I wake every morning faced with the challenge of survival. Negotiating a series of hurdles before I can either get back under the duvet or obsessively research botched IVF debacles when Stevie's asleep. I try hard for Stevie, but it's a front. Breakfasts. Dinners. Bills to pay – or not, as we're now on reduced maternity rate. Attending Sing and Learn group, pretending we're absolutely fine. Tolerating Wan's off-the-scale-irritating parents. Avoiding going to my mother's, because that's awkward too. Afternoons are punctuated by an online bank balance check. Maybe a trip to the ATM for a cash uplift on the credit card if the account has gone overdrawn. Sometimes you stop by, Jode, which is lovely but also excruciating, because I don't want you to see me like this. I don't want anyone to see me like this.'

She looked at me blankly. Poor Jodie. Still, she listened.

'When you stop by to take Stevie around the park, Wan looks so hopeful, it's painful – or he did for a while. Maybe we could 'use the time' for a quickie, but no. I've pushed him away so much, he's stopped asking. Or if he does, I'll pick a fight so there's nothing on the cards. I'm a regular bunny-boiling bitch from hell. We're spectacularly miserable.'

'How's the IVF debacle research going? Anything Mrs Jennings could use in your defence?' Jodie had obviously heard enough about the reality of my existence.

'If you're asking if I've found any cases like mine where there's a happy ever after, that would be no. I haven't found a single incidence of a child – or children – whose identity has been confirmed resulting in anything but a return to their biological parents.' I exhaled loudly, exhausted by my own circular ranting.

We let the words sit there. I wasn't after reassurance or platitudes, and Jodie was wise enough to know that.

'What's the deal with going back to work? How long have you got left?' Jodie asked gently, daring to move the conversation forward.

'I'm supposed to go in for a meeting with Lynda next week, but I don't think I can.'

'What – you'll delay going back or go on sick? What's Wan think?'

I shrugged, trying to keep my default angry tone from creeping in. 'Jode, with respect, what the fuck does it matter what Wan thinks? It's *me* that's got to go back and face everyone, not him. What is it with everyone worrying about Wan when it's me that's dealing with the brunt of all this?'

Jodie leaned over and orchestrated a toy reshuffle for Stevie, who was growing tired of gnawing the corner of the Very Hungry Caterpillar board book.

'I worry about both of you. You know that. In fact, I'm worried about the two of you in a way that I never have before. Yes, and being single, I'm in no position to offer couple's advice …'

I was about to jump in, but Jodie put her hand up and stopped me.

'Just listen, then you can speak. You've always held each other up – like a pair of crappy roller skaters, propping one another up when you need it. But you aren't letting Wan pick you up. You're falling and refusing his arm no matter how hard he tries. And I'm gonna name it, seeing as that's where we are. You've hit bottom before, and I can't bear to see you there again.'

Jodie's tears threatened to brim over as she rummaged for a tissue.

'It's shitty, yes. But I've got a child to care for. Even if we lose Stevie – and I cannot imagine anything more painful – I'll have Phoebe Rose to care for. I'm not going to kill myself, if that's what you mean.'

'And who's going to care for Wan while you're in self-preservation mode?' Jodie asked gently. 'Because you aren't helping him by blocking him out. He is grieving. Just in a different way to you. While obviously being a sanctimonious health prick!' she added.

Fresh racing commentary started downstairs. I didn't have a response. Like the wise and loyal friend that she was, she'd said her bit, and I might at some point begin to process some of it. Moments later the key turned, and Wan, mid phone call, saluted a hello to us all – back early from his meeting and heading straight to his studio. His smile was fleeting and aimed squarely at Stevie, who enthusiastically beamed back.

***

Evie's birthday loomed. I'd tried to reflect on Jodie's observations, although she couldn't possibly put herself in my position. Nobody could, which smarted, because I thought I was doing an amazing job of simply existing. However, I decided that rather than marching on with Evie's birthday (or Death Day, as I named it last year) plans, I would see how Wan felt about things. Walking through the park on the Thursday before the court hearing, I raised it. I was trying to be nice. I didn't *feel* nice – it was incongruent, but I figured better than nothing.

'I don't know. Last year was pretty grim: you, me and a cake. I think our grim quota has been exhausted this year, don't you?' Wan looked sad. And thin.

'Our cup of grimness has truly runneth over,' I agreed. A light grey drizzle fell, to Stevie's delight. I quickly pulled her rain cover down as she tried to catch the raindrops as they landed. She screeched loudly, prompting me to peel back the cover and let her enjoy herself. In the grand scheme of things, it was just a little rain.

'Do you really want to know what I think, Lana? And I don't mean that in a difficult way. Just that Evie's birthday will be another reminder. A loss. I know we've remembered her birthday for the last two years, but I'm not sure I can go there after all that's happened. That said, I worry that whatever I say or think just gets your back up, so if you need to do something, just crack on and do it. You know I'll be there.'

We continued to walk. That was fair enough.

'The last thing I want to be is difficult, Wan. I know I've always been the vocal one. A bit "my way or no way". That kind of worked before. Maybe it's the teacher in me, I don't know.'

'Or maybe you're just a bossy cow?' Wan grinned. Turning to me, he reached out to pull me inside his jacket. Stevie saw and made the heartfelt 'aww' sound we use when we cuddle her tightly.

'I'm sorry I've been such a bitch, Wan. I just don't know what to *do* with my feelings. I struggle to be remotely positive about this shitty situation. It doesn't help that we're keeping this between us. I don't know. It feels like a time bomb that nobody else knows is ticking. No wonder we're losing it.' This isn't new territory in our well-worn dialogue.

'It feels like we've enough on, with court next week and whatever else follows, to think about Evie's birthday.'

'Maybe if we had something to focus on other than this it might be easier? Surely it couldn't be worse. I don't want a party or anything. But something – a walk or even a few beers, I don't know. I would just like to *feel* something other than this. Which is crushing me by the day.'

'Talking of "feeling" things …' Wan laughed and held me close.

'I know. You might as well be in a relationship with a nun. At least a nun might talk dirty to you – if God wasn't listening!'

It felt good to be held after pushing Wan away for so long. We probably looked ridiculous, the ever-shrinking Wan trying to encircle my ever-increasing bulk.

'Part of it is that I'm reaching seismic proportions. I don't want you to see me like this. I don't really enjoy demolishing family sized bags of crisps and boxes of biscuits,' I whined. 'It's just kind of become a habit.'

We both grinned wordlessly at the 'habit' pun. Lovely Wan. We were almost back at the house.

'Everything just feels so futile. I literally feel helpless, like I'm going through the motions of normality, but it's ridiculous. I'm continuing every day, putting one foot in front of the other, and for what? I'm going to lose Stevie. I can't even say the words without feeling like I've been punched in the stomach.'

Wan nodded solemnly as we walked. The situation hadn't changed, but it felt good to be able to name just how wretched I felt.

***

'All rise for the court.' I'd been to crown court for school purposes, nervously giving evidence in the context of parental neglect. I was relieved in family court to be spared the wigs and shenanigans. Wan and I had dressed as 'upstanding parents', whatever they were. I wore my tired school flats, dark pleated skirt and a poorly fitting polyester jacket – just accommodating my size. Wan had on his funeral suit, which he'd 'transformed' (not) with a pale blue tie. Feeling every bit the poor relation, I tried to focus on the task at hand; this was about Stevie and Phoebe Rose. All they needed from us today was to help the judge arrive at the best outcome for them. Even if I'd already selfishly decided that. I needed to remember that this was also about Wan. Since Jodie's gentle dressing-down, I'd been trying hard to move out of 'moody cow' mode. It wasn't easy.

Tilda looked uncharacteristically flustered. She had someone different with her. An older guy. Stevie would be disappointed. I hoped that, without Ellie, Stevie would fuss if we were able to meet after the hearing. I looked forward to seeing how maternal the Ice Queen would prove herself to be without her sidekick. Phoebe Rose looked as beautiful as ever and immaculately, if stuffily, dressed. Her tufty curls were captured far too tightly into pigtails close to her scalp. My stomach contracted as I took in her demeanour. I squeezed Wan's hand tightly, urging him to look closely at our girl. The older guy held her close. Was it unfair of me to be suspicious? He looked like a drinker. Was it Tilda's father? His ruddy complexion contrasted with Phoebe Rose's skin tone. The guy looked across with interest at Stevie. I glared until he looked away. A paedophile until proved otherwise.

There was some back and forth between Mrs Jennings and Tilda's solicitor, Mr Dreyfuss, his shiny gold cufflinks competing with his cosmetic smile. They stood before the judge like a comedy duo. Spiffy and Fleabag. My gaze kept returning to Phoebe Rose, trying to pinpoint exactly what worried me. There was no spark. Her eyes were dull, no sign of inquisitiveness despite her surroundings. She hung limply from Possible Paedophile's arm rather than curling into the cuddle she usually craved. Was she ill? Would we have the right to know if that were the case? The judge looked impatient, and Mr Dreyfuss's body language suggested he wasn't at all happy with what was being said. Mrs Jennings looked unperturbed. She'd been at this much longer than her opponent and wasn't about to blow over anytime soon.

'The court will adjourn due to some ... *oversight* from the counsel. We will reconvene in thirty minutes.' The judge beckoned both solicitors to the bench. Did I imagine that Mrs Jennings looked slightly smug as she stepped forward? My heart skipped with hope. We filed out and left the three of them talking animatedly, the judge's tone clearly unhappy.

As we gathered awkwardly in the foyer, Tilda spoke first.

'Shall we grab a quick drink – speedy baby exchange?' She looked towards Stevie. 'My friend would love to meet the fair Stevie.' Tilda beamed, but I raged at her insensitive words. The 'fair Stevie'. What the actual—?

Wan joined the queue while we found a table and organised the infant exchange.

'Is Phoebe Rose okay, Tilda?' I felt her chest under her elaborate jacket. 'She feels hot. She doesn't look right at all.'

'She's fine,' Tilda said dismissively and focused on Stevie, holding her aloft, her fair hair illuminated by the neon bulbs hanging from the ceiling of the hipster café. I held Phoebe Rose close and whispered into her tiny ear: Motherese, words only we could hear. Without asking permission, I removed her jacket, a ridiculous velvet affair with a starched Peter Pan collar. She was radiating heat, an angry weal at the nape of her neck where the collar had been rubbing. How could I bear to see Tilda's neglect? It was torturous.

Stevie, to my horror, was giggling at the creepy man's efforts to entertain her. He stuck out his fat tongue, which she thought was hilarious. Tilda glowed. I busied myself showing Phoebe Rose the book we'd brought for her – *Baby's Busy Day*. Babies of different cultures, universally bound by parental love. Phoebe Rose snuggled in as we read, her eyes darting from the book to my face as she listened, finally breaking free from her stupor. Phoebe Rose possessed a stillness – and not just today, when she was clearly off. A presence far removed from Stevie's boisterousness. A kind of reserve that I hoped was grace rather than neglect. I thought of the *Amazing Grace* book I'd read to my nephews and nieces so many times. Tears brimmed, but today I'd promised myself I would keep them in check.

The question that Wan and I dared not ask hovered. Seeing Tilda today with this guy and their obvious delight in Stevie made me feel it wasn't one we could ask at all. *Of course she wants her. Why would she be jumping through these exhausting and expensive hoops if she didn't?*

Tilda leaned in, nodding her thanks for the coffee.

'Lana, Joel, this is Edwin, my friend. He will be an important part of Stevie's life, so I'm introducing you,' she stated formally.

My stomach churned. 'Where's Ellie?' I asked, hoping it would remind Stevie that a key member of the party was missing.

Selfish, I know, but maybe she would fuss and keep this old man at arm's length. 'And Rosa. How are they doing?'

Tilda's pause made me query the honesty of her reply.

'She's good, thanks.' Tilda glanced quickly at her watch and commented on the time, clearly closing the conversation down.

My stomach churned as Edwin reached over and grasped Phoebe Rose under her dress. 'Does she need a nappy change, Tild?' he queried. Wan and I exchanged mortified glances.

Tilda shrugged without even looking Phoebe Rose's way.

'Edwin, do you see me in her at all? I do try to play down that she has my mother's nose!'

Edwin made a 'good luck with that' face and Tilda laughed loudly. They were more than friends.

Edwin had taken Stevie over to the enormous fish tank that sectioned the tables from the lounge area. He tapped on the glass and encouraged Stevie to do the same. Ignorant twat. He made a face like a fish and Tilda laughed even though he looked more horrific than amusing. I couldn't help myself and took Phoebe Rose to the opposite side of the tank.

'It's important not to bang on the glass, Babba. It gives them a headache,' I said pointedly.

Even through the murky glass I saw the eye roll from Tilda and the muttering that followed. Edwin placed an arm on her shoulder, a sneer across his purple, possibly (definitely) paedophile complexion.

Phoebe Rose's eyes were heavy lidded, barely focusing on the fish. I loosened her collar further. I'd tucked a piece of tissue against the weal on her neck, hoping to reduce her irritation.

'Time we were going,' ordered Tilda, nodding in our direction for an infant swap.

'Aw, Babba, you don't seem yourself at all. I hope you feel better soon.' Reiterating my concern, I kissed Phoebe Rose's plump cheeks and reluctantly handed her to Tilda. I really couldn't let it go.

'Well, she's not fussing or whining, so in my book it's all good,' Tilda stated brusquely, giving Stevie a squeeze goodbye and proffering her to Edwin for a final kiss. I looked away, nauseous. No tears today for me – my simmering anger was holding them at bay. Tilda seemed interested in the older guy's response to Stevie. I didn't like anything about this guy's vibe, not at all comfortable that he might be someone close to Stevie. I couldn't help where my mind went thinking about an older guy with a younger woman and his interest in her child. More fodder for my tortured mind.

Reconvening, we listened as Judge Sullivan described 'last-minute' parent concerns that ought to have been brought to her attention prior to this morning. Tilda stiffened visibly. Wan and I looked at one another desperately. Had Mr Dreyfuss found out about my undercover trip to London? I tried to calm myself, remembering Mrs Jennings's body language and expression earlier. Instead, Judge Sullivan began citing legislation and described feeling uncomfortable with the polarised perspectives of the solicitors. Mr Dreyfuss was pushing for compressed contact and an accelerated exchange. Mrs Jennings, referencing developmentally sympathetic research, was suggesting a longer period of adjustment in the interests of the children rather than the parents – whom Mr Dreyfuss had been accused of prioritising. But she had mentioned parent concerns? Had Mrs Jennings somehow communicated our doubts or queried Tilda's attachment to Phoebe Rose? While she couldn't explicitly identify the source of these, further assessment might buy us time and ultimately expose Tilda's lack of investment and emotional availability.

'On the matter of extending the period of transition, I am left with no choice but to take the recommendation that where doubt exists around one or both party's ability to meet the needs of the child, then transition timeframes remain as such until the completion of capacity occurs. Furthermore, in line with *Kalmar v. Drake* 2017, I will request psychological evaluation of both parties, which should be returned for my attention prior to the next hearing. I expect these to be completed at least fourteen days before the next session to allow for my timely review, particularly given the polarised views of both parties.'

The relief was overwhelming. We had been granted a stay of execution. What had Mrs Jennings said? I was beyond grateful. Without further comment, we were instructed to stand as the hearing drew to a close. No overnights, no unsupervised contacts. Surely we would sail through our assessment; hadn't Dr MacKinnon said as much? The doubt was excruciating. Had we read this right? Was the concern around Tilda rather than us?

Tilda quickly got to her feet and scooped up a startled-looking Phoebe Rose. Her face was furious. Mr Dreyfuss followed in her wake up the steps. Wan and I hugged unashamedly, and Stevie clapped her hands excitedly, joining her parents' delight. The others strode from the courtroom. Mr Dreyfuss ushered them into a side room.

Wan and I beamed at Mrs Jennings, but her attention was focused purely on Judge Sullivan, whom she was trying to engage as she prepared to leave the bench. My tears threatened, but I fought them back. *Dwell on the here and now. Don't you dare water those seeds of doubt.* Wan and I made our way to reception. Tilda's response to this development wouldn't be hard to predict. She'd be raging. The gloves would well and truly be off. We were desperate for contact with Phoebe Rose today but could not see how that would work now. Tilda would surely see us as her enemy rather than parents trying to get things right. In any case, Judge Sullivan had stated that contact would now need to be supervised. Knowing Phoebe Rose was so near made it unbearable. I longed to hold her close.

Mrs Jennings had asked us to wait in reception until she'd spoken with Judge Sullivan. If Mrs Jennings had somehow raised our safeguarding concerns around Tilda's care, how would Tilda respond? Could we still play nice? Would she demand my head on a platter before the next court appearance? We were torn between willing Tilda to appear with Phoebe Rose while we waited and willing her not to. Fifteen minutes and still there was no sign. We roamed reception, playing a hushed version of the Stevie Loves game. Our new and improved version now extended to 'Mama loves' and 'Dada loves' – much more interesting and developmentally supportive of other perspectives.

'Dada loves …' I began.

'Mrs Jennings,' Wan filled in, and we laughed loudly. Stevie joined in, clapping her approval.

'Mama loves Stevie, Dada and Phoebe Rose!' Wan sang. It was all too much. Grabbing the buggy, I installed a now over-excited Stevie, and she and Wan skidded exuberantly down the length of the deserted foyer. It was a small win in the battle, but stalling overnights and unsupervised contacts was surely a triumph. The psychological reports were another hurdle but hopefully one that would work in our favour.

Stevie and Wan were mid turn when the formidable figure of Tilda appeared in the corridor, closely followed by her harried-looking 'friend'. Phoebe Rose looked immediately excited, but it was short lived. Tilda quite deliberately removed her from our line of sight.

'Tilda, can we arrange the next contact while we're here – get some dates in the diary?'

She would have continued walking had I not spoken. Stopping mid stride, she looked furious. Glancing at the expensive-looking timepiece dangling from her bony wrist, she offered no eye contact.

'We're rushing for a flight. I'll text you.'

'Going somewhere nice?' asked Wan, trying to keep things civil.

'Home,' she replied curtly. Without a glance at either us or Stevie, she strode off. Phoebe Rose's cries echoed up and down the corridor from her car seat, dangling from Edwin's arm, Tilda indifferent to her distress. What would this do to our daughter? What damage would be happening? The magnitude of the question was impossible. We had fought for a longer transition period, buying us time to allow the cracks to appear in Tilda. But at what cost to Phoebe Rose, desperate for a mother's – or, frankly, anybody's – love? And if our worst fears were realised, what horrors might be in store for our precious Stevie?

Tilda

Edwin said his goodbyes at the airport. He told me he was staying the night in Manchester, then heading to France in the morning. Seeing a friend, he said. I was grateful he'd supported me today, but it was obvious that there was little left between us.

The business lounge was teeming. A kind steward found space for us and brought toys over for Phoebe Rose, no doubt picking up on my teetering mood. Leaving Phoebe Rose in her baby seat, I placed a stuffed toy in her lap. She simply gazed at the bright bunny apathetically. I figured she was as disillusioned as I was after today. As I settled myself onto the exquisite leather couch, the young steward brought over a well-deserved complimentary champagne. Sipping the honey-coloured drink from the delicate glass, I exhaled loudly. I congratulated myself. I was holding it together. Somehow.

I allowed myself to process. What the fuck? What about my views? So we were to have a protracted transition, and all because of the over-protective Lana. Where did my needs come into this? *My* need to start afresh, to care for my own flesh and blood, not someone else's. It was unbearable. So, the defence had requested a psychological evaluation for me. Dean had alluded to information from the defence that he wasn't able to disclose that had prompted a concern. Fuck me sideways. Yes, I'd had some issues – some fairly recently – but surely the progress I'd made with Nurture would outweigh any challenges I'd experienced – indeed, overcome? I took a moment to breathe. In. And out. The relentless scrutiny from Lana and Joel felt worse than ever. With each contact, the blaze of their silent condemnation wore me down a little more. Their judgement of me was vile, like they were willing Stevie not to like me, darting over the second she looked upset. It was horrific. I nodded for a top-up.

Phoebe Rose had drifted back off. I'd found if I avoided her gaze, she tended to do that. Hopefully she would sleep through the flight. The verge of not coping felt close. Eyeballing another drink, I promised myself it would be my last. Unless I could spend the rest of my life in this business lounge. Did they have a crèche?

I fleetingly wondered when the baby had last eaten or drunk. *Did she have something at the café? I think Edwin tended to her.* Somehow we had missed lunch getting through the airport. She'd survive. It was too much fussing that made babies demanding. Bloody Lana, suggesting Phoebe Rose was ill. I hated her default that I couldn't be trusted. *She probably thinks I'm not feeding her enough because she doesn't weigh in like Sumo Stevie.* Well, I'd be sorting that out as soon as I was able.

Phoebe Rose stirred as we boarded. My heart fluttered; could I find the energy to mother her on the flight? The rows were rammed. I could get neither business class nor a window seat and found myself squeezed mid row. Most unpleasant even for a short flight. The passenger to my right was a talker, her 'off' switch clearly faulty. It was relentless.

'Is she always so laid back?' The woman to my left joined in. Stereo.

'Look at her, just taking it all in. I've had four and none of them so chilled. How do you do it? What's your secret?' She laughed. I didn't respond for fear she'd try to talk at me through the flight. Maybe she'd think I didn't speak English.

Phoebe Rose gazed absently towards the window, although there was little to see but heavy cloud. The passenger to my right maintained her commentary for Phoebe Rose, describing all she could see (very little) and where we were flying. It was incessant. I felt beyond irritated. Even Phoebe Rose looked uninterested.

Did she look a little flushed? Loosening the buttons on her bulky coat, I debated when she'd last had a nappy change. Had Edwin changed her at the courts? She'd let me know when she needed it. Feigning interest in the duty-free magazine, I attempted to block out the droning neighbour's narrative. I craved the peace of the apartment. The last few weeks I'd been grateful for Edwin's presence. He hadn't stayed over beyond the first night but had propped me up, dusted me off and been supportive in a way I hadn't known he was capable of. It had all been very platonic. He'd held me without attempting a kiss. He'd supported me in getting sober and kept me that way, feeding me decent food and taking Phoebe Rose while I slept. It was all very fatherly. And disappointing.

Declining further drinks (but ordering carry-off duty-free tequila), I picked at the meagre mozzarella salad which had appeared despite the brevity of the flight. There was an offer to heat a bottle for Phoebe Rose, but I wasn't sure I had one.

As the plane began its descent, the cabin pressure quickly dropped. Phoebe Rose let out a horrific but short squeal of pain, then settled. I was grateful for a peaceful landing, the thought of my own bed and a small tequila.

The taxi journey again featured an overly chatty travel companion. Rav, the driver I've used for years, had endless questions. What was so fascinating about my business?

'Long time no sees!' he exclaimed, his English still poor after three years in the UK. He'd seen Phoebe Rose before but enthused like he'd never seen a baby before.

'Where's the boss? Where's Mr Edwin?' he asked, laughing, for no reason that I could identify.

'Edwin— he's ... we're ...'

What were we now?

The last two weeks, he had saved our lives. I hadn't enjoyed his sanctimonious scolding or ruthless disposal of my Grey Goose vodka down the U-bend. Which was probably why he hadn't stayed over. An evening was incomplete without alcohol for him, and clearly he couldn't imbibe around me. Edwin had been different from how I'd remembered him, like our connection had broken this time. I recalled the morning after he landed, his bewilderment at trying to process the image of a non-Caucasian infant in a crib and a woman barely able to look at her. I'd attempted to explain the extraordinary story, but Edwin's expression had indicated that he could not reconcile my behaviour towards Phoebe Rose, irrespective of how the situation had arisen. Why did no one believe that things would be different when I had care of my own child?

***

The apartment felt lonely. I turned on the radio, the station blaring a discordant jazz note, still tuned to Edwin's favourite channel. I lit candles and ran a bath, pouring expensive oil into the tub. My new life with my daughter felt close but so precarious. I might be exposed – humiliated, in fact – in court. The psychological assessment would probably be damning, and I would be left with nothing. Without Ellie, everything seemed flat. And futile. And what if, against the odds, I was granted care of Stevie? What if I couldn't bond with her either? Where the fuck would that leave me? Phoebe Rose remained tightly furled in her seat. Awake but silent. It struck me that she'd spent most of her day there. Had Lana been right? She did seem listless. Pulling her from her chair, there was none of her usual energy, her neediness. I placed her on her playmat. She lay completely still. Toys within arm's reach held no interest; her eyes were unfocused.

She must be hungry. In fact, we both needed food. The food/champagne combo had left me lightheaded. Not tipsy, but not on point either. I searched the cupboards for some formula. *Damn you, Edwin.* He'd promised to collect some but clearly hadn't. That was why I'd breastfed initially, to avoid this faffing. I offered boiled water and Phoebe Rose sucked furiously for a glorious minute, then fussed and batted away the bottle. She was too young for cow's milk, but what about diluted? I had oat milk; would that work? The thought of weaving my way to the shop under the critical gaze of Stan held no appeal. *What has she forgotten now? Or has she run out of wine?* Finding Phoebe Rose a sleep suit, I quickly changed her for bed. Her nappy was completely dry. Anxiety prickled. When had she last taken a bottle? *Did* Edwin feed her at the café? Her last definite feed had been at 6 a.m., before we'd left for the airport. I tried again with heated oat milk, which she again refused. Feebly arching her back, she whined pitifully. Maybe she needed space after being confined all day. The sound of cascading water came from the bathroom. I ran to the overspilling tub, swearing loudly. Grabbing towels, I attempted to absorb the pooling water.

By the time I'd returned, Phoebe Rose had crashed out on her mat. As quietly as I could, I plucked the bottle of tequila from the noisy duty-free wrapping. I could order an Uber Grocery delivery of formula: problem solved. Pouring a generous measure and taking the bottle for company, I headed for the tub. It had been such a long day. I'd order some formula after my bath. Dimming the lights, I dipped beneath the surface of the water.

***

Shattering glass ricocheted around the bathroom, jolting me awake. Fragments of crystal from the tumbler lay scattered across the porcelain tiles. The bath water was freezing, my teeth chattering. What time was it? A knot of pain gripped my stomach, followed by a wave of nausea, my oesophagus burning. I tried not to focus on the tequila level hovering just below the bottom of the label.

Phoebe Rose. Oh my God. The desire to vomit was strong as my mind backtracked. She'd been dozing on her playmat. I'd changed her into sleep stuff. It had been such a long day. Tears brimmed.

Stepping shakily from the bath, I dry retched. Grabbing a towel, I skirted the shards of glass and headed for the lounge, beyond terrified of what I might find. The clock, illuminated, showed 5.43 a.m. My legs shook violently with each step. Phoebe Rose remained on the playmat like a starfish, her small hands splayed. She'd gotten herself onto her back. A patch of vomit pooled at her side, her dark curls crusting in the bile-like substance. I leaned in close. *Fuck. Fuck. Fuck. Please be okay.*

Phoebe Rose was breathing. Faint and rapid but breathing, her skin clammy to the touch. With trembling fingers, I struggled to feel her temperature under her poppered suit. When I slid my fingers in between the poppers, Phoebe Rose emitted the same high-pitched squeal that she had on the flight. Only this time it didn't stop.

Reaching for my phone, I quickly dialled Edwin. *Please fucking pick up.* The dial tone continued. Edwin's voice rumbled down the phone. He'd call me back as soon as he got the message.

Grabbing a throw from the sofa, I wailed pitifully, pulling the French doors wide as the morning air rushed in. A violent pain struck, and a fountain of tequila-tinged fluid splattered a perfect arc against the balcony wall. I stepped out. The city was waking below. Early traffic and commuters. I used to be a person. I used to function. Kind of. The solution felt blindingly clear. Who would I land on? I would be a dead weight. The physicality intrigued me. The sound of my head exploding as it hit the pavement like a bomb going off filled my mind. The nothingness such an attractive option. No demands. No failure. No judgement. A solution just a moment away.

The exploding head sound was displaced by the persistent and piercing cry from the apartment. I couldn't even fantasise about suicide in peace. I made my way, slow motion, to the source of the sound; scooping up her small body, I held her close. Guilt can make you behave in strange ways. Edwin still wasn't picking up despite my speed dial efforts to reach him. The baby radiated a furnace-like heat.

'Right,' I commanded, still pissed. 'Call the doctor at 8 a.m. For now, a bottle.'

Then, like a terrible Groundhog Day, I remembered that we had no formula. Propping Phoebe Rose on my hip, I tried to comfort her to no avail. I tried again with the boiled water combination, again the relief palpable as Phoebe Rose fleetingly took the teat. It was short lived. Her eyes shot wide open, and her high-pitched cry resumed. Surely she would drink if she was thirsty or hungry? Could she even swallow? She would be so dehydrated. Could we wait for the GP, or did we need the hospital? How could I sit in A&E without vomiting? We could both have a vomiting bug! If the tequila fumes went undetected, that could work. My mind was racing.

'You are an idiot!' I shouted, landing my fist on the glass coffee table. Another sharp pain ripped through my stomach. Yellow-orange vomit dripped from the table and seeped into the ivory-coloured rug below.

***

Doctor Spencer looked ridiculously young. Her eyes accused me from the moment she began to examine the listless Phoebe Rose. Pinching the skin at the nape of her neck, the doctor's eyes widened. So many questions: what had she eaten/drunk, when was her last bowel movement? I could barely stand, let alone field her questions.

'I think I have the bug too. If that's what she has. We've both been ill. I've been vomiting all night.' I sensed that I would get little sympathy from this medic.

Doctor Spencer nodded her head – disbelief or contempt, I couldn't decide. She continued her examination. Stripping Phoebe Rose off hardly seemed necessary, but she persisted.

'Do you think she might need a drip or something to pick her back up? She fussed all day yesterday, wouldn't drink at all.' Did that sound like I was blaming her? Still no response. The doctor paged a colleague and told – not asked – me to wait in the seating area. I held out my arms to take Phoebe Rose, but she indicated it would just be me who would be leaving the room. My unsteady legs delivered me to the cheap plastic chairs. Placing my head in my hands, I wondered for the myriadth time how this had become my life. And where the fuck it was heading. After the longest time, a stern-looking consultant strode from the examination room. Dr Spencer summoned me back in, her face a mask.

'Your daughter is severely dehydrated. We're admitting her now. She'll be placed on a drip and monitored over the next twelve hours. Why did you not bring her in sooner? She's clearly been unwell for some time, judging by her fluid levels. How could you have failed to notice?' The doctor sounded incredulous, refusing to meet my eye. I tried to speak but she cut me off.

'We'll be informing children's social care as a matter of routine. You can stay with your daughter on the ward, but under no circumstance must you remove her from the ward. A social worker will inform you of the next steps of the enquiry.'

'What are you suggesting, Doctor?' I was livid. How dare this *girl* accuse me of neglect? 'I've been unwell too, you know!'

'You can take that up with the social worker. *We're* now going to take care of your daughter.'

Phoebe Rose looked worse than ever, a noticeable decline even since we'd arrived at hospital. Her eyes were glazed; her small body sagged listlessly in the doctor's arms. If anything happened to her, would that mean I wouldn't get Stevie? Was that a terrible thing to think? I wasn't sure if that would be the end of the world or the best possible outcome. Still, there was always Plan B. The balcony nosedive.

Phoebe Rose was whisked away. I tried to keep pace with the gurney, conscious that I needed to keep my distance if the tequila were to have any chance of going undetected.

***

Hours passed. I sat at Phoebe Rose's bedside willing her to be well. I didn't pray but came close. The ward nurse agreed to watch Phoebe Rose while I spoke with the social worker, Mary. Mary, bless her burned out, retirement-countdown soul, was less scary than Dr Spencer. She swallowed my story of us both having a horrible bug. Clearly, if I'd been well, I would have responded differently. I hadn't realised how *quickly* she could deteriorate. Mary had been a single mum herself. She understood the challenges. I wept profusely and theatrically. I was devastated to learn that there would still need to be a Child and Families Assessment. It was standard procedure following any concern flagged by medical staff, but the news was a blow. This would surely come to the attention of the court. Would I look negligent? The kind but weary-looking Mary insisted it was just procedure, but I was hollow with fear, because, fuck, I really had been so negligent.

Mary and I looked in on Phoebe Rose. Thankfully, she was looking more like herself, managing a brief eyelid lift and a fleeting gummy smile. I held her tiny hand and she clung with the other, Babinski style, to my sleeve. My heart fluttered.

'Is there anything I can do to convince you that further assessment is not warranted? I don't think you understand how important this is to me.' The thought came to me in a blinding flash. 'My mother. She bequeathed money to the renal wing of this hospital. She still does through the Stand Foundation.' The cadence of my voice was high. Mary looked at me, confused.

'The hospital relies on the kindness of benefactors. She must be a very generous woman.'

'She is. Well, she was. Does that not count for anything?'

Mary looked at me, either unclear what I was suggesting or pretending that she was. She continued to pack her files away and left the conversation quite deliberately there. What was I thinking? Could I make this any worse?

Lana

The psychological evaluation was dreadful. A stranger asking the most personal questions was exposing beyond belief. It felt as if our future hung in the balance based on the interpretation of our responses, each one a potential grenade.

Wan and I treated ourselves to pub food on the way home, lacking the energy and the inclination to cook. Wan made an artform of sampling the craft ales, and Stevie made a new friend at the next table, a huge child squeezed into a highchair. Stevie loved everything about the pub we chose, an old favourite from our childfree days, although she ate more of the free wax crayons than her carrot sticks. We both felt too wiped to argue with her.

'Do you think the judge requested psych reports because he thinks *we're* unhinged or Tilda is?'

'Not much in it, really!' Wan laughed, relaxing into his ale. I couldn't disagree.

Stevie launched a crayon and laughed hysterically, which set us all off and spread like a Mexican wave to the next table. I wiped away the tear that was never far from my eye. My beautiful girl was now seven months old, becoming aware of her ability to beguile all she met. My heart ached with love and the horrific but looming possibility of losing her.

Wan and I compared notes and responses to the *very* personal questions the clinician had bombarded us with.

'What did you say about our sex life? I so wanted to tell him to keep his filthy beak out!'

'*Does your partner satisfy you?*' Wan boomed, a perfect mimic of the serious clinician. No extra charge for providing entertainment to surrounding tables.

'Do you think we came across as sane? I managed all the questions about childhood, parents, siblings – obviously with slight embellishment. You won't have had to, with your Henry Normal family. Did they ask about my "incident"?' I asked, lowering my voice.

'Yep. As rehearsed, I explained it was completely out of character and in the context of losing Evie. I don't think they're trying to catch us out, you know – just make sure we're in good enough shape to cope with what's happening.'

'Wan,' I breathed. 'I keep getting this awful feeling that Phoebe Rose won't want us. She's been so used to self-soothing, meeting her own needs – what if she can't love us? What if our love overwhelms her? I've been reading about psychopathy …'

'I'm going to need psychiatric help to deal with your catastrophising if you carry on!' I hoped Wan was at least half joking. 'To be fair, I'm actually amazed at how you've handled things over the last few weeks. Since court, I feel like I've got the old Lana back. Of course, it's a bonus that you've stopped being a psycho bitch with me.' Wan laughed.

The judge ordering the psychological reports *had* been the catalyst. I knew that presenting before a psychologist with low mood, overwhelmed and on sick leave would not work in our favour. I was also buoyed up by the possibility that Tilda's report might expose her difficulties. I was almost disappointed in myself for thinking that way, but there was far too much at stake.

'I told him how helpful Dr MacKinnon has been. I don't know what I'd have done without her.' Her requesting a phased return to work for me had made a world of difference to how I felt about going back. Although I wasn't sure about the timing of my return, three days before the next court hearing.

'You'll survive, and what doesn't kill you makes you stronger,' Wan muttered into his ale, then looked mortified at his choice of words.

I owned it. 'Unless, of course, it kills you – then you're just a goner.'

'I'm so glad it didn't,' Wan said softly, taking my hand just as the server arrived to clear our plates.

Tilda

Stan gave me a heads up. Our guest – Eleanor the social worker – was on her way up. After an eternity, the bell rang loud and long. Her unnecessary bell lean would not throw me. I steeled myself as the same strong South African accent I'd heard on the phone bellowed down the intercom.

'Mateelda Asquithh-Hyeeed?' the voice barked.

Smiling sweetly, I opened the door, Phoebe Rose on my hip, welcoming Eleanor into the apartment. The front room had had a child-friendly makeover; toys and baby paraphernalia were spread across the floor. It looked like a bomb had gone off – like Ellie's house used to, which she swore was the sign of a healthy parent.

Phoebe Rose clung to me, unused to callers. Eleanor and I chatted about the trials of central London traffic, and I shared some lesser-known shortcuts that I hoped she'd appreciate before we got down to business. I'd prepared a pot of tea and bought some luscious Florentine biscuits, which I hoped would win her over. She looked like she was fond of a biscuit. Or two.

Eleanor exchanged babble with Phoebe Rose, who lay among a sea of toys on her mat. I sat protectively beside her. Eleanor plucked a crocheted rainbow teddy and jiggled it in front of Phoebe Rose, who flapped her arms with excitement. Eleanor's almost brusque tone towards me was skilfully juxtaposed with her soft baby babble.

'I understand, further to a conversation with your solicitor – whom incidentally I thought a very rude individual ...' Common ground was good.

'I couldn't agree more, Eleanor. He's not a nice human.'

'... that your situation is complex. I need to understand how this may be impacting your care of Phoebe Rose, however long she remains here.'

'Complex is euphemistic, Eleanor, but thank you for the acknowledgement.'

Phoebe Rose sensed immediately that Eleanor was baby-friendly. She reached her small arms out, and Eleanor responded. Her oversized hands seized Phoebe Rose's tiny body and swung her skywards. The look of joy on their faces made me uncomfortable; I made my excuses and went to the bathroom. Yet another human with the ability to nurture. I returned to find Phoebe Rose sitting contentedly in Eleanor's lap, chomping on the exotic-looking pendant lying between her enormous breasts. Eleanor didn't seem to be concerned that a pool of saliva was seeping over her blouse. I took to the sofa. I might as well experience the third degree in comfort.

Attempting to condense the last six months into a coherent narrative was difficult. Phoebe Rose's babbling in Eleanor's direction was so loud at points that I could hardly hear myself think. Eleanor had no problem zoning between the two of us. She explained that she needed to understand how this 'one-off' medical incident was far removed from Phoebe Rose's day-to-day care. She kept harking back to the here and now, endlessly asking about my support networks, who my 'go-to' people were. Like it was a weakness to be independent. Maybe in other people's worlds there's a family queue ready to scoop up your bundle. Was it my fault that wasn't the case for us? I was doing Phoebe Rose a favour, sparing her from my horrible family. Surely it's better not to expose your child – or someone else's – to unsuitable family. Seems like you're damned if you do and damned if you don't. The ducking stool of modern social care.

There was no end to Eleanor's multitasking. She was now making notes. As she leaned forward to steady her laptop, she caught the edge of the tea tray with her left hand. In slow motion I saw the contents of the tray shunt sideways, teapot and cups leaking tea over the carpet.

'I am *so* sorry,' Eleanor declared. Relieved it wasn't me who'd almost scalded Phoebe Rose, I still struggled to contain my response.

'How?' I shouted before my brain moved into gear.

Eleanor looked embarrassed and shocked at both our behaviours. Phoebe Rose whimpered at the commotion.

Did this mean that I had 'something' on Eleanor? As a child protection social worker, she'd almost scalded my child. Or had I just completely overreacted to spilled tea? My brain was unable to land on which might be the case.

After I'd attended to the worst of the spillage, Eleanor picked up our conversation exactly where we'd left it. She'd used the time to update her notes. Phoebe Rose was now unperturbed and had made her way up Eleanor's sizeable body, trying to perch her head on her shoulder.

Feeling less certain than I had *prior* to the tea incident, I tried again to explain just how impossible our situation had been.

'If I *have* distanced myself from Phoebe Rose, it has been as a form of protection – for us both – so we didn't get too attached.'

'She is *somebody's* child. Biologically not yours, but one who needs *you* to take care of her until she is with her real mama – not keep her at arm's length, literally.' She wasn't mincing her words.

'It's been such a difficult time. I've received so much judgement when actually I think I've handled things rather well. I'm hoping you can focus on how things will be when Stevie, my daughter, is in my care and Phoebe Rose with her rightful parents, because what you see currently is circumstantial – not remotely the parent I intend to be with my own daughter.'

My mouth had gone into overdrive; my carefully prepared responses had evaporated. Eleanor made no effort to disguise what she thought of my behaviour.

'Ms Asquith-Hyde, your neglect on the day in question is the focus of my assessment. If you were unwell, why would you not enlist others to care for Phoebe Rose? You were actually in court that day. I'm certain Lana and Joel would have jumped at the chance to look after her. Wouldn't you agree?'

'She seemed fine until later on, when we got home.' I could feel a red flush creeping up my throat, knowing that Lana would have been vocal about Phoebe Rose seeming unwell and her insistence that this was the case.

Eleanor waited, no doubt for me to implicate myself further. I resolved to say as little as possible given the hole I was digging.

'I will ask again: if you found yourself to be unwell, why would you not ask a family member or friend to help?'

'I did,' I lied. 'It was late, and people were either unavailable or ill themselves.' More gibberish.

'Can you show me the calls, Ms Asquith-Hyde. Let me see for myself.'

The red flush was now spreading across my cheeks.

'I ...' Tears filled my eyes. 'I changed my phone recently. I've no proof. You will just have to believe me.' I sounded nothing short of petulant. And untruthful. She tapped at her keyboard.

Eleanor steered towards less contentious areas as I provided her with Phoebe Rose's up-to-date health record and positive documentation from the midwife in the early months. She made noises indicating that the visit was wrapping up, although my attempts to prise Phoebe Rose from her as she packed away were unsuccessful. As we stepped towards the door, I distracted Phoebe Rose with a toy before prising her grip from Eleanor's collar. She emitted a piercing cry. I kissed her head gently as Eleanor disappeared through the door, Phoebe Rose's high-pitched wailing echoing down the corridor.

***

Antenatal Kate, Corey's mum, had – reluctantly, I think – agreed to have Phoebe Rose. As awkward as asking had been – we really weren't that friendly – there was no one else. It specifically stated in the letter that I should be unaccompanied for the psychological assessment. Short of getting a childminder, I was stuck. I figured it would look worse on my evaluation if there wasn't a single friend or family member whom I could ask to care for Phoebe Rose.

Arriving early for the appointment, I was flicking apathetically through a *Cosmopolitan* from 2021 when I received the text. How was this possible? I read and reread the words.

> My dearest Tild. I will keep this succinct. I think we both realise that our relationship has run its course. I probably haven't been the best partner for you and hope that you find someone suitable. You deserve that. I didn't feel able to share with you last week but it's

important you should know. I am in the early stages of a new relationship. It's someone I've known for some time, a retired colleague now living in Provence. Please know I will always care for you. I can be around over the phone if you need support during this difficult time but wanted to be clear regarding my situation. Life has enough complexity for you without ambiguity regarding our relationship. Take care of yourself.

Regards

Edwin

How had that geriatric fucker gotten himself a piece of skirt? *A retired professor living in Provence? Are you kidding me?* I'd spent the last twelve hours honing a zen-like mindset ready for this fucking evaluation and now I get this, right before my appointment. He didn't even have the balls to call me. I bet it was Jan from Classics. He'd always had a thing for her. Every Christmas do I was suspicious. The bastard. The mindful breathing exercises I'd been practising all morning were not helping. How could I go in there and pass for normal feeling like this?

I imagined Edwin in some rustic farmhouse, playing his shitty Edith Piaf vinyl, trying to impress Jan with his atrocious French accent and spouting his flaky knowledge of French wine. *Uurgh, he makes me ill. Why did he not just tell me like a grown-up at the airport?*

'I can be around over the phone if you need support during this difficult time but wanted to be clear regarding my situation.' I'd had less impersonal job rejections.

The fantasy I'd created of Edwin: pushing Stevie on a swing, teaching her to ride a bike, persuading her to eat her greens. What a fool I'd been. He'd been a selfish twat throughout our relationship, so why I'd thought that would change, I have no idea. He'd barely had contact with his own grandchildren, so how I'd deluded myself was unfathomable. I couldn't go ahead with the appointment. If I was a donkey on the edge before, I was now a donkey that had stepped off the cliff edge and was now in freefall. I'd tell the doctor I was ill. I was in no fit state to talk to anyone. Grabbing my bag, I turned to see a weary-looking older man proffering a wrinkly hand in my direction.

'Miss Asquith-Hyde? I'm Dr Jackson. Lovely to meet you. I'm running slightly late today in clinic. I'll be with you in about ten minutes. If you're able to fill out these questionnaires while you wait, that would be helpful.' He sounded like a robot.

He turned before I could respond, leaving me open-mouthed in the waiting room. What to do now? He'd seen me, halted my escape. I could still leave, of course. But what would he think? An involuntary groan escaped as I sat helplessly back in the chair.

Use your senses to ground you. I could hear Jenna (fuck her too) and her ridiculous suggestions. The irony of 'grounding yourself' when your world was falling apart. *I'll give you five things, Jenna.* I could *hear* a toddler laughing with his mother across the waiting room. Trigger. I could *see* posters on the walls: 'Baby loves breast best', a besotted-looking mother feeding her (no doubt biological) infant. Trigger. I could *touch* the sticky residue on my fucking designer coat where a child – who wasn't mine – had emptied her snot-filled cavities moments before I'd dropped her with a relative stranger. Trigger. I could *smell* my own fear. The thought of raising my child completely alone. And it scared me shitless. Trigger. I could only imagine the *taste* of Chablis, rolling back and forth in a way that I no longer even enjoyed, with no one to drink with and carnage when I did. Trigger.

Dr Jackson returned, and I followed like a lamb to the slaughter. I found myself wearing a fake smile, apologising that I hadn't completed the forms, my jaw aching with the effort. The doctor's left eye twitched violently, his irritation clear. He assured me that it was fine. I knew it would be anything but.

***

The robot analogy makes sense to me. Robots don't have feelings: just be a robot. Remove all emotion from the situation and simply function. I completed the psychological evaluation, delivering neat responses in a tone I didn't recognise as my own. It could have been worse. I was able to get through the questions, somehow shelving the Edwin bombshell and remaining present. Maybe all the therapy had actually paid off. I would gain custody of Stevie. I would pick right back up where my life had left off, seven months ago in the delivery room. Without the complication of incubating and birthing someone else's baby, none of this would be happening. I just needed to focus on the life that I *should* have had and still could.

It was six weeks before we were due back in court. I tried not to calculate: how many more nappy changes must I offer this child? How many more 'smiles' when someone tells me how beautiful my 'daughter' is? How many more times would I have the balcony debate – if the world, and two children in particular, would be better off without me in it? How long before I'd be publicly informed that I was unfit to care for a child? Walking home from the surgery, I was too depressed to even want a drink. A new low for me. The thought of collecting Phoebe Rose from perfect Kate was unbearable, but somehow I found myself going through the motions.

Kate's driveway was ostentatious – sparkly granite flags, faux concrete pillars and arches. All that money and no taste whatsoever. My leaden legs carried me to the doorstep.

'Kate, thanks so much.'

She appeared with a baby on each hip, her strained expression clear.

'How's she been?'

'She's been okay,' Kate stated flatly. I wasn't sure what that meant and didn't have the energy to enquire. 'Can I get you a drink or something?'

I could be interested. 'That's the best offer I've had all day.'

Kate looked blankly at me. 'Tea or coffee? Or juice?'

'Coffee. Thanks. White, no sugar.' This wasn't an invitation to bond over a glass, then.

I followed her through the grand hall to an open plan kitchen, further gleaming granite and white chandeliers. I took Phoebe Rose from her as she prepped the coffee. Phoebe Rose looked surprised as I mechanically planted a kiss on her head.

Looking around the cavernous kitchen, I caught sight of Kate's wall planner, the only thing in the place that wasn't straight from a showroom. Her diary looked as empty as mine, but I was drawn to an entry in red pen. NCT BIG NIGHT OUT. Friday 25 March. I checked again. A week on Friday.

Kate saw my expression and winced. She quickly recovered.

'Are you out with us next week?' she asked without making eye contact.

'Don't think I knew about it,' I said bluntly, tears threatening to brim. 'Have fun,' I managed.

'Didn't you get the email? Jo sent it ages ago.' Kate still couldn't meet my eye. She fiddled with a thread of cotton on Corey's shirt.

'I get loads of emails from the group, but no, I didn't get this one.' I wrestled a level of composure back into my voice.

'I'll forward it to you – let me check.' Kate reached for her phone.

'No. Actually, I won't have a sitter anyway, so there's no point.' I fastened Phoebe Rose's open changing bag, my rollercoaster mood dropping by the second. 'Let me know if you want me to have Corey at any point. Do you have a sitter for next week?' I asked facetiously.

'Thanks, but my mother-in-law would murder me if she thought there were others in the queue before her.' Kate looked genuine before she realised how insensitive her words were.

'I'm going to leave the coffee. Thanks for today.' I needed to get out of the house. I felt like someone had disconnected my motor, like I was slowing completely down. I had no clue how I would reach the bottom of the drive, let alone home.

Kate and Corey waved from the door. It took all I could muster not to give her a big fat V sign.

Lana

Wan gripped my hand tightly as we took the steps to the courtroom together. It felt good to be shoulder to shoulder with Wan again even in this perverse situation. I had no clue how Tilda was coping without a partner. Seated on either side of the courtroom, we looked like warring parties rather than families trying to get things right for their children. Mrs Jennings, as usual, looked more like a homeless person who'd wandered in off the street than my legal representative.

Tilda was on her own today, it seemed, just her and my daughter. As usual, Phoebe Rose remained bundled in her seat, facing outwards. Did Tilda ever stop to think how this looked? The bonus was that we could see her. I lifted Stevie's hand in a wave over to Phoebe Rose, who looked at us blankly. Tilda, noticing the movement, bobbed her head, a clinical salute in our direction, and stared ahead towards Mr Dreyfuss at the bench. He gestured 'one minute' and continued his conversation with Mrs Jennings.

It had been a surreal few weeks. Nursery had offered a staggered transition for Stevie and me, which had gone well. Short sessions had increased to half days in anticipation of my return to work – three full days per week. The process, like most of my recent experiences, was bittersweet. Seeing my little girl becoming increasingly independent was hard – the tears and devastation of first leaving her giving way to a new attachment; Stevie's lovely key worker, Marge, had been quick to form a bond with her. Marge was warm, loving – yes, cuddles and squeezes – both kind and no-nonsense at the same time. All that I hoped I was – and everything I knew Tilda wasn't. I couldn't help but compare.

The Year 5 class that I would be teaching were a collective delight. The same class I'd taught in Reception, my first year of teaching after graduating. Surely Lynda had orchestrated this? Year 5 were hands down the easiest year group in the school. I'd sworn Lynda as headteacher to secrecy – or at least professional confidentiality – as I'd explained the context to my return from maternity leave. Aside from Jodie, no one within my friendship group was aware of my situation. But I knew that if I was to survive a return to school, I would need understanding from the headteacher.

Being back in the classroom was lovely. I hadn't realised how much I'd missed it – the kids and staff, anyway. Not the long hours, of course, or the tedious lesson planning, but it was lovely to be someone other than mum and partner. I tried not to torture myself handing Stevie over to Marge each morning. Knowing that one day soon there would be a permanent handover crushed me every time. Each morning my tears flowed as I hurried back to my car, balancing a seesaw of emotions. I clung to an irrational belief that I wouldn't have to part with Stevie – contrasting with the reality of the swift legal progression towards her being removed from my care. Wan and I would be more than open to maintaining contact between the girls, but Tilda had not given any indication that she wanted anything but exclusive rights to her 'daughter'. And given the lack of compassion she showed for Phoebe Rose now, I couldn't imagine she'd be interested in any aspect of her future. I clung desperately to the hope that Tilda's psychological report would question her ability to meet the needs of a child whose attachment would already have been affected.

Wan and I looked over at Phoebe Rose sitting lethargically in her seat. Stevie would have had none of that. She'd demand a cuddle or stimulation beyond the ridiculous gadgets that Tilda attached to her seat – anything to spare herself interaction. At least she didn't have that terrible starched outfit on this time. I waved excitedly, but Phoebe Rose stared vacantly back.

'All rise for the court,' the usher instructed, and we dutifully obeyed for the presiding god of our world, Judge Sullivan. The omnipotent one with the power to both give and take away.

'I'm grateful to the counsel for their timely acquisition of assessments within a tight timeframe. I thank both parties for their compliance with assessments and a process that at times will have felt most invasive. I'm aware that contacts have been scheduled and adhered to, which ought to have today led to being able to set a date to finalise the exchange of infants to their rightful birth parent and parents. However …'

Would my heart stop? Wan squeezed my hand as Judge Sullivan looked unusually awkward. Pausing, she frowned at the documentation before her.

'Yet again, it would seem that an outstanding assessment – not ordered by this court – has been requested in a way that we could not have anticipated.' Tilda held herself like a statue. Wan and I looked at Mrs Jennings desperately. It was the suicide attempt. It had caught up with me. Months of fooling myself that it would come to nothing. Fuck …

'Whilst I am in receipt of psychological evaluations for both parties, it would appear that a Child and Families Assessment is occurring independently of court regarding Matilda Asquith-Hyde's care of Phoebe Rose. Of which I have *only just* been informed.' Judge Sullivan peered over her glasses towards Mr Dreyfuss.

'Objection, Your Honour. This is a specific and isolated medical incident which occurred when my client was also physically unwell with a debilitating—'

'Overruled, Mr Dreyfuss. This is a live social care assessment around allegations of neglect which left the infant hospitalised. Furthermore, your failure to disclose this matter ahead of this hearing can only be seen by the court as deceitful.'

'What have you done to our daughter?' I was on my feet, yelling and pointing at Tilda before Judge Sullivan had ended her sentence. Mrs Jennings stepped forward and silenced me, motioning me to be seated.

'Your Honour. Forgive my client; the considerable strain is impacting. This intrusion will not happen again.'

I sank back into my seat, dumbfounded by what I'd heard.

Judge Sullivan turned her stony gaze in my direction. 'Mrs Edwards, I am not able to provide further detail beyond this scant statement. And I pardon your outburst on this occasion. Although Mrs Jennings is correct. It will not happen again in this courtroom.' Judge Sullivan's expression hardened further as she shifted her focus towards an increasingly uncomfortable-looking Mr Dreyfuss.

'I will speak to you in counsel, Mr Dreyfuss, regarding the lamentable late admission of information in this already protracted hearing. We shall explore the barriers together that have led to your belated admission. Unfortunately for the children, I have no choice but to ask that court reconvene when this assessment is complete to allow full consideration of the facts. Contacts should continue to occur under full supervision in the interests of safeguarding both children.' Judge Sullivan's tone was not to be argued with. Mr Dreyfuss took his seat.

'My understanding is that social care will require a further ten to fourteen days to complete their assessment. We will reconvene after this date. Parties can expect that I will have made a decision – taking into account all representation made thus far, along with the final report. Time is of the essence and the children's needs must come first, not the needs of the adults. This court is dismissed.'

'What the fuck? I knew it! Didn't I?' I hissed into Wan's ear, trembling violently and scrutinising Phoebe Rose for obvious signs of harm as Tilda snatched up the seat and strode from the room.

'Why is she still in her care if there's the *slightest* doubt?' Wan welled up too, wrapping a protective arm around my shoulders. Would this ever end? In a messed-up way, however, this was good news. There was a query; there must be doubt in the minds of others regarding Tilda's ability to care for *either* child. *I knew it all along.* A mother's instinct, not that Tilda would have the slightest clue what that was. A sharp pain ripped through my stomach. Leaving Wan with Stevie, I made my way to the bathroom. If Tilda appeared, I wouldn't be responsible for my actions. Bursting through the door, I vomited into the nearest hand basin, breathing hard and sobbing. *How bad was this? What was she doing to her? By the time we get Phoebe Rose, what harm will have occurred?* A second wave hit and I retched again, a spectacular splatter reaching high on the splashback. The outer toilet door shifted. Clenching my fist, I prepared myself. A startled-looking court usher asked if I needed any help. The relief that it wasn't Tilda vied with the disappointment of not being able to smash her perfect teeth into her head. The usher wordlessly ran a bowl of warm water and offered paper towels, for which I was grateful.

Tilda

'Why the fuck didn't you tell me? Did you think it wouldn't come up?' Mr Dreyfuss closed the heavy wooden door behind him before spitting out his words.

'I don't like your tone or your language, Mr Dreyfuss,' I hissed, gesturing down at Phoebe Rose in her seat.

'And I don't like your dishonesty, Ms Asquith-Hyde.' Mr Dreyfuss exhaled slowly.

'This was not dishonesty. This was an omission of information which is merely an unfortunate red herring. The assessment will come back without concern. I am neither neglectful nor abusive.' My confident tone belied my raging shame.

'With respect, Tilda, at this point in the proceedings I don't think Judge Sullivan or the Edwards will see it that way. And that's before we've even come to your frankly borderline psych report.' He thrust a copy my way. 'Now that Judge Sullivan has had sight of these, we are permitted to see them. Buckle up.'

'Well, that's why I pay you the astronomical fees that I do. Over to you and your expensive spin. I'm guessing it hasn't declared me completely unfit, or we wouldn't be having this conversation.'

Mr Dreyfuss shrugged, looking deflated.

'I've been able – due to the astronomical fees I charge – to find an expert witness prepared to place your behaviour within a trauma context. Namely that environmental factors have driven your behaviour rather than anything organic. "With support", there is no reason why you would not be able to meet the needs of your biological child. The expert witness is expensively charismatic. It will be a sizeable addition to your fees.'

He wasn't done.

'How can I make it clear for you? You aren't helping yourself if different people – or worse still, like today, no one at all – supports you in court. The psych report highlights your limited family and friends network. Bring someone next time. I don't care who. Bring the cleaner if you like, but bring a body.'

'I'm an independent woman. I'm sure the report identified that as a strength.'

'It doesn't look good. Dress that up any way you want. We shall await the Child and Families Assessment. In the meantime, try to monitor Phoebe Rose's health and make sure you look after your own.'

'Don't insult me, Mr Dreyfuss. I don't pay you for that, and I will thank you to remember it.' Trembling with rage and shame, I gathered Phoebe Rose and stormed from the room, the door crashing noisily behind us. Head down – God forbid that I should see Lana and Wan – we strode from the courts and back to the car. The thought of the sober drive home after the day from hell was exhausting. I could hardly have a cheeky glass somewhere, though. Adding drink driving to my portfolio wouldn't be the wisest move. *Fucking Mr Dreyfuss, fucking Judge Sullivan, judgemental arseholes. Walk a mile in my shoes and let's see how sane you'd be.* Loneliness swept over me as I pushed the car's power button on autopilot. The engine throbbed to life. I could call at Archie's, wave an olive branch. Maybe the overweight one and his offspring would join me in court next time, evidencing my family network. Archie would be beyond astonished to see me at his door, infant in tow, not of the Asquith-Hyde colouring. It would almost be worth it just to see his expression. Maybe it would be enough to stop his cholesterol-clogged heart in his barrel chest. I let the car warm up while I gathered myself. Phoebe Rose babbled gently in the back.

'Well, one thing's for sure, Phoebe Rose. We've another month together. Let's check out some nurseries. I don't think we'll survive otherwise. What do you think?'

Phoebe Rose babbled some more, which I took as a thumbs-up. Mr Dreyfuss had suggested that I hold off on nursery, as he knew Judge Sullivan was old school, and was surprised that Lana would return to work in the circumstances. Clearly I needed any advantage going. I'd couch it in terms of planning ahead. Phoebe Rose would be attending childcare when Lana went to work. It would be the least I could do to reduce the impact of this. In reality, it was a very necessary means of survival.

As we neared the turn-off for Archie's, I found myself wrestling with the steering wheel. How low I had stooped. At the last moment, pride got the better of me and I sped past the cul-de-sac, heading for the motorway back to the south. I had a small glimmer of hope that tomorrow I would find a nursery for Phoebe Rose. Even if it went against me in court, the thought of another day of caring for someone else's child was unbearable. I couldn't bring myself to even try to bond with Phoebe Rose. I had never believed in the investment and less so at this stage – for Phoebe Rose's sake, of course.

***

Thanks for nothing, NCT group, but your collective sanctimonious judgement.

'I wouldn't leave Henry with anyone but family, and even then, it isn't for long. You hear real horror stories about private nurseries, Tilda. Are you sure this is what you want in these early few months of life?'

'I can recommend a childminder, but she only takes children on a part-time basis. Are you sure it's full time that you need?'

'There's such a long wait list for the decent nurseries. Did you not register Phoebe Rose before she was born?'

'You'll struggle to get a nursery that's halfway decent if you're looking to send her immediately. You wouldn't believe how bad some of them are. Nothing will be like the care that you can give her one to one.'

The reality was that I was at breaking point and whoever could offer something first could have her. Maybe the kennels would take her. I knew the group didn't think I was good enough. It came through loud and clear in their poorly veiled comments. Their privilege was not lost on me. The privilege of support networks ready to share in the joy and care of your baby. The privilege of not having a seriously screwed-up family. The privilege of birthing your own infant and getting to raise her from day one.

I googled childcare and nurseries within a kilometre of my home. Somewhere in my mind a rationale hovered that if the nursery was within walking distance, I could have a cheeky afternoon glass of something if needed.

There seemed to be something seriously wrong with the childcare industry. Little Angels. It sounded more like a brothel than a nursery. Dream Big, Little One. Dream about anything you like as long as I'm not involved.

As it turned out, the first nursery that we viewed with availability accepted Phoebe Rose on a full-time placement. So much for the naysayers. Although I doubt it would have met with the NCT members' lofty approval. I'd done my homework. Ofsted described them as 'improving' (2018). I hoped the rating wouldn't come up in court, but it was the highest-rated place with availability. I looked beyond the depressed nursery nurses, their expressions as enthusiastic as mine at the thought of spending a day surrounded by little people. I guessed they were competent enough. Besides, if the staff were apathetic, that would work in my favour. I certainly wouldn't want Phoebe Rose overstimulated, or who knew what she'd expect when she came home?

Lydia, her badge announced, looked about twenty-five and managed the nursery nurses. She addressed me in a bizarre sing-song voice. I wondered whether she had a learning disability, such was the level of her communication. Even I was aware in that moment of how unkind my narrative had become. I thought back to pre-birth days, when I'd tried so hard to reinvent myself as hopeful, altruistic, kind. I longed to gossip with Edwin about the staff. He would have understood, had he not been shagging a post-menopausal ex-tutor in Provence (who would provide none of the banter that Edwin and I had enjoyed). Although, to be fair, Jan wasn't raising an infant that wasn't hers *or* asking Edwin to play grandad. Quite the advantage in her flabby-arsed favour.

Despite a drawn-out transition involving leaving Phoebe Rose for increasing periods of time, by the end of the week I received permission to leave her in the hands of the team. It was all I could do not to conga from the nursery. Phoebe Rose had been declared 'sufficiently attached' to her key worker to allow a full-time start the following week. The irony was that our own attachment needed no such assessment. I felt positively giddy at the prospect of filling my week any way I pleased. Of course, on paper – and as far as the courts were concerned – I had returned to my post at Nurture. In an ironic way I was nurturing myself for the first time since giving birth all those months ago.

The missed calls from Richard were racking up. I'd messaged back stating that Phoebe Rose had been ill, which was true. Then I'd been unwell, which also wasn't wide of the mark. Despite my texts, the calls continued, but I couldn't face a conversation. I texted a response that I hoped would keep him on side until court proceedings were concluded. The nursery place was a 'necessity' for the position I held at Nurture. The reality was that I'd lost all appetite even to explore IVF errors/shortfalls and had no appetite for the exposé that I'd planned. If I could have turned back the clock and severed any connection I'd made with IVF, I would have. If I gained custody of Stevie, so be it. If I didn't, there would be no backward glances. So often I had doubted whether I even wanted Stevie, terrified that I might not be capable of loving her. How could I separate what had happened from how things might have been? All I had was the here and shitty now. I sent a meeting request to Richard for a time that I could see from his diary was unavailable, stalling further still. The next four weeks were set out before me like impossibly high hurdles.

Jodie

I bloody love the bones of both of them, but sometimes it feels like I devote my life to worrying about one or the other. I had no problem organising Lana's maternity do. It was entirely my pleasure. However, their latest request has blindsided me. A memorial party for Evie's third birthday. Okay. The bit I'm wrestling with is where in the agenda do we announce Stevie's birth identity? What would work best: before or after we cut the cake? Or maybe we just pop a note in the party bags? Christ, Lana, seriously. Lana told me she and Wan couldn't agree on a plan for Evie's birthday this year and they were shelving it. I'm not sure why Lana has resurrected the idea and thrown it into my lap. I certainly have misgivings. Her rationale was that the celebration of Evie brought tears anyway, so why not use the opportunity for people to say their goodbyes to Stevie?

To be honest, I'm terrified where this will end. I've seen Lana like this before and it didn't end well. When she was pregnant with Evie, her mood could not have been higher. If she'd been on ecstasy, she couldn't have been more pumped for the whole nine months. Of course, when Evie died – and I cannot imagine her pain – she fell like a dead weight. I worried at the time that she would harm herself. But Joel got her through.

Since all this started, Joel has aged about a decade, his mood a mirror image of Lana's but behind a mask that he feels he must hide behind. I don't think he's properly grieved for Evie, let alone being in any mental shape to be managing this pressure. I asked him a while back if he'd been able to talk to any of his friends about how he felt. He tried to sound casual, explaining that his friends seemed to have the opposite problem. While he and Lana struggled to 'keep the babies in their care' – his words – his mates wouldn't understand.

'Jode, I've got one mate whose partner's pregnant and his bit on the side has just delivered twin boys. I've another who has four teenagers, and his missus has just found out she's pregnant. They're over the moon.'

It's a fair point.

I don't think Lana can withstand the pain of losing Stevie. It's as simple as that. Even with Phoebe Rose in her care, I can't see how she won't implode, the sum of the grieving parts just too great for her. And there isn't a thing I can do to make it better.

Lana

Evie's third birthday loomed. Just two weeks before the final court hearing. Given that Stevie's identity was known only to a handful of people, we – or I – thought a single announcement to everyone might be easier. Wan had wanted to tell people way back that Stevie wasn't our child, but I'd not been able to go there, unable to process this for myself, let alone with others. To me, she was, and still is, all mine.

'If we get everyone together and they all hear it at the same time, it means it's done,' I offered pragmatically. In case celebrating Evie's third birthday was not sufficiently sad, we could add another layer. Give them a glimpse of our world.

'Babe, we don't *have* to do anything. Evie won't object if we don't celebrate her birthday with a party. And the only wellbeing I'm concerned about right now is yours and mine, so let's just pause and think about this. Having a "party" so close to court will be overwhelming, even without this horrific agenda.' Wan brought me close and enveloped me in his lovely warmth. A tug on the bottom of my skirt saw a very first Stevie stand as she clambered to join our hug.

'Aw, Babba Stevie!' I squealed, lifting her between us. 'Who's our clever girl just for her mama and dada!'

'Stevie loves standing up!' Wan joined in, and we jigged in a circle, to Stevie's delight.

'I have no clue if this is a good idea or a car crash of an idea,' I said simply; the impossible task of telling others would break me either way. I couldn't face letting people know individually, like a never-ending loop of the worst information we could ever share. I'd thought about a collective Facebook status or a letter that we post to everyone. At least this way people could say their goodbyes to Stevie there and then. In some cases, hello and goodbye, for those who still hadn't met her. I couldn't bear for the next two precious weeks all and sundry knocking at the door with their tears and condolences. I neither needed nor wanted them. I just wanted to enjoy the last few weeks of Stevie's life in the most normal way possible. We could pop to my mum's for Sunday brunch, have lazy weekend mornings with her favourite books on repeat, play the Stevie Loves game all day if that was what she wanted to do.

Tears were streaming down our faces. We huddled together to spare Stevie our sadness as usual. If Stevie had memories of those times when she was older, they would contain many of the moments when we'd attempted to hide our tears – the smallest act of mercy we could offer her in those helpless times.

'We could ask Jodie to organise it?' Wan suggested.

'That's an idea. To be honest, I haven't the energy to arrange it. I don't want it here, though. Somewhere we've no attachment to.'

'We do have the C and F assessment to come back. It's not beyond the realms of possibility that the decision might not be favourable for Tilda,' Wan dared hope. Because he's the optimist. And I'm the realist, aware of the power of her solicitor; that Tilda's money could still sway this. *Everything* can be bought, including Judge Sullivan's decision. It's only the faintest hope I hold of anything but Stevie going to Tilda. I know we won't be empty-handed. Phoebe Rose will be in our arms where she belongs. But the pain of a Stevie swap ... is unbearable.

***

'Jode, it looks ace! I bloody love you!' Jodie had singlehandedly transformed the seedy Labour Club. Colourful balloons and badly crayoned butterflies festooned the ceiling. A large stuffed koala was perched precariously on the stage.

'Ah, you know me, love a project.' Jodie grinned modestly but was clearly pleased with herself. 'I know this is Evie's party, but I couldn't resist a Stevie koala!'

I gently placed Stevie at Jodie's feet and pulled her in for the hug that she'd rather not receive. 'Thank you,' I whispered. Stevie sprang up, grabbing Jodie's knees for balance.

'Whoa, little one! And when was I to be informed of this development?' she shrieked, scooping up Stevie and burying her face in her tummy.

'It's old hat, Auntie Jode. Mastered that last week.' I laughed. Stevie squealed in delight. 'Seriously, it looks great. You even used child labour too!'

'Of course, art being central to the curriculum.' She laughed and stole away with Stevie to show her the decorations. It was a relief to drop my fake smile, if only for a moment.

To describe myself as distressed wasn't accurate. I'd moved through that phase. I was now simply numb. The party build-up had been unbearable, remembering our precious firstborn and all that had happened on the day of her birth. Her three-year-old presence with us today as ever. I never told Wan – he would insist it wasn't real – but I *see* her all the time. Disappearing down the hallway when I'm heading back to bed after a night feed. Peeking around aisles in the supermarket. Sometimes she appears at Stevie's bedtime, listening around the corner to the tail end of her story. The dog-eared copy of *Amazing Grace* – the book my mum bought for Evie, that we read to her stillborn body – is now a go-to read for Stevie. Evie's curly hair is often just visible at the periphery of my vision as I read. When I turn to look, she's always gone, her departure a literal blur. The sightings are not my imagination. But I didn't think Wan would understand. And besides, I love the idea that she only comes to me. Her first, last and always mama. A sharp tap on the shoulder hauls me back into the moment.

Wan's parents had arrived. Jean crossed the room, looking distraught.

'It's a day for happiness, Jean. Don't start me off!' I chided. She knew the drill from last year. 'Only smiles in memory of our beautiful girl.' For now, at least. Wan's dad hugged me and steered Jean off towards the buffet.

Wan was at the decks, his safe place. I felt alone with Stevie off with Jodie, and vulnerable to others' emotions. As the room began to fill, I was struck by the absurdity of the event. I had no desire to even speak to anyone, let alone tell them that Stevie wasn't ours. A double baby loss. What had I been thinking?

***

I found myself on the high street. It was pouring down; large raindrops quickly darkened my purple skirt. I was sporting a highly random outfit even by my standards: silk top teamed with a winter hessian skirt, which looked terrible with my Converse. I hadn't thought about clothing until this morning. It seemed to work earlier, reality only now striking home on so many levels. I walked quickly, checking behind me that no one had seen my escape. The House with No Name looked inviting. Never a busy pub, but it looked deserted. Taking the seat next to the jukebox, I flicked through the tattered food menu, relieved to be alone. A double whisky appeared that I barely remembered ordering. The burn at the back of my throat felt good – the only thing I wanted to feel right now. I was emotionally spent. I wished

Stevie was there, though. She'd help me choose some cool tracks from the jukebox. I'd have to get used to this feeling. Learn how to do stuff without my Stevie-shaped sidekick. Would Phoebe Rose want to play the 'Phoebe Rose Loves' game? It didn't have the same ring to it. I waved a note in the landlord's direction. I wanted to disappear. Nothing drastic, just to not *be* here at all. *I should text Wan. Tell him I can't do it anymore, the pretending I'm okay.* Why had I thought this celebration of Evie could still go ahead? And how the hell had I agreed to announce that Stevie wasn't mine? She *was* mine … she *had* to be …

Slumped in my seat, my head almost touched the grubby table, every ounce of energy draining from me. The phone in my pocket vibrated. *Where are you? Are you okay?* No. The official answer was no. I needed to go home. Unless I could fade into this greasy sofa and become part of the furniture. I could spend the rest of my existence listening to other people's conversations. Hearing their problems, sharing their hopes. I could do that. If it didn't mean facing my own.

'Another!' I mimed and the landlord again delivered.

The pub was filling up. I was horizontal on the bench, my legs curled against my chest, my nose within sniffing distance of the threadbare sofa. I was apathetic despite the musty smell filling my nostrils. Slowly I removed my phone from my pocket. Eleven missed calls from Wan. Three from Jodie. So many unread texts.

'I'm sorrrrry. Hope the music's going okay. I havennn't done anything don't worry. I just couldn't stay. X 't ell everyone to give Stevie a big hug and that weee'l see them soon but without her. Don't forget to let them d n know we will have different baby with us then. See you at home. Sorry.'

God, I'm pissed. Such a lightweight. At least Wan knows I'm okay. In an 'I'm not going to kill myself' kind of way.

I could picture the scene. Wan left the sanctuary of his booth and headed over to Jodie, committing the unforgivable DJ sin: using a generic playlist. He and Jodie exchanged words. Tension rippled around the room. Jodie held Stevie in her arms. Good old Jode. Stevie had fists full of breadstick that she was crumbling into Jodie's lovely chiffon shirt. Wan looked panic-stricken, his face ashen. I would have done anything to make this situation better, but I was quite unable. Wild horses couldn't drag me back into that room. Wan would like that. A Rolling Stones nod. One for Evie's awful third birthday soundtrack.

The guests: parents, siblings, friends, nieces and nephews got wind that something wasn't right. Wan looked fleetingly relieved when he received my text. He and Jodie whispered between them, hatching a plan. Jodie seemed insistent about something. Would they pretend I was ill? Maybe I'd been urgently called away. But why? All the people I cared about were gathered in that room. Wan's dad looked awkwardly into his phone. He was Face Timing Jake. Good luck with that.

Wan headed for the door. I saw him turn on to the high street and do a circuit round the park. Pulling his coat around his narrow shoulders, he looked so sad. For a moment I worried that *he* might 'do' something. I'd never thought about that, so consumed by my egocentric grief. He was shouting something. My name, I think. *You won't be able to find me, Wan, even if you track me to this very pub.* I was now lying full length unashamedly, my body out of sight, obscured by the table above me. I was quite safe.

Wan looked angry, his park reccy unsuccessful. That was more like it. I'd take angry over sad. He tried his phone again – a call vibrated in my bag. Wan headed back up the street and I guess towards the Labour Club, defeated. Jodie had taken charge in his absence. She'd turned the music down and asked everyone to gather. Wan joined her, looking stunned. As he spoke, the crowd around him gradually silenced. I saw sadness, incredulity, disbelief. Did I see anger? *Why didn't you tell us sooner? We could have helped.* But nobody could or can. Which was why I had to leave. Telling others makes it worse, bringing reality that step nearer. There were tears, of course. Wan's dad wordlessly ending the FaceTime call. The little ones became irritable. Hungry, needing the loo, desperate to race up and down the shiny floor again. Just like Evie would have done, egged on by her boisterous cousins. If she were still here. Jodie practically pushed Wan out of the door with Stevie. 'Go home.' She would take care of things. His ridiculous mother followed.

Tilda

I was trying hard to stay afloat. Pretending to the world that I could behave like a mother. Phoebe Rose and I strolled through Hyde Park, trying to pass for normal. Enormous metal sheets glinted on the art installation in the weak March sunshine. I pictured Stevie alert in her pushchair. We were playing peek-a-boo, her deep chuckle filling the air.

'There's Stevie ... where's she gone? There she is.' Stevie was delighted by her reflection in the steel sheets. A couple heading our way couldn't help but smile. The guy put out his tongue and Stevie giggled. Everywhere, people were jealous of our happiness. They passed by the pushchair nudging one another, in awe of my beautiful girl. Stevie's fine blond hair ruffled in the breeze. We paused, breathing in the moment. Stevie's pale blue eyes were stunning against her violet dungarees. I rearranged the suede tassels of her pony-skin bootees to fall evenly on each shoe.

Phoebe Rose began to wail. I was snapped cruelly back to the moment, to the cry that escalates within minutes. She'd be full pelt any second. Tired, hungry, or needing something that, despite my best efforts, I can never quite figure out.

'Look, Phoebe Rose.' I pointed to the metal to our left, but a cloud had moved across the sky above us. There was no metallic glinting. Phoebe Rose wasn't interested anyway. All she ever seemed to want was food. Or to be held. An old man shuffled past smelling of piss. He tried to catch my eye, but I bent down quickly, straightening the tassel on Phoebe Rose's shoe.

I'd not thought to bring a bottle. My castle of motherhood was showing signs of crumbling. I felt so alone. Pre-child, 'bring a bottle' had meant something completely different, but dinner invitations and parties were not something that featured in my current existence.

I wandered ghost-like through the final week before court, avoiding everything. The phone rang occasionally. There were calls from Richard. A couple from baby club people. Unknown numbers that I could not bear to answer. I checked, crestfallen, every time, hoping it might be Ellie. Or even Edwin. I could focus on nothing but the hearing, my entire life hanging in limbo. Everything would be riding upon the C and F assessment, of which I wouldn't know the outcome until court. I knew it would not be favourable. How could it be? Even sleep brought no peace. Fragmented images, vivid dreams of how my life might end, awkwardly hoisting myself onto the glass balcony of my apartment, trying to sleep while perched precariously on the divide. Other times I fall gracefully like a leaf wending its way to the ground until I land gently on the pavement. Sometimes Phoebe Rose is by my side, other times not. When I fall, I land somehow intact, but Phoebe Rose breaks apart like an egg, her dark blood spreading over the pavement.

I fought the urge all day but caved around teatime. *Mr Dreyfuss, if there is even an ounce of decency in you, you will let me have this one small favour.* I ask the question that I know he can provide the answer to.

'I can't tell you anything you don't already know in advance of tomorrow. How many ways do I need to say this?'

Damn him. He's no stickler for rules. I've just pissed him off and now he's being an arse.

'I don't think it's unreasonable the evening before the most important day of my life that I seek reassurance from the world's most expensive solicitor. Can you not even give me a verbal summary?'

Dreyfuss remained silent. Of course he did. I could hear the vulgar chewing of gum.

'I have received a precis, but I am not able to share the contents. I could lose my licence. The judge specifically stated this.'

'You can't leave me dangling. Why would you say that if you can't comment?' I'm pleading now.

'Just trying to be transparent.'

'Transparent? You could hardly be less transparent. You *know but won't tell*. It's not going to be *you* with egg on your face tomorrow, is it?'

'Actually, Tilda, it will be. You've been dishonest with me throughout this entire case. That absolutely impacts me and my reputation. We will follow due process at court tomorrow and Judge Sullivan will decide what's best for the children.' I could hear blinds closing, the click of a light. Dreyfuss was leaving his office.

Could this information come at a price? I wondered. Was this the route he wanted to go?

'Name your price!' I hissed.

'Tilda, I'd love to extort money from you. But sometimes there's a decency bar, and you've crossed it. Money can't always get you what you want. If it transpired that I'd been anything but honest in the context of such a sensitive and high-profile case, it would be professional suicide for me. You haven't given me any reason to trust you throughout the whole of these proceedings. You will learn the outcome tomorrow.' Mr Dreyfuss cut the call, leaving me seething.

For the last time, walking on autopilot, I collected Phoebe Rose from nursery, clamouring for control, my mind seeking a solution. Pre-empting that tomorrow's decision would not be favourable, I had choices that didn't include public humiliation. *I could not show up. Or I could choose to settle out of court. Leave Stevie where she is, and Phoebe Rose can live with people who will love her.* The temptation to end my suffering – which may only just be starting if I was given care of Stevie tomorrow – was never far from my mind. *What if even Stevie doesn't want me? Why would she?*

Phoebe Rose's face shrivelled as she realised it was home time. I stood awkwardly in the dingy nursery reception, curly edged indecipherable paintings lining the walls. I was grateful that it would be the last time I would feel this shame. The child in my care was distressed at my very presence. Lydia brought out a miserable-looking Phoebe Rose and prised her from her torso.

'See you tomorrow.' I feigned cheeriness. Fraudulent on so many levels even towards the nursery staff.

Phoebe Rose and I wandered slowly through Selfridges for one last time. She wouldn't be getting decent food in the land of toast and beans. We should have a last supper. Of course, the real reason for the Selfridges detour was to pick up a commiseratory/celebratory bottle of vino. Whatever my new life might bring, I deserved that. Landing at the corner of the aisle, we found the high-end New Zealand Marlborough. Oaky vanilla within sipping distance. Would there be anything that I would miss about this baby? I pondered at the checkout. I could come up with nothing. It wasn't her fault. Or mine. We'd just been in survival mode from the outset. There would be so much that I would *not* miss. Not waking in the small hours with a feeling of freefall, my life so out of control, it felt I would never find my feet. I would not miss the guilt and shame that shadowed my every step. Would it ever change? *If Stevie lands here tomorrow, will this be Groundhog Day? But with a different child?* The possibility that this wasn't at all about Phoebe Rose but about me was terrifying.

Picking though the olive and mezze platter, I played music and changed Phoebe Rose into pyjamas for the very last time. There was no sadness. I was performing a chore that I'd engaged in every day for seven months, each time as disconnected as the last. The wine was exquisite. It would have benefited from a quick freezer blast, but even so. Who said money couldn't buy happiness?

Phoebe Rose went down easily, as always. A quick bottle feed and she was done, asleep before the dreadful musical toy she was so fond of had ended. *Of all the toys she has, this crappy thing, a gift from Ellie, is her go-to.* When the music finished, it was goodnight from me, as if the last of my emotional energy had expired on the last note. Phoebe Rose knew that and didn't fuss.

I was three glasses in when reality hit. I needed to decide. Not tomorrow. But now. There would be a trajectory tomorrow irrespective of my decision. Locus of control, that's what Jenna used to talk about. You need to feel in control of your situation. Not like a pawn or a puppet with no mastery over your existence. That was what had been so horrific about this journey – my life being dictated by others' behaviours and decisions.

As I drained the bottle –I'm a firm believer in the adage - good wine will never give you a hangover – my weary brain retraced its neural steps, the ones I'd turned over like pebbles the last few months. Tearfully, I remembered the early excitement of choosing Stevie's sperm donor, Ellie's low alcohol threshold giving way to hilarity as she swiped and shrieked at my donor possibilities. I could still hear her voice.

'Will it be scenario number one …' I smeared a tear across my cheek. A tear that was never far away when I thought about Ellie.

'So, what will happen tomorrow? Will Tilda recognise herself for the human train wreck that she is in *advance* of court? Will she do the right thing?' I said aloud. It wasn't a fun game without Ellie. *But seriously, do I offer care of Stevie to Lana and Joel? She deserves better than I can give.* And (take away the feeding element) Joel and Lana were good people. She would be *loved*. I could send money – which they were clearly short of.

'Will it be scenario number two?' Did I have a bottle of emergency wine at the back of the fridge? 'Hold that thought.' Unsteadily, I got to my feet. Nestled between out-of-date broccoli and an oversized jar of red cabbage lurked a bottle of champagne.

'Well, how fitting!' I declared, skilfully and silently opening the bottle. Always with a Vic radar in mind.

I settled back on the sofa, glass in hand.

'Where was I? God, I'm pissed. I roll with the dice. If Judge Sullivan decides I'm able to care for Stevie, then I give it a go. I'll be like every other mother and their baby, Mini-Tilda and me, just like I'd imagined. We could still go to Chile, open that vineyard. I could still expose all things IVF and seedy, close the Manchester Clinic. Or maybe I'll just become a normal mum, whatever that is. Last glass,' I admonished myself, reaching for the bottle.

With both scenarios out there, I was forced to consider the remaining option.

'Scenario number three. I will spare the world, any children, future partners and even myself from further distress. I will remove *myself* from the planet.'

The balcony swan dive. Teasingly just a moment away. I could do it in the small hours to avoid traumatising the wider public. I hoped Stan wouldn't find me. I wouldn't wish that on him. Maybe Vic would. That would be good. He'd be full of remorse for his unkindness, forever traumatised. But that would be the Disney version. Although if Disney were shooting this, I wouldn't be ending my life. Disney would never have mixed up the eggs in the first place.

My phone vibrated. I dared to hope. Edwin? Or Ellie. Always optimistic. Always disappointed. Vodafone. *At this fucking time? You can shove your upgrade up your platinum-and-diamond-encrusted arse.* Deleting the voicemail, my clumsy fingers bizarrely dialled Ellie, second number down from voicemail. *Fuck.* I cut the call. The thought of hearing her voice after all these months was still painful; my shame at letting her down was never far away.

Topping up my *very* final glass, I mulled over my options. *Do I assign points for the worthiness of each scenario? Or do I just go with my gut?* Tiptoeing through to Phoebe Rose's room, I hovered near the door. She was fast asleep and smiling in her dream. *This beautiful girl will tomorrow receive the love that she deserves. Because she is such a good girl. It's me that isn't.*

My ringtone filled the lounge. Quickly closing the door before Phoebe Rose stirred, I stumbled over to cut the noise before she woke. The phone ringing was not a common sound in our home. My heart raced as Ellie's name glowed on the screen.

'Hello?'

'Hello.' It was good to hear her voice.

'Tilda, I had a missed call from you?'

'Hi. I'm so sorry. It was a pocket dial, sorry. I know you don't want me to contact you. Huge apologies.' I'm trying hard not to sound pissed.

'Oh.' Did she sound disappointed? 'I was only thinking of you today. I wondered how you were.'

'Okay. All right. The big day tomorrow, actually. Final hearing.'

'Wow. Is that why you called?' Ellie said kindly, far removed from her tone when we'd last spoken.

'No, it was a pocket dial.' I paused. Seconds in and already I wasn't being honest with her. I stopped myself. 'I'm sorry, Ellie. I did call you. I was desperate to speak to someone I cared for before I fucked everything up.'

'I needed to keep my distance, look out for myself and Rosa – time to lick my wounds.' Did she sound more sad than angry?

'I can't tell you how sorry I am. I'm so ashamed. How's Rosa?'

Ellie's smile poured down the phone. 'She's great. Little Miss Sass, but I wouldn't have her any other way. How's Phoebe Rose? I miss that giggle of hers and her super-tight snuggles.'

'She's fine. Ready for her new mama, even if she doesn't know it yet. I feel so bad, Ellie, that I haven't been able to bond with her. Every time I look at her, all I think about is Stevie. Then I get this horrible pang that Stevie won't want me …' My efforts not to cry were unsuccessful.

'Hey, you've had to cope with a huge amount of pressure. You've done your best. So, Stevie will be with you tomorrow, is that right?'

'I'm not sure. I'm not sure of anything, Ellie. But yes, in theory.'

'I'm sorry I cut you off like that, Tilda. I've wanted to call so many times. The last few months must have been difficult. Did the NCT group help you out?'

'No. I don't think Phoebe Rose and I are NCT material,' I snuffled.

'Well, if you will join the far-right version of antenatal groups ...' Ellie laughed her lovely laugh. I'd missed it so much. I could hear Rosa stirring in the background. 'My perfect night sleeper has gone rogue. Waking at all hours. So, what's the plan tomorrow?'

'I don't know. I'm not sure ...' My tears were back.

'Tilda?'

'I'm just hoping that the right thing will happen tomorrow. That the decision will be a good result for the girls.'

'And for you. You'll have your daughter and your new start and ...'

Wiping tears, I pretended Phoebe Rose had woken and I needed to tend to her.

'Lovely to hear from you, Ellie. You can't know what a difference it's made to me. Like I'm someone, not no one.'

As I ended the call, a huge sob burst forth, an emotional furball of distress and fear. And alcohol.

A fresh drink somehow appeared at the same time as my brain seemed to be edging towards a decision. The anxiety and uncertainty of the next day combined with my belief that Stevie would be better off with Lana and Joel seemed to point to only one solution.

Grabbing the hotel notepad that Edwin had brought, I began to scrawl.

> Dear Tilda
>
> It was nice knowing you. It wasn't always nice being here. I wish we could have met under different circumstances. I wish someone could have understood you. Cared for you. I wish you hadn't had the privilege that afforded you not to function. I wish you'd never ever met Edwin. Have you been depressed? Are you a monster? You are an alcoholic. Is it too late?
>
> Yours faithfully
>
> Tilda

I was on a roll.

> Dear Lana and Joel

As I reached for the paper, my glass tipped, sending the hotel logo ablur. I grabbed another sheet.

> Dear Joel and Lana
>
> I want to write how thankful I am that my fertilised egg chose your womb in which to accidentally implant itself, as weird as that sounds. I'm very pissed right now and ideas and words on paper are separate entities.

Scrap that.

Dear Lana (actually, this is not about Joel. This is mama to mama)

I'm sorry I haven't been a better mother to your beautiful girl. I'm hoping that what I've decided to do goes some way to making things right. I hope it doesn't make things worse. That isn't my intention. I've got lots of things wrong in my life. I hope this decision is the right one for the girls. Please look after my daughter. I'm sad that I didn't get to do that and didn't do a great job of looking after yours. She will be headstrong like me. Please know that when she's being stroppy, she will need you the most. Please know she won't mean all the unkind things she might say. Like me, she will be a prickly hedgehog, sharp on the outside but soft and sensitive on the inside. I'm not sure I was ever understood by anyone. And maybe that's why I've ended up this way. Please understand her and love her and Phoebe Rose. And do all the things that I didn't or couldn't.

Tilda

Ellie

'Thanks, Mum. I really hope I'm overreacting, but I can't leave it. There's Calpol in the fridge. She can have a couple of spoons if she needs. Or just settle her back down. She should be fine.'

At 10 p.m. the roads were clear. My feet juddered on the pedals. I should have reached out sooner. I knew the timeframe. God, Tilda. Something in her tone wasn't right. Her attempt to appear sober was hopeless but didn't surprise me. It was her tone that worried me, the vagueness of her plan for the most important day tomorrow. Like she didn't intend going to court at all. What did she say? 'It matters more than you'll know that I'm not on my own'? I hit redial but met the same unavailable tone. *Ellie, you've been such a cow. She's been depressed.* How *could* she have coped? How would I have coped without my support network when Rosa was tiny? *You were her entire support network.* I pushed 50 in a 30 zone. 'Fuck the cameras,' I breathed.

Stan waved me through. I didn't need to ask. The lift took forever, stopping for an elderly couple moving at gravity-defying speed, wheelchairs and walking frames blocking my way. Barely containing my irritation, I stabbed at the close button just as the wheelchair exited the lift.

I rapped hard. No answer. My heart raced. I rapped again. 10.30 p.m. She was probably in bed. I felt like an idiot. Catastrophising that Tilda would harm herself just because she was emotional the night before court. I'd take that over the reality any day. Still there was no sound other than my hammering heart.

'Tilda,' I shouted through the letterbox, putting my ear close to the door. She wouldn't harm Phoebe Rose, would she? What had she said? 'The girls will be in a better place tomorrow.' What did that mean? Panic filled my chest as I simultaneously hammered on the door and dialled her mobile. After an age, I heard the smallest sound. Or had I imagined it? The door creaked open ever so slightly. Tilda looked a state. Dried vomit down her Gucci blouse, her hair plastered against her head. She stunk, booze radiating from her.

'Ellie!' she whispered.

Steering her carefully to the sofa, we navigated a pool of vomit that had spattered over the armchair and floor. Vomit-drenched papers were strewn across the carpet.

'Dear Lana,' I could make out at the top of one, but the writing was all over the place.

'Jesus! Tilda, how are you going to get to court in this state? What time do you need to be there?'

Tilda was motionless. Silent, she turned her face from me and into the cushion.

'Have you taken something?' I shook her shoulders. Tilda gave an imperceptible shake of her head. Could I believe her? I made my way through to Phoebe Rose's room, where, thankfully, she lay peacefully, stirring only briefly as I peered through the darkness.

I prepared coffee and a pint of water. It was a good job I hadn't had a drink myself. I tried to get my head together as I waited for the machine to finish its filter. Was this a pre-court wobble or was this her new norm? Guilt prickled as I tried to figure out the quickest way of sobering her up. I knew how vulnerable she had been. Why had I cold shouldered her? She was depressed, for God's sake. What had been the impact of my cutting her off like that? In a way, I was responsible for the whole IVF decision.

If we hadn't hooked up, would she even have considered a baby? She'd have had that vineyard well under way by now.

Placing the drinks on the table, I nudged her and squeezed in next to her. She squeezed me back in return.

'Operation Sober, my friend.'

Jesus, we were going to need a miracle.

Tilda groaned but didn't resist as I propped her skinny frame upright, forcing the pint glass into her hand.

'Were you organising your affairs?' I picked up the non-vomit-covered pages and tried to decipher the scrawl. 'Hope I got something.'

Tilda half smiled but her eyes remained closed, her lids puffy like she'd had the worst crying jag. She sipped half-heartedly from the glass.

'I was only writing to people I'm in touch with,' she slurred.

'Seriously, have you taken anything? Don't piss about.'

Tilda opened her eyes and looked directly at me. 'No.' She paused. 'I was going for the direct approach. Thought I'd take the scenic route via the balcony.'

'God, Tilda.'

'Ellie. I'm fucking terrified. What if Stevie doesn't want me? I'm no Lana and Joel. I'm odd, socially awkward, spoiled. I have nothing to offer her other than my depressive genes.'

'You've missed out how irritable you are.'

'That too.'

'Seriously? If you want to "do the right thing" – how is that killing yourself? You've poured all that love, that energy, into creating Stevie. You've cared for Phoebe Rose despite it being so overwhelming. You've never had a model of maternal behaviour and done all this without a partner. You're amazing, Tilda! How can you begin to pull apart how much the trauma has affected you? You'd have aced it being Stevie's mum. You *can* ace this! It would have rocked anyone when Phoebe Rose popped out.'

'I feel bad for Lana and Joel ... depriving them of Stevie will kill Lana. They love her like she's their own.'

'Does it have to be so black and white – no pun intended? Didn't you mention those couples in the US who became a blended family, sharing the kids between them?'

'The girls won't want to come to me! I'm not a patch on Lana and Joel.'

'Oh, stop it with your wallowing. And besides, the girls will want to come and see Auntie Ellie and Cousin Rosa. You can't argue with that!'

Pouring coffee into Tilda's mug, I could only hope she might keep it down. At least the water had stayed put.

'Tomorrow, I'll be driving – you'll still be pissed. Your two jobs will be not to puke in the car and work out what will be the right thing for you and Stevie. The solution of killing yourself is ridiculous. And it's the only outcome I won't hear of. Your daughter *needs* you in her life. Now and when she's older. And I'm not just saying that because I'm your friend.'

'*Were* my friend. Before I ruined it.'

'I *am* your friend. I was just hurting. How will Stevie and Phoebe Rose feel when they grow up and find out what happened? That you'd killed yourself the night before court? You think finding that out as a young adult will be helpful? Character building? For either of them? Stevie doesn't need you to be perfect, Tilda. She just needs you to be around, being the best version of you that you can be. Loving her, being her perfectly imperfect mum. You will need to kick the booze, and you will. You've got this!' Frustration filled my voice, which meant I was entering lecture mode. Which wouldn't be helpful for a recently— currently suicidal person, for all I knew.

Tilda shrugged, struggling to keep her eyes open. She looked exhausted.

'I'm running you a bath, Tild. Don't get comfy. And I'm binning these. You won't need them.' I waved the non-vomit-drenched letters in her direction and headed for the kitchen. My head was running in a thousand directions. I was projecting a confidence that did not reflect my inner state; I was shitting myself. Doing a quick reccy of the bathroom for lethal means – pills, sharps, other – I declared it a safe space but settled on a propped-open door.

Tilda

I couldn't quite land on a word that described how I felt that morning. If Ellie hadn't come over, there wouldn't have been a morning, for me at least. I'd have been spared today's likely humiliation in court and/or the possibility that I would ruin my daughter's life chances by having her in my flawed care. Had I told Ellie last night about the C and F assessment, the small issue of neglect that had been thrown my way?

I didn't feel hungover, more 'out of body'. I ought to have had the mother of all hangovers, but the gods had been kind.

I felt like an observer, going through the motions under Ellie's instruction. Dress, makeup, hair, baby bag. Thank God Ellie had sorted Phoebe Rose out. I found myself in the passenger seat, Ellie at the wheel of my car. I think because it's bigger. Or maybe she didn't want to run the risk of me vomiting in her car. I wondered briefly if the car seat would end up going with Phoebe Rose today. Or would they have their own? Would there be an infant on the return journey other than Rosa? My mind felt puréed, half-formed thoughts passing through. We collected Rosa en route, and although the time frame was tight, we found ourselves almost on track for 3.30 p.m. Manchester Court.

The journey was surreal. We played music, but there was no road trip feel. Ellie tried to help me think through what I wanted to propose. Or if I was comfortable waiting to hear the judge's decision. Comfortable was not a state I'd experienced in the longest time. I shared my version of events with Ellie regarding the unfortunate A&E trip, explaining that I would only learn the outcome of the social care assessment today and the bearing this would have upon the judge's overall decision. Staring straight ahead, I could only imagine Ellie's expression as she listened. Minutes passed.

'For what it's worth, I think you've been post-natally depressed. Given what's happened, you need support and treatment, and the psychologist should make that clear. Just take a moment and think. This isn't you. It doesn't define you. You've responded to a traumatic event that was not of your doing. That makes you human, not bad or mad. You're an alcoholic with no support network. That's an illness. Try and gather your thoughts in a text or on paper. What's manageable, doable? With support, I think you can be every bit as fabulous a mum to Stevie as Lana. Just hold on to that.'

Her words were kind. But how could I take that gamble? If I messed up, how would that be fair to Stevie? After all that had happened. I felt beyond wretched. A feeling of panic began to build in my chest, my airways closing with each ragged breath. My entire body felt like it was collapsing in on itself.

'I need air,' I gasped, wildly jabbing at the window control to my left. It wouldn't budge. I lunged across Ellie, frantic for air, pressing buttons randomly, wrenching at the door handle. Screams filled the car. We weaved across lanes, Ellie with one hand on the steering wheel, the other frantically fielding my efforts, and pulled over onto the hard shoulder, hazards blinking.

'Tilda. Sit back. Breathe,' she shouted, sending the window down effortlessly. She took my hand and stroked gently as she counted, sitting and breathing, waiting for the panic to subside. The white noise from the barely audible radio and the motorway traffic was strangely soothing. The racing of my heart and the terror of being unable to breathe slowly began to subside.

'We need to move, Tilda. It's not safe to be stopped here.' Eventually I nodded. Ellie calmly restarted the car. We ignored the satnav announcing that we were way off schedule for 3.30 p.m. court.

Lana

It was a beautiful March afternoon. Sun streamed through the courtroom, which belied the angst filling the room, a grim version of *Sophie's Choice* playing out before us.

Stevie, at nine months old, was vocal and, ironically, at the stage of development when she was suddenly wary of separation from us, understanding for the first time the concept of object permanence – that if something disappears, it isn't gone forever. Would she wonder why we had lied to her? Mama and Dada might leave the room, but they would *always* come back. Only this time they wouldn't. What else would she need to delete from her slate of trust?

Since my spectacular combustion at Evie's birthday, I hadn't been able to return to work. Despite my resolve and momentum, I'd crashed and burned. My beautiful Stevie – the second child of mine that couldn't stay, as perfect and loved as her sister before her. Today she too would leave our care. It was unbearable. The thought of holding Phoebe Rose in our arms later did nothing to reduce the pain.

Stepping into the courthouse was overwhelming. Since our – actually Wan's and Jodie's – 'live disclosure' my mobile had not stopped pinging with concerned texts and calls. I hadn't responded to a single one. I'd asked Wan to pass on to everyone who'd reached out that I was grateful. But I'd stepped into a vortex and had no intention of surfacing.

The courtroom was crammed, as many as at Evie's birthday. I looked up briefly and Wan's brother waved a small sun-tanned hello from the right of the benches. My tears and resolve quickly gave way, the love and emotion in the room flooring me. Wan placed a protective arm around Stevie and me and we made our way to the front bench. Stevie looked excitedly around her, beaming and waving to all who loved her. For her, it was like Christmas. For us, it was a funeral, a wake. Clutching Stevie tightly, I sobbed. I could not bring myself to look to the right of the courtroom where Tilda, Phoebe Rose and her solicitor would be seated.

It was difficult to read Judge Sullivan's body language. I could see on my periphery a couple of Wan's DJ friends, Virginia from Sing and Learn, Lynda, others from work, so many people. It was too much. Who gave them permission to be here? Did Wan know they were coming? I didn't need an audience for my pain. Judge Sullivan banged her gavel. Parties were asked to rise. I remained seated. I hoped that Judge Sullivan would understand. I couldn't move. All I knew was that I could not part with Stevie. Today or any day. That was as far as my mind would go. I must have Phoebe Rose, and Stevie had to be mine. No trade-off.

'Permission to be seated.' I felt the weight of Wan beside me, his arm quickly closing around my shoulders.

Words echoed around the courtroom. I had no energy to process what was being said. My world felt like it was shrinking. A text landed and my phone vibrated. So much kindness, but I remained numb.

There was a murmuring from the back of the room, unheard of in Judge Sullivan's court. I looked at Wan anxiously but couldn't read his expression. Judge Sullivan looked beyond perturbed, slamming her gavel down furiously.

'Silence,' she demanded. For the first time since entering the courtroom, I dared to look towards Tilda and Phoebe Rose. My stomach turned over. What was happening? Mr Dreyfuss sat alone, turning awkwardly in his seat.

Mrs Jennings approached the bench. There was an exchange.

'Where is she? Where's Phoebe Rose?' Wan asked quietly. 'What's going on?'

I did a visual circuit of the room. So many people. But no sign of Tilda or Phoebe Rose.

The clock ticked a clear 3.45. Court had convened at 3.30. Where were they?

Mr Dreyfuss held a mobile to his ear, looking increasingly disconcerted. There was a burst of sound from the back of the courtroom and all eyes landed on the embarrassed usher entering the room.

I checked my mobile, although Tilda texting me would be unlikely. A somersault of emotions coursed through me as I refused to process what their absence might mean. Mr Dreyfuss left the bench without the judge's permission, taking two stairs at a time as he took the call. The noise level steadily rose as the courtroom grew restless.

Judge Sullivan again used her gavel thunderously.

'This court will reconvene in twenty minutes.' Her tone was ominous, her face incredulous that there would be a complication at this final hearing.

I was touched at the turnout but felt so exposed in the goldfish bowl that our life had become. Wan, Stevie and I remained in our huddle. I had no desire to interact with anyone behind us. Jodie would have been the exception, but of course the teaching profession does not make term-time exceptions, even for me. It was just us three amigos. Family and friends were dispensable extras as far as I was concerned. I was astonished to see a text from Tilda. I nudged Wan urgently and we read together. My hand shook and Wan steadied the phone on the bench in front as we scrolled. It felt like time had stopped, our lives in freefall as we read. And reread. In disbelief. Wan and I held one another as we tried to make sense of the information.

Tilda, Phoebe Rose, Ellie and Rosa entered the courtroom. The relief of seeing a wriggling Phoebe Rose brought tears to my eyes as they made their way to the front bench. Tilda looked unkempt. The situation was surreal, like something from a bad TV drama. Wan and I continued to try to understand the text. Could this happen? Legally? Would Judge Sullivan allow it? There had been so many U-turns and stalling, it felt like we would never reach a conclusion.

Judge Sullivan returned, flanked by Mr Dreyfuss and Mrs Jennings, calling us to order and demanding silence.

'All rise for the court,' cried the usher.

Wan took Stevie from my arms. And this time I found my feet.

Head bowed, I hung on to Judge Sullivan's every word.

'I am ...' Judge Sullivan's voice faltered. 'Deeply sorry *again* to update the Edwards, Mrs Jennings and Mr Dreyfuss. However, I am informed, despite my clear directive that there must be no further delay in proceedings, I *still* have late information submitted.' Could Judge Sullivan accept this?

'I'm informed that Ms Asquith-Hyde is relinquishing her parental rights to Phoebe Rose to Lana and Joel Edwards *without* a directive from the court and *without* request to receive care of her own biological child, Stevie.' Even Judge Sullivan sounded taken aback, pausing to reread the statement before her.

'Again I find myself in possession of new information, and as such must revise my prepared ruling. I trust that this will satisfy all parties. Ms Asquith-Hyde, rather than assuming custody of Stevie, has requested a formal and legally binding arrangement be drawn up to allow regular contact moving forward between herself and Stevie Edwards. This is to be requested monthly by agreement of both parties. That said, I will insist that any contact between Stevie and Ms Asquith-Hyde needs to occur initially with supervision until such time that Ms Asquith-Hyde has accessed intervention and support around her alcohol misuse. Mr Dreyfuss, Mrs Jennings, please discuss with your respective clients and provide me with written confirmation within forty-eight hours.'

I wept. Loudly. A howl of relief and overwhelming joy. I buried my face in Stevie's fair hair, for once allowing her to feel the painful emotions we'd worked so hard to protect her from all these months. Wan sank to his haunches, filling the court with a terrible keening sound. Tilda approached with Phoebe Rose, tears streaming down her face, truly distraught. I made room for them both within our huddle. We remained as a unit, oblivious to the court around us. Phoebe Rose's small fists clung tightly to her new family.

Salvaged letter by Ellie from the night before court:

> Dearest mother
>
> I can't remember writing you a letter before. i've written a few this evening and didn't want to miss you out. im tired, it's my last letter so pls forgive typos and garammatical errors. I know you are a stickler. Probably more so with time on your hands in the afterlife.
>
> I was never able to talk to you about anything, was I? I still can't – you're dead. If you weren't, this is what I'd like to understand.
>
> why you loved my brother so much more than you loved me
>
> what was with all the men? You humiliated us all
>
> how you could turn a blind eye. You knew the man of the cloth, your lover, was not only interested in you. I was 13 years old. Why did you look away?

Nathan

Lab Technician

18 Dec 2021

Manchester Clinic

'Good morning, Nathan. How are you doing? Getting used to us all, I hope.' Dr Brown looked like a charismatic TV doctor, a weird blend of sleazy and earnest. Fortunately, his pleasantries were rhetorical as he walked straight past my desk, which was handy. Because if I'd opened my mouth, I wasn't sure that anything coherent would come out.

Shit. Shit. Shittingtons, Von Shit. Accepting the offer to be Dan's plus one at the corporate last night was a retrospectively terrible idea. Being moderate is difficult, full stop, but when there's a free bar … well … And that final line of coke, the temporary livener, leaving my brain so fuzzy. Phoning in sick would have been the sensible thing to do. Only in your first week it's not the best idea if you want to keep your job.

Adrian was gloved up, prepping the samples. Of course he was. Mr Brown-Nose gets in early every morning. His left eye twitched as he glanced at the clock. I didn't have to answer to him. Ignoring the tremor of my hands, I snapped on surgical gloves.

'I've removed and prepped today's inseminations. They just need your signature for double check. When you're ready.'

I tried to focus on the spreadsheet, but my eyes refused to cooperate. The words seem to lift off the page, like my mind was clicking and dragging. Fuck.

Seven embryos were lined up in the 'go basket'. Each long ID number was perched against each vial on a neon sticker, ready for me to check and attach. I turned up the high beam overhead, which helped marginally. Sensing Adrian's impatience behind me, I pulled up a chair and attempted to gather myself. Why the hell was I here and not in bed? My breathing remained fast and shallow as I tried again to focus on the chart.

The door clicked and, thankfully, Adrian stepped into the neighbouring lab. I could hear his clumsy attempts to flirt with the trainee. God help her. Carefully removing each sample, I worked from left to right, checking, initialling and attaching the ID stickers. I was about to replace sample number four when a powerful spasm of my hand sent the 'go basket' flying, spewing the samples across the workbench. I quickly gathered them, but not before two had disappeared into the half-full sink. Within seconds I'd retrieved them and held them in my trembling fingers. No harm done. They appeared intact. I tried hard to read the barcodes to assign the tubes to their rightful places, but the numbers swam before me. I closed my eyes for a second. To my horror, when I opened them, everything was clear except the smudged barcodes on both tubes. As I smoothed my thumb gently over one of the codes, the paper began to tear. *Fuck. What to do? I can't just throw them away.* My bowels churned violently. Would I shit my pants here and now? What to do? Tinkling laughter from the embarrassed trainee carried through as the door opened. I had to make a call. One that didn't involve telling Adrian I'd messed up.

For no reason other than proximity, I assigned one test tube to each rack. Adrian loomed, and I wordlessly presented him with the completed chart. I made my way to the bathroom. If I was going to get through the rest of the day, I would need a little helper.

Edwin

You will have heard bad press about me. Much of it will be true. I didn't pause to think about Tilda nearly as much as I ought over the years. She's a fascinating but complex creature. She's kept me younger than my years, kept me on my toes at many points, made me laugh harder than anyone I know, and frustrated me beyond belief. I'm not proud of some of my behaviour if I reflect. And not just related to Tilda. I was never paternal – in fact, Tilda received more nurturing from me than either of my own children. I ought to be ashamed of that, but I didn't *know* I wasn't paternal until I'd gone down the married with children route. It's a shame you can't have a 'try before you buy' taster. A bit like that noose of a timeshare I had back in the eighties. It was protracted, but at least there was an opt-out, which my solicitor did well to spot. That's why Tild and I got along so well. Egocentric kindred spirits that we were.

Tild was far more wounded by her mother's behaviour than she would ever admit, not least to herself. Oh, her mother was a sow. Constantly fawning over the horrific Archie. If life were a fairytale for her mother's emotions, he was a prince and Tild was Cinderella. Without the fairy godmother. The poor girl never got a look-in. She'll tell you that she never bothered with the Stand Foundation, which simply isn't true. In the early days she tried desperately to impress her mother, holding true to elements of the charity that she could barely tolerate – attending Church commissioning events and steering groups made up of clergymen who held on to her hand just a touch too long and indiscreetly undressed her with their eyes, just as they had her mother before her. Alas, it was never good enough for Cynthia. She criticised, belittled and ridiculed Tild's every effort. In the end, Tild simply gave up. It was easier for her to believe that she'd never really tried.

And as for alcohol, well. We loved to drink. Together and apart. When I retired, that hedged into dangerous territory. I tended to go for the slow soak whereas Tild would oscillate between desperate stabs at sobriety and terrifying binges. Between her mother and I, we drove her to that I think, but I was beyond being able to reach her when she got to that point. The self-loathing in which she bathed after a bad binge was horrific to observe. All I could do was feed her, launder her vomit-stained bedding without judgement and wait for the aftermath to abate.

Tild was obsessed with the idea that I would be unfaithful to her. Which was ridiculous. She was the one turning heads, not I. Given her mother's frightful infidelity, I would never have cheated on her. Tild experienced such humiliation on behalf of her father. He seemed strangely inured to Cynthia's behaviour, but Tild was humiliated by her father's acceptance of her mother's strangely public affairs.

I wasn't surprised to receive an inebriated crisis call – several, actually, each more desperate than the last. Of course, the child was a shock. When I heard the whole sorry story, I was devastated for her that such a courageous step had turned so complicated. I think with the right support – and removing the unfortunate variable of Tild giving birth to another woman's child – it might have been the making of her. She deserved that chance after so much else in her life had been so unfair.

Support

It's almost fifty years since Louise 'Joy' Brown was born - the world's first baby conceived using IVF. And the world has never looked back. Millions of families have since had the ultimate 'Joy' of a child being brought into their lives using IVF, which otherwise would have been impossible for them.

Whilst IVF continues to be a fantastic solution for many families, with amazing outcomes, like any human endeavour it is not without its failings. Fortunately, these failings are extremely rare.

I hope that in writing this book, I have dealt sensitively with the topics of IVF, mental health and the improper use of alcohol. If you, or any of your loved ones have been affected by these, then please reach out to your GP and those close to you for support. Additionally, I hope that some of the following resources may be helpful:

>https://fertilitynetworkuk.org/
>
>https://www.nhs.uk/conditions/ivf/support/
>
>https://www.mentalhealth.org.uk/explore-mental-health/a-z-topics/women-and-mental-health
>
>https://www.fathersnetwork.org.uk/supporting_fathers_mental_health
>
>https://www.thecalmzone.net/
>
>https://www.alcoholics-anonymous.org.uk/

If you would like to get in touch regarding the book, or see news about what I am pursuing next on my literary adventure, then please visit:

>   https://www.sharonnoble.co.uk

Printed in Great Britain
by Amazon